THE
SOLACE

a novel

Robert Madrygin

OF

TREES

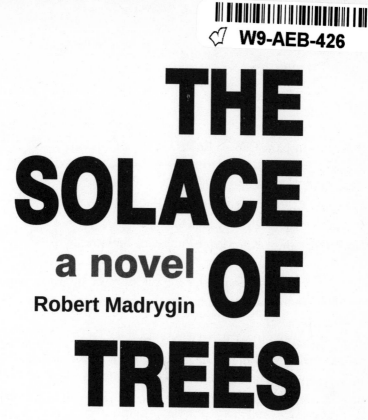

New Europe Books

Williamstown, Massachusetts

Published by New Europe Books
Williamstown, Massachusetts
www.NewEuropeBooks.com
Copyright © 2017 by Robert Madrygin
Front cover art © 2017 by Julia Madrigan
Interior design by Knowledge Publishing Services

This is a work of fiction and, except in cases of historical fact, any resemblance to actual persons, living or dead, is purely coincidental.

ISBN: 978-0-9973169-0-2

Cataloging-in-Publication data is available from the Library of Congress.

First edition, 2017

10 9 8 7 6 5 4 3 2 1

For my wife, Susan

and

for Amir and all the silent victims of war

Prologue

They kept asking him the same questions, over and over. Questions they already knew the answers to. He felt so tired, so impossibly sad and broken. All he wanted was to sleep. To let his eyelids fall, his mind shut off. But they wouldn't let him. "What is your name?" they asked for the thousandth time. "Why did you return to Bosnia?" "What do you do for Zakariyya Ashrawi?" "Where are you really traveling to?"

Amir answered the questions, but they dismissed anything he said, as though no response he could give would please them. He was so weary that he would say anything they wanted just so he could close his eyes. They asked him again, Why had he come back? He answered that he had returned to visit his country. "*Your* country? What do you mean, *your* country! You are American now, aren't you? Why are you here?"

He had no answer to this other than what he'd already told them. The two men interrogating him turned to speak to each other. They talked in hushed voices behind the chair his body was slumped on. Amir heard a lighter being struck, and the smell of cigarette smoke filled the room. He closed his eyes. If only he could keep them shut. But at least he had the few minutes until their cigarettes burned low and they resumed their questions.

American or Bosnian? The truth was, he felt neither completely the one nor the other. It had been nearly ten years since he had been relocated from the land of his birth to the United States. Yet each of those years might as well have been a decade in itself for the distance he felt from the painful, sad memories of those times. He had been ten when the Bosnian War began, the history books having assigned the date of April 6, 1992, as the beginning of the conflict. He had been eleven when, nearly a year later, it reached the doorstep of his family's home with brutal and savage intent.

December 14, 1995—the day of the signing of the Dayton Accords—marked the end of the war that had decimated the land of Amir's birth. But for him, as with all victims of war, there was no simple, finite ending—no day, month, or year that closed the door on the past with reassuring finality. Human souls were not history books, couldn't relegate the past to letters and words, couldn't disappear traumatic events into paragraphs of analytic explanation. What had been suffered lived on, remained a part of you, like an arm or a leg, for the rest of your life. There was no use in denying it, for then it became like a phantom limb, an invisible appendage whose pain could be felt but not eased. The struggle to come to terms with it was made all the more difficult because the world seemed only too happy to forget.

While the smoke swirled about the room and his interrogators continued to chat behind his back, Amir's mind traveled back in time. . . . He was a child wandering the woods alone. He didn't speak, and couldn't if he'd tried. His ears could no longer hear the singing of the birds, the sound of his own feet touching the earth, the wind blowing through the trees.

A loud voice startled him. "What is your name?" it demanded.

Amir's eyes struggled open, his mind disoriented.

"What is your name?" the second interrogator repeated, shouting the question even louder than his compatriot.

"Amir," he answered, confused why they would demand he speak his name again and again when he'd spoken it so many times already.

"What-is-your-name?" the first interrogator asked once again, this time in a slow, angry voice.

"Amir. Amir Beganović-Morgan," he answered hoarsely, distantly . . . his mind still wandering in the memories of his lost childhood.

Chapter 1

He awoke at dawn's light, cold and confused. At first, Amir couldn't understand how he had come to spend the night in the tree fort he had built in the woods behind his house. The disorientation of waking up not in one's bed but in the resting place of birds, however, was soon subordinated to the sense that something was drastically wrong with his head. It felt pressurized, and he could hear nothing at all. Images slowly began to appear in his mind . . . men shouting, charging past the front door of his home. There were the cries of his mother and sister, and an ear-shattering explosion. His father had been shouting, yelling for him to run.

Amir struggled to find his bearings, to draw the images wandering about his mind into focus. Were they fleeting fragments of a nightmare, or were they shards of real memory to be put whole again? A part of the boy's mind rebelled in opposition, not wanting to pull the clouded visions closer into view, but rather calling out to abandon them until they disappeared and became indiscernible from the gray, murky atmosphere that enveloped them.

Hesitantly sitting up, Amir looked around at the tree limbs that surrounded him, as if by doing so his eyes could somehow find the sounds his ears could suddenly no longer hear. He struggled to remember the cause of his deafness, at the same time he fought to keep its memory at bay. Between the push and the pull of opposing impulses, bits of recall slipped into his mind.

There had been the sudden rumble of an approaching vehicle followed by the sound of gravel tumbling over itself as an armored truck sped in and jerked to a halt in front of his home. Stunned, he and his family had found their legs unable to move as they listened to the shouts of men charging forward on feet that, unlike theirs, raced ahead with confidence and purpose. Amir's father had quickly gathered him, his mother, and his sister by his side, then stepped in front of them to face the home's entryway. The door was propelled inward by the boot of a man who, rifle in hand, couldn't bother to simply lift the latch of the unlocked door and swing it open.

A fleeting image of the lone, shod foot entering his house flashed into Amir's memory. His family stood in the main room of their modest farmhouse struck by an almost physical shock, as though they, and not the door, had been splintered and slammed into the wall. Yet it was the face of the boot's owner that fully brought home the horror of the situation: the look that gazed over them with a perverse combination of hate and pleasure; the smile that leered its violence with lust and undisguised anticipation. The eyes of the eleven-year-old boy held the moment, like the click of a camera shutter snapping the scene, indelibly printing it upon the soft tissues of his startled young mind. But the child couldn't understand what it all meant. He could see only that the terror on the faces of his family broadened the man's smile.

After a time Amir climbed down from his perch, and his feet took him in the direction of his family's house. As he approached the edge of the woods, Amir saw the charred remains of the simple one-story farmhouse smoldering in the morning's early light, its steep, orange tiled roof collapsed within the now-blackened whitewashed sidewalls that once supported it. Without venturing any closer, Amir walked back in the direction from which he came.

Turning back into the forest brought him some sense of relief. He stayed there for most of the day, maundering close by, and then later, without thought, began to make his way toward the village that lay several kilometers from his family's farmstead. If he had paused to consider the direction he had taken, Amir would have realized he was heading to the house of his mother's brother, Murat, his wife, Ajka, and his cousins, Tarik, Reko, and Refik. The boy spent a second night in the woods, though this time more comfortably, in a hollow, covering himself with leaves and branches. Tired, disoriented, and weak from hunger, he fell into a deep and dreamless sleep.

When he reached his uncle Murat's house early the next morning he could see it was empty of life and had been ransacked. The village was deserted. Amir began walking on the road leading away from town, with no idea where he was going. Freshly rutted truck tracks led off the main street toward the Omerbasics' field. Amir followed them to where they ended. It was there that he found his cousins, aunt, uncle, and both of his grandparents.

He found them in a ditch with other villagers he knew. They were piled one on top of the other like old rag dolls, soiled and ruined, discarded in a heap. It was as if an old collection of someone's childhood playthings, uncared for and neglected, had finally been abandoned by its owner—the dried blood on the clothing and bodies looking like dirt stains, the eyes and mouths of the frozen faces as if painted by some artist's hand . . . surprise, fear, disbelief, the last moment of life forever fixed like a doll's face in a single, solitary emotion.

Amir's eyes wandered over the death mound in a shocked, fixed stare. He was able to make out the body of his oldest cousin, Tarik, and then the youngest, Reko, three years old, looking more like a doll than any of them. He had a hard time recognizing Refik, the cousin the same age as him. Refik's face was hidden by the crumpled corpse of an elderly man, but eventually Amir made out his clothing, the shape and size of his body. He couldn't find his Aunt Ajka, but he saw a head, mutilated and bloodied by gunshots to its face, that might have been his Uncle Murat. To the far side of the mound lay his grandfather, the elderly man's arm draped around his wife as though embracing her against the cold.

The boy's body, numb and immobile, stood as still as the air about him, his eyes the only part of his physical self that moved. And though his body held its place, standing upright upon the ground, his mind swooned, the scene of lifeless horror in front of him disappearing into a blur of muted color. After a time, Amir could feel sensation returning to his limbs. He turned from the ditch, and when he got back to the main road he no longer followed it but instead returned to the forest.

In the woods, Amir met others fleeing from the war, but he always saw them before they saw him. They took the easy ways, walking through the trees and undergrowth on well-worn paths. They never waited hidden in the shadow of the land as he did— guardedly, patiently looking for movement in the distance.

The small group of relatives and neighbors had been hiking since dawn, and the muscles of their legs, not used to so long a march, were sore and stiff. In the preceding twenty-four hours the classification of "refugee" had suddenly been made relevant to their lives. It was no longer just a word seen in print in the newspaper or used in conversation about others who had been displaced. The war had spread around them like a plague, but they had believed with false hope that it would never reach them. In the peaceful quiet of their slumber, between the time of having lain down to bed and waking, their world had been abruptly and quite literally turned upside down—mortar and artillery fire raining down upon their homes, crumbling walls and shaking them from their beds. Behind the boom of explosions they could hear a barrage of automatic rifle fire slowly but steadily coming their way. The families had grabbed what they could: food and clothing, as well as some things that made little sense for people fleeing for their lives. Half-asleep and panicked, they stuffed their belongings into whatever was at hand and fled into the heavily forested hillsides that encircled their town. Hidden among the trees, they huddled together, waiting to see what the chilly spring dawn would bring.

When light finally came, those in the small group began to make their way deeper into the forest, doing the best they could to keep to the faint paths of animal and mankind that crisscrossed through territory none of them previously had reason to travel. Without leader or direction, they were disoriented, frightened, and wary of being found by the men who had chased them from their town and who may have been, at that moment, pursuing them.

As they stumbled their way through the trees, a squirrel suddenly leapt onto the forest floor to scurry from one tree to the next—momentarily stilling their bodies and silencing their whisperings. Frozen mid-step, they glanced in the direction of the noise to seek its source, their eyes darting from point to point, like woodland prey wary of the presence of a lurking predator. At the realization that it was but a small creature, a bushy-tailed rodent, that threatened their path, the group released an audible, collective breath. Quiet, nervous laughter followed, and the tired travelers decided to rest and gather their strength. It was then that they came across the thin, pale boy, though in fact Amir had seen them first and watched their progress for a time to ascertain whether or not they were friendly.

Amir's ears could hear no sound, so he could not tell from the timbre of the people's voices whether their words might be gentle or angry. Only when he had seen them so easily frightened by a squirrel had he let his presence be known. That he was unable to find his voice and could not speak caused the boy no frustration or concern. It seemed somehow fitting to the circumstances surrounding the loss of his hearing. They spoke to him, but he remained silent, his face as blank as his ears and voice. After a time they rose and continued on. He joined in with the displaced families without acknowledgement on either side that he should do so, assimilated into the party of refugees by virtue of common privation.

It was apparent to Amir that there was neither rhyme nor reason to the direction these people were traveling. They roamed the woods following paths that provided them no road sign to indicate destination, and they seemed hopelessly lost and confused. Yet it didn't bother him that they wandered about without bearing, for he had no destination of his own toward which to travel.

Even though he could not hear the sound of their steps, he could see that these people were disturbing the peace of the forest, and he found this distressing. After he had walked with them for some time, they halted in a small clearing to rest and fuel their bodies from the meager provisions they carried. A loaf of bread was pulled from a rucksack and divided among the group, the silent boy given an equal share. He accepted the small slice of bread with a thankful nod.

Amir was glad of the break, for now the forest could return to peace without the interruption of so many feet tromping the undergrowth unaware of the disturbance they caused. He sat by himself, away from the others, and ate his ration, comforted by the peacefulness of the forest, a place where he had always felt as much at home as within his family's house.

Looking down at the ground by his feet, Amir watched a colony of ants as they suddenly appeared from the undergrowth and converged on a few tiny crumbs of bread that he had dropped on the ground beneath him. He looked upon the ants as if from afar, his eyes focused in a distant gaze. Sitting upon the soft moss cushion of an old tree stump, he held his small body still as he watched the tiny soldiers march single file through the undergrowth with intent and unfaltering determination. He stared at them silently, his muscles poised in perfect balance between tension and calm, no stirring of body nor mind to betray his presence. His eyes recorded it all without comment or judgment, neither thought nor inner dialogue interrupting the scene that played out in front of him. There was only the image of what he saw reflected through pupil to retina, streaming the trail of optic nerve to brain, leaving in his mind the picture of what was, and nothing else.

The ants moved with precision and resolve, though the blades of grass that hindered their way must have seemed to them an interminable forest. They advanced on the tiny crumbs of bread like an army to a siege. It had been like that with the men who had come to his home. Crumbling more bits of bread onto the ground, Amir watched as the ants carried them away.

Chapter 2

When it came time to continue onward, one of the men among the group tried to rouse the silent boy by touching him on the shoulder. Amir didn't respond, but continued staring at the ground by his feet. A mother handed over her infant to an older woman, who might have perhaps been the baby's grandmother, and walked over to Amir to gently pull at the sleeve of his coat. Amir's arm gave a few inches before it retreated to his body and crossed with his other arm to lock tight against his chest. He briefly glanced up in the woman's direction and met her eyes with a blank stare, then returned his attention to the parade of ants marching past his feet. After another attempt the woman gave up and returned to reclaim her child. The small caravan of refugees moved on without the boy.

None of them knew the boy's name or how he had come to be alone in the woods. Yet they could guess it: the dirty, raggedly dressed boy was from one of the nearby mountain villages and had been separated from his family by the same men who had attacked their town or, worse yet, had been orphaned by them. It wasn't for the want of caring that they knew nothing of the child. They had asked, but the boy hadn't answered. He seemed unable to hear their words or to speak in response, his mouth sometimes opening as if to reply, but no sound emerging.

On another day, in different times, they wouldn't have left the child to himself so easily, with nothing more than a sigh of regret, the image of his face erased from their memory with the turn of a shoulder. They would have searched for someone who knew his family or, at the very least, contacted the authorities. But now the question of who the authorities might be was far from clear, and it was even less clear whether they would offer help or deadly persecution. No, there would be little chance of finding the boy's family. The men who had chased them from their homes had seen to that. The destruction of family bond and the eradication of all that united them through their common ancestral blood was one of the principal strategies of those men's war. The boy wandering the woods alone was proof enough of that.

The next day, Amir happened onto another group and traveled with them for a short time before he separated from them as well, hanging back until he was left behind. His life now seemed to have no connecting parts. One thing was linked to the next by only the flow of its motion at best and, much of the time, by nothing at all, as though passing through a doorway that served neither as entrance nor exit, but whose purpose existed only as a notion of itself.

How his world could have altered so swiftly never entered Amir's thoughts. The mental faculty to compare the one thing to the other seemed to have disappeared along with his family and all that he had once known. The last thing he remembered of that life was the concussive blast of an explosion that was like a thunderclap going off inside of his head. . . . The explosion had come from a grenade thrown by one of the men who had invaded his family's home. The exact details of what had led to that remained mercifully inaccessible. He remembered only his father, Asaf, crying out for him to run to the woodbin at the side of the fireplace, where they stored the winter's firewood. Inside the woodbin alcove was a hatchway that allowed the bin to be filled from the outside.

Amid the chaos of gunfire and men shouting from all sides, Amir's legs finally managed to move him toward the woodbin. Just as he had ducked down into it, an explosion had filled his head with a terrible ringing. Somehow its force had pushed him through the hatchway, to the back of the house, and without bothering to conceal himself, he made his way into the forest, to his playing grounds, where his feet carried him instinctively and without thought. He was alone—his father, mother, and sister still inside the house.

Dazed from the grenade's detonation, Amir had not run far into the woods before coming to a stop. His mind wasn't able to function clearly, nor did his legs have the strength to continue. He knew he was escaping from something but was no longer sure what it might be. His head felt as if it had been compressed into a ball of pain, his consciousness slowly slipping away. He only had a few minutes' lead on the members of the paramilitary band who were at that moment racing through the woods in search of him.

Working on pure instinct, Amir carried himself to a tree and forced his body to climb it. The tree, a large pine, was one he knew well. High above, where two large, sturdy boughs grew next to one another and then spread wide, he had, with his father's help, built a tree fort: a place of play, of make believe, of dreams, and now of refuge.

Amir had earned the nickname Little Squirrel for his love of the woods and the amount of time he spent playing there, climbing trees and building forts. His mother would complain of the difficulty in cleaning his clothes of pine pitch and dirt, but it was really the worry of her son falling from a tree that caused her to try to rein in Amir's enthusiasm for climbing. He would play in the woods by himself or with his cousins Refik and Tarik, when they visited. Hide-and-seek had been his favorite game to play with the boys because they could never find him. He was just as happy to play on his own, though, and could occupy himself for long periods of time in one of his favorite trees, silently gazing down on the forest life that ventured out unaware of his presence.

Asaf would tell Emina not to worry about the boy: "He's sure-footed and strong. He knows what he is doing. Amir can climb the tallest of the trees just like he was born to it."

"It's just that which worries me," Emina would respond, not comforted by her husband's reassurances. "He always wants to climb the biggest tree and go all the way to the top. He isn't really a squirrel, you know. He's just a boy."

"He's about as likely to fall from a tree as he is from walking on the ground with his two feet," Asaf replied with a laugh.

Unconvinced, Emina shook her head. "What can I expect from the man who taught him to climb in the first place?"

Asaf had instructed his son in the same way his own father had taught him. *If you want to see forest life, you have to become part of it. Walking around making noise, you will never see anything. All of the birds and animals will run and hide. You have to be silent and, above all, patient. You have to sit in a hollow, unmoving, for hours, downwind from the place you watch. Find the paths that the forest life walks. Find their resting places, where they feed, and you will find the animals. Here, climb up that tree. Sit up there, quiet as a rock, and when I return tell me what you have seen.*

At first the eight-year-old boy was excited to be up in the tree. Then he grew tired, his muscles sore from holding the same position for so long. He became bored and, though he felt restless, forced himself not to move, because his father had told him to be still. Amir always listened carefully to his father's words because of the way Asaf talked to him. He spoke to his son with respect, always assuming the boy's intelligence, strength, and integrity, without showing even the slightest doubt of the child's ability to do whatever task might be placed in front of him. Even when Amir came up against a thing he was unable to achieve, his father always treated his son's effort at it as the true measure of the boy's success.

After a time, Amir thought about climbing down from the tree on his own. Perhaps his father had forgotten him, to leave him there so long. It was then the doe and her fawn came by. Soon after, there came a pair of squirrels. An owl, eyes closed, sat camouflaged only a few trees away. Why hadn't he seen it sooner? It must have been there the whole time. By the time Asaf finally returned to the tree to retrieve him, Amir's boredom had long disappeared, replaced by a calm dreaminess that seemed to transform the boy into something of the forest itself.

Amir had so many things to tell his father. "Papa, I saw a doe, and she had a little baby," he cried excitedly. "There was an owl, too. I thought it was just a squirrel's nest, and then I saw it had eyes!"

Asaf smiled broadly as his son laughed with joy. Thereafter, it was hard to keep the boy from the trees. With his cousins Refik and Tarik, he had scaled practically every tree in the hillsides surrounding their home, particularly the big ones that had called out their challenge.

After parting from the second group fleeing the invading soldiers, Amir went in the opposite direction. He had no idea where to go. It seemed to him that life had slipped away, and there was only the dream of it now. In this dream world there were no destinations, no fixed places, just interconnecting circles that led him round and round without meaning or purpose. For a time, it appeared as if his feet were following this same logic and that the ground itself revolved in a kind of circular concurrence, leading him nowhere and to nothing. Yet as much as the world seemed a dream, it was not, and Amir's solitary wandering was interrupted by his arrival at a place where the forest ended.

Amir became aware of the town before he saw it. The forest growth became more ragged and intruded upon, debris and other signs of human habitation leaving their mark. Amir felt hungry, though his hunger had become almost a food in itself, the physical ache dulling that of his mind and heart. He skirted his way around the areas of the most obvious human intrusion until he reached a hillside that overlooked a roadway. From his vantage point he could see the town several kilometers to his left, to the northeast.

Hidden in the scrub, he sat quietly observing the road for some time. Only occasionally did a motorized vehicle pass. More carts and horses traveled past than cars or trucks. To the boy, coming from his mountain village, this seemed only natural, though to the inhabitants of this larger town it was anything but. The greatest movement along the road was by people on foot. That their ethnicity was the same as those who had attacked his home didn't register in his thoughts. There were no soldiers among them, no armed militiamen. Their appearance, the way they dressed, and the way they walked was exactly the same as if they'd been people from his village.

Amir walked down the hill to the road, his hunger having turned into a kind of feeble delirium. His mind, impaired by lack of food, saw the people on the road as a continuation of the refugees he'd met in the woods. His body carried him toward the town. After only a few minutes, he stopped and sat by the roadside. He felt dizzy, his steps unsteady, unsure that he could continue walking, one foot able to follow the other.

Chapter 3

Sonja Ćosić didn't hurry the mare. She was in no more of a rush to return to her farm than the weary horse that pulled the empty cart homeward, fresh from being freed of a ponderous load of firewood. It had taken Sonja the better part of the day to load the wood, drive it into town, and sell or barter it for whatever she could. The chill of early spring was quickly fading and people had higher priorities than firewood to spend their money on. Sonja was tired; she seemed to wake up tired, go to bed tired, and spend the time in between feeling the same way. All of her children were gone from home and there was no one to help out with all of the work. Her husband never allowed her a moment's rest; he treated her in the same manner that had caused their daughter and two sons to escape as soon as they were old enough to do so.

The boy, small, thin-limbed, and brown-haired, sitting on the roadside, barely caught her attention. His head hung down as if he was dozing; he didn't even look up when the horse whinnied and the cart was near to passing.

As she approached, Sonja considered him. There was more work at the farm than she could ever possibly keep up with. She prepared to pass the boy by, figuring that he would not do for her, but then reconsidered: Her husband, Zoran, had his Josif to help him. But would he share that boy? No, there were always too many of her husband's chores for the helper to do, so that the man could go off with his friends to drink and boast of his role in a local paramilitary group.

Stopping the cart a few meters from where Amir sat, Sonja called out to him, "Hey boy, if you're hungry, there is work at our farm. If you work well, you'll be fed well."

The woman leaned over the cart and waited for a response. The chicken coop needed cleaning. But there were other things that needed her attention more. There always were, and the floor of the coop just kept rising higher and higher with the chickens' shit. It was a harder job now than ever.

When the boy made no response, Sonja stepped down from the cart, thinking the child asleep. Coming closer, she saw his head move, and she could see that the corner of the boy's eye closest to her was open.

"Hey boy," Sonja called once more, a moment passing before Amir gave a start and jerked his head up to stare at the woman.

The older woman realized almost immediately that the boy hadn't reacted to her call but rather that it had been the movement of her body drawing close that had caused him to look upward.

"What's the matter, you didn't hear me? Don't be frightened. I have work to offer you," she said, observing the child closely as she spoke, a suspicion of something in her face, a distant memory whispering an answer.

Amir watched the woman talking to him, saw the realization dawn on her after her words went unanswered. When Sonja was a little girl, a deaf-mute boy had lived on the farm nearest her family's. Sonja remembered the look of his eyes. They held a wider, more intent gaze than she was used to seeing in others. They watched and waited with an open candor, innocent of any agenda they might impose on others. Eyes of ordinary people didn't do that. They looked, then quickly scurried to some inner place to peek around from, to peer out from where they couldn't be seen.

Sonja raised her hand to her mouth three or four times, as if holding a spoon or fork, her eyes looking directly into Amir's. It was not so difficult talking to the deaf. Maybe it was even easier, clearer. There was room for only the simple, the truth. She remembered the neighbor boy. One of his smiles would have been worth a hundred of Zoran's. If she had only known then.

She saw that this boy understood immediately. Next, she mimed the act of shoveling, taking three scoops of air and depositing them in a nonexistent wheelbarrow. She repeated the eating again, then once more the simulated shoveling, until she was sure he understood he would get food only for work. Acting out a nod in question to his agreement, Sonja waited for his answer. A feeble movement of the boy's head came in response, and Amir attempted to rise, only to almost immediately fall back into a sitting position. He was very weak. Sonja worried whether she would get her worth's out of him and thought to just leave him there and go on her way. Then, looking at the boy's hands, she saw that they had known work.

The woman grew angry at herself, at how she'd come to think like Zoran, and helped the boy up into the cart. She'd take the boy home and feed him. After a good meal and a night's sleep he would be able to work. To hell with what her husband would say. Let him breathe the acrid, rotten egg–like smell of a winter's worth of chicken shit if he didn't like it.

Despite the courageous words of Sonja's inner dialogue, she hid the boy up in the hayloft of the barn after feeding him, signaling him to sleep and not to move until she returned. She would have the boy begin his chores the next day. Then Zoran would see. When her husband returned from the woodlot, where he was felling next winter's fuel supply with his helper, Josif, her boy would be well into the cleaning of the chicken coop, and Zoran would see that the new boy could work. He wouldn't be able to protest much then. And there were plenty of other jobs for the boy as well. If he worked hard she'd keep him for the summer. He could help with the haying. Even her husband would see the wisdom in that. With the war producing so many lost and homeless walking about the countryside, it made sense to take advantage of the available extra hands. There was only the cost of the food, and in summer they provided much of that from their own gardens. After the final haying was done the boy could move on to whomever or wherever he might belong.

Chicken shit was not nearly so easy to clean as cow shit. Its smell burned the nostrils even after sitting for a long time, the ammonia so strong that Sonja always wore a scarf to cover her mouth and nose when cleaning the coop. Cow shit, on the other hand, soon lost its edge, even taking on a pleasant earthy, musty smell. The cow shit would come up in nice, big clumps even when layered thick like a wedding cake, tramped down between months of neglected bedding. The chicken shit wouldn't do that; it would break up small, glue the bedding hard, raise a dust in the air that filled your nose and lungs. Zoran knew that. The cow work was his, man's work. The chickens were always the work of the woman, everyone knew that. At least that was Zoran's idea. Women do the chickens, men the cows. That was unless the woman did the chickens and the cows and the man went off to something more important, like drinking with his friends. But Zoran liked his cows.

The next day, after her husband left for the woodlot, Sonja retrieved Amir from the loft and set him to work. The boy had cleaned a chicken coop before. That much was evident, though Sonja had hoped for a better output than the new helper seemed able to muster. It wasn't for the lack of the child trying. He was still weak; he needed another day and more food. This would never do. Zoran would come back and laugh at how little the boy had done. She could say the new farmhand had started late, though even then, her husband would say how tired the boy looked for so little work. There was nothing to do but for her to help and say that her new helper had done it all on his own.

Sonja worked with the boy until the lunch hour and then served him a large meal. Her husband would rave if he saw how much she fed the child. She left the boy to finish the work by himself and returned to the house to prepare Zoran's favorite food for the evening meal.

"What's that in the coop? You let a stray cat in with the chickens?" Zoran asked, stepping into the kitchen upon his return home. Small wood chips spit from a chainsaw speckled his clothing. His face looked tired and annoyed. "I told you: no more help. Josif is enough and hardly worth the food it costs to keep him. There's time for you to do all you need to do. Next, you'll be wanting a maid so you can watch television all day."

"The boy costs nothing," Sonja replied, her defense mapped out in advance, and, though predictable, one she was confident would work. "A few scraps of leftovers, that's all. And as for all the time I have, if I'd had to clean the coop myself there wouldn't be stuffed cabbage and yam pie on the table for dinner tonight."

Her husband didn't bother to acknowledge her words, his look saying that nothing she might have to say would be of any justification. Yet, he left it at that. Sonja saw his nose sniff the air, his mouth already salivating, tongue licking his lips. She'd won that round, though of course she couldn't show it. God, what kind of life was it to feel pleased, like a cur receiving a pat on the head after being kicked, like a servant rewarded by a benevolent smile from the mighty master? She'd keep the boy as long as she wanted. If Zoran didn't like it he could go to the barn with his cows, not that it would be any great displeasure to him.

The next day nothing more was said about the boy. Not even when Zoran called out to him and was about to cuff the boy for ignoring his words before Sonja stopped him and explained that the child was deaf-mute. Her husband shook his head in disgust and walked away with a look that said, *He's your problem, not mine, just keep him out of my way.* From then on Zoran treated Amir as if he were no more than one of the farm animals. There was nothing of worth in the boy that he could see. Which couldn't have been better for Sonja—her husband wouldn't be stealing him for his own use.

If Sonja's husband paid the new boy no mind, it was the opposite for the man's young helper, Josif Babic, who was excited at the prospect of having someone to talk to. A distant relative of the couple— so distant that the exact relation could not be named—Josif had been working on the farm for nearly a half year and would not wish himself there another half day, no less the remainder of the year, as had been agreed upon. It wasn't the work. That was difficult though bearable. It wasn't even Zoran's constant disparagement of his intelligence—the man's treating the boy as if he was nothing more than an indentured servant, barely worth the food it took to sustain him. Josif could live with that. It had been that way for him since the age of thirteen, when, effectively orphaned by his parents' divorce and his mother's alcohol addiction and mental instability, he, his brother, and two sisters had been parceled out to whichever relative could be talked into taking them. No, what bothered him was the sheer loneliness of the place, his only human contact that of Zoran's embittered wife and her callous, uncaring husband.

It didn't matter to Josif that the new boy could neither speak nor hear. In some ways that was even of benefit. He could say whatever came to his mind or fell out of his mouth without fear of judgment or belittlement, of being called an idiot, or simply told to shut up. These were the predictable outcomes of any conversation that might occur with Zoran. His distant relative preferred talking to listening, and certainly so with a fifteen-year-old who had no more than a fourth-grade education. Josif spent his hours with the older man, a captive audience of one. At night when his work was done, the young teenager retired to his room in the barn to listen to his prized possession, an old, dented cassette player, his arms flailing the air with make-believe drumsticks, dreaming of the day he'd be able to escape his life, run away to Belgrade, and join a rock band . . . to a time when he would finally have friends and a life of his own. Signaling the new boy to enter what served as his room—two stalls boarded off from the rest of the barn; a doorway, a single, hinged window, a few built-in shelves, and a bunk its only amenities—Josif shared his secret passion with Amir.

"Come, feel this," Josif said, leading the new helper to the small, timeworn metallic machine he'd spent his entire savings to purchase. Placing the younger boy's hand on it, he asked, "Can you feel it, the music? Wait, I'll put it louder. Can you feel it?"

Amir looked at the older boy, unsure what was being said. Peering past Josif's question, he looked beyond the older boy's smile and into his eyes. Amir nodded his head yes. The older boy grinned broadly, happy at sharing his private escape with someone, someone who might be able to understand.

"Listen, feel the bass . . . *bom, bom bom, bom.* It's good, isn't it? Yeah, I love it."

Josif's hands rose into the air, invisible drumsticks beating out the rhythm. He looked over to his new friend, and for the first time he saw the younger boy show a semblance of a smile. The older boy began to drum harder, going fully at it now for the benefit of his new friend, his right foot joining in to pump an invisible bass drum, his head and body bouncing wildly to the music. A great grin broke out on Josif's face as he looked to see Amir's reaction. A small but true smile shone on the face of Sonja's young helper. Josif, laughing, took Amir's hands and showed him how to drum the air.

"You don't have to sleep up in the loft," Josif said to the boy, signaling him by pointing to his bed. "It's big. You can stay in this room. Zoran doesn't really care. He told you to sleep up there to show his wife who the boss is. He doesn't care about me having to share the bed. That's not why. Anyway, I don't care. It's OK to stay here."

Amir watched Josif talking to him, his eyes reading the expression of the older boy's face and gestures. *Alright, thank you,* he nodded in response, the slight upward bend of his smile broadening. The aching inside Amir's head was almost gone. It seemed as if he'd been deaf for his whole life. Amir never questioned why his speech should have gone as well. It seemed to fit that, along with his hearing, it too had disappeared from his life. Just like his family. In a strange way it comforted him, made living in the world possible. Josif continued talking, though now Amir had no idea about what.

The woman was pleased with the way things were working out. The boy was bright and did his work well. She had barely to show him the task before he would nod his understanding and go about it. He must have some education, and he knew farm work, that was clear. She did sometimes wonder how he'd come to be along the road like that . . . yet as soon as the thought entered her head, she quickly ushered it out like an unwanted visitor. These were times when it was better to know less than more. The work was getting done, and that was the important thing. Sonja occasionally rewarded the boy with what little extra food might be about. He always saved it, bringing it back to the room to share with Josif.

Amir knew to keep a careful distance from Zoran. There was something in the man's eyes that frightened him. Amir watched him in the same way he had been taught to observe animals in the forest. To look without being seen . . . going more than quiet . . . going still. . . . His father, Asaf, had taught him that in the woods the hunter learns that his invisibility needs to be more than simply to the physical eye. The hunter must also be imperceptible to the instinctual eye, the one that is felt in the body, whose sight is sensation. Amir had experienced this more than once: an animal's head suddenly jerking upright, coming alert, even though the boy was downwind and securely out of sight. In fact, his father had counseled, it was more important for the observer to be hidden to the instinctual eye than to the physical one, whose tendency to inattention was much greater.

The farm was running smoothly, summer making its way past spring. Amir's body recuperated quickly, but his mind's ills were still too tender and, to him, distant, to begin their healing. Amir knew he didn't belong where he was. Yet where did he belong, now? As soon as the lights went out and Josif and he lay down to sleep, dark images of men dressed in battle fatigues crept their way into Amir's consciousness like hunters threading their way through the forest, stalking their quarry. Scenes from the last few minutes he had spent with his family, before they had disappeared into oblivion, played through his mind. One of the dark men reached out for his sister, Minka, his hand roughly taking hold of her arm. Their mother, Emina, was crying and pleading, but the men dressed in the colors of the forest were laughing as they dragged the young girl away. Asaf, his father, stood with quavering knees. The scenes came and went with no linear sequence or sense. There was fighting and gunfire—the remembrance of the sounds reverberating deep within his unconscious.

Chapter 4

Sundays were supposed to be days of rest on the farm, though Zoran often found reasons for Josif to work at chores that he said the boy had neglected to do or done so poorly they'd have to be done over. Even so, Zoran needed rest from himself—from the energy it took to bring everything around him down to a level that he could stand above, allowing him to lord over those beneath him.

The day was hot, the sun bright, and Josif felt like a bird freed from its cage. It was Sunday, and Zoran hadn't bothered to come up with any extra chores for Josif to do, so the young farm worker luxuriously slept in until mid-morning, even though it meant missing breakfast. There would be nothing put aside for him, of course; neither Sonja nor Zoran was willing to indulge the farmhand to that degree.

When he awoke, Josif was pleased to find a plate of food by his bedside—bread, jam—and a glass of tea complemented with a splash of milk and a spoonful of honey. It was a rare treat somehow procured by the younger boy. Josif knew better than to take his good fortune for granted. As soon as he'd finished eating, he signaled Amir that they were going to go off on their own, away from the farm. The older boy knew not to try his luck, not to look relaxed and happy in sight of Zoran. Having fun kicking a soccer ball around the yard would invite his boss's attention and at the very least bring some scornful, sarcastic comment, if not a sudden forgotten chore in need of tending to.

Taking Amir by the hand, Josif led him out the back of the barn and indicated they should take a path into a small clearing where the cows grazed—away from the dirt lane that led from the farm out to the main road—to avoid being seen by Zoran. Once in the clearing, the two young farmhands cut through the woods to the road and a large grin spread across Josif's face.

"Yeah, we're free now, man!" Josif laughed. "No more fucking Zoran saying 'do this, do that. No, wait. Do that and then do this!' Ha, what shit that guy, huh?"

Amir looked back, the expression of his smile and eyes saying, "Yes, I am glad to be getting away." Even if the younger boy couldn't hear the older boy's words or read his lips, he seemed to understand. "What are we going to do?" Amir asked with a tilt of his head and a furrow of his brows, not so much because he cared one way or the other, but rather wanting to give support to the happiness he could see in Josif's face.

"We're going to go swimming," Josif said, his smile broadening at the quizzical look on the younger boy's face. "I know a good swimming hole just up the river from town. There's a place you can dive off the rocks into the water."

"OK," Amir smiled back timidly, understanding by the motion of the older boy's arms snaking through the air, one following the other, that they were going swimming.

"You know how to swim, don't you?" Josif asked with a questioning look, as he repeated his mime of a swimming stroke.

"A little," Amir answered with his fingers.

"OK, no problem. I'll teach you to swim like a fish," the older smiled bringing his two palms together in front of him, weaving them back and forth as though a fish swimming through the water. "Look," he said, "it's like a dance. I've just invented it!" And with a great laugh Josif began to move his feet along with the movement of his hands, stepping to the beat of a silent song.

Amir could see by Josif's laugh and his body's gyrations that his friend was making some kind of a joke. Although he had no idea of what had been said, Amir shared the moment's humor with a small, silent laugh of his own.

"Come on friend, let's go before Zoran comes along and finds us." Placing his arm around the younger boy's shoulder, Josif led him down the road in the direction toward town. Amir's body nestled into that of Josif's, the warmth of the older boy's arm drawing him in.

Josif liked his new friend. It was what he had come to name him, "friend." It was a simple term for want of a real name. Sonja and Zoran called the new helper "boy," though there was a clear difference in the tone of voice with which they addressed him. Zoran, when he bothered to at all, used the term with a derisive inflection. Sonja's tone was neutral, almost too purposefully so, as if she might be hiding some hint of affection, not just from her husband's ears but from her own as well. Neither of the farm's owners had attempted to ask Amir what his name was. Nor had Josif, though not for the want of caring, as with Zoran, or the fear of knowing, as with Sonja, but simply because it hadn't seemed relevant to him given the fact his younger friend could neither speak nor hear it.

"The swimming hole is just up a little farther," Josif said upon arrival at the river, speaking loudly so his voice carried over the sound of the running water. "It's a shame you can't hear the river. It's so beautiful. It's like music. Look," the older boy paused, turning to Amir and pointing at the coursing water. "It's really nice, yeah? It's still running strong. It's going to be fun diving into it."

Amir followed the motion of Josif's hand as it moved in a gentle arc, taking in the nature surrounding them. The younger boy's head nodded in appreciation of what he saw. He had in fact been in a heightened state of awareness from the moment they set foot on the narrow trail that wound its way through the trees and over the rocks that bordered the bank of the river. Josif had been only partially right in thinking Amir couldn't hear the running water. His ears, it was true, no longer picked up the sound . . . yet the sight of it, the spray of the mist rising in the air and wetting his skin, the smell of the water and the taste of it upon his tongue, all unleashed a memory that sang out like a choir of healing hymns to his soul.

"I like it very much. I am happy to be here too," Amir said by way of his smile.

"There are a few good places to swim in this river," Josif indicated with a sweep of his arm. "We'll keep going until we get to the last one. It's got the best place to dive from."

There were no other bathers at the swimming hole when they arrived. The boys, in fact, had seen no one else at all, war having drained the local inhabitants' spirit for such summer pastimes. The look on Josif's face, however, showed no weakening of enthusiasm for enjoying the bucolic setting of the river running through field and woods in a countryside that had changed little in the centuries since it had been first settled.

"Yeah, this is it!" Josif shouted in glee when they finally arrived. He gestured to the younger boy to follow as he raced along a narrow path leading up to a small outcropping of rock sitting above the deepest part of the swimming hole. "Come on, come on," he cried.

Reaching the highest point of the rugged rock formation, Josif began dancing on one foot, then the other, as he removed his shoes, and then his pants. A small grin broke out on Amir's face as he watched the older boy hopping about in such a rush of enthusiasm that he appeared to be attempting to jump right out of his clothing.

"Come on, don't be scared," Josif laughed as Amir stood to the side, watching him with a timid smile. "We'll jump in together. It's not as far down as it looks."

"I don't know," Amir answered with a doubting look, stepping toward the edge of the rock and peering down at the nearly thirty-foot drop to the water below. He wasn't a strong swimmer, barely able to do more to keep himself afloat than paddle about with arms and legs.

"Ha-ha, you're scared," Josif joked good-humoredly. "It's going to be fun. You'll see. You can't think about it. You just have to do it."

Stripping off his shirt, Josif stood clothed in only his underwear and gestured impatiently to his younger friend to follow his example. Sensing both the abandonment of the moment from the older boy and a hesitant warning of rational restraint within his own mind, Amir slowly did as Josif had encouraged. "OK, OK," he said, using his hands to express his hesitation, "I'm coming, I'm coming."

"Yeah, alright. Look down there, man. This is going to be fun!" Josif exclaimed after Amir had shed his clothing and finally stood beside him ready to take the leap. "Here, take my hand. One, two, three . . . go-o-o-o!"

Unable to hear Josif's countdown, Amir could nevertheless feel the anticipation of their leap by means of the tension transmitted from the older boy's hand clasped on to his own. Amir wanted to speak out, to say "wait," but even if the deaf-mute boy had been able to verbalize his hesitation, there was no time. Pulled by the weight of Josif's leap, the ground disappeared from under Amir's feet and was suddenly replaced by nothing but air, the two boys' bodies rapidly plunging downward in free-fall. And then, as abruptly as the leap had been taken, the flight was broken by the impact of the splash, the sensation of falling through air now displaced by the feel of total submersion in clear, cold liquid.

Josif surfaced first, a shout of delight exiting his mouth at the very same moment he took in a large inhalation of air. Amir's head and shoulders broke through a second later, the small panic he felt at being closed in by the water quickly being overridden by the relief of surfacing and the sight of Josif's face manifesting his joy in smile and shouts of adrenaline-inspired delight that echoed about the pool. There was happiness in the laughter coming from deep within Josif's lungs, its pulse rippling outward like the water from his dive. At heart, Josif was a person drawn to the wonder of life, even if his lot had been one of difficult and too-often loveless experience.

As the sound of Josif's laughter traveled through the air it found entry into the boy whose ears could not detect its melody. Amir felt the sound's emotion gain access to his own senses through his chest, a sensation of warmth arising from his solar plexus and spreading wide. The younger boy could feel his heart breathe in Josif's joy like the great gulp of air his lungs drew in upon surfacing from the water. For a glorious moment, Amir felt himself freed of the cast that had formed around his fractured psyche—the invisible plaster that kept his mind whole and held all of its pieces together temporarily replaced by the happiness on his friend's face and the beauty of the nature that surrounded them.

Josif and Amir raced back up the rock wall several more times, jumping feet first or with legs pulled into chest for maximum entry splash, until the older boy gestured with arms outstretched in front of his head that they should try a real dive.

"We can go from there," Josif indicated, pointing at a ledge about halfway up the outcropping. "It's not so high."

Standing on the rock shelf with Amir by his side, Josif lifted his arms upward, palms spread open. The older boy momentarily lowered his right arm to point at Amir and then to his own eye in spontaneous sign language. "Watch this," he said, a small look of pride peeking out from behind his smile. Standing with his body erect and his back arched, the memory of once having seen a professional diving event on television playing in his mind, Josif raised his arms yet higher above his head, then lowered them to his side and pushed off the ledge, trying to imitate a classic diving pose as best he could. As his body neared its goal, Josif tucked his head between his extended his arms, his body breaking the water's surface with a clean, neat incision. Stepping out from the pool, Josif pulled up his sagging underwear before raising his arms and pumping them up and down in victory celebration. Standing on the ledge, Amir gave him a thumbs-up and smiled broadly.

"OK, now you try," Josif yelled, his arms mimicking the action of his dive.

"No way," Amir replied, his head moving back and forth.

Before Josif had a chance to say anything more, Amir leapt into the air, his legs curled into his chest, wrapped tight by his arms. The splash of the younger boy's cannonball rained over Josif, and it was Amir's turn to raise his arms in victory. Back up on the ledge together, Josif, feeling himself the expert from his first dive's success, persisted in getting Amir to try it.

"Look, you do it like this," Josif demonstrated in encouragement. "Yeah, come on, friend, you can do it!"

The expression on Amir's face looked doubtful. Nevertheless, he began to imitate the older boy's pose and, cheered on by Josif, he leapt outward from the lower ledge. Amir flew out parallel to the water and looked like he might stay that way, ending up with a belly flop, until, at the very last moment, he was able to make an adjustment, tucking his head downward and tilting his body at a sharper angle, to hit the water with a reasonable facsimile of a proper dive.

"Yeah man, cool. Really great," Josif called out to Amir when he surfaced. "Hey, look there! Your underwear!"

The impact of the dive had removed the old, ill-fitting underwear from Amir's body. Laughing, Josif dove at the floating piece of cloth and took hold of it just as his hands breached the water. He emerged from the dive holding the briefs up teasingly toward Amir and, still laughing, threw the garment over the younger boy's head, up onto the rocks at the pool's edge. Seeing Amir's embarrassed surprise, Josif's grin grew larger, and he spontaneously reached down to take hold of his own underwear, which had slipped low on his waist, and removed it, then threw it over his young friend's head as well, giggling with drunken delight. Their breath bursting forth from their lungs in laughter, the boys raced up to the shore to gather their underwear. Reaching his first, Josif took hold of them and covered the area of his crotch, grinning and pointing at his younger friend's nakedness. Then, as though playing peekaboo, Josif kept moving them away from and then back over himself, giggling at a blushing Amir, the older boy's knees buckling as if he were about to fall down laughing. But all of a sudden Josif's jesting ceased, something about the younger boy's nakedness catching his eye.

"Oh, my god," Josif said. "You're circumcised. Your worm is cut."

Amir returned his older friend's surprised expression with a quizzical gaze. Josif was clearly pointing toward the area of Amir's pubis. At first instant he thought his friend might be teasing him for lack of any body hair there, but in the very next second his eyes caught clearer focus of the older boy's penis. His immediate reaction was that there was something wrong with Josif's member. It didn't look right. In the very next beat of his heart, though, Amir understood what Josif's surprise was all about. He, Amir, was circumcised, and Josif was not.

Seeing the blush of embarrassment on his younger friend's face change to the flush of fear, Josif sought to assuage the boy and tell him there was no need to worry. It was lost on neither boy that, in their land, to be circumcised was considered a badge of Islam. In a time and place where the violence of war had come as suddenly and swiftly as it had in their country, the fact of one's being circumcised or not could mean the difference between life and death. That the presence, or lack thereof, of a small piece of foreskin could hold such significance seemed an absurdity. Yet now, for the two boys, things had changed.

The surprised look on Josif's face quickly changed to one of concern and was followed by a moment's silence. A thought came to Josif, and he bent to his knees and lowered himself to the ground, his body prostrating forward the way the Muslims did at prayer. Josif then looked up at his friend with a question in his eyes.

"Yes," Amir answered in kind, his eyes meeting Josif's, "I am Muslim."

Josif went quiet, though after a moment his smile returned, a softer one than the earlier, more playful grin.

"Come, let's dive again," Josif said speaking more to himself than to his friend, his thoughts trying to come to terms with what this revelation might mean.

That night in bed, Amir could see Josif's lips moving, though barely so. Whether he was talking to himself or to Amir was unclear. Feeling the warmth of Josif's body next to his, Amir fell off into dreams while Josif lay awake, continuing to speak in quiet whisper. After a time the older boy no longer spoke out loud, and his thoughts retreated to silent wanderings. Above all, Zoran must not know. Josif must bring his friend to town. He had heard that buses sometimes passed through to take the Muslims to what were called "the safe areas," the places where the blue-helmeted foreign soldiers were stationed. But he remembered Zoran drinking one night with his friends, some of whom were soldiers. They joked about the buses. Some would get lost, they laughed. A drunken Zoran spoke of the things he and his soldier friends had done to the people on the buses, things that made Josif shiver.

No, he must not let Zoran know. He needed to get his friend away. To the town authorities, that would probably be best. Then again, maybe not. Josif's thoughts began to mingle one into the other: the war, his silent friend, Zoran, the unhappiness of his own life . . . all mixing in jumble and then dispersing . . . and suddenly, in the moments before sleep took hold, he found himself in a rock-and-roll band. He was in Belgrade. He was onstage, and below him were hundreds of kids his own age dancing wildly to the music. The last thing Josif remembered before falling into dream, he was sitting in the drummer's seat, his body pulsing like the skin on the drum to the reverberation of the beat, sweat dripping from his head to his feet, his heart as happy as music itself.

Chapter 5

Amir closed the door on Josif dancing to a popular Belgrade rock group's hit song, this time the older boy pantomiming the guitar solo instead of taking on the role of drummer. The younger boy headed in the direction of the cow stalls, to go past them through the large double doors, to the place where he and Josif went to relieve their bladders under the night sky. The house had an indoor toilet. The boys had but a fetid, uncared-for outhouse that they avoided whenever possible.

Walking through the barn, Amir came to a sudden, though noiseless, stop just as he came onto the stalls. He sensed a presence, a movement, and too, there was the faintest of sounds breaking through the obstruction that hindered his hearing. Brief flutters of noise, like a smell so indistinct as to seem odorless, a thing too distant for the eyes to distinguish from the horizon, had recently begun to make their way in but made no impression on his conscious mind.

Scanning the evening gloom, Amir saw Zoran standing tall in silhouette inside one of the stalls. The farmer was standing on a pair of milking stools placed side by side, his pants fallen down around his ankles. The man's body swayed back and forth, his hips moving rhythmically. His head was bent back with open mouth and moved in counterpoint to the motion of his hips. In the shadowy darkness of the barn interior it seemed to the boy as if he were looking upon the strange dance of a puppet backlit on a darkened stage. Amir stood silently watching, the invisible hands of the puppeteer pulling the strings from somewhere behind a hidden curtain.

Zoran's hands rested on the cow's rump to give him balance, his left hand serving double duty, keeping the cow's tail flipped to one side. Forward and back, the farmer swayed. Amir looked on as Zoran approached the climax of the event, his head lolling to the side, tilting just enough to catch sight of the boy standing there, only ten meters off. The young deaf-mute's eyes were like the darkness of the night; they saw, but said nothing. A sardonic smile intermingled with Zoran's look of pleasure, his head returning front on. Back and forth . . . the cow contentedly chewing grain from the feed bucket Zoran had placed in front of it, the action of the farmer's penetration lost to the sweetness of the grain's taste. Then, all of a sudden, Zoran's eyes rose up in their sockets, his head no longer moving in opposition to the rhythm of the hips but tensed back, face toward the ceiling. His groan floated past the boy's ears unheard.

"Oh, Lepa, you're a good one," Zoran murmured while lifting his pants up to his knees.

The farmer stepped off the stool, patted the cow's rump, then took a rag hanging on the bars of the stall and wiped off his penis. Pulling his pants up all the way now, his body sedated and laconic, he shoved the stools back into the stall with his foot and turned to look at the boy who stood in the shadows as still as a mouse. Zoran gave the boy barely a moment's consideration, as though the child held little more concern to him than might an actual rodent.

A week had passed since Josif's discovery of Amir's Muslim heritage. Nothing more of it had been communicated between the two. Amir was, to an extent, innocent of its potential danger to him at the farm. The younger boy felt secure in his trust of Josif, protected and cared for by his older friend. If Josif was not by nature drawn to, nor fully cognizant of, the rationale for the violence that had ignited the war, he also wasn't ignorant of its dangers, nor the precariousness of his friend's situation, living in such close proximity to a man like Zoran. He decided he needed to help his young friend escape to the safe haven provided by the blue-helmeted soldiers of the United Nations, sooner rather than later.

That Sunday, Zoran came up with several hours' worth of chores to occupy Josif on what was supposed to be the boy's day of rest. "So you don't become accustomed to laziness," the man gave for reason. "And take your pet rabbit with you to help out," he added with derisive glance in Amir's direction, indicating that the younger farmhand was not to escape the lesson.

After lunch, when their last chore had been completed, Josif told Sonja that he wanted to take the boy into town. "He's never seen it," Josif said, by way of reason.

"How do you know?" Sonja asked. "That's where I found him. Just outside of town."

"I asked him," Josif answered. "He shook his head no."

If Josif had been speaking with Zoran, the man would have said something like: "You can't ask a question of a rock. And a rock certainly can't answer one. Go away and talk your foolishness to someone else stupid enough to listen."

Sonja didn't take the conversation any further but just nodded her head, more in thought than in assent. Questions of the boy's origins hovered at the back of her conscious thought, where she had sent them to keep her nagging suspicions at bay. The farmer's wife would rather know less than more. She had lied to her husband when he had asked where the boy came from. Instead of telling the truth, that she didn't know—a fact that would have drawn more inquiry from Zoran—she'd made up a vague story of the boy being the relative of a friend of a friend, insinuating an ethic origin that would have the child coming from the "right" side. This was enough to assuage both Zoran and her own mind.

"Can we use the bicycle?" Josif asked, distracting Sonja from the question of going to town to that of using the bike, as though the former had already been answered in the affirmative.

Sonja hesitated before saying yes . . . not for any fear of loss or damage to the old, rusted bicycle itself, but rather, her thoughts traveled to her children. She remembered them riding about the yard, playing freely in rare moments when their father wasn't bullying them about. She wondered where they might be at that very moment and prayed that wherever it was, it was far from this damned war, a war stirred up by men like her husband, only ones far more clever and ambitious than he.

"Yes, you can take it," Sonja said, reluctance struggling with generosity, the kinder part of her winning over. "But be careful not to leave it unattended. Things disappear quickly these days. You can't be too careful. And be back well before dark."

Unable to keep a smile from his face, Josif raced off to the barn to collect the bike. He had already pumped air into its tires and sprayed oil on the sprocket and chain. Knowing Zoran had gone off with friends, he had assumed there would be a good chance of talking Sonja into letting him and the boy have the bike. Josif hopped onto the bike and rode it around to the back of the barn, where he had left Amir waiting.

"Hey, look," Josif laughed. "I got it!"

"Hah, great," Amir smiled.

"Come on, then," Josif said. "Let's go."

"Where?" Amir asked by way of opening his palms while hunching his shoulders and tilting his head to the side with a quizzical expression.

"To town," Josif answered.

"Where?" Amir asked once more, not sure of what his friend was saying.

"To town," Josif repeated, this time more slowly and mouthing the words broadly, his arm signaling the direction they would go.

When he understood where they were to go, Amir hesitated, the idea of going into town somehow disturbing to him. "I don't know," Amir said with a doubtful shake of his head. "Let's go swimming instead," he suggested, his arms miming the stroke of the crawl.

"Yeah, maybe later," Josif lied. "But we have to go to town now. I heard Zoran talking to one of his soldier friends last night. He said they are taking some of your people to the safe place today. To where the blue helmets are. The buses will be passing through town this afternoon. We need to get you on the bus so you can get away from here. You'll see, it will be good."

Amir had no idea what his friend was saying. He could sense, though, that Josif had something in mind and seemed agitated. "OK," he shrugged and mounted the bicycle's crossbar, sitting in front of the seat, Josif's feet holding the bike steady.

"Yeah, it's going to be OK," Josif said with reassuring smile. "You'll see. Everything is going to be alright."

With the younger boy securely nestled between his arms and the handlebars, Josif began pedaling toward town with purpose. They were almost there when the older boy caught sight of three buses coming their way. Two military jeeps escorted the larger vehicles, one in the lead of the buses and the others taking up the rear. Most of the men riding in the escort vehicles were dressed in military fatigues, the rest in regular civilian clothing. All of them but the drivers carried weapons. As the convoy drove by, Josif stopped pedaling, his feet coming to the ground to hold the bike upright. The lead bus was nearly full, its occupants only men. Bleak, frightened-looking faces stared out the windows, a few turning to look at Josif and Amir, most gazing off into the distance. The next two buses were filled with women and young children. At the sight of soldiers Amir felt his body seize in fear. His eyes closed to shut out their image.

"Damn, we're too late." Josif spoke with a look of disappointment on his face, the buses already moving past them into the distance.

Amir felt the breath of Josif's words on his neck. He opened his eyes and then turned to look at the older boy. "What?" his expression asked. "I don't understand."

"I was going to send you with them," Josif responded, realizing at that moment that if he had succeeded it would have meant returning to the farm alone. The idea of losing his friend, of returning to Zoran's to once more live at the farm without companionship of any kind, suddenly felt unbearable to the older boy. At that moment, he knew he was finished with them. He was finished with being shipped off here and there to people who just used him as a servant. It was time for him to strike out on his own. To Belgrade. Yes, to Belgrade, to find a job playing drums in a rock group. He could take his friend with him. The boy could help in the band, be what they called the roadie, carry the equipment, set it up, and break it down. But no, it wouldn't work. Josif needed to get Amir to the place of the foreign soldiers, to where his own people were.

"Hang on. We're going to go after them," Josif said, pointing in the direction of the buses. "We'll ask people on the road where they passed to. We'll find the safe area ourselves."

"No, I don't want to," Amir answered with a firm shake of his head. "Let's go back."

"Look, don't worry. I'm taking you to your people. It's going to be OK. You can't stay at Zoran's. It's too dangerous. He's going to find out. You have to trust me. Come on, now, it's going to be good. I promise you."

Amir didn't understand what Josif had said, but the look of caring and confident resolve on his friend's face eased the tension in the younger boy's body and mind.

Giving Amir a thumbs-up and a reassuring smile, Josif swiveled the bike around. Feeling his young friend's body relax into his, Josif raised his feet to the pedals and began pumping for all he was worth in the direction the buses had gone. After a time, the boys lost thought of all destination and fell into a world of their own imagination.

They took turns pedaling, sometimes madly as if racing against an imaginary challenger, at other times slowly and lazily, beguiled by the summer day's promise of endless sunshine and eternal warmth.

Nearly two hours later, legs tired and their energy on the wane, the boys saw a small cloud of dust rise ahead of them. Soon a lone, empty bus emerged from the billowing opaqueness. It was headed in their direction and escorted by a military jeep, the lead vehicle's passengers looking like tired workers whose shift had just finished. They seemed not to notice the two boys, mounted on their bicycle, who were staring at them from the side of the road. Weapons at rest, several of the men could be seen laughing and joking while the others looked off into space with blank faces. The fine mist of dust drifting earthward signaled that they had driven out from a side road just ahead.

Josif quit pedaling and lowered his feet to the ground. Touching Amir's shoulder, he pointed down the dirt road, holding his thumb and index finger close together to sign that they must be almost at their destination.

"We must be close," Josif said, trying to look hopeful. "That's only one of the buses. We'll catch up with the others soon."

"No," Amir shook his head. "Let's keep going straight." The younger boy pointed ahead of them, away from the turnoff where the bus had come from, not really knowing why, some instinct within him reacting in alarm. "Let's go that way."

Josif placed his hand gently on his young friend's back to calm him. "Look, it's OK. I promise you. It can't be far to where the blue helmets are now. You'll see. I'm glad we missed the bus. This was more fun anyway. You and me together. Wasn't it?"

Comforted, Amir saw the question in Josif's eyes, unconsciously understanding the deeper query whose answer the older boy sought. Amir nodded his head in affirmation. Whatever the question's words, he knew the answer was yes, the two of them were good friends.

As Josif's legs began pumping the pedals with renewed vigor toward the side road he was sure must lead to the UN camp, a thought came into his head. He might not have to leave his friend so soon after all. He had an idea how they might still be able to remain together, at least for a time. His imagination, flying, soon slowed. The road was narrowing, the gravel looser, rougher, and more potholed. This wasn't right. The road should be bigger and better maintained, not like an abandoned country lane. Josif was sure the two vehicles had come from this way and that the other two buses must still lie ahead. Yet it looked as if the road ended at the clearing they had just come upon. Stopping, the boys dismounted, and Josif laid the bike down on the edge of what seemed to be an abandoned quarry. The older boy spied something at the far side of the open land. Foot tracks pressed down through the grass and headed in that direction. Josif signaled to Amir that they should go forward to investigate. The younger boy went no more than twenty meters when something became clear to him, something that still wasn't clear to Josif.

"No!" Amir shook his head vigorously and stopped in mid-track.

"Come on," Josif responded, his voice less than sure, his hand reaching out to take Amir's arm.

"No!" Amir shook his head yet even more emphatically and pulled his arm from Josif's hand. The older boy looked into his friend's eyes, something within him sensing that it wasn't so much fear expressing itself in the younger boy's face as some kind of terrible knowledge. Josif turned to proceed on his own. After about fifty meters the older boy began to understand Amir's refusal to go forward . . . the distant colors, the shape of the formation becoming clearer. His legs took him closer and closer, some invisible force pulling him even though he knew he should turn and run, never see what lay in front of him.

They numbered twenty or more. It was difficult to say exactly how many there were because the ditch into which they were piled hid most of them from view. The bus with the men and boys had been detoured and their journey ended in brutal fashion.

Josif had never really believed the stories he had heard from Zoran and his friends, tales of disappearing buses and the things done to those trapped inside: knives drawn across throats and other brutal murders hard to believe possible. Yet the young teenager now understood that the stories he heard spoken in drunken swagger were not of minds speaking in idle boast but were real acts, the results of which he was now witness to. Looking onto the piled corpses—the faces of men and boys who a short time ago he'd seen gazing out the window of their bus—Josif was overcome by a sudden wave of nausea.

Turning away from the death mound, Josif felt his knees go weak and was unsure he would be able to continue walking without lowering his body to the ground. He made his way as if in a trance toward Amir, who now came toward him. The sudden realization hit Josif that if his young friend had been on the bus, he would, at this very moment, be among the dead piled in the hole.

"Did you see?" Josif asked, his eyes searching those of Amir's. "I didn't know. I didn't know. . . ." The older boy's words slipped by Amir's ears unheard.

"Come, we must leave," Amir said by way of a small turn of his head, hands pointing the way. Josif started to follow but paused as the younger boy's steps began to lead away from the road they had entered on and instead headed in the direction of the woods.

"Wait. Where are you going?"

"This way, to the woods," Amir answered, his arm pointing toward the trees.

"But the bike," Josif said. "We can't leave the bike." It took a few seconds for Josif to realize the disoriented state of his mind. He was worried that Sonja would be angered if they didn't return the bike. Yet after what he had just seen, he suddenly understood the borrowed bicycle was as if nothing—only rusty, old lengths of metal welded together. It was all nothing. He felt like someone had reached into his body and pulled the life from within him and then thrown it into a dark, endless abyss. No, no, he could never go back to Zoran's farm now.

Abandoning the bike, Josif followed Amir into the woods. They had no more than entered into the tree line when the older boy heard the rumbling of a motor in the distance. He signaled Amir to wait. The sound of the engine grew stronger, and soon they saw a backhoe driving down the track they had just left, come to finish the soldiers' work.

The two boys passed the evening in the woods. Amir made a bed for them from what loose material he was able to gather from the forest floor, and the boys huddled close to share the warmth of their bodies against the chill of the night. They awoke the following morning at dawn, cold and hungry and thirsty, not knowing where they might go— only that it should be in the opposite direction from where they'd come.

It was Amir, not Josif, who led their way through the forest. The boys exchanged no communication as to who should lead. They had simply and instinctually fallen into line with Amir in front.

The two had been walking for a number of hours when Amir raised his right arm and signaled Josif to stop. The older boy looked at him questioningly but could see by the look on the younger boy's face that the pause wasn't a casual one. Amir pointed to their right, put a finger to his mouth, and squatted low. It was only after another few seconds that Josif finally heard a distant movement and saw figures moving through the trees to their north.

There were three of them. Two younger men and one older. The younger appeared to be in their mid to late twenties. Neither they nor the older man carried weapons. Their shoulders were burdened by backpacks stretched full, and it was clear to Amir by the hesitant, cautious step of their gait that they were the hunted and not the hunters. Amir seemed content to watch and let them pass by; Josif, however, had already had enough of the woods.

With Josif sitting behind him, Amir was unable to see the older boy's mouth open and move. He knew only by virtue of their startled response that Josif had called out to the three men.

"Hello-o-o," Josif sang out once more. Amir turned around to see Josif standing with his arm in the air, waving in their direction. The demeanor of the frightened men quickly changed upon seeing that it was only a pair of young boys who had interrupted the quiet.

"Shut up!" the taller of the two younger men hissed as they came close. "Are you crazy or just stupid? There are snipers all about here just waiting for idiots like you. Do you want to get us all killed?"

Josif's face flushed, and his eyes blinked and looked past the man as if in search of something behind him. The shorter of the young men glared at him. The older man held the palm of his right hand toward the ground, raising and lowering it in short brief strokes to calm his traveling companions. They were all on edge, their nerves anxious and worn thin. The taller man, who had spoken harshly to Josif, took a deep breath and closed his eyes for several seconds. Raising his eyelids, he looked to the older man and nodded, then continued walking onward through the woods.

Without anything being said, the two boys fell into line behind the three men. They walked for about an hour, until they came to a place where light flooded into the landscape along a wide horizontal break in the trees. Just beyond the tree line was a paved roadway. The men whispered among themselves, arguing about what to do. They sat waiting for what seemed an eternity, watching to see if there was anyone about. Finally, one of the younger men raised himself into a crouch. He nodded to his companions and then sprinted across the road. The two remaining men continued to wait. There was no movement anywhere. They rose and quickly crossed the road, the two boys right behind them.

A short time later they came to a meadow. The men debated whether they should stop and rest before continuing on. Deciding to take a break, they opened their backpacks and began to pick through them for food. Ignoring the boys, the men shared what little they had with each other until the last few bites, when the older man finally looked toward Josif and Amir. He turned back to his companions and gave a brief nod of his head in the boys' direction.

"Here," one of the younger men said, handing a few morsels to the boys without further word.

The boys gratefully received the offering—a couple of pieces of pan-fried bread and a few slivers of raw onion—wolfing it down quickly from hand to mouth. Josif thanked the men and asked them where they were going.

"Where do you think?" the shorter of the two younger men answered sarcastically. "The same place as you. Away from here, before we get killed."

Josif said nothing, his eyes opening just the slightest bit, as if trying to take in the import of the man's words. Not knowing what else to do, he nodded his head as if in agreement and struggled to come up with something to say that might make sense.

"Yes, we are trying to get away, too," Josif responded to no one in particular.

"Hey, you," the taller of the young men said, turning to Amir, "pass me the pack next to you."

Amir was staring straight out in front of him. Josif nudged his young friend's arm to get his attention, then pointed at the backpack and then at the man who had spoken. Amir didn't understand. He could see the man was talking to him, saying something, but he wasn't able to make out any of the words from the movement of his lips or mouth.

"What are you staring at me for? Just give me the fucking pack, will you?" the man said.

"I'll get it for you," Josif responded, quickly reaching over for the backpack and handing it to their newfound traveling companion.

"What's the matter with your brother?" the man asked with an annoyed look as he took the pack from Josif.

"He can't hear," Josif answered. "He can't speak, either."

"A deaf-mute?"

Josif nodded. He didn't bother to refute the labeling of Amir as his brother. He accepted the man's labeling of the younger boy as his brother as if indeed it were true . . . as how it really was between them.

The three men looked at each other with unspoken words. Traveling in enemy territory was dangerous enough without having the burden of a deaf-mute child on their hands.

"Where's your family, then?" the older man asked.

Josif paused to think, but then just answered with the simple truth. His truth. There was no family anymore. No mother, no father. There was only him and his younger brother.

"And your grandparents? Your aunts and uncles?"

Josif thought about Zoran and Sonja.

"No, there is only my brother and me. No one else. They are all gone."

"What are your names?" the older of the men asked, his compassion slipping past the barrier of his fear's defense.

"My name is Jusuf," the older boy answered, using the Muslim form of his name, unsure of what the men's reaction might be to the Serbian variation of his real given name. Nodding toward Amir, he spoke the first Muslim name that came to his mind, "My brother's name is Muhamed."

After speaking, Josif looked at the ground, not wanting to make eye contact with any of the men. They in turn looked away, reading into the boy's words their own experiences, their own losses. That the boys were orphans was not shocking news. The men didn't need to know more. Didn't want to know more. The men couldn't afford to become involved. Self-preservation allowed no room for the indulgence of pity or the binding complexities of attachment. The three men rose, slung their backpacks over their shoulders, and began walking toward the woods at the far side of the meadow. They didn't look back to see whether or not the boys followed.

By day's end, they had wandered close to an outpost where peacekeepers had been deployed by the United Nations in an effort to create a humanitarian corridor leading to an area protected from the war. About an hour remained before sunset. The day had been long and arduous. When they finally came within view of the UN camp, the men and boys could see that the main road leading to it had a Serb checkpoint blocking any direct approach. The three men argued about whether to simply take the road to the camp and brave the checkpoint, or find some other route in. Surely the Serbs wouldn't do anything confrontational that might be seen by the UN observers, one of them had argued, to the cynical looks of the others.

In the end they all agreed it would be best to find an alternative route in. They skirted the camp, to where a wooded hillside led almost all the way down to the outpost's perimeter, leaving a distance of only a couple hundred meters without cover. The men made their way as quietly as they could. Unable to hear, Amir could nevertheless see by the way the men were walking that their feet would speak their presence to any who might be carefully listening.

A quiet, peaceful scene from long ago appeared in Amir's mind, the memory floating into his consciousness. He and his father were about to enter the woods behind their house, and his father was speaking. Amir could hear the words inside his head. His father was telling him about the secrets of the forest . . . saying that to understand them, one needed to be able to engage the depths of nature's silence.

"When you are on the hunt in the woods, everything you do must be done in silence," he'd counseled the boy and then asked, "And do you know the most important thing of all to be done in silence?"

"Is it to walk?"

"No, son. The most important of all is to see in silence." Asaf paused. "Do you understand?"

Amir was quiet for a moment before responding. "No, Papa," he answered truthfully.

Asaf smiled, his heart warm with fatherly pride and love for his son. Amir couldn't understand why his father would appear so pleased, when he had been unable to answer the question. Asaf's hand came to rest gently on his son's shoulder, his thought suddenly traveling back in time . . . to words his own father had once spoken to him as a child, to the Sufi aphorisms his father had been so fond of quoting.

His mind returning to the present, Asaf looked down at the top of Amir's head, the fine, dark-brown hair, and at the small, delicate round of shoulders yet to gain their form. He thought to repeat one of his father's favorite sayings, but the boy was young. There would be time later, when Amir was older. Father and son continued quietly on in pursuit of the wild mushrooms they had promised to collect for Amir's mother, Emina.

Chapter 6

The men sat at the forest's edge for nearly half an hour before deciding to make their way down to the UN camp. They argued about whether to wait until it was dark or to cross the open land while there was still enough light for the peacekeepers to see them. The older man, Ismet, was afraid that in the black of night they might startle the sentries, causing the soldiers to fire on them.

"What are they saying?" Amir asked Josif with his eyes.

Josif shook his head and gave a slight shrug of his shoulders. "It's not important," his gesture spoke.

As the sun began its final descent to the horizon, the men gathered together at the tree line and made ready to dash across the meadow that separated them from the UN outpost. There was a heavy silence as they waited one last minute before stepping out into the open and exposing their presence to any snipers that might be about. The men stood and adjusted their backpacks. Josif tapped Amir on the shoulder and pointed out past the wood's edge to indicate the direction they were to go. Taking Amir's hand in his, Josif followed the men as they began to make their way across the open field at a trot.

Nearing the halfway mark, as they closed in on their destination, Amir could see smiles of relief breaking out on the faces of their traveling companions. He glanced toward Josif to see if he too was smiling. Josif's eyes met his. "It's OK," they said, a wide grin shining on the older boy's face. Feeling the courage of hope within Josif's eyes, Amir responded in kind.

One of the boys' older traveling companions let out a laugh of relief and began to wave his right arm in the direction of the camp to signal the peacekeepers of their arrival. Josif felt the surge of adrenaline passing among them all as they drew close to the camp; the boy's stride becoming light, he felt like a deer bounding through the high grass.

Signaling his joy, Josif's hand closed tighter around Amir's, and with a bright grin he said something the younger boy couldn't make out. Amir looked back with his eyebrows raised in question only to see his friend's smile suddenly disappear, the older boy's happy expression replaced by a look of astonished surprise that leapt out from his face as though some great thought or perhaps disturbing news had just entered his mind. At the same moment, Josif's body jumped abruptly forward, lurching ahead and causing his hand to separate from Amir's.

The men distinctly heard the gunshots that the deaf-mute boy registered only as a faint rush of air passing near the surface of his skin. Panic, arising from some instinctual place of fear, welled up within the men, momentarily freezing their march. Amir, reacting at the instant, lunged ahead to retake Josif's hand but halted his thrust forward because his friend was inexplicably falling. Spinning round in his descent, Josif landed on his back, his eyes staring into the darkening sky until a second later Amir's face appeared inches from his own, blocking out his view of the heavens.

Josif saw his little brother looking pale and shocked. Josif didn't want him to be afraid. He smiled that it was all OK. He felt so funny. Everything tingling and numb.

Freeing himself from the paralysis that had seized him, Ismet screamed for everyone to run. He had seen Josif hit the ground, the front of the boy's shirt going dark with red. The little deaf-mute was kneeling beside his fallen brother, shock and confusion on his face. The older man ran to their aid.

The younger boy would not let go of his brother's hand. Ismet could see the life fading from the older boy's eyes. He reached out his arm to grab hold of the younger boy, to lead him to safety. But the silent child wouldn't release his grip and held onto his brother with a fierceness of strength unimaginable for one so small. Ismet began pulling both boys toward the camp, one arm wrapped around the small, shocked body of the young child whose only words were the tears that ran down his cheeks, and with the other dragging a body that would never cry again.

Yelling, Ismet called out to the others for help, through the rifle shots whose sounds filled the air all about them. His two companions quickly joined him, taking hold of Josif. They struggled toward the camp with their burden as fast as they could. The sound of rifle fire continued, but the bullets could no longer find their mark, the refugees being now beyond the snipers' range.

At the sound of the rifle fire, the camp sentries ran in the direction from which the shots had come. The peacekeeping force had their weapons at ready, but by the time they reached the group straggling in to the perimeter of the outpost the firing had stopped. A paramedic quickly went to the aid of the wounded boy. A soldier knelt down beside the child who sat rocking next to the bloodied body, his small hand clinging to that of the injured boy.

"Come, come," the man said softly, bending down toward Amir. "It's alright. He'll be fine. Come with me. What's your name, son?"

Ismet spoke English. He now stepped forward to intervene, his hand reaching out to touch the soldier's shoulder.

"He cannot hear you," he said, his voice no more than a hoarse whisper. "He is deaf and neither can he speak. Let him be with his brother. It is all that he has left."

The look in the refugee's eyes spoke the obvious. Josif was all but dead. The soldier hesitated. The older man looked down at the peacekeeper, not sure whether the man understood. Anger crept into Ismet's voice as he repeated, "The wounded boy is the deaf-mute's older brother. Their entire family has been killed. There is no one left. No grandparents, no aunts, no uncles, no cousins. No fucking nobody. You understand? Nobody. They have killed them all."

The medic stepped in then, telling the assisting soldier they needed to evacuate the wounded boy to a nearby field hospital as soon as possible if they were going to have any chance to save him. The soldier nodded and quickly moved to arrange the transfer.

"OK, OK," the medic spoke softly to Amir, moving to detach the boy's hand from Josif's. "I have to help your brother now. You can stay. Just sit to the side. Look into my eyes now. See, I'm going to help your brother."

Amir's expression was blank, his eyes hollow, his face wan and shocked. He let his hand be moved without resistance.

"I need you to translate for me," the medic said, addressing Ismet. "I have to keep this boy conscious. Ask him how he feels . . . whatever you can think of. Just keep him awake."

Ismet nodded and bent forward to speak to Josif. Blood bubbled from the boy's mouth. His face was moribund and his eyes glazed. Ismet told Josif that everything was going to be OK, that the doctors would take care of him. He asked the boy how he was feeling. When there was no response he came closer still, until he could make contact with the wounded boy's eyes. He asked once more, and this time Josif moved his mouth, but the only sound that came out was a gasping and the gurgling of blood bubbling forth from his lungs. The medic cleared the boy's mouth and made sure his tongue wasn't obstructing his airway. Ismet sat, silent, a deep, weighted sigh escaping his mouth. It was too much. He couldn't try to talk with this dying boy and still maintain the buffer of emotional distance that was the only protection left to his sanity.

"Talk to him . . . talk to him," the medic admonished in an urgent voice.

Despite the pain it cost him to do so, Ismet continued to speak to the wounded boy until a vehicle arrived to transport him to the hospital. The medic transferred Josif to a gurney and with the driver's help carried him to the makeshift ambulance. Ushering Amir into the van, the medic jumped in and closed the rear doors, doing what little he could to cushion the patient during the slow, rough ride over the bomb-cratered roads that led to the field hospital.

Midway there, Josif's eyes seemed to liven for a few moments, and he turned to smile at Amir, who sat curled next to him. The younger boy's eyes were closed, and his head lay on top of Josif's left hand. When his friend's hand stirred, Amir looked up. Their eyes met. Amir smiled back. Some moments later the medic saw Josif's respiration stop. He attempted to resuscitate him, to no avail. The boy's eyes had a glassy, fixed stare, his pupils had become abnormally large, and his pulse was gone.

The medic lowered Josif's eyelids with his hands, and Amir gave the man a questioning look. The medic shook his head. A lone tear fell from the corner of Amir's eye. And then another. He lay his head down on Josif's chest. After a few moments Amir's back began to rise and lower, his chest heaving convulsively from the great gasps of air entering and exiting his lungs. After a time the sobbing stopped, and the child lay quietly with his head resting on the lifeless body of his friend.

When they pulled into the UN compound and stopped in front of the tent housing the field hospital, the medic stepped out of the vehicle to speak with a young woman who held a two-way radio in one hand and a clipboard in the other. He informed her that the gunshot victim was dead and that there would no longer be need of emergency medical services—only a body bag and a tag. The woman nodded and spoke into the microphone of her radio, instructing the voice on the other side to fetch the body and deliver it to the morgue. Her voice was calm, and she spoke with a clear, precise, accented English.

Pia Struch was in her early thirties, held a graduate degree in international relations, and prided herself on her professionalism and composure in difficult circumstances. It was her second time as a UN volunteer but her first experience working in a war zone. This particular chore done, Pia began to move on to the next item on her list, but then she noticed that the medic who had brought in the gunshot victim stood there, looking as if he expected more.

"Is there something else, then?" Pia asked.

"Yeah," the medic responded, nodding toward the vehicle he had arrived in.

Pia looked through the early evening light into the rear of the van. From where she stood she couldn't see anything other than the shape of the prone body of the victim.

"I don't understand."

"I've got his brother here," the medic replied, leading Pia toward the vehicle.

He pointed toward what had, at first glance, appeared to Pia to be a pile of clothing on top of the corpse but that now, at closer inspection, turned out to be the slumped form of a child.

"Why did you bring him with you? Is he injured?" Pia asked, her tone of voice changing to one of reproach when the medic answered in the negative. "Then he should be processed at the camp he entered. You know that."

"It just happened. I didn't think. I just put him in with his brother," the medic said with a shrug as he stepped into the van and gently shook the boy by the shoulder, the emotional exhaustion of the ordeal having caused the child to retreat into sleep.

Amir awoke to his body being jostled. Disoriented, he saw a woman speaking to him. Josif lay next to him. The memory of what had happened returned to his mind.

"He can't hear you," the medic informed Pia as she greeted the boy with a soft hello. "He's a deaf-mute."

"Oh, my god," Pia sighed.

"The kids' names are Muhamed and Jusuf," the medic offered. "The men who came in with the boys said the rest of the family are all dead."

"Who are these men?" Pia asked, her mind attempting to buy time with which to think.

"I don't know."

"You have to bring the boy back. They must be relatives of some sort. He should be with them."

"Those guys found the kids in the woods," the medic countered, shaking his head. "I can take the boy back if that's what you want. But the people he came in with are in no shape to care for him. And if I bring him back to our camp they're going to process him and probably just send him back here anyway."

"We're at capacity," Pia countered.

"So are we."

Pia drew in a large breath. One more thing to add to a never-ending list: an unaccompanied minor, likely an orphan, and on top of that, a disabled one. Focusing her attention on the reality at hand, her mind began to order the necessary steps needed to deal with this unexpected turn of events. The boy would have to be processed and placed with the other unaccompanied minors at the camp until arrangements could be made to send him elsewhere. Turning to the van, she looked inside. The rumpled pile of clothing was now sitting upright, staring at the body lying on the gurney by his side. From what she could see of him, the surviving brother looked to be about ten years old. His clothing was stained with dirt, grime, and the blood of his brother's wound.

Two men showed up from the medical tent that housed the temporary morgue. They helped the medic pull the gurney with its lifeless load from the back of the van and lower its wheels to the ground. Amir's eyes followed the exiting cot as though under a hypnotist's spell, his face now fully turned in Pia's direction. The boy's eyes were a deep ocean green, and their gaze momentarily intersected her own without touch or acknowledgment, offering no emotion nor anything of personal note. Yet it was the very emptiness of the child's expression that caused the UN volunteer to waken from the buffer of her professional posture.

With the wheels of the gurney set in place, the men prepared to move. As they took their first steps, the boy, who still sat in the ambulance, grew agitated and began to breathe out in sharp, rapid exhalations.

"He'll want to take a last look," the seasoned medic said and then lifted the sheet he had placed over the dead boy's body.

Pia watched as the cloth billowed and rose. Her mind, caught off guard, had no chance to process thought, no time to object nor call out for pause to consider the act's propriety. There, suddenly, before any reaction could surface to voice itself, lay a truth that could no longer be veiled by emotional detachment or the weariness of war: a dead boy's face gazing up into the sky through eyelids lowered and shut tight to the world of the living. There would be no more life for him, she thought, no matter how many cries of compassion, calls for justice, reason, or revenge rang out.

The UN volunteer felt her stomach constrict and her throat go numb. She wanted to look away but found herself immobilized by the pallid beauty of the dead boy's face. Her lungs held tight to her breath, and her body seemed to float as though gravity had suddenly lessened its force. The medic's lifting of the boy's shroud had seemed to her like the graceful sweep of a magician's hand, the cloth rising high in the air and the thing it covered dematerializing into the ether. Yet it wasn't the object beneath the sheet that had disappeared but rather that in which it and all materials things were held—time itself. In the vacuum that followed, the corpse seemed to speak its final words. Ones that were in a voice too hushed for any to hear.

As she looked on, Pia had a fleeting vision: the pale, inanimate features of the boy lying on the gurney in portrait with the child looking down upon him, the two faces meeting in a realm beyond the clock's reach, in a place of neither death nor life—silent but for the rustling of one heart's whisper to another.

With the drop of the cloth, the medic broke the spell. The white sheet now back in place over the slain boy's face, the men dutifully began wheeling the gurney away toward the morgue. Pia shook herself, her shoulders and head giving a small shudder. Her eyes refocusing, she saw that the young boy was now looking at her. He held her gaze for a second before turning away to watch his brother being carted off.

Pia lifted her two-way radio and spoke into it briefly. "Yes, I'll bring him right away," she said, signing off.

"Alright then, I'll be going," the medic said, giving a nod in Pia's direction.

"Wait. Which one is which?" Pia asked.

"What?"

"The boys," Pia said, looking down at the notes she had scribbled on her clipboard. "Which one is Jusuf and which is Muhamed?"

"I don't know. Sorry. The guys the kids came in with said one was named Jusuf and the other Muhamed. That's all I remember. I never got anything out of the older brother before he died. And the younger one, well . . ."

Pia sighed and looked away. Reading annoyance in her face, the medic shrugged as if to say the obvious: this was a war zone, not a buttoned-down, orderly bureaucracy.

Pia asked, "You'll get me the names of the men who accompanied the boys, then?"

"Yeah, no problem."

Pia nodded, thanked him, and then approached Amir as the medic moved to close the ambulance door.

Placing her hand gently on the boy's shoulder, she led him along a path that threaded its way among the barracks of a small, former military base where the UN had set up the camp. Hundreds of low-lying white tents spread out surrounding the old wood and metal buildings, like daisies overtaking a yard. Laundry drying on ropes that secured the tents to the ground fluttered like flags in the breeze. People could be seen mulling about the tents, some just standing as though lost in thought, others tending to family—the rest of the camp's inhabitants hidden away in their canvas abodes. A few children ran about playing, others could be heard crying, huddled in their tent with a parent lost in grief.

As they made their way to the administrative building where the new refugees were processed, Pia tried to comfort Amir as best she could with a compassionate look, a touch of his shoulder, and comforting words that she knew would be lost on his ears. When they arrived at the old airplane hanger that now served as the camp's central administrative office, Pia sat Amir down at a table and began the work of filling out the intake forms. She marked him as an "unaccompanied minor" and then wrote an account of the circumstances of his arrival at the camp.

Looking at her notes, Pia took a sheet of paper and slit it in half. On one piece she wrote "Muhamed," and on the other she wrote "Jusuf." Taking the first half and placing it in front of the boy, she looked at him questioningly. When there was no response, she took the paper back and drew a question mark after the name Muhamed and then pointed at him, her eyes seeking an answer.

Amir didn't understand what the woman wanted. And even if he had, there was little in him capable of responding. The names written down in front of him made no sense. He didn't know why the woman had written them. Looking downward, Amir felt his mind shut off. He didn't want to answer questions. He wanted to be with Josif. Although his rational mind understood that his friend had just died, there was yet a more powerful sense of Josif still being of the world, present somewhere nearby, though exactly where was not clear.

Amir rose from his chair to find Josif. He saw the woman rise as well and felt her hand on his shoulder, holding it with a gentle pressure directing that he stay seated. He shook off her hand but sat back down. The woman started to put more pieces of paper in front of him on which she'd written words for him to look at. He briefly glimpsed her way and saw that she was talking to him. Amir's eyes once again sought the comfort of the floor, its clear, simple lines . . . its safe, unambiguous purpose. After a minute he began to feel himself blend in with the grain of the long, narrow wood slats, losing himself in the play of the linear patterns running the length of the boards like empty, peaceful roads.

Chapter 7

Pia's attempts to gather information from the boy went nowhere. The child didn't seem able to read lips, or perhaps he was simply too traumatized to respond to the questions asked of him. Guessing his age at about ten, she wrote that down with a question mark. Unable to go any further, Pia led the boy to the barracks where the unaccompanied minors were housed. He showed no emotion at being left there, no recognition of her leaving and being replaced by yet another person under whose charge he was placed.

Returning to her office, Pia began the process of sorting out the child's long-term placement. Her primary job in dealing with unaccompanied minors was to reunite the children with their family or relatives as soon as possible. In instances where the children were too young or too debilitated to be able to provide relevant information about their family, she would, as the administrating agent, give the case top priority.

The situation became still more difficult when Pia discovered that the boy had no ability to communicate through sign language. Among the refugees at the camp, Pia had found a schoolteacher who was fluent in Bosnian sign language and arranged for her to meet with the deaf-mute child. After spending some time with him, the woman informed Pia that the silent boy seemed to have no knowledge of any sign language whatsoever, neither that used in Bosnia or any of the other regional dialects.

With so little to go on, and the communication so challenging, Pia turned to a colleague, Teresa Fried, for help. Among her several university degrees, Teresa had one in art therapy and had been using art in her work with the refugees to surprisingly good results. In addition, she was fluent in Serbo-Croatian. If the deaf-mute child couldn't sign, at least he could hopefully read. Pia arranged for Teresa to meet with Amir in the hope that she might gain enough information to help trace his background and ultimately find one of his family members.

Pia's colleague had set up a small art space in the corner of one of the administrative tents. There she had gathered a folding table, a few chairs, several rolls of art paper, and some colored pencils. When Pia had brought him to her, Teresa had begun her session with Amir by writing down simple questions in the boy's native tongue: *Do you like to draw? Can you write your name?*

When confronted with queries about who he was and where he came from, Amir, however, had responded as he had with Pia, his writing hand heavy at his side and his gaze distant. The words on the paper were like those spoken out loud and inaudible to his ears; his eyes saw them but did not seem able to register their meaning. Recognizing that the boy was beginning to shut down, Teresa decided to turn to simple drawing as means of communicating with him. At first she had a difficult time getting Amir to pick up the colored pencils she placed in front of him.

Amir had been trained to show respect to his elders by being shown the same from them. His mother and father, Emina and Asaf, tried to never speak ill of others nor fall prey to the temptation of gossip that came so easily to village life. When he got angry at his sister, at one of his cousins, or at playmates and reacted with negative actions or words, his parents didn't lecture him about politeness but showed their understanding of his feelings, then they did the very same for the person who had drawn Amir's ire. When their son did something that hurt another's feelings, they didn't scold him—their disappointment said more in its silence than a thousand reproving words. Amir understood that the two women were trying to help him. As pained and constricted as his emotions were, Amir knew he must make the effort to show appreciation, no matter how small a response he might be able to muster. His hand reached out and took a green pencil. He drew a tree, and then another. To the right of the trees he drew a pasture and added a cow. With a brown pencil, he filled the background with mountains. He wound a road through the pasture and the hills.

The act of drawing calmed and soothed him. His body relaxed as it lost itself to the rhythm of his hand going from one colored pencil to the next, the pencils moving as if on their own across the paper in front of him as the images appeared.

"Very nice. It looks like your road is high up in the hills," Teresa said, looking over Amir's picture. She used her hand to indicate the meaning of her words by curving it back and forth in progressively higher motion.

"Yes," Amir nodded.

"Pia and I have something for you to look at," Teresa continued. "It's a map of the towns higher up in the hills. Can you look at it?"

Amir could see that she was asking him to look at the sheet of paper she was unfolding on the table. Pia, standing by her side, looked on.

"Alright," Amir nodded. It was a map. After a few seconds he began to recognize some familiar names written next to the small dots designating towns. Then Amir saw a name that caused a rush of air to fill his lungs and linger for a time before it rushed out in one long current of breath, the sound lost to his deaf ears. He now knew what they wanted.

After his finger had pointed to the village where his family had lived, he looked away from the map and the women, his breathing becoming audible. He felt the gentle touch of a hand resting on his shoulder but didn't respond. When he finally turned his head back, he could see the two women speaking. The one who did the drawings with him picked up a piece of paper, wrote something down, and placed it in front of him. It said "name." The other woman had also done this the first day he had been there. But he had been confused; the names Muhamed and Jusuf had been written on the paper, and he didn't understand to whom they might refer.

Seeing the boy hesitate, the art therapist took the paper and added another word so that it now read "your name," and then added her own, Teresa, and pointed from it to herself. She handed the paper to Pia, who did the same. They could hear the air enter and exit the boy's throat. He picked up a pencil and wrote "Amir."

"Amir?" Pia asked, mouthing the name carefully.

"Yes," the boy's nod spoke, "my name is Amir."

Now it was the UN volunteer's turn to be confused. She had been told the boy's name was Muhamed. After some back-and-forth with him, it was clear he understood the question. The women repeated the exercise of writing their names down, the boy following suit, once again his hand speaking his name, "Amir."

Seeing his name on the paper in front of him, Amir could feel no connection to it, no special familiarity to its presence before him. He had taken up the pencil and written down his name as he might write the answer to a history question in a classroom quiz. The only thing of note that he felt as the word emerged from his own hand was his lack of emotion at seeing it. A name, especially one's own, he knew, should have special significance, should be filled with meaning. Yet a name was just a word like any other if there was no one to speak it with love.

"And your last name?" the art therapist asked, both she and Pia adding their surnames to their given name. Nodding his understanding, Amir began to write his family name with the same feeling of emptiness with which he had written his forename. As the letters appeared one by one, however, the sound of the name began to ring inside his ears . . . Beganović . . . like a pebble tossed into a pond, traveling waves of emotion rippling outward toward his conscious mind.

"No." Amir's internal voice spoke with a shake of his head, his hand letting go of the pen. "No," he repeated, this time more resolutely. "No," he repeated again and then again, the internal sound of the negation like a dam holding back deep waters—a flood of emotion threatening to drown him in sorrow. Feeling the weight of the moment, the two women refrained from intervening.

Breathing in short, sharp inhalations, Amir closed his eyes for a time and then opened them again, his anxiety lessening. Collecting himself, Amir reached down and took the pen in hand once more. Placing the tip of the pen to the paper, he wrote his family name, "Beganović."

The next day Pia and Teresa met with Amir again, this time to try to gather information about what had happened to his family. The men who had accompanied Amir and his brother into the UN camp had said the older boy told them that their family had all been lost to the war. But the men had also said that the boys' names were Jusuf and Muhamed. The two women well knew that misinformation, both from error or purposeful, abounded in war zones. It was important that they get as much firsthand detail from the boy as possible.

The art therapist began by indicating to Amir that she would like him to sketch a simple picture of his home. He was hesitant to do so, his hands remaining rigidly by his sides when she offered him the pencils. Taking a sheet of paper, she drew a picture of a house and showed it to Amir. Underneath the drawing she wrote, "my home." Teresa offered him the pencils once more. This time he accepted them and began to draw a picture of his family's house.

The resulting drawing seemed to confirm the story that his family had met a tragic end. The picture showed a small farmhouse that appeared to have collapsed upon itself, with no people to be seen either inside or out. Next to it was a barn. Like the house, it was colored black and seemed to be lifeless. Beside the barn was a cow on its side. Teresa gently pushed for more information.

Showing the child a series of photos depicting families standing together in pose, she wrote down the word "family" and indicated by sketching a picture of her own family members that he should attempt to do the same of his. Amir drew his picture as had she, using stick figures to portray the people. Yet while her drawing showed everyone in standing position, his figures, like the cow beside the barn, were all drawn in horizontal position. What was even more disturbing than the prone position of the family members was that they were drawn one on top of the other, as if stacked in a pile.

When she had finished, Teresa picked up the picture she had drawn of her family and wrote a name beneath each figure. She took a separate piece of paper and asked Amir to do the same. The art therapist looked on as Amir took the pencil in hand in what almost seemed a trance and wrote down his family's names. "Asaf. Emina. Minka."

"And your brother?" Teresa asked after a moment's pause, taking the paper, writing the words "brother" and "Jusuf," followed by a question mark. But Amir suddenly grew agitated and unresponsive. Letting go of the pencil, he lowered his head and stared at the ground in front of his feet. The UN worker reached over to touch Amir's shoulder in an attempt to bring his gaze back up.

The art therapist spoke the name Jusuf slowly and repeated it several times so that she was sure the boy understood the word.

"No," Amir shook his head in a rapid, brief movement meant to end the encounter. "I don't know what you want. I don't want to talk about this," his body said, speaking his emotion as clearly as any words.

Amir understood that the woman had been talking about his friend. He knew Josif's name because Josif had written it down for him once, and he'd seen it spoken on the lips of the man and woman whose farm they had worked at. Somewhere in a far-off region of his mind Amir realized there was some kind of misunderstanding. But he didn't want to answer questions about his friend, didn't want to think about Josif in the specific, in the here and now. Because that would mean thinking about what had happened. That would mean accepting that Josif was dead, a thought Amir dared not approach for fear of touching yet another pain, one even sharper and deeper than the loss of his friend.

Thoughts of Josif, triggered by the woman's questions, brought unpleasant images to Amir's mind. But his emotional remembrances, those held in his heart, were different. They brought Amir comfort. They carried a sense of his friend as though he were still there, as if Josif's smile still hovered in front of him, his body still radiating warmth, the imprint of his arm hooked affectionately round Amir's shoulder, the smell of him, his skin and hair, still lingering in the air. Unlike thoughts, these feelings traveled to neither past nor future but hovered in a kind of amorphous present and could live in a world of their own, in a place without time or demands.

Why could he hold his feelings for Josif so close to the surface of his consciousness, but not the memory of his family? If the loss of his family was an open wound yet to scar over, Josif had been the salve. Josif had provided him a refuge, had created it by braving his own place of pain to share with Amir his hope and what little love he had been able to find in the world. The woman who had Amir make the drawings kept mouthing Josif's name. He could see by the woman's eyes that she wanted to help, wanted him to let her in. But there was no room. What little there had been, had been made by Josif, and Amir knew he must save it for his friend. It was the only way to keep Josif from completely disappearing, as had his mother, father, and sister.

Having both the boy's full name and that of the village he came from, Pia was hopeful that she would find some connection to Amir's family. Her hope, though, was short-lived. Even with the more detailed information they were able to get from the boy in subsequent sessions—the names of other family members, the fact that Jusuf was in fact not his brother but a friend whose real name was Josif—she was unable to find anyone in the other nearby UN refugee camps who recognized the boy's name or photo or knew anything of his family.

Speaking with an officer aligned with an intelligence unit, Pia learned that Amir's village lay in an area of heavy conflict. Specific information was spotty at best. There had been no aerial surveillance scheduled over the small hamlet, and little intelligence data existed other than a single eyewitness report. It had come from a Muslim inhabitant of the village who had been lucky enough to be deep in the forest cutting firewood when his home had been invaded by a large paramilitary unit. What he recounted was disheartening. The village had been "cleansed" of its Muslim residents. After the paramilitary left, the man had sneaked back into town, to find his family gone and his house ransacked. Searching frantically, he eventually found them in a death mound located in a killing field just outside of the village. If his story were to be believed, the invading paramilitaries had massacred everyone they found—man, woman, and child.

"But the boy escaped, as well as the man in the woods," Pia said, struggling for some small foothold of hope. "Couldn't some of his family have gotten away as well?"

"Of course," responded the intelligence officer. "There are very likely a number of residents who either escaped or evacuated the village before the attack. But we won't really know what happened there until we're able to access the place. We try not to rely too strongly on a single testimony. That said, the witness account seems solid. It fits the profile of what we know has happened in other towns in that area. In general, the Bosnians have very strong family bonds, and if the boy was, as you say, wandering the countryside alone, it's not a good sign."

Later that afternoon, Pia found a few precious minutes to herself. But thoughts of work continued to churn in her mind. The faces of the refugees she worked with kept replaying in her memory. The images arrived unbidden. Exhausted physically and emotionally, Pia took a walk through the camp and came to rest in a small alcove formed by a pair of old plum trees and dozens of empty fuel barrels stacked at either side. A board bridging two halves of a barrel invited her to sit. Not far away, a newly erected tent drew her attention, and sitting outside of it, his eyes staring blankly out to the distance, she saw a man she'd helped process the night before. His tale was one Pia wished she had never heard.

The man himself had been unable to tell his own story. He had not spoken for days. A friend who had been with him at the internment camp where they had been held had to speak for him. Pia had previously heard reports about the castration of Muslim prisoners, but this one was a particularly gruesome account. If she hadn't seen the face of the nearly catatonic victim for herself, she might have been able to put the story aside as simply one of propaganda. It was easier to do so than to believe that such acts were humanly possible.

The man, called Sevko by the refugee who accompanied him through the processing, was a victim of castration, though in his case not of losing his testicles but perhaps something even more integral to his being than that. The friend who spoke for him recounted how they were taken to the internment camp's maintenance building and ordered at gunpoint to drop their pants. One by one, the prisoners were offered a choice. A gun was held to their head and a knife to their testicles. When they got to Sevko, his knees buckled and he fell forward. Angered by his fainting spell, the soldiers dragged him to a nearby motor oil pit and shoved his head into it, nearly drowning him. One of the guards, already bored with the castrations, had an idea to make things more interesting.

Dragging Sevko back to the line of prisoners, they forced him to perform the next castration, commanding him to open his mouth.

It was hard to say which of the victims of that particular castration suffered more: the man who'd had his testicles bitten off . . . or Sevko, forced to gnaw them with his teeth until they were no longer attached to the victim's body and then to eat them.

After recounting the story, Sevko's friend began to report other instances of forced cannibalism that he'd witnessed. Pia began to feel nauseous writing her report, as the silent man's friend seemed unable to stop talking. She tried to tell him that all she needed at that point were the general details necessary to fill in the information on the intake form. But Sevko's friend seemed possessed, as though he was retching a flood of unimaginably foul, evil substance from his gut. When he got to the story of the decapitation by chainsaw, Pia was no longer able to stay at her desk and had to ask one of her coworkers to finish processing the man.

Pia's thoughts went from the lost, silent man sitting outside the tent in front of her to the deaf-mute boy whose stark drawings she had just filed away. The image of the boy looking down upon his slain friend floated into her mind. It was a memory she fought to keep at bay. Never before had she witnessed anyone's passing so closely, no less a boy whose death mask framed its innocence in a kind of suspended animation, the smooth, silken skin of his face drained pale of blood. His face was all the more the stuff of haunting nightmares for the surreal beauty of its expression. Then there was the face of the younger "brother." Like Sevko's, the young boy's visage was colored by a sadness that traveled beyond his own personal suffering, the eyes of both victims, the deaf-mute boy and the older man, speaking a horrible truth.

It was one thing to see such a look in the eyes of the older man; to have seen it in the eyes of the child was almost more than Pia could bear. It was an impossibility to her that acts of inhumanity could happen on such a scale, impossible that wars were sanctioned, that they were tolerated. That people believed in their inevitability.

Before coming to Bosnia, Pia had thought she understood war, understood its causes, its evolution in present-day reality—death and destruction somehow more civilized now with the advent of cleaner, more efficient means of delivery.

Pulling her breath deeply into her chest, Pia rose from the makeshift bench to return to her desk. She had people to take care of, a job to do. Free time was not good for her. It gave her mind too much room to think. Without the veil of distance, the shield of her comforts, and the pattern of ordinary life to distract her, the place she found herself in—this hideous war in this lovely countryside— was too much to ponder without her own heart and mind falling victim to its brutality.

Chapter 8

With her efforts to find any of the boy's relations, even distant ones, frustrated by the chaos of the war, Pia began to focus on securing a visa for Amir to a host country where he could receive the kind of professional help he would need. But the UN volunteer quickly found herself running into one roadblock after another. There were few allocations for foreign placements: the involved international governments, with the exception of Germany, all accepted only token numbers of Bosnian refugees.

Pia knew that if the boy were to stay in his homeland, the best that could be hoped for was placement in an orphanage, which, with the ongoing war, would have few resources to deal with his physical and emotional impairments. Eventual adoption was highly unlikely. Foreign adoptions were rarely permitted by the Bosnian government, and to make matters more difficult, the large number of war orphans resulting from the ongoing conflict made domestic adoption an extremely remote possibility as well. As elsewhere, most couples wishing to adopt preferred younger children and ones who didn't bring along with them the extra burden of being both hearing and speech impaired. Amir was likely to end up a ward of a state under siege—a country unable to even offer its people a stable food supply, no less provide a future for a boy like him.

Disheartened, Pia approached her supervisor, Madelaine Ellis, an American woman who had many years of experience and deep connections within the vast UN bureaucracy. Despite initial reservations, Pia's boss was won over by the volunteer's heartfelt effort on behalf of the boy. After several meetings with Pia and Amir, Madelaine became personally involved, calling in favors and creating a new debt or two of her own. Pia was delighted when the woman called her several weeks later to relay the news that she had found a religious charity in the US willing to sponsor the boy. Yet, as happy as she was to see Amir relocated away from the war zone, the day of his departure came all too soon.

"I've brought you a piece of luggage for your clothes," Pia said, mouthing her words slowly and carefully lifting up a small suitcase for Amir's viewing. She had, on several occasions, prepared him for his departure as best she could, having communicated by both written word and photographs the information that he would be moving to a new home in the United States. Amir had nodded his understanding, but at best the news had registered only as an intellectual concept having little to do with his present-day reality.

"I've brought you a few new things as well." Pia smiled, laying the suitcase on his bed, opening it to show him the underwear, socks, and shirts she had procured for his trip.

Amir was beginning to look uncomfortable. He looked at Pia as though he didn't understand.

"These new clothes are all yours," Pia indicated with a sweep of her hand. "We'll just pack your other clothing in with them, and then you'll be all ready to go."

The UN volunteer bent down and pulled a small box from under his bed. It contained the things the staff had given him when he first arrived at camp: a few items of clothing, a toothbrush, a pair of shoes.

Amir felt a growing alarm rise inside him. The idea that his clothes would be removed from their "home" made him anxious. He wanted Pia to put his things back in the box, under the bed, where they belonged.

"It's alright, Amir. It's alright," Pia spoke in a soothing tone. "You're going to a place where there is no fighting. You'll have a new home there."

He couldn't make out what her mouth was saying, though he somehow understood the basic point: he was to leave. But he didn't want to go anywhere. He wanted his box back in its place under the bed with all of its contents. He wanted to stay where he was.

"No, please put my things back," Amir indicated by a shake of his head, his hand pushing the box back under the bed.

"Oh, Amir," Pia sighed. "It's going to be OK. You're going to the United States. It's very nice there. You'll like it. See? Look at these photos I've brought you."

Having suspected that Amir would be disturbed by the change, Pia had asked her supervisor for photos of the woman's homeland to show to the boy.

"I want to stay here," Amir said with the stare of his eyes, his hands staying at his side, not rising to accept the proffered photographs.

"You'll get to ride on an airplane," Pia smiled, the flat of her hand gliding upward like an airplane's ascent from the tarmac. Bending down, she pulled the box of clothing back out from under the bed and began placing the items one by one into the suitcase she'd brought. She wanted to tell Amir that she would miss him but refrained from indulging her own emotions in front of the child, who was struggling with ones far more complex than hers.

"OK, that's done. I wish I could pack so easily," Pia laughed, trying to lighten the moment. Closing the suitcase lid, she took its handle and stood. With her other arm she reached out to take Amir's hand. When he didn't respond, she paused for a moment, transferred the suitcase to his hand, put her arm around his shoulder, and very gently ushered him forward.

For Pia Struch it was a bittersweet parting. On one hand, she felt as if she had succeeded in finding the boy a good home far away from the violence of war, in a place where he could receive proper care. On the other, she would miss him. For Pia, the slight, silent child was a creation of beauty amid a world of ugliness. Sad though Amir's situation was, she found hope in him, as though somehow the boy's overcoming of his suffering could make both him and the world a stronger, better place, validating the ultimate goodness of humanity . . . a belief she was struggling to maintain under the weight of what she had experienced and witnessed since arriving in Bosnia.

There was none of the excitement typical for a child boarding an airplane for the first time: for peering out the window to look out upon the world so far below; for seeing the clouds at eye level and wondering what it might be like to walk upon them; for awaiting the food served from carts that roll down the aisle and placed by smiling, stylishly uniformed people on trays that fell from the seat right in front of you.

Amir experienced the event as though it were not he flying but someone else. The first of the two airplanes they sent him on had been a military transport whose flight seemed to end almost as soon as it began. The second plane was like those he'd seen pictured in magazines and movies, full of people on their way to far off places sitting in comfortable seats whose backrests reclined so you could sleep if you wanted. He knew he should be excited to ride in one of the silver planes that he had only ever seen from afar streaking across the sky. He had always wondered what it would be like to ride in a thing that moved so fast, so high above the earth. He could see that the faces of the others in the small group of refugees with whom he traveled showed some emotion—hope, fear, relief—but he could find no feelings of his own.

Even when he felt his stomach rise up toward his chest as he looked out the window as the plane began its descent into Boston's

Logan International Airport—seemingly as if it might touch down upon the sea instead of land—he felt nothing but the physical sensation of gravity's pull. Amir disembarked from the plane with the other Bosnians and was accompanied through immigration by an official who had been waiting for them at the end of the gangway connecting the plane to the terminal. There was a newness to everything he saw and a movement all about him like the buzzing of flies. Still, he could not find it in him to be awed by the momentous change that had come to his life.

The agency responsible for Amir's care had given special consideration to his case. Normally an unaccompanied refugee minor would, if possible, be placed with a family of his own ethnic and cultural background. However, the needs required in dealing with Amir's speech and hearing impairments took precedence over all other criteria. The resettlement agency placed Amir in a group home located in an outlying town west of Boston. The situation was temporary, until they could complete a thorough medical examination and find him a permanent placement. The foster parents at the group home, a couple in their early fifties, were both certified in taking care of children with special needs, and the wife, a registered nurse, was fluent in sign language.

Amir was driven to the group home by his caseworker, who soon grew accustomed to the child's withdrawn and silent presence and spent the drive listening to the radio and giving the boy an occasional smile. Arriving at the house, the caseworker stepped from her car, pausing momentarily to admire the setting. The 150-year-old, white-clapboarded New England farmhouse spread out along an east–west axis, overlooking fields to the north and south. Three small additions telescoped outward from the main building and tied into an old post-and-beam barn painted deep red. Sitting on about five acres of open land, the one-time farm was surrounded by a small, wooded nature preserve. As the caseworker stood surveying the scene, the door to the home opened and the foster parents, Howard and Joy Thorenson, walked to the car to greet her and their newest foster child.

"Hello, Howard. Joy. Shall I introduce you to Amir?" the caseworker asked. Opening the passenger door, she took the silent boy by the hand and led him to meet the couple.

"Well, hello, son. How are you?" the foster father asked with kindness as he bent down and extended his hand to the boy.

Amir looked at the man and then glanced at the wife, observing her face as he had the husband's, with a quick blink of his eyes, like a camera shutter opening and as quickly snapping shut. Amir let the man take his hand and give it a few shakes.

"Hello, Amir," the foster mother smiled. "Come on in, and I'll show you your new home." She repeated her words in sign, and though the boy had no instruction in American Sign Language, he seemed to understand and followed her in.

Inside the house, Amir viewed its layout the way he might have scanned a forest floor, searching for signs of its life—the clues to the patterns of movement that might tell its story. Coming from the refugee camp, and even the comfort of his own family's house—which had been furnished well, but with simple, practical furniture—Amir perceived the interior of the new home to be that of a wealthy family. The living area was filled with large, stuffed chairs and sofas, desks and tables with lamps, and numerous small items—baskets, plants, flowers, photos, little carvings, and ceramic bowls. There was a room just for the television. It, too, was filled with soft, cushioned chairs and had a large, L-shaped couch. And the television was bigger than any he'd ever seen.

Everything in the place was neat and ordered, unlike the farm where he had lived with Josif. There, things had been gathered together in piles, pushed into corners, or stuffed into closets . . . a sense of angry denial and resentful reproach lying behind a superficial orderliness. The kindness in the woman's eyes here was not begrudging as had been Sonja's, and he could see no meanness in the man's face as had been carved in Zoran's.

After his tour of the main living area, Amir was led up to the second floor, where he was shown his room. It was small but bright, painted a comforting pale yellow, and it had a window looking out to the fields and woods. There was a small, single bed, a simple wood wardrobe and bureau for his clothes, and a small desk with a lamp on it. After being shown his room, Amir was introduced to the other foster children living in the house— three older boys of high school age. Two of them, like him, were from Bosnia, and the third was from Latin America. They greeted Amir cordially, their eyes meeting his as though all were wearing bifocals, the focus of one lens a common greeting taking in the image of a new acquaintance, the other a seeing of silent knowing, a recognition of damage done, hurt and pain hidden beneath the surface of what was readily visible.

For Amir, the transition into yet another living place, while no less stressful, had become easier to navigate with each succeeding experience. A numbness of both emotion and body had been with Amir since the death of his family. It came in varying degrees of intensity. At times it registered as but an almost indistinct tingling of his body's extremities, at its worst as a narcosis of spirit that left his body feeling like an uninhabited shell. Now, in this place so far from home, his emotional self retreated to a detached, passive place of emptiness where it found shelter in an inner harbor so still there there seemed not a ripple of emotion to be detected anywhere on its waters.

Amir was an easy child to care for. He moved about noiselessly, asked no questions, made no complaints, and did his share of the work and more. Even when he was present it was easy to overlook him. There was something in the way he held himself that made you forget he was there. He rarely inserted himself into any family event or communication but rather sat looking on, as a spectator might watch a show. Yet the boy rapidly learned the patterns of the household, going about on his own, knowing what time to come to the dinner table, what chores to do. The boy was always there when he was expected; he was "out of sight and out of mind" much of the rest of the time.

Amir's foster mother worked diligently to teach him how to sign, an effort complicated by his ignorance of English. Having the two older Bosnian boys to help with written translation made it easier. Her newest ward seemed hesitant to communicate through the written word, however, even though the older boys from his homeland were encouraging and patient. That the boy didn't have any ability in ASL, American Sign Language, didn't surprise the foster mother. But that he had no knowledge of any formal sign language whatsoever, did. She knew it would be a complex and challenging task to teach the boy American Sign Language. Even if he had spoken English, it would have still been akin to learning a foreign language. The ASL grammar and syntax were completely different and its meaning was expressed through the use of hand shapes and facial expressions.

Raising her eyebrows and tilting her head slightly forward, Joy Thorenson signed the word for swimming, her facial expression serving as a question. "Go swimming?" she asked, bringing her hands up in front of her and then spreading them as if in a simple swimming motion.

Amir first responded with a question in his eyes, but when his foster mother repeated the sign again, he remembered it from one of their lessons. With a hesitant expression he nodded his head and signed the letters *o* and *k*.

"Good," his foster mother's hand spoke in reply and then signed that they would be leaving in fifteen minutes. She was pleased with the boy's progress in the basic signs. His mind was sharp, and he seemed to have an instinctual ability to observe physical movement and record its form, playing it back in accurate imitation.

Nodding his head, Amir turned and went upstairs to change his clothes. His body movement showed his ambivalence. It was clear that he would rather stay close to home and wander about outside the house, but he knew the invitation to go swimming had not been a request so much as it had been a polite way for his foster mother to say she wanted him to get out and do something with his foster brothers. While sensitive to his withdrawn behavior, the Thorensons made frequent attempts to involve him in activities with the older boys under their care. Although Amir always acquiesced to their efforts, his participation was often lackluster, and his social interaction with the others was passive. The Thorensons were patient, believing their youngest foster child would eventually feel secure enough to begin emerging from his shell.

Amir appeared happiest when alone doing chores, feeding the chickens, or out in the pasture with the Thorensons' two horses. From his first days at the foster home, the deaf-mute child had been drawn to the woods that bordered the fields surrounding the house and barn. He often gravitated toward the area of the yard east of the barn that lay closest to the woods, where several grand, old sugar maples formed a natural portico leading into the forest. The foster parents would frequently find the young Bosnian boy stationed in that part of the yard looking into the woods, as though waiting in expectation of something.

Trying to find and encourage anything of interest, Mr. Thorenson showed Amir the paths that led through the woods to the adjoining properties and were sometimes used as a shortcut to the town center by the older boys. After walking only a few feet into the trees, the man could see Amir's countenance change from neutral and passive to something brighter and more colorful. After several more excursions into the woods, when the Thorensons were sure he knew the lay of the land, Amir was allowed to venture alone among the trees to wander and play.

"Stay close home," his foster mother had instructed him. "Trees OK. But see house. Understand?"

Amir signed back his agreement, the small flash of happiness coming from his eyes rewarding his guardian's decision to broaden the boy's freedom.

Though he was unable to hear any of the forest's sounds, there was such a familiar comfort to its environment that the absence was filled by the intensity with which Amir's other senses drank in its visual and tactile riches. The cool, gentle breeze that wove its way through the trees washed his skin in rich, humid air, awakening the memory of the sound of rustling leaves. His steps upon the soft, deep mat of the forest's slowly decaying subsurface recalled the timbre of quiet feet walking on the woodland paths behind his family's home. The sight of birds, squirrels, and insects unlocked a discordant, beautiful harmony inside his head; there came a remembrance of song . . . of warble, caw, and trill . . . of chatter, buzz, and percussive pulse. It was a world he knew and loved. The only one that for him, now, made any sense.

For the Bosnian war orphan, anxiety always lingered just below the surface of his consciousness; it felt like a deep, lingering doubt, the images of his family's faces shimmering beneath the surface of the feeling of total emptiness. If such people could be so easily extinguished in a moment's passing, how could a boy like him survive? And why would he want to? Did he? But these were questions too complicated for him to articulate in any rational form; there was only the sensation of their hovering presence—the child left to wait either for their dissipation or distant answer in some far off future time. Until then, he was a passive witness, and he lived in the custody of others. He saw what was required and did it, knowing that he would then be left alone. It had been this way at the other farm, where he had met Josif. In his mind, it would be the same in this place as well.

Amir had been living in his new foster home for barely a week when he began climbing out from his bedroom window at night, onto the roof of the back porch that stood just beneath it, to watch the stars and feel the cool evening air bathe his skin. He didn't like being indoors. The young orphan's dreams often seemed like the color of night itself, Amir waking in the morning with no memory of anything but black, vague feelings of anxiety and unease. At times, though, his dreams would be backlit as with thin shards of a crescent moon's light . . . hints of things seen, silhouettes of familiar forms strangely obscured in meaning. The images that visited him in sleep sat unmoving in an ominous silence, like the form of a figure lurking in the shadows of a darkened alley.

"Minka!" a voice called out into the dark, the sound of his sister's name ringing deep within the cavern of his psyche. It was, he realized, his own voice that had called out for her. She had been there, so close that he could still feel her presence. She had been frightened. Desperate. In need of something or someone.

Those were the nights Amir woke up in a sweat, breathing in short, sharp gasps of air, his muscles cramped. Then he would slide out the window and into the night. From the porch roof beneath his bedroom window, he was able to step onto the limb of an old sugar maple that grew next to the house. After climbing down to the ground, he sat silently in the yard or walked over to the edge of the woods, where he waited, listening . . . watching for shadows of nocturnal creatures moving quietly through the dark. One evening, on the night of a full moon, he ventured into the forest. Stepping into the woods, he came onto a trail. The wonder of the moonlit landscape drew him farther and farther along. Painted all about the woodland floor were magical replicas of daylight's shadows: as clear and precise in their outlines, but softer in form and beautifully eerie.

Walking slowly, carefully along the path, Amir came to a stop. If any forest animals were about, he wouldn't be able to hear them. He would have to stand quietly, make no sound, and then, if he was lucky, he might catch sight of some nocturnal animal wandering the woods. Looking about him, he felt as though he was on the inside of a film in which a boy stood alone in a strange but beautiful forest—a remote, otherworldly landscape where he could feel, if not at home, at least a sense of belonging.

Standing there, bathed in moonlight, stars showing through the gaps in the canopy of leaves above, Amir was carried back in time and space. Comforted, held in the arms of nature, he approached a memory that he had held at bay, its remembrance calling forth the faces of those who filled it and the impossibility of their absence from his life now and forevermore.

"Mama i Tata," he spoke, his lips forming the words but their sound not exiting his mouth. "Mama i Tata," he repeated, the image of his mother and father appearing in his thought, the first time he'd dared to consciously call them forth since they'd disappeared from his life.

"Gdje si ti? Gdje si ti?" Amir asked of the sky as he peered up into it. "Minka, gdje si?" his lips soundlessly whispered. And though there was no response from the heavens as to where his family might be, he sensed a distant, unfathomable answer coming from somewhere beyond his human reach . . . something touching him somewhere.

Amir's chest filled with a deep and heavy breath, the air filling his lungs tinged with a sadness that entered his body and sat there inside of him, weighting him down into the earth. He let out his breath and then breathed deeply again, the effort of his questions having drained him of all energy. After a time he turned from the woods and made his way back to the foster home, where he climbed the tree that grew next to the house, then stepped onto the porch roof and through the window into his bedroom. Lying down on his bed, he closed his eyes. Now the world kept its distance, no sight, nor sound, nor voice interrupting his mind's journey into the refuge of sleep.

Chapter 9

When Amir had first arrived at the foster home, there had been no sense that his free-fall into a world dictated by the laws of chaos, begun the day of his family's death, had ended. For the young orphan it felt like just another stop along a road that seemed to have no direction, destination, or apparent purpose. If some people had difficulty in identifying with him, an orphaned child who could neither hear nor speak, then the emotional isolation Amir felt within himself was even greater than that coming from those who couldn't see the person behind the disability.

To Amir, his silent relationship with the world seemed right and just. Amir always assumed that his hearing had been lost in the explosion that had come when the soldiers had invaded his home—the deafening sound that was the last memory he held of life with his family. His inability to hear thus felt proper and reasonable. The strength of this sensibility overrode even the physical healing of his ears. That the vibration of sound waves had over time begun to make their way back to Amir's brain was lost to his conscious mind.

There was no rational explanation for the loss of Amir's speech. Yet there was no question within the boy as to why that sense had been lost along with his ability to hear. Something within him understood that his muteness helped anchor him, supported his deafness, and provided a ledge of emotional and mental stability where he might safely rest from the tumult of a world he no longer understood. In Amir's mind his ability to speak was simply gone, as though it had never been there in the first place, so he neither questioned nor lamented its absence, even though he understood his condition placed him at a disadvantage.

Of the five senses, sight, hearing, and speech are those by which people predominantly come to know one another. And because the radar of people's speech received no echo back from him, there were those for whom Amir's presence registered but the weakest of blips. They could see him with their eyes, but with the absence of his ability to speak or hear their words, he was, to an extent, only partially visible to them. That it might be their own perspective that was limited, and not the object of their view, rarely seemed to cross their minds.

Amir did not question where he stood with regard to being normal or a somehow lesser being in the eyes of others. Amir, at eleven years of age, lived in a world that had not yet become so finely defined. He felt, rather, afloat in a consciousness much larger than his own . . . a lone specimen of life treading water in an endless expanse of sea, with no land nor vessel of safety and security in sight. To him, the world of humanity was not what it seemed. It was a mirage of forms and meanings that posed as a rational, reliable, and constant place but was actually filled with gaps of polar opposite, flashes of erratic and random moments marked by chaos and denial. Amir had experienced both the deepest of love and the darkest of hate—confused and damaged, he no longer knew what to believe in.

The young Bosnian orphan's stay at the Thorensons' was meant to be temporary. The foster parents' house served as a transitional residence for children on their journey from whatever trauma had taken them from their birth family's home to what would be their permanent placement while under the care of the agency responsible for them. In the case of refugee children coming from foreign countries, a complete medical exam was required before any determination of a final placement could be made. Amir's initial physical examination resulted in his being referred to a pediatric eye, ear, nose, and throat specialist.

The eye, ear, nose, and throat physician told Amir's caseworker that his exam of Amir had shed more light on the boy's condition by what he hadn't been able to determine than by what he had. His report stated that he had found some evidence of scar tissue in both of Amir's inner ears, indicating that at some point there had been an external source of damage, though not enough to cause any permanent loss of hearing. The specialist hadn't been able to find any other structural damage that might account for the boy's deafness. The doctor reported that Amir's vocal cords seemed to be in perfectly functional condition and that he couldn't find any apparent cause of either the child's hearing or speech impairment. The specialist ended by recommending that Amir see someone experienced in treating children with symptoms of post-traumatic stress disorder.

With summer ending and the school year about to begin, Amir's caseworker and the Thorensons agreed that Amir should be enrolled in the local elementary school, and they met with a counselor at the school to discuss the boy's special needs. Given the still-unresolved nature of Amir's ongoing medical examinations, any question as to whether or not the boy would be at the school for more than a brief period complicated any long-term planning for his education. In the end, it was decided to put him in an age-appropriate class and arrange for an interpreter, tutoring in American Sign Language, as well as other logistical support to help with his integration into his new school and culture.

The school where they sent Amir was big, and he felt confined within its walls and maze-like, windowless passageways. There were many people, he spent many hours locked within, and he worried that the other kids saw him as an oddity. He was lost in a strange land filled with many things and much going on, all moving so fast that he felt dizzied by its blur. As soon as the large yellow school bus delivered him home, the first thing he would do, after meeting the obligation of greeting his foster parents and eating the afterschool snack they had prepared for him and the other boys, was to go off on his own into the wooded area at the back of their home.

"Merhaba vjeverice, sta ima ba?" Amir greeted the gray squirrel, the words of his native language speaking soundlessly within his mind.

The small mammal twitched its tail nervously, then, recognizing the boy, stilled its movement. Its large round eyes looked back at the silent smiling boy who sat a few yards distant, like it, resting on his haunches. Its face seemed to respond to the "Hello squirrel, what's going on?" in a neutral answer. "Not much," it said in a quick series of brief chirps. Amir's smile broadened. Though he could not hear it, he could see the sound emerge into the air by the expression of the animal's face.

Amir's greeting had not been one of random introduction but rather one of acquaintance. He had come to know the squirrel from his daily forays into the woods. He recognized it by its coloration, its size, its partially missing tail, and most of all its body language, which responded to his presence in friendly trust. Amir had carefully observed the places where the squirrel had built its nests and knew the location of some its many food caches.

"Kako si, jesi dobro?" Amir asked.

"I'm fine, everything is OK, but I am very busy," the squirrel seemed to respond before running off to continue its foraging.

"Vidimo se," see you later, Amir said, then rose to continue on his way as well.

He walked farther into the woods until he came to a place that had long ago been a homestead, the only remnants of which were an old stone foundation now fallen in on itself and half-filled with rocks, decomposed plants, and leaves come to rest there during the many years since its abandonment. When he had first come across it, he knew before even seeing the collapsed foundation that the place had once been somebody's habitat. The trees were larger than any others in the surrounding woods, they grew at evenly spaced distance from one another, and the undergrowth beneath them was sparse and open. The woods here reminded him of his home in Bosnia.

The trees and undergrowth were different, the landscape and views not as dramatic, but the sense of people once having worked the land by the sweat of their own bodies was the same. It had been that way with his family. He could feel it here, too . . . some family, once upon a time, had lived here as if planted into the earth, just like the crops they grew and harvested with their own hands.

One tree in particular called out to him: an ancient red oak that stood tall and broad, its great round crown calling out to the heavens. Supported by a trunk still sturdy and strong after nearly two centuries of life, it stood out like a venerable, wise monk among a gathering of young novices. How it and the others spotted about the old property had survived was a mystery and near miracle for trees such as these, whose beauty, for some, lay in the value of their flesh cut and stacked into boards of wide, clear, unblemished wood.

When he had discovered the tree, Amir sat for a time looking at it and the land its majestic presence stood tall in protection over. He lay on the ground, still and quiet, looking up into the great crown of leaves above him, the nerve endings in his skin alive and attentive, listening to a language of sensation that came from the large life form that loomed above him. Trees could speak. In his child's mind, unhindered by intellectual bias, he knew this. And even before he had lost his powers of hearing and speech, he understood that the communication came in a silence that could be heard only with a stillness of being as great as that of the tree itself.

Amir had a deep and instinctive respect for these monarchs of the plant world. He could visualize their slow, persevering growth through the ages and the extremes of weather they must have endured—floods, winds, lightning, the freeze of winter wind, and the heat of burning summer sun—not to mention diseases, the assault of humankind, and all the surrounding plants birthed by nature and competing for survival. On his tenth birthday, the year before the war had landed on his family's doorstep, his father, Asaf, had given Amir a book about trees, with illustrations of some of the world's monumental species.

"Papa, look at this!" Amir had called out excitedly. "They say this tree is nearly five thousand years old! Can you believe this? Can that be true?"

"I'm sure it must," Asaf had answered, "but I had no idea a tree could live so long. That is older than anything I can think of, except the earth itself."

"And look at this one!" Amir continued excitedly. "It says the tree is one hundred and fifteen meters tall. Could I even see the top of it then?"

"Ha-ha," laughed Asaf. "If you stood near it, I suppose not. I think you would have to stand at some distance to see the very top of it. But then the other trees around might block its view."

"These old trees must be very wise from having lived so long," Amir said, his face suddenly turning contemplative.

"Yes, I think you are right," Asaf smiled in reply. "They must be very wise indeed."

The first time Amir climbed the old oak in the forest behind his foster family's house, he roamed about it with his body, just as his eyes had initially wandered its form. Amir explored its branches not only to find a vantage point from which to look out onto the surrounding landscape, as he liked to do, but also to know its body, as a blind person might touch the face of a friend to better know him. Several days later, when he came across some old flooring boards his foster parents had discarded, Amir thought to build a small platform in the venerable oak, like the ones he had in the trees behind his home in Bosnia.

Gathering enough boards and some rope with which to lash them down, he returned to the long-abandoned homestead. He knew just the right place to fashion his platform. Just over halfway up the eighty-foot tree grew two sturdy boughs whose close proximity to each other made them perfect supports for his observation post. Carrying up one board at a time, he tied the planks securely to the limbs until he had made a platform large enough for him to comfortably sit or even lay down upon, with his legs extended out onto the smaller branches growing from the boughs.

Having finished its construction, Amir sat upon the boards of his perch with a sense of satisfaction—a task taken on and completed, a thing now existing that just hours before hadn't. He looked outward through the gaps between the curtained layers of green leaves moving and shifting in a slow dance with the mild and pleasant autumn wind. The breeze washed over his skin gently and peacefully, the scent of the earth carried on its breath. Amir lay down and looked upward to stare into the tree's great crown. The maple leaves had already begun turning, to shades of red and gold, but the green oak leaves seemed more determined to hold their color, though soon enough they would follow suit. Amir could already see the paling of some oak leaves to translucent green, on their journey to more flamboyant dress.

The daydreams that drifted in and out of his consciousness, like the clouds passing high over his head, were quiet, slow, and of gentle form, unlike the visions that sometimes visited him in sleep. As he stared up into the leaves his sister, Minka, appeared in his mind. The image came from deep within his emotion's recall, and he smiled at the clear, innocent beauty of her face. She used to like to run her fingers through his hair to straighten out any unruly strands. If it was particularly unkempt from play, or perhaps from a late afternoon nap, she would take a brush to it instead, stroking gently across his scalp and finishing with a kiss to the top of his head. There were times, too, when she would get annoyed with him. Sometimes he would follow her and her friends and not leave them alone. If he felt rejected by her, he would sometimes behave badly, make irritating comments or say something stupid that made no sense at all, just to insert himself into a conversation he hadn't been invited to in the first place.

Minka's face was round, with clear, soft, pale skin and hazel eyes like his. Her lips, like her eyebrows, were thin but were held in a gentle, kind manner. Her features were elegant and soft in form and to Amir seemed like those of women whose photos he had seen in magazines modeling clothes for others to admire. Her hair was like his: fine, smooth, and chestnut brown; it was beautiful on its own, even without the face it accentuated.

As the picture of his sister grew fuller and clearer, Amir began to shift his mind to other thoughts. He was afraid to let the image of Minka come any closer, knowing that the presence of her memory had been triggered by another remembrance of her the prior evening, one that was not sentimental and gentle as this, but disturbing and ridden with anxiety. It had come during the hours of his sleep, and whether it had been just the product of dream or the play of actual memory, he could not say. The images had been too painful to bring forth from the archives of his mind into conscious thought. It had begun with the anxious look of his father, telling him to hide the hunting rifle.

"Take it down to the lower pasture and bury it behind the big boulder at the far end," his father, Asaf, had commanded.

The order had confused Amir. Why would he hide the hunting rifle? But his father didn't have time for explanations. "Please, please just do it," Asaf had shouted, his face showing his fear. In Amir's dream-memory, just after he had hidden the rifle and returned to the house, the soldiers came. One of them kicked open the door. The progression of images that followed played out in Amir's mind in a fast-forward matter of seconds. In real life, the experience unfolded in tortuously slow and painful ordeal.

At first, when the paramilitary barged in through the front door, it was as though everything was moving in slow motion. The men who filled the room were like the presences in Amir's dream, but in real time they didn't shift in sharp, angular images, one after the other in rapid-fire frames, but rather seemed to loom in a kind of slow, hovering threat, as though moving through a viscous atmosphere. The leisurely, measured ease with which they moved inferred their intentions with a horrible certainty.

Amir's father, Asaf, felt a chill of fear invade his body. He was paralyzed, unable to move, and his knees wanted to give way and lay him on the ground. He felt his wife move close and lean upon him. She took his arm with a shaking hand that silently begged he make the nightmare disappear. Asaf's fingers, touching hers, spoke back mutely, trying to give comfort where there was none to be had. Some frightened bird of illusion momentarily flitted through his mind. He looked at his wife and his children and saw their beauty and innocence with more clarity than he'd ever known. The men wouldn't do them harm. Their humanity wouldn't let them. There was hope.

"What have we here?" one of the men asked, stepping forward from the rest. He spoke calmly and smiled as if greeting an old friend. There was about the man a confident, almost pleasant demeanor, one that carried the unmistakable look of command, though more like that of a university professor than a soldier at war.

The father remained silent as the leader of the paramilitary group walked toward him as though in approach to shake his hand. The rest of the men stood quiet, relaxing the grip on their weapons as an unspoken look passed between them. It was their calmness that sent fear coursing up Asaf's spine.

"Seska, search the house for weapons," the commander ordered, stopping in front of Amir's father. The man's eyes, scanning the family, lingered on the daughter, Minka. "How old are you, girl?"

Minka hesitated, her voice lost. She willed herself to find it in order to get the man's eyes off of her, a lone word forcing itself out in strangled voice. "Fourteen."

"Ah, a lovely age," the commander smiled. "And you, boy," he asked, turning to the son, "how old are you?"

His eyes fearful, Amir looked away from the man to his father and then unconsciously out the window to the lower fields. There was no one down there, and they wouldn't find the rifle anyway. He had been very careful. Where he had buried the rifle, he had brushed the ground with a fallen limb to make the setting look undisturbed and natural.

"Boy, I asked you a question," the commander spoke coldly now, no pretense of kindliness in his voice.

"He has just turned eleven," Asaf answered, seeing that his son's eyes were like an animal's caught in a trap.

"Eleven, old enough to be a soldier then. Are you a soldier, boy?"

Terrified, Amir shook his head, finally getting a word out, "No."

The leader smiled, his head nodding up and down in slow motion, the languorous movement of his gesture belying the menace of his eyes.

"Stogan, search the father," the commander directed one of his men.

The paramilitary leader took a folded piece of paper from his shirt pocket and scanned its contents. The information it contained had been provided by a local resident aligned with their side, and it listed the name of every Bosniak in the village. The names of the ones thought to be participating in the resistance had been circled and annotated with detailed information about their activities and whether or not they might have access to arms.

"Nothing," Stogan reported, after running his hands over Asaf's body.

The commander looked at Asaf as if with some interest, studying his features: a man in his prime, in his mid-thirties, of healthy complexion. His face was marked by a broad mustache, and his dark hair contrasted with the green eyes that had found their way from some ancient heritage into the gene pool of Bosnian Muslims. Of average height, he looked capable and agile. Just the sort of man who would have given them trouble. The smile on the captain's face hardened, then disappeared altogether.

"Well," the commander said, looking at the report in his hands, "there is a rifle listed here. It must be hidden somewhere." Turning to the soldier who had searched the father, he commanded, "Stogan, search the girl, then. Maybe she is concealing it."

Stogan moved quickly from the father to the girl, clearly happy to follow the ludicrous idea that an object as large as a rifle could be hidden within the confines of her clothing. The soldier ran his large, calloused hands over the girl's shoulders and from there moved under her arms, his fingers spreading wide, taking in her breasts as he moved down her body. Jerking backward, Minka cried out, trying to move away from the soldier. His hands grasped her before she made even half a step, and he pulled her roughly toward him, bending his head to her ear to whisper something in it. The parents could not make out his words, but the daughter thereafter remained paralytically still.

Asaf forced himself to keep from going to his daughter's aid. He could feel the soldiers waiting for him to make a move. His wife clung to him with hands pleading in their grip. Both his daughter and son now had tears falling from their eyes, but the father knew he could neither intervene nor divulge the location of the rifle. A weapon would be used to qualify him as an enemy combatant and condemn them all, if in fact they were not already so marked.

"Nothing," Stogan reported with an affected, officious tone after having finished the search.

The commander's face once again took on the demeanor of the kindly professor, pausing a moment as if in thought before responding to his student. "Well then, go help Seska search the rest of the house for weapons. We'll wait here. And take the girl with you. Perhaps she'll be able to assist you."

"Of course, Captain. Good idea," Stogan replied with a broad grin and narrowed eyes.

"Please, please," Asaf pleaded, taking half a step forward, the words falling like tears from his mouth . . . all hope, as remote as it had been, drained from his being like rain into desert sand. He knew now, rifle or no rifle, what was in store for them. But before he could speak to tell the weapon's hidden location, the soldier nearest to him let the flat end of his rifle butt fly into the side of Asaf's face. Asaf resisted his body's wish to fall. Grunting in pain, he struggled to hold himself upright as blood began running down his face.

"It's in the field," Amir blurted out in quivering voice.

He was a boy of good nature. Well-educated, he knew never to speak out unless signaled by a parent to do so. Yet, distraught at the violence to his family, the words escaped him. His eyes ran to his parents, seeking some kind of sign, either of consent or condemnation for revealing the secret that had fallen from his mouth. But there was nothing, only the weeping of his mother and the dazed, bleeding face of his father.

"Below the lower field," the words continued to spill from the child. "Below the lower field, by the big rock."

"Ah, you see," the commander spoke in the stern voice of a righteous parent, "you should have said so in the beginning. A weapons cache, then. Stogan, tell Seska to quit searching the back and go take the boy and retrieve the arms."

Amir's eyes darted back and forth between his mother to his father, reflecting fear and confusion and the guilt of having spoken the rifle's hiding place. All these things were clearly written on the poor child's face. If there had been time, Asaf would have explained to his son that it was alright, that he too would have spoken out, in fact, had been about to when the soldier struck him.

Amir could see his father looking in his direction. His face was saying something but the child couldn't understand what. Was it condemnation for Amir having blurted out their secret? "What? I'm sorry, Papa. I'm sorry. What?"

But there had been no answer to his question then, nor upon waking from the dream-memory in a strange house so impossibly far away from all that had once been his. His eyes opened to the dawn's soft light, the vision fading and soon disappearing altogether. Blinking away any remaining threads of memory—lingering traces of the dream world that he would not follow even if he could—Amir quickly found his place of comfort: the deadened silence that would shelter him throughout his day.

Chapter 10

Waiting for the wheels of bureaucracy to turn, Amir's foster parents tried to make the best of the situation until an appropriate long-term placement could be found for their newest ward. Overall, Amir's social headway at school and home, although improving, was decidedly slow and came in small spurts that felt like they might end altogether at any moment. There was a sense of detachment about Amir that his sensory impairments alone couldn't explain. Whether it was something of his nature or resulted from his experience of war was far from clear. It was likely, his foster parents suspected, something of both. The Thorensons had been caring for children for nearly two decades and understood that the circumstances of Amir's past experiences told only part of the story. There was, as well, always the individual to be understood. People reacted to difficult conditions in different ways. With Amir's emotions so deeply obscured, his foster parents attempted to better understand the war that had brought Amir to their home.

Like most people who kept up with world news, Howard and Joy Thorenson knew the name of the country Amir had come from as Bosnia. Yet the underlying politics of the region were unclear to them. To the best of their understanding, Bosnia had once been part of Yugoslavia, which they rememebered as having been a satellite of the amorphous communist nation the USSR, a country they knew simply as "Russia," now broken apart and struggling to redefine itself. But much of their understanding departed from historical fact. They were as unaware of Yugoslavia's split with the Soviet Union following WWII as they were of the country's ultimate breakup in the early 1990s that had one after another of its six republics declaring independence, with Bosnia and Herzegovina doing so on March 3, 1992.

Amir's foster parents began to pay more attention to the nightly news, but the media's updates on the war in Bosnia provided them little more than snippets of historical fact or present-day horror, shedding little light on what was going on in that faraway place. Even occasional, extended media coverage of the conflict was confusing. There seemed to be an expert for every side of the story, and the sides seemed to multiply by the number of experts with theories to expound. The images and sound bites felt distant, delivered by newscasters whose faces were like those of onlookers standing at a safe distance. The sympathy in their voices seemed calculated to reassure the listener, passive compassion overriding the need for action. In the comfort of their living room, the Thorensons felt they could do little more than listen with growing alarm to the stories coming from the land that had once been their young foster child's home and be glad that he had escaped it. It was better now, they thought, that Amir's past be forgotten.

As time passed with no news from Amir's case manager about a permanent placement for the boy, the Thorensons grew increasingly disheartened. The likelihood that the Bosnian war orphan would end up staying with them in a long-term holding pattern or be transferred to a larger institutional setting grew with each passing day. Yet, while their discouragement painted a less-than-hopeful picture of their foster child's future, fate's workings seeded a very different destiny for the boy.

Margaret Morgan was retired, widowed, and by nature reserved. Feeling herself content to live out her retirement in the quiet, secluded comfort of her old New England farmstead, she had cut her links to Boston—and to city life—where she had been a noted professor of psychology at one of the nation's top universities. Yet despite her declarations to friends and family—and even more emphatically to herself—that she was perfectly happy in her retirement, she felt a growing sense within herself that something was missing from her life.

The truth of the matter was that Margaret Morgan wasn't happy. But she couldn't blame her unease on her voluntary retirement from her teaching career. The feeling of slow, gnawing dissatisfaction had, in fact, been what prompted her to accept the generous early retirement package proffered by the university to all of its senior professors. Margaret had been one of the few who accepted the offer, having long ago promised herself she wouldn't end up being the kind of fossilized academic who stood selfishly blocking the aisle, keeping the younger teaching professionals from moving ahead.

The retired professor recognized she was caught in a kind of internal conundrum, one she had avoided thinking about until the circumstances triggered by her retirement forced it upon her. She was too active a personality to simply fade off into the sunset, write the occasional article for a professional journal, and tend to her country gardens. Yet her years in academia had done nothing to prepare her for any other role, nor given her imagination fuel from which to consider any other possibility.

If Margaret Morgan's retirement did nothing to worsen her internal discomfort, neither did it do anything to alleviate it. Margaret was left, as she might describe it, to tread the water of complacency, even if she was not content with the ever-growing realization of an impending ending that would bring no new beginning. In her childhood, time had seemed to have the physical properties of gas: indefinitely expandable and able to occupy so large and far-reaching a space that it seemed infinite. But Margaret's understanding of time had changed along with the years. Time for her had gone from a gas, to a thing liquid and flowing, to something solid and finite. Now in her mid-sixties, its boundaries had become frighteningly visible. The trap for her, of course, would be to attempt to fill as much of those bounds as possible with as many activities as might give the illusion of youth's immortality.

But it wasn't the mirage of a plenitude of time that Margaret needed. Her spirit called out for some meaningful, if small, experience of life before having to leave it all behind. Yet Margaret felt nothing remained for her but to begin a life of retirement, pretending to herself that it was exactly what she wanted. She tended to her gardens and enlarged their scope. She wrote an article for a leading psychology journal, maintained correspondence with her former colleagues and students, and attended enough events and social gatherings that her calendar felt as full as ever.

At a party hosted by one of her former colleagues, nearly a year to the day she had retired, Margaret was introduced to a woman who worked for a religious social services organization. Jane Coleman, the director of the charity's children's programs, fell into easy conversation with Margaret, the two having much to share in the way of professional experience. After a time they were joined by other guests, and the topic of conversation drifted to shoptalk, the politics of work, and from there to the politics of government and the latest human indignity to occupy the evening news—the Bosnian War.

As the guests spoke about the lack of international intervention in the conflict, Margaret was struck by how the sympathetic dialogue coming from herself and the others mirrored the political rhetoric: neither the involved governments nor any of the partygoers were doing anything of real import to help halt the genocide in progress. Both offered only words of sympathy, abhorrence, and outrage in place of any real action.

Among the people attending the gathering, however, one was actually doing something to make a difference: Jane Coleman, part of whose job was to manage a program that provided homes for refugee children separated from their families. During the conversation they had shared earlier, Jane mentioned that a growing number of Bosnian minors were included among the children being sponsored by the religious charity she worked for. Margaret made a mental note to send that particular charity a donation. It was a good cause and, she thought, the very least she could do.

Her donation was substantial enough to have crossed the desk of the department's director. Jane Coleman, remembering Margaret from the recent gathering, phoned her to thank the former professor for her generosity. "I wish I could do more," Margaret said.

"Well, we're always looking for host families for our children. If you or anyone you know might be interested in helping in that way, there is always that opportunity as well," the program director responded. Margaret noted the casual tone in which the administrator delivered the opening, with neither pressure nor expectation in her inflection.

"I'll certainly pass the word on to those I know," Margaret replied. "As for myself, I'm afraid my age would disqualify me."

"You would be surprised at the wide variety in age and background of our foster parents," Jane answered. "Some of our most successful host families have been grandparents."

"It's true, we old folks do have some experience to make up for our declining firepower. But it's been years since I've practiced my mothering skills. My daughter grew up and left home more years ago than I care to remember."

"Well anyway, give it some thought. I always mention the possibility to anyone who shows interest in our programs. We are constantly in need of good homes for our children."

"I'll keep it in mind. I think what you're doing is wonderful, and I applaud your agency's efforts."

During the next twenty-four hours, Margaret Morgan's conversation with the children's program administrator played back in her mind several times. The weight of her own words, while externally polite and correct, internally felt superficial, the complacency they implied leaving a feeling of shallowness that pained her conscience.

At home alone on the evening following her phone conversation with Jane Coleman, Margaret sat drinking a glass of wine, her conversation with the director of children's programs replaying in her mind yet another time. *My god,* she thought, *is tossing money like a bone the best that I can do? Will I spend this last leg of my lifetime only in the pursuit of self-comfort? Can't I afford to give something more?* Certainly, she could help the charitable agency on an occasional basis by offering her professional services, if they had use of them. And what about becoming a foster parent? Was the noted academic too exalted a personality to take on that role? Wasn't she the teacher, the coach who sat on the sidelines and instructed others how to play, never dirtying herself in the game? Here in her thoughts, Margaret's irritation with herself turned to a smile, a caricature coming to mind: the pompous professor tripping over her own feet as she walked to the podium. Her humor lightening her mood, Margaret thought back upon her recently abandoned career. *You were a good teacher,* a voice inside of her acknowledged. *You were diligent, caring, and dedicated,* the voice continued.

A second voice, doubtful and unsure, entered the conversation: *Should I really have retired? Had it been a terrible mistake to leave a lifetime of professional identity behind with nothing there to take its place?*

No, the first voice answered, *it had been right for you to stand down and make way for new talent. In any case,* it said in finality, *retirement didn't have to be an ending.* Yet the doubting voice was not comforted. *But if not an ending, then what is it?*

Margaret Morgan had grown up in a wealthy family, never wanting for anything except for the experience of living in a world away from the fenced-off grounds of her privileged, safe haven. As she grew into her adolescence she longed for an opportunity to join the world at large, not be sheltered from it. But her parents and the times didn't allow for any experimentation in the integration of class or race or culture. Her childhood might have been without material struggle of any kind, but emotionally it had been just the opposite. Small fissures of unhappiness, unnoticed by any but herself, began to appear beneath the enviable, gilded lifestyle that held her up.

In her adulthood, Margaret worked diligently to free herself of the bounds of the propriety her parents had imposed on her childhood. But the postwar years of the 1950s were not encouraging of women who wanted to pursue an independent path. Her parents never expected her to complete her college education; her attendance was, after all, more to find her a good husband than to procure a degree, which would have little use in her future as a mother and homemaker. Yet Margaret had other ideas. She was bright, she had an inquisitive mind, and she cared about others and the world. As the times and social mores changed, Margaret was among those who fought to bring the progression about. She graduated from college and went on to pursue a postgraduate degree, ultimately earning her doctorate and, eventually, even her parents' grudging admiration. After she fell in love with a young, successful attorney, got married, and gave birth to a child, they felt everything had finally fallen rightly into place.

But if Margaret believed she had broken free from the confines of a life of stifling security, she was never quite sure whether or not she had escaped the grounds of the prison itself. Her years in her chosen profession had taught her that internal enclosures were no less difficult to free oneself of than their external material counterparts. Had she escaped the conditions of her past only to find that now, years later, she had walked in circles and ended up back in the very place from which she had sought to free herself?

Several days after her conversation with Jane, Margaret found herself picking up the phone. "Hello, Jane," she said. "I'm calling to see if you might tell me a little more about what's involved in hosting a child."

Happy to hear of Margaret's interest, Jane Coleman explained the process involved in becoming a foster parent and answered the retired professor's questions. She then added that the agency was in need of someone of Margaret's professional capacity who could volunteer time to consult on several of their more complicated cases. It was, she suggested, a good way for Margaret to see firsthand some of the issues that might be involved in being a caregiver to a child before she made a final decision whether or not to enter their program.

There was, Jane mentioned, a case they were having particular difficulty with. The program director had remembered, from her conversation with Margaret at the party, that the retired professor had experience working with hearing-impaired persons and was conversant in American Sign Language. The child in question was a war orphan from Bosnia, a deaf-mute boy who had been placed in a temporary residence and was having trouble adjusting. Would Margaret be willing to meet with the child and give her professional opinion of his condition to help the agency determine the most appropriate setting for his permanent placement?

"I'd be happy to," Margaret readily replied, though a part of her was caught off guard at how quickly she'd gone from an exploratory phone call to actual involvement.

"That's great, Margaret. Thanks so much," Jane said. "As you might be aware, all refugees entering the country go through a standard health screening. The results from this boy's screening have left us with more questions than answers. If it's OK with you, I'll forward the case file to you today so you'll have all of the necessary background information, and then, if you're willing, we can set up an appointment for you to meet with the child. His name is Amir Beganović."

When Margaret received the Bosnian orphan's file, she was struck more by what information it didn't contain than that which it did. The general and cursory medical report described his health and sensory impairments. There was scant information concerning his history before arriving in his host country. The file stated he had been transferred from a refugee camp in Bosnia, yet there was nothing of detail pertaining to how he had come to be there or what his life had been like before the war.

Driving to the foster home to meet with the boy, Margaret considered her role in the case. For a number of years early in her career she had maintained a small private practice while teaching at the university as an adjunct professor. But after working her way up the ladder to become a tenured professor, her responsibilities at the school grew, and she had let the practice go. It felt good to be back in that role again. The sun was out and the sky clear, the beginnings of a beautiful Indian-summer day. Margaret felt more enlivened than she had in a long time. After meeting with the boy, she would continue into Cambridge to visit with her daughter, who lived there. As she pulled into the Thorensons' driveway, Margaret felt at ease and as if, once again, she had something to offer the world other than the forced contentment of her smile.

Chapter 11

The retired psychology professor's first visit with the Bosnian war orphan went well. The child had not been particularly responsive, nor had he exhibited much emotional reaction during their time together, but he had been polite and respectful and displayed, from her experienced perspective, an intelligent demeanor. Margaret's initial impression of the boy came from the simplicity of her practiced, uncomplicated observational skill. As Amir entered the room, led by his foster father, she had noted the way he carried his body, how he held his head, the musculature of his face and mouth, and the movement of his eyes. He was slight of body, his face passive in its expression, and his eyes, as they briefly met hers, were shielded by a reserve that maintained their distance.

Amir watched as Margaret introduced herself, signing "hello" with a wave of her hand. She introduced herself by spelling her name with her fingers, but he wasn't sure of all its letters. He signed back "hello," the movement of his hand timid, and then he sat down at the kitchen table with Margaret and his foster parents.

His foster parents served tea and cookies to their guest. His foster mother poured him a glass of milk, then put some cookies on a plate and placed it in front of him. Amir looked on passively as the woman visitor sipped her tea and spoke with his foster parents. Even though she knew his signing skills were limited, Margaret signed her words as she talked and glanced in his direction so that he might feel included in the conversation. Though he added no comment of his own, she would occasionally smile at him as if he had spoken, yet never with the look of expectation that he need actually do so.

Amir ate his cookies with his eyes directed at his plate, stealing a look at the woman for only the briefest of moments. He could see that she was aware of his glances, just as he was aware that, although none of the adults at the table directed more than casual attention in his direction, he was the reason the visitor was there.

"How school today?" his foster mother signed, attempting to engage the boy in the conversation.

"OK," Amir's hands replied, spelling out the two letters, their movement reflecting the ambivalence of his feelings.

Joy Thorenson nodded her head and searched his eyes for a brief second. "Good, or just OK?" she asked with a smile.

Amir shrugged in reply and looked briefly downward as if the answer to the question was to be found written on the ground by his feet. He then raised his head and once more signed the letters *o* and *k*.

"School big or small?" Margaret asked, signing her question as she spoke. Her face expressed a casual curiosity, her head tilted to the right, her eyebrows arched, and her shoulders raised upward.

"Big," Amir responded, bringing his hands close together and then spreading them wide apart, his gesture indicating that he considered the place very large indeed.

"I see," Margaret signed back, her face showing her curiosity satisfied.

With the ice broken between the boy and the visitor, the conversation at the table continued on more at ease until, after a time, Margaret could see Amir's attention beginning to wane. She excused herself and thanked the Thorensons for their hospitality. As she drove toward Cambridge she considered the myths many people held about foster parents and the children they cared for.

The children themselves were often considered "damaged goods" beyond repair and the foster parents in it just for the money. The truth was that the great majority of children under foster care, though struggling to overcome very difficult circumstances, were resilient, polite, and bright children just like you'd find in the homes of your friends. And if the Thorensons were any example, the idea that foster parents were in it simply for the money was uninformed. In fact, for the Thorensens it was just the opposite. Both held jobs. She was a nurse and he was a real estate appraiser. The truth was they financially augmented the charity's foster program and not the other way around.

By their third meeting together, Margaret felt Amir beginning to become more responsive to her. They had passed the point of being strangers, and the comfort of familiarity had begun to grow between the woman and the boy.

"We have a fun project today," Margaret signed. "Want to try?"

Amir looked back at the woman, his brows furrowed and his face showing he didn't understand her.

Realizing her signing had been beyond the boy's still-basic skills, Margaret signaled for him to watch. Taking a stack of tissue papers of assorted colors from her bag, she placed it on the table. She then removed a small tub of glue and brought it over to the Thorensons' kitchen sink, where she diluted it with water. Sitting back at the table with Amir, she demonstrated what they were to do.

"Take any color paper you like," she signed. "Cut or tear big or little, then put in glue and place on the poster board. See, just like that. It's simple."

Amir was not sure. It wasn't the woman's signing that confused him now, nor the process itself. It was the end product he didn't understand. What was he supposed to make by putting the tissue paper on the poster board?

"I don't understand."

Margaret smiled at the quizzical look on the boy's face, the tilt of his head and the ever-so-light lift of his shoulders that spoke his thoughts as clear as any words.

"You can make picture," Margaret signed.

"What kind?"

"Any kind. Anything you like."

"But what kind?"

"The picture makes itself. Don't worry. Just have fun."

Amir looked at Margaret doubtfully but began to work on his project all the same. Reaching for a pair of scissors, he cut out pieces of tissue paper of various colors, laying them out on the notebook-size sheet of poster board the woman had placed in front of him. Margaret could see that the pieces he was cutting would make the pattern of a landscape. The boy was carefully laying out each piece and putting it in place in preparation for gluing it down. The retired psychology professor smiled but said nothing. The art process she had chosen to engage in with the boy was not a medium meant for replication of the literal but rather one intended to open the imagination to forms whose meanings were beneath the surface of conscious thought.

Instead of showing Amir what he might do with the materials at hand, Margaret focused on her own work and allowed him to continue unimpeded. Still not quite sure of how he was to proceed once he'd cut out the pieces to his picture, Amir looked to the woman to see if he should begin gluing his cut-outs one at a time, as he made them, or finish cutting all of them and then glue them down in sequence. What he saw surprised him. The woman was tearing off bits of tissue paper without the scissor's help, dipping them in the glue solution, and then placing them in seemingly random locations upon her sheet of poster board. Only occasionally did she use the scissors to cut the tissue, and even then, when she placed it on the poster board, she didn't lay it down flat in a position that might make sense with the others around it, but rather, she let it soak in the glue solution until it was saturated and completely pliable. She then bunched it up, swirling the material about so that some of it was elevated on the sheet and looked like a small hill rising from the ground beneath it.

His face expressing both his curiosity in what the woman might be doing and his doubt about his own process, Amir looked to Margaret.

Margaret, seeing the boy hover between the world of the literal and that of the imagination, smiled in response. But she did nothing more, leaving him to choose which realm he wished to enter.

"But I don't understand," the look on the boy's face spoke.

"Just have fun," Margaret signed to Amir.

"What are you making?" Amir signed back.

"Don't know. I am waiting to see what the picture wants to be."

Amir paused momentarily to ponder what the woman had signed, not sure what she meant. "How do you do that?" his hands asked, pointing to a textured rise in Margaret's creation.

"This?" Margaret queried, pointing to where her tissue paper bunched, intermingling one piece with the next.

"Yes, there."

"I don't remember. I think something like this," she said, attempting to recreate the spontaneous technique.

Amir turned away from the woman and considered the ordered pieces of tissue paper that lay in front of him and the idea that they could be set in place by no other mandate than his whimsy. Hesitantly taking hold of a piece of paper, he submerged it in the diluted glue solution and let it soak for a few seconds as he had seen the woman do. Lifting it, he then laid it on the sheet of heavy paper. It didn't look right to him sitting all alone by itself. It seemed out of place. Nevertheless, he continued, gluing one piece at a time, his poster board soon beginning to look less like an empty, disjointed canvas. But still, he could feel no fun in what he was doing . . . until he accidentally caught the edge of the last piece he'd placed, bunching it up with the one he was currently laying down.

Just as a feeling of frustration began to rise at the mistake, he saw the woman glancing in his direction. Looking at his sheet of paper, where the two pieces, one blue and the other green, had accidentally merged, she gave him a thumbs-up, as if his fumbling of the tissue had been an artistic triumph. Amir turned his gaze back at his botched work and saw that where the two differently colored pieces of tissue paper met, a third color had been created, turquoise, and that the wrinkling of the bunched paper gave it a texture that made it look like gentle waves gracefully traveling across a pond. Strangely, it looked more real to him than an actual photo of ripples on a body of water.

Taking another piece of tissue paper, Amir let it soak extra long in the solution. He laid it down on the poster board and then, doing as he'd seen the woman do earlier, swirled it around on itself in a circle. It didn't create the rise of a small hill, as it had in the woman's piece, so much as it did the roll of sand dunes you might see in a desert. It looked good, and he liked the feel of it under his fingers.

"Like this?" he signed.

"Are you having fun?"

"Yes."

"Then, yes. Just like that."

After Amir had finished using all of the pieces he had cut out for his landscape, now spread about his poster board in what seemed to him a disordered chaos, he began tearing additional strips from the sheets of the tissue paper with his hands, leaving the scissors resting on the table. While his mind still sought to make some sense from the mix of colors and shapes that had grown upon his canvas, his hands continued their work.

As he placed the new pieces of torn and irregular shapes on the board, Amir began to see how they took on a life of their own, revealing a hidden world beneath the veil of the obvious. It was just like looking at clouds moving slowly across the sky. At first, all you saw were great white puffs standing out against the backdrop of the blue ceiling high above them. But then, the more you looked, the more you could see. Curious shapes would begin to emerge within the amorphous billows of white, vague images that soon took on the appearance of the familiar: eyes, noses, cheeks, and hair—human, animal, and other shapes arising in phantasmagoric shiftings of scenes that set his imagination free to wander in magical realms. It was just like that with the picture growing from the pieces of colored tissue paper he placed on the poster board, Amir's mind no longer directing the action, his eyes watching, waiting to see what emerged from his imagination's flight.

Margaret Morgan waited several days after her third visit with Amir to begin to write the conclusion to her report. She told herself that the delay was to better consider the boy's situation, though she knew the nebulous, unformed questions hovering about in the background of her thought had as much to do with her interior state as they had to do with the child's. It wasn't until she finally completed writing her evaluation that the retired professor became aware that her postponement of the process had, in fact, been because the report would mark an end to her involvement with the boy. Putting the thought to the side, she submitted her evaluation to the charitable agency.

Margaret followed up her report with a phone call to Jane Coleman, ostensibly to discuss any questions the program director might have regarding it, though behind that straightforward act sat the motivation of a far deeper and complicated urge. Margaret began her conversation with Jane by recounting the general details of her three visits with Amir. She went on to tell the administrator that she found indications of emotional disturbance within the boy's behavioral pattern. Exactly how profound, and stemming from what, remained to be seen, but she had noted clear symptoms of anxiety, difficulty in concentrating, detachment, and emotional numbness. He appeared, Margaret added, to be of above-average intelligence and beneath his quiet, withdrawn demeanor showed signs of a healthy, bright curiosity. Margaret didn't believe the boy's best interest would be served by placing him in any kind of institutional setting. Despite the complexities of his case, the retired psychology professor concluded, a long-term, individual care environment, where Amir could receive both the attention and the freedom of movement he needed, would be the best option for his care.

The clear, concise, and professionally neutral demeanor in which Margaret delivered her opinion to Jane Coleman belied the feelings that strained within her. The visits with Amir had stirred a profound force inside her. Had the child's disabilities triggered her empathy for the trauma of a child caught in war? Did his story spark her professional interest? Her sympathy? Or something else? Strangely, there was something of her own need calling out. The retired professor was weary of her own issues. She worried that she had lived a life too far removed from risk—the secure, fixed comfort of her identity coming at the cost of growth and spontaneity. Her career had been marked by maturity, intellectual advancement, and the attainment of society's respect. Had the safe and the certain become her spirit's master? Privilege bred privilege and, left unchecked, bred a complacency that smothered the instinct of real compassion, leaving only a veneer of caring. It was a trap she'd fought against the whole of her life. Had she really managed to evade it? Or had she simply become so accustomed to it that she no longer was even aware of being caught within it?

A battle flared up in her mind, one part of her decrying another, a determination growing to surrender neither to apathy nor to false contentment. If the dimensions of her hope had retreated and shrunk, if doubt and fear had reduced the boundaries of her possibilities to the known and sure, then at least she could help provide an opportunity for someone else to find the place of their promise and follow its lead into the future. Margaret tried to imagine what that struggle might look like for Amir. If her own hope had become a mountain of daunting height to scale, then what must the experience of hope be like for the orphaned boy? She imagined, given all he had suffered, that for the child, hope might be infinitely more distant . . . a planet so far away it was but a speck in the night sky, at one moment its tentative blink signaling a presence, only to vanish the very next second into the vast blackness of the cosmos. Yet, as repressed as Amir seemed, she sensed that in the depths of his inner life, hope persevered.

In the end, there would be no battle of mind and heart for Margaret Morgan. As shocking and illogical as the idea of becoming the boy's caregiver seemed to her, a voice within her called out that it was the right thing to do—despite another, opposing voice, speaking in practical tone, declaring that she was acting irrationally. Pushing aside all doubt, after she finished giving her assessment to Jane Coleman, Margaret asked the program director if she might be considered to become the orphaned boy's foster parent. It was only when the call had ended and she had replaced the phone on the receiver, Jane Coleman's positive and enthusiastic affirmation of her request still sounding in her ears, that Margaret began to grasp the enormity of her decision and the depth of the change it would bring to her life.

Chapter 12

Some years before her retirement, Margaret Morgan had bought her country home as a place of retreat from the dense constancy of city life, even though her principal residence sat in an oasis of metropolitan privilege surrounded by its own, small slice of nature, affording her both privacy and escape from the harder, less yielding lines of an ever-growing cityscape.

Her country property was a very manageable two-hour drive from her Cambridge home and was located within walking distance of a small village center whose rural quaintness had been as much the reason for her purchase as the house itself. The center-chimney colonial home was surrounded by nearly ten acres of cleared land, most of it on the south side of the residence. The property was accessed by a private driveway lined by a stand of sugar maples. The driveway ended in a clearing where the house sat on a small plateau overlooking the valley that cradled the village.

A wooded area occupied the area north of the house. A brook wandered along the wood's edge and worked its way downslope, past a small orchard of old apple trees at the far end of the field. Although the village offered little in the way of the amenities and activities she had grown accustomed to in her many years of city life, Margaret's country home was less than a half-hour's drive from a large university town rich in cultural and commercial resources.

Amir showed little reaction at leaving the Thorensons' house and being shuttled to a different one. Howard and Joy Thorenson hugged him good-bye, the dual feelings of sadness at his departure and happiness that he was going to a good home apparent in their faces. Of the three older boys who had been there when he arrived, only Andrés, the Nicaraguan boy, remained. The two older Bosnian boys each had recently found placements in Bosnian households, one in the suburbs near Boston and the other in Connecticut. They would soon be replaced by a brother and sister whose mother had been incarcerated on felony drug charges. For the Thorensons, the emotional pain of losing children they had become attached to was mitigated by the arrival of new foster children in need. It was how they coped with being short-term caregivers and having to face the ultimate removal of the children they had bonded with. As he drove away with Margaret Morgan, Amir looked out the car window at Howard, Joy, and Andrés waving good-bye. He raised his own hand in farewell, moving it back and forth twice, and then turned his head.

For the first few days at Margaret's house Amir felt like he wasn't really there. It was as though his body walked about the place empty, the rest of him floating off somewhere in the distance, looking down upon his physical self with no sense of ownership or relation. Even as Margaret showed him about and made every attempt to make him comfortable, Amir's eyes looked out upon his new world dulled and without shine or spark, as though jaded at having seen it all a thousand times before.

It had been apparent from the very first moment he'd set eyes on the house that it was one of wealth and privilege. It was not so much that the structure was large, though that it housed only one person surprised him. Rather, it was the quality of everything about it, both on the outside and within, that had made him feel discomfited to live in such a rich environment.

It had previously been explained to Amir on a number of occasions that the place to which he would be moving would be his new home. Yet upon seeing it he could think of no other logical explanation that he should be taken to live in so grand a property, other than that he had been brought there to work. This made perfect sense to him. The woman was old, and he had to earn his keep. When she had taken him upstairs to show him the bedrooms, the woman led him into the one across from hers and signed to him that he could stay there if he wished. It was large, its furnishings were old and of fine quality, and it had its very own bathroom. He felt strangely insecure in such a big and fancy room. The woman must have seen the discomfort on his face. Smiling, she signed for him to follow her down the hall and showed him a smaller room off by itself, this one just large enough for the bed, a bureau, and a small writing desk. It had two windows on each of the exterior walls, and they looked out onto the fields on one side and the woods on the other.

By the end of his first week at Margaret's, Amir began to relax and feel freer to enjoy the many aspects of the place that had drawn his interest but in which he'd initially been too withdrawn to engage. Of all the things about his new home that impressed Amir, nothing did so more than the property itself. The fields and gardens surrounding the house were beautiful. It was clear that they were very well tended and cared for. A large barn stood as strong and sure as the house itself, everything within it neat and ordered. Not far from it, a small brook ran down from higher ground along the edge of the field, its waters clean and cold, reminding him of the streams and rivers he had known in Bosnia. All of the cleared land was bound by stonewalls, carefully laid, solid and strong.

Walking the perimeter of the fields, Amir found the places where the hollow of the ground revealed the pathways of the forest animals as they traveled from woods to field in search of food. There was no more popular trail, it seemed, than the one that traveled through a break in the stone wall that led from the forested area to the old apple orchard that stood in graceful pose at the far side of the fields. The trees, pruned and healthy, held a bounty of fruit that now, late in the season, dropped plentifully to the ground for the birds and animals to feast upon. Amir was surprised that the apples should be left for animals and not harvested by the woman to sell or store.

Informed by his previous foster parents that Amir loved the outdoors and handled himself well there, Margaret had indicated to him that he was free to roam about outside, her only injunction that he not travel far into the woods until he came to know the lay of the land. Though she understood from the Thorensons that Amir spent a great deal of time outdoors, she was still surprised at the number of hours he occupied himself wandering about the property. At first, it felt strange to see him roaming the fields, walking along the brook, or moving in and out of the woods. It was as though she had spotted a new animal among the regulars who visited her land. The way the boy walked, lightly and with care—his body's posture vigilant and aware—seemed more akin to the creatures of the bordering forest than it did to someone of her own species.

One warm, sunny fall day, sitting quietly on her patio, Margaret looked up from the book she was reading, sensing a movement in the distance, and saw Amir emerging from the woods at the far edge of the fields. She watched her new foster son as he crossed into the orchard, losing sight of him as he wandered among the apple trees. Neither seeing him exit its other side nor within the orchard itself, she became perplexed. After some moments, her curiosity roused, she rose from her patio chair and walked out to the orchard.

Coming up to the first row of trees, she guessed that he had come in on the deer track that wound its way into the orchard from the woods. Looking around, she was mystified as to what could have possibly become of the boy. He had been there one instant and was gone the next.

Margaret walked, scanning the trees as she went, then stood quietly for a moment without looking about. Finally, with a slight shake of her head, she started to take her leave. No more than two steps into her return, an apple suddenly fell softly nearby, its descent bringing with it the distinct sense of the object having been gently propelled, not fallen of its own accord. She turned and looked up in the direction of its fall. It took several seconds of gazing up through the leaves for her to make out the face of the boy staring back down at her. His expression at first appeared blank. But then the subtlest of smiles rose from the corners of the boy's mouth, momentarily breaking through the strange, sad seriousness that often marked his face, and it seemed to Margaret that something of his spirit had shyly emerged from its place of quiet.

It had been a spontaneous action. Amir saw that the woman was leaving, and his hand had reached out by its own accord, though even then, when it was about to make him known, it took the apple soundlessly. When her eyes found him, she made no move in his direction but, like himself, was content to simply observe. What he saw in her face had made him smile.

"Many apples," Amir's fingers spoke, pointing to the fruit-laden branches around him as he looked down to the woman below.

"Yes," Margaret smiled, her fingers answering back, "many apples."

"They are falling to the ground," Amir indicated by pointing to the ground.

"Animals like them. The deer come here to eat," Margaret signed, raising both her open hands to her head and placing thumbs to forehead in mimic of antlers.

"And you?" Amir asked. "Do you like apples?"

"Yes, I do," Margaret answered.

"I can pick them," Amir responded, gesturing toward the apples as if plucking them from their branches.

Margaret smiled at the enthusiasm of the boy as his hands demonstrated how quickly and easily they could harvest the fruit.

She signed to him that it would make her happy to have some apples to eat. She had not before seen such animated display of emotion in her new foster son and was glad of its arrival. Amir climbed down from the tree and indicated that he would walk down to the house with her. He remembered seeing some old apple crates stacked in the barn. He would need them to store all of the apples he would harvest.

Back at her seat on the patio, Margaret watched as the boy ran off to the barn and emerged with a wheelbarrow piled high with the old wooden apple crates left over from times long past, crates that had seemed so much a part of the barn she'd never had the heart to throw them away. She was bemused to see the boy carrying the ambitious reservoir of storage containers and thought to intercede. A small bag of apples would more than suffice to meet their needs. Yet, seeing the happiness in the focused rhythm of Amir's movements, she held back. Observing Amir push the heavy load across the field with determined perseverance, Margaret was struck by a powerful sense of the reality of his sudden presence in her life. How had it happened? The fact of it seemed strange, wonderful, and frightening at the same time.

Watching him struggle with his load up the small rise to the orchard, Margaret strained to feel some tangible sense of the child as her foster son, or even just of him as a person called Amir. But the only solid connection her mind could grasp was that of him as being simply the boy who was now living in her home. They had yet to come to know each other. Without speech between them, there was no distraction of the spoken word to fill the voids of awareness between the one person and the other, no easy chatter to distract the mind and quiet the emotion's precarious vulnerabilities.

Margaret continued to watch as Amir reached the orchard and unloaded the crates. Taking up an old, thin canvas drop cloth he'd scavenged from the barn, he fashioned a harvest bag, folding it in half, knotting its ends, and tying it around his waist. In another second he disappeared up the trunk of one of the trees. Smiling, Margaret returned to her reading while Amir continued up and down the apple trees, filling one wooden crate then the next, his foster mother unaware of the growing number of boxes the boy was loading with steady and focused pace.

Amir liked being up in the apple trees. He liked the idea of working, of being productive at something he knew. And although he wasn't able to express it, he enjoyed the sense of independent well-being coming from life reduced to the essential: his body at work, his mind fixed on the task at hand, and his heart at peace in nature. Carefully stepping out onto the trees' stronger limbs, he picked their fruit with sure, graceful movement as he slid carefully along their branches. High up in the trees, Amir could feel the pieces of his diffused emotional self coming together, touching with the sensation of wholeness—a reminder of times once known that had vanished into oblivion.

Every fall he had harvested apples with his father in his family's small orchard, much the same size as the one he was working in now. His mother and sister helped. They packed some of the fruit for storage and some to be turned into a rich, thick apple butter. Later they would all be busy in the kitchen peeling and cooking the apples, the house filling with the smell of the simmering fruit. There had been purpose in their work, in his life, a bounty of love there. Lost to the cadence of his hand moving back and forth from apple to bag, Amir's mind wandered from his task, obscured images flowing in distant thought.

Amir didn't notice Margaret's approach until she stood beneath the tree he sat in, her hand holding forth a glass with tiny beads of condensation clinging to its side. Descending from the tree, Amir received the cold drink his foster mother had brought him and signed his thanks, the fingers of his right hand touching his lips and then falling slightly back in her direction, his face smiling in affirmation.

Returning Amir's smile, Margaret glanced at the crates he had filled and gave a mock look of shock to indicate she was very impressed with his efforts. A shy grin of boyish pride broke out on Amir's face along with a hesitant blush. He paused for a moment between the small, careful sips with which he drank as his mind searched for some comment or piece of conversation to add, but he came up empty. When he finished his drink, Margaret took the glass and left without any further communication other than her smile.

After she had gone, Amir returned to his work, though the image of the woman stayed for a time in his thoughts. She knew, Amir understood, how to approach a wild animal in increments, earning trust with patience—to acclimatize it to human presence by containing oneself in quiet stillness until the animal came to accept the human as part of the natural order. He liked this in the woman.

"My goodness, what in heaven's name are we going to do with all of these apples?" Margaret declared, looking at the full crates Amir had wheeled back to the house. He had been up at the orchard nearly the whole of the afternoon and still would have been there if Margaret had not gone up to signal him back to the house.

Amir looked back at Margaret, his palms flat and open to the sky, his shoulders hunched in question.

"Sorry," Margaret signed with her hands, realizing she had been speaking out loud without their translation. "Many apples. What to do?"

"Eat," Amir indicated by holding an imaginary apple to his mouth. "Cook apples," he added, his right hand coming to rest upon his upturned left palm, flipping it like a pancake being turned.

"Yes, good idea," Margaret smiled and signed back. "Tomorrow, make pie. My daughter is coming. Cut apples now to eat, OK?"

"Yes, OK," Amir replied.

"Tea and cookies too, OK?"

Amir signed his assent and followed Margaret into the house. His foster mother indicated that he should wash up while she prepared the tea and snacks. Putting the kettle on to boil, she placed a few cookies on a platter and then sliced two of the apples her foster son had harvested. Tomorrow her daughter, Alice, would come and they could make a pie from the apples. The activity would be a good icebreaker. Amir liked doing practical things, keeping his hands busy. It seemed to make social situations easier for him. It would be the first time the two would meet. Margaret was as excited at the prospect as she supposed Amir might, himself, be reticent. Alice had been genuinely happy for her mother's decision to foster Amir, had supported the idea from the first, though she had been surprised at how quickly it had all come about.

"Tea in library?" Margaret asked when Amir appeared back in the kitchen, clean and tidied up.

"OK," Amir replied, taking the plate of cookies and sliced apples Margaret held out to him while she transported the tray that held the tea set. Of all the rooms in the house, the library was Amir's favorite. When he had first come to live at Margaret's and she had shown him around the house, Amir had entered the library and been awed by its voluminous contents. The room had seemed to him like something one saw in the pages of a magazine, the place of some famous scholar or person of wealth, replete with furniture covered in the finest fabric and rich, dark shelving made of the most expensive hardwoods. It was a library perfect in its comfort, a place to sit and read among the seemingly uncountable volumes lining every wall of the room, even framing the two large, mullioned windows overlooking the gardens outside. Everything in the room—the paintings, the photographs, the small sculptures and art objects—was encircled by the books Margaret had been collecting for the better part of her life. There hadn't been even a small library in Amir's village. An individual having her very own room full of books seemed an amazing luxury to him.

Following Margaret into the library, Amir placed the plate he was carrying beside the tea set she placed on the antique butler's table that sat between two of the armchairs circling the room's old brick fireplace. His foster mother took hold of one of the cups by its handle and carefully poured tea into it, asking Amir if he would like milk or sugar. Amir signed back that, yes, he would like a little sugar but no milk. Margaret added the ingredients, gracefully stirring the cup and placing it on a saucer in front of the boy.

Amir could see by the manner in which his foster mother had poured his tea and attentively set it in front of him that he was being treated with the special care afforded a respected guest or friend. Nodding his head in acceptance of her offering, he met Margaret's eyes in thanks, briefly holding them before taking his cup in hand. She felt in this, and in the way the boy sat carefully sipping his tea, as though in recognition of its ceremony, a hint of something that drew her curiosity. If Margaret could have asked, and if their relationship had developed enough for the boy to share his past, Amir would have told her that in the Beganović home the arrival of a guest had been an exciting event. In the Muslim tradition, a visitor would have been given the very best foods to be found in their kitchen.

But for Amir's family, the real measure of their hospitality had always been in the offering of coffee, and along with it, the time they shared with their guest, no matter the never-ending work of their farm. His sister, Minka, would help her mother in the preparation of the coffee, the beans finely ground into a powder, as in Turkish coffee, but the way it was prepared was slightly different, proudly Bosnian. While the brew was being made, Amir would pull out the round iron tray it would be served upon, arrange small ceramic cups on its outer circumference, and then add a dish of sugar cubes and a glass of water to complete the service. When the coffee was ready the small, long-necked copper-plated pot was set in the middle of the tray. His father would carry it into the main room, and the whole family gathered to honor the visitors and make them feel welcome—

as much a chance for themselves as for their guests to enjoy a pause in the routine of their lives.

Sipping her tea, Margaret smiled at Amir. Taking hold of the food plate, she placed it in front of him. From the boy came a small, timid smile in return. Amir reached forward and took a cookie, although he was hesitant to do so. To have refused the offer would have been disrespectful to his host. It was not that he wasn't hungry enough to eat one or that he didn't like them, rather it was the sensation of the woman's gentle touch having found its way into his feelings that was disturbing. Since losing his family he had been the recipient of various acts of kindness from others, yet this was more than an extension of sympathy or even compassion. There was a lingering sense of something else, something deeper, the possibility of an emotional bond tying him to another. Yet it frightened him. He could not afford any more loss. In the boy's mind it was safer to have nothing than to have something that could be taken from him yet again; for each loss had given him the sensation that yet another piece of him was disappearing, breaking off from his being, that soon there would be nothing left of him at all.

Chapter 13

Margaret's daughter drove to her mother's house without her husband, Paul, who, though eager to meet his mother-in-law's new foster son, had been called to the office that Saturday to deal with pressing work. Alice had not pushed her husband to join her, the truth being that she looked forward to the solitude of the journey and a chance to spend a few precious hours alone. Setting out from her house in Cambridge, Alice turned on her radio and headed west on the highway, though she had not driven very far before she reached over to lower the receiver's volume and then finally shut it off altogether. Too much talk, too much news, too much of too much.

Letting out a sigh, Alice suddenly felt released, the road gliding beneath her, the white run of painted lines guiding her along the ever-flowing river of black tarmac that focused her attention from outside intrusion. Two hours of downtime and only one thing required of her: to keep the car on the road. A real Zen experience. Alice smiled. She laughed to think of herself intent upon beating the rat race by outrunning all of the other rats who themselves sought the same. How many of the other drivers were hurriedly running along on a hamster-wheel of haste, and how many, like herself, were attempting to escape it? A modern-day retreat, she thought with a sigh—asylum in a steel-capsuled hermitage rocketing along the highway at seventy miles an hour.

Her thoughts slowly drifted in the direction of her mother, to their relationship past and present and to what it might still become. Alice recalled the times, up till her early teens, when her own path and her mother's coincided in an easy, graceful arc. Then, without either being fully cognizant of its happening, their directions began to diverge: the surge of Alice's teenage years gained velocity, taking her faster and farther afield; her mother's career in academia found success with the publication of several well-received books and tenure in a major university.

During Alice's teenage years, it seemed the bond she and her mother once shared had never really been. They couldn't spend more than a short time talking before a simple conversation turned disagreeable. Alice thought that her mother's counsels about her scholastic and social life had been full of veiled judgments and lacked confidence in Alice's ability to make her own decisions. She understood that her mother's early years had been emotionally difficult, that her grandparents' conservative view of the world, their adherence to "proper" behavior and a manner of living befitting their station in life, had been stifling to her mother. But Alice didn't feel trapped by her family's affluence the way her mother had. Alice lived in a different time, with different attitudes and ways of life.

As their disagreements grew more frequent and more intense, Alice's father found himself taking on the role of arbiter between mother and daughter. Alice had just begun her first year at college when her father suffered a sudden heart attack and died. Over the following years, now living apart and without the relational bridge provided by the father, the daughter's and mother's trajectories diverged further, both women aware of the increasing separation of their parting paths but neither able to navigate a correction. There had only been the time shared on the occasional holiday, a day or two's visit at most. Alice had taken up life and medical school in the Midwest; her mother had become ever more involved in her own work.

Only recently, since her mother's retirement and Alice's return to Boston, had their paths once more found a common intersection. The slow atrophy of their mother-daughter bond finally reversed, their relationship was once again able to find a place of growth.

Alice stepped out from her car in Margaret's driveway and stood for some moments in the yard before venturing inside, letting the chill of the air and the quiet and peaceful beauty of the setting wash the lingering drone of spinning wheels from her head.

"Margaret?" Alice called out, entering the house and, hearing no response, called out again, "Mom?"

"Hello," Margaret responded from a distance. "In the kitchen."

"Hi! Well, you're looking quite domestic," the daughter smiled at the sight of her mother busy at work, an apron hung over her clothing. She walked into the room to embrace the older woman.

"I know," Margaret laughed. "It's not the image of me that I'm used to. Paul didn't come?"

"No, today it's just the two of us girls and Amir," her daughter replied.

"That will be fun. It's been a while since I've had you all to myself."

Alice broke into a smile, like one she might have had upon hearing those same words as a young girl. "Almost all to yourself," Alice laughed, correcting her mother. "Where is Amir? I'm dying to meet him."

"He's outside playing. He loves the outdoors. Spends almost as much time wandering around the property as he does in the house."

"How is it going? Has the adjustment been difficult for you?"

"Yes and no. It's all still new. We're slowly feeling each other out and getting to know one another. Can you pass me that bag of flour, please?"

"Sure. Apple pie?" Alice asked, scanning the ingredients on the counter in front of her mother.

"Yes. Amir picked some apples. Actually, quite a few. He was very proud of his accomplishment, so I thought I'd make a couple of pies in recognition of his effort. One is for you to take home."

"Thank you. That's very thoughtful. Paul will be very happy to see it. Now, where is that boy? Is he ever going to come in?"

"Unlikely," Margaret laughed. "I'd go get him, but my hands are covered in flour. Can you find him? He'll be somewhere close at hand. Try the fields or along the brook. I told him not to go far because you would be coming, so he shouldn't be too difficult to locate. The sign for 'hello' is basically the same as it is in the hearing world, just a casual wave, sort of a very informal salute with your hand side to side, like this." Alice's mother demonstrated the movement. "Amir is getting good at reading people's gestures and faces, so no need to worry about him understanding your meaning."

"OK, got it," Alice said, repeating the gesture.

Happy to step out into the bright autumn day, Margaret's daughter walked slowly around the house and barn in search of Amir. Not seeing the boy, she called out for him, "Amir!" before she caught herself in embarrassed silence.

Realizing that finding Amir might require more attention than she had previously considered, Alice began to look about with a keener eye. *My god, what a beautiful day*, she thought, pausing in appreciation of the nature all about her. There was a chill in the air, but the early cold front that had brought it had also cleared the sky of any obstacle to the sun's rays. Light rained down all about, heightening the colors of the autumn leaves and giving Margaret's daughter the sense she had entered a wonderland found only in fairy tales.

As she walked out into the fields Alice's eyes scanned the pale green plane of their expanse. Not seeing the boy, she cast her gaze along the stone walls that bordered the grassland. Turning from the fields, she walked toward the brook that snaked its way down along the forest's edge on the north side of the property. The sound of running water grew in volume as she approached, and she suddenly spotted the form of a small boy among the trees that grew along the stream's edge. He was sitting on a rock with his back turned toward her, hunched over and holding something in his right hand that he was poking into the running water.

The flow of water was ceaseless, strong and free. Carried along in its current were branches, twigs, and leaves fallen or blown into the stream by gusts of wind that had just recently begun to clear the trees of their colorful cover. Amir sat on the bank by a small eddy watching the current slow and then reverse itself, trapping leaves and twigs in its lull. A stick in hand, he worked at freeing whatever was caught in the circular flow so that it might continue its journey onward. He then watched the loosened objects as they made their way floating and bobbing among the boulders until they disappeared from sight.

Sometimes, if a branch he'd freed got trapped or wedged between the stones downstream, he would go set it loose once again or take hold of it and break it into smaller pieces so that it wouldn't create a dam and catch the things he had liberated farther upstream. Watching a leaf or twig float off into the distance, riding the heave and drop of the current as it bounced from boulder to boulder unhindered, engendered the feeling within the boy that he too had somehow been released from the obstructed swirl of emotion within him.

Amir was lost in meditation, his eyes following a leaf cupped like a saucer, whose stem seemed like a rudder steering it past the obstacles that hindered its way while it floated boat-like down the stream. He was unaware of the woman who had approached him from behind and who now stood waiting in hope he would turn and see her.

Had it been someone other than Amir, Alice would have called out over the loud drone of the coursing water to avoid startling him. The boy sat on a rock jutting out into the brook such that she was unable to make her way toward him from either side. As her hand reached out to gently touch his shoulder, something within the boy felt a presence, breaking the soothing, peaceful trance that had transported his mind from the present world to one distant and without need of vigilance. Startled, he abruptly turned.

The boy's reaction caused a reciprocal response from the woman: Amir's head jerked involuntarily, as if avoiding being struck, and Alice stepped backward, nearly tripping over a stone as she did so. When she recovered her balance, her immediate instinct was to apologize, but the impulse was superseded by another spontaneous inclination, one that saved the moment, changing abashed confusion to comical encounter . . . Alice broke into laugher at her own awkward ballet in attempt to stay upright.

Looking back at her timidly, Amir smiled, his hazel eyes blinking in the smooth plane of his face.

"Sorry," Alice said, interrupting her laughter. Remembering her mother's lesson in sign language, she waved hello to the boy.

Amir waved back while continuing to look at Alice, his knit cap pulled down low over his ears, eyes no longer blinking but focused and intent, as if in search of something. His cheeks were flushed from the cool air coming off the stream. He wore an old hand-me-down coat that had come from his former foster family and, though clean, it added to the look of the waif about the boy. His thinness was noticeable even through his clothing, the sparse body of a person who ate only in afterthought. The boy's eyes softened, in nearly simultaneous timing with Alice's.

"I'm Alice, Margaret's daughter," Alice said, pointing at herself, hoping the boy would understand her words.

Amir nodded his understanding. He had seen her face framed in photos on Margaret's desk in the library, on a side table in the living room, and hanging on the wall in her upstairs bedroom. Margaret had shown him a recent photo of her daughter so he would understand who was coming to visit. In it the daughter had sat, smiling, next to the woman, her arm draped around her mother's shoulder. Her hair was long, like her mother's, but let loose, not tied back like the older woman's. The clothing and jewelry they wore followed in the same pattern, the daughter's appearance more stylish and expressing a more extroverted fashion, while the older was clothed in a simpler, understated dress, her face and hands adorned with only a pair of earrings and a gold wedding band.

In the photos the daughter's face appeared more angular and symmetrical than her mother's. Her hair was light brown, the color Margaret's must have been before it had gone to gray.

In a large framed photo that Margaret had shown him, one taken some years ago, he had seen the daughter standing between her mother and her father, who was no longer alive. He could see both of their faces in the girl's. But while the father's smile and attractive features were easily noted in the daughter's face, it was in the eyes of the two women where the most striking resemblance was to be found. Grayish-blue in color, the mother's and daughter's eyes looked out from the photo with sharp and focused gazes, both formidable and caring. It was this look in her eyes that Amir first noticed about the woman speaking to him, confirming in his mind that she was indeed his foster mother's daughter.

"It's very beautiful here," Alice indicated more by the look on her face than by her words as she gazed about the setting. "I can see why you like spending so much time outside."

A small blink of a smile appeared on Amir's face in response to Alice's comment. He hadn't understood what she had said, though he could feel her expression all the same.

After a few moments of shared, silent appreciation, Alice looked at Amir and nodded her head in the direction of the house. Her smile saying, "Shall we?" the two turned to walk side by side in easy stride down to the house.

"Well, I see that you found each other," Margaret remarked with a smile to her daughter and foster son as they entered the kitchen. "Here, let me take your coat, Amir." Margaret signed its removal, and that of Amir's knit cap, with her hands.

"Come, sit here." Alice's mother patted the seat of a stool next to the island counter and held up an apple for Amir to see. "We're making pies from your apples."

"Alice, could you hand Amir the bowl of apples, please? He likes to keep busy. He can peel them while I finish making the crust."

The daughter passed the bowl to Amir, handing him the peeler along with it.

Amir received the bowl of apples, looking at the peeler as he did so. After several passes of the peeler he shook his head and handed it back to Alice.

"What? You don't want to peel them?" Alice queried, her face showing her question.

Amir responded by making a circular motion with his right hand around the apple he held in his left.

"What's he saying, Mom?"

"I'm not sure," Margaret said, turning the palms of her hands upward, hunching her shoulders, and giving the boy the look she used to indicate that she didn't understand.

Amir shook his head once more and hopped down from his stool, skipping quickly over to the far counter, where a wooden block held the kitchen knives. Selecting a small paring knife, he mimed the action of drawing the blade back and forth across a sharpening stone. Margaret pointed to a drawer, her smile growing at the boy's animation. He seemed unusually happy that day.

Working the knife over the stone with precise, quick strokes, it was clear the boy knew the art of keeping a cutting tool sharp. Coming back to the counter, Amir took an apple in his hand and then looked up to Margaret and Alice as if to say "watch" before returning his focus back to the red fruit. The paring knife began its circumnavigation of the apple with sure and expert movements, the razor-sharp knife blade peeling the fruit even more closely than the peeler could have. When done, Amir held a long, unbroken strip of apple peel in the air, its length spiraling downward. A tiny grin of pride appeared on his face as the women applauded appreciatively. The boy picked up another apple to peel while Alice cut the first into pieces to fill the pie shell.

Later that evening, during dinner, Alice noticed how little Amir served himself, even of the pie whose filling he had so proudly harvested and helped prepare. His eyes scanned between her and Margaret in short, brief glimpses before returning to his meal, or he directed his gaze at the center of the table, where two lit candles flickered in their silver holders.

The clinician in Alice observed the boy's behavior, his attention, the movement of his eyes, his hands, and their reactions to the stimuli that engaged them. Uncharacteristically, her mind began to wander, straying from her practiced clinical observation to a more distanced perspective, where she saw the boy simply as himself without reference to any symptomatology that might define him.

With dinner finished, the three retired to the library, Margaret lighting a fire from the wood Amir carried in and stacked next to the fireplace. While the boy paged through one of the simple children's books Margaret had given him to help in developing his English skills, mother and daughter relaxed into casual conversation. Later, after Amir had gone to bed, the topic turned to the boy and the change he had brought to Margaret's life.

"What are your impressions of Amir?" Margaret asked her daughter.

"Well, I can see why you fell for him," Alice responded with a smile. "Beneath the silence, there seems to be a lot going on in there. I like him a lot."

"I'm glad of that. It was apparent that he liked you as well," Margaret said, rising from her chair to stir the coals of the fire and add another log to its flames.

"Was it? It was difficult for me to get a read on how he felt toward me. But maybe that's just him being shy. I was impressed by how polite and respectful he was. At first I wondered if his politeness was a kind of emotional shield, but on the other hand it felt very natural and genuine."

"Yes, the depth of his politeness is unusual for a child of his age. At least in our culture. However, I think that's not so much the case in the society he grew up in. But I do think there is also something of a buffer in his deference. While there's no question in my mind that his politeness is genuine, it is reasonable to expect, given all he's been through, that he would be prone to also using it as a defensive mechanism. His behavior is sometimes almost too good to be true. Hopefully, he'll begin to feel secure enough to be able to be less than perfect." After a pause, she added, "Would you like some tea? I'm going to make myself a cup before bed."

"Yes, that would be nice. I'll help."

Returning to the kitchen, Margaret filled the teakettle with water and placed it on the stove, while Alice took out cups and placed a teabag in each, not needing to ask her mother what kind she wanted. A cup of peppermint tea before bedtime was one of her mother's long-established rituals.

"By the way, Mom," Alice said, continuing their conversation, "I'm curious to know: has it been determined whether Amir was born deaf and mute?"

"The results from his initial health screening indicated that it isn't a congenital condition. The attending physician recommended that Amir be sent to someone experienced in dealing in post-traumatic stress disorder for further examination. That's actually something I wanted to talk to you about."

"You're looking for a referral?" Alice responded.

"Yes," Margaret answered with a nod. "The agency in charge of Amir's care is a good one, but they have many constraints, financial and otherwise. Given his past, I'd like to see that he gets the most thorough examination possible, with someone who's experienced enough with children like Amir to understand the possible complications."

"A behavioral pediatrician would probably be the most appropriate starting place, rather than a referral to a psychologist," Alice said. "Behavioral pediatricians have the advantage of their medical training as well as their subspecialty training in developmental and behavioral problems. They'd be able to consider both the medical and the psychosocial aspects that might affect a child."

"Yes, I agree. That would be best."

"I'll make some calls and see what I can come up with," Alice said after a pause. "Mom, you said that Amir is living with you as a long-term placement. What does that mean? Six months, a year, two years, more?"

"There's no defined time limit. It's difficult to say in Amir's case. His relocation to the US is based upon an agreement that he'll be repatriated back to his homeland as soon as the political situation becomes stable there. Right now it's a war zone. Who knows when it will be stable enough for him to return? It could be a year. It could be two or three or, most likely, even longer. The big question in Amir's case is to what and to whom he would return. Are you concerned that caring for him will be too much for me?"

"No, not really. I'm more concerned that you're going to grow very involved and then he's going to be removed. I'm worried that will be very difficult for you. I think it's going to be hard keeping yourself from becoming too attached to him."

"Yes, there is that," Margaret acknowledged. "But somehow it doesn't seem a worry for me. Maybe it's just a denial of future possibilities. I don't know. Given all of the change that caring for the boy has brought to my life, thinking about his leaving someday seems very distant. And if that should come to be, the agency has other children in need. Just think of it as me getting good practice at becoming a doting grandmother. How's that going, by the way?"

"We're working on it," Alice smiled. "Paul has to keep reminding me not to be anxious about it, that we should enjoy the process. He says it with a leer, thinking he's cute. It's very annoying. But my ovulation seems to have improved, so we're hopeful."

"Well, I am too," Margaret said, pausing a second in thought. "A child can be said to be a universe of its own. There is so much there to learn . . . for both the child and the parent. Sometimes it's hard to say who's teaching whom. It took me too long to realize that."

"We survived it," Alice laughed, "and now here we are chatting away like a couple of old girlfriends."

"We did, didn't we?" Margaret smiled, taking her daughter's arm in hers, the two slowly making their way upstairs to bed.

Chapter 14

The first few weeks of sharing her home with Amir had been a time of exploration, the orphaned boy and retired professor slowly getting to know one another, finding in the quiet, deliberate manner of their ways a sense of kindred spirit. But the honeymoon, Margaret knew, was drawing to a close. There was so much for her to do. The issue of where Amir would attend school grew more pressing every day. Should he go to public school, private school, or continue with the homeschooling she had begun in the interim? Would they find that none of those options would work well and that Amir would ultimately be better off in a school for the deaf? In order to make that decision, they needed to better understand his disabilities.

With the agency's approval, Margaret's daughter sought out a behavioral pediatrician experienced in war trauma. Alice, a pediatric surgeon at a major Boston hospital, had a number of contacts in the field. With the help of sympathetic colleagues, she was able to find a well-respected behavioral pediatrician who was willing to fit Amir into his already-overloaded schedule the following week.

On the day of the appointment, Margaret drove to Boston with Amir, first stopping to drop off their overnight bags at her daughter's home in Cambridge. The house, which had been hers before she had deeded it over to Alice, held a host of memories. She and her husband had purchased the property nearly forty years prior, worried that they'd taken on too big a challenge in fixing up the run-down, large white Victorian, a white elephant that could drain their incomes and savings. But they persevered through a series of small renovations, one project at a time, and in the end the house became a home.

Pulling into its driveway, Margaret felt both immediate and distant, as though she was, on the one hand, stepping back into the rhythm of daily routine, and on the other, returning to a childhood home whose absence was measured in decades. Visions of the past rose from the front walkway her feet had traveled countless times. The plants and shrubs, planted by her own hand seemingly a lifetime ago, greeted her like old friends. The house called out its welcome as well, and as Margaret stood outside gazing upon it in fond remembrance, she could recall the view from each window as though they were old, familiar paintings. Though the interior of the house had changed since her daughter had moved in—the walls now of brighter, more uniform color, the old drapes replaced with ones less formal in look, its furnishings of a modern style suited to a young professional couple—the smell and the feel of the home remained as she remembered it.

While Margaret's mind wandered in memories, Amir marveled at the grandiose scale of the houses he had seen in the Cambridge neighborhood. These buildings were even larger than the ones in the town where he lived with Margaret, an idea he found difficult to reconcile against the memory of the modest village homes he had known in Bosnia. Walking into the spacious foyer of Alice's home, he wondered how many people lived in it, even though by this point he had learned that in his new country the size of a home didn't necessarily correlate to the number of inhabitants who might live there. That only Margaret's daughter and her son-in-law would live alone in such a grand house seemed to Amir an unfathomable idea.

After dropping off their overnight bags at Alice's, Margaret drove Amir to his appointment in Boston. The hospital where she took him felt vast and impersonal to Amir, and the rooms where he waited had the feel of places of internment to him: boxes formed of windowless walls, painted in bright colors, with tubes of ersatz sunlight strung across the ceilings that filled him with cold instead of their promised illusion of warmth. Margaret noted a distinct closing down of the boy's emotional state the moment they stepped into the large medical complex, and she gently took his hand in hers so that he might feel the touch of human warmth to ease his anxiety.

The behavioral pediatrician who Alice had arranged for them to meet, Dr. Richard Caron, was experienced in working with children suffering from war trauma. After sitting for a short time in a waiting room, Margaret and Amir were ushered into an examination room by a friendly nurse. The two sat down on metal-framed chairs, Margaret resting back into hers, Amir sitting on the edge of his. Margaret signed to Amir not to worry, that the doctor would come soon and that there was nothing to be afraid of. Amir nodded his understanding, but his body stayed rigid and his hands fidgeted as he nervously looked about the room.

When the doctor entered a few minutes later, he introduced himself and greeted the two warmly, engaging both Margaret and Amir in casual conversation, with Margaret serving as translator for the boy. The behavioral pediatrician scanned the report written by the eye, ear, nose, and throat specialist Amir had previously seen. He then ran a series of tests to assess Amir's sensory, motor, and cognitive skills. With Margaret translating his words into sign, he asked Amir questions about his general state of health and how he was adjusting to life in his new country. At the very end of the examination, Dr. Caron asked Amir several general questions about his life in Bosnia, carefully observing the boy's reaction to the mention of his former homeland. When he had completed writing down his observations, he gently asked Amir to sit in the waiting room while he and Margaret discussed his findings.

"OK, let's see," Dr. Caron said, looking to the notepad he held in his hands, "to begin with, I noted some ageusia, analgesia, and apraxia—taste loss, insensitivity to pain, and the inability to engage in purposive acts. Amir's thinness appears to be anorectic, and I noted that he exhibits a general unresponsiveness as well as some loss of organic function."

Dr. Caron paused, looking from his notes to his watch and then to Margaret. He was aware of her professional history, having been told by Alice. He knew that Margaret had taught at the graduate level and authored several psychology texts. She didn't need him to lead her from A to B. "Look, I can go through a number of the other details from my notes if you want, but my guess is that they will only corroborate your own observations up to this point, so if it's OK with you I'll cut to the chase."

Seeing her nod, the physician continued. "Some years back, I worked with an organization up in Lowell providing services to the Cambodian refugee population that arrived in the aftermath of the Khmer Rouge. Amir exhibits a number of the symptoms that I saw in the Cambodian children who survived that war. I'm sorry to say that I think it is very likely the trauma Amir suffered in the conflict in Bosnia is even more severe than his records indicate.

"Given the loss of both speech and hearing capability without any severe physiological trauma to explain its cause, it's my feeling that we might want to begin exploring the possibility of somatoform dissociation. It's fairly rare, and there's very little historical data available on it. It's a syndrome that can last a week, a month, or years, but that in its physiological manifestation, at least, generally goes away."

"I see," Margaret replied, keeping her voice steady and reasoned. "Could you run through some its symptomatology for me?"

"Yes, of course. Essentially, somatoform dissociation is the loss, or deficiency, of normal integration in a person's sensory or motor components. There's not been a lot of study on this as it relates to war trauma. But there is some history of mutism and deafness as being part of the symptomatology. Somatoform dissociation can also affect seeing, movement, and feeling. It's not an easy thing to diagnose. The symptoms sometimes appear to be inconstant or even contradictory. They can initially occur as the result of an actual physical experience—a concussion, an explosion, those sorts of things—as well as from the experiencing of horrific acts."

Margaret listened as the doctor continued speaking, but her thoughts began to wander, visions of what Amir might have suffered interrupting her focus on what the physician was saying.

"I know," Dr. Caron said, seeing Margaret's attention drift, "that it's not easy to think about what your foster son might have experienced in Bosnia. Hearing the stories that come from these children, I often find myself trying to make sense from something that has none, to find some kind of rational explanation for the most irrational of human acts."

As she listened to Dr. Caron's words, a sigh came from deep inside of Margaret's being and exited her lungs audibly.

Dr. Caron paused and smiled gently at the woman sitting across from him. After a quiet moment, the two talked about the treatment options available to Amir and arranged a date for a return appointment. Margaret already knew from her conversations with Jane Coleman that the agency didn't have the budget for Amir's long-term therapy. She would cover the expense herself. This time, though, when she wrote the check, it wouldn't be a gesture coming from a distance. As Margaret stood to leave, Dr. Caron handed her his card. Thanking him for his efforts on the boy's behalf, Margaret absentmindedly slipped it into her purse, the mystery of Amir's past and what he might have suffered in the war weighing heavily on her mind.

Later that evening, seated at the dinner table, Amir shyly observed his dinner companions, looking first to Margaret, then to Alice, and finally to Alice's husband, Paul. Not since he had last sat down with his own family, the night before they were killed, had he experienced the taking of a meal with such feeling of communion.

Little in Amir's expression demonstrated the happiness he actually felt in their company. And though his emotions were unable to express it, he was glad to have the others turn in his direction and speak to him, even if he could not hear their words, the three using their smiles, laughter, and the gestures of their hands to include him in the conversation. The man who sat next to Margaret's daughter attempted to speak to him. He looked to be in his mid-thirties, about the same age as Amir's father. He was taller than his father, his skin whiter, his hair lighter in color but with gray just beginning to appear. The hair around Asaf's temples had also begun to lose their darker color to age. Alice's husband wore a suit. His father had a dark blue sport coat he sometimes wore, though never with a tie. It was apparent to Amir that the man sitting next to him found his work in an office and not on the land—his hands were soft, accustomed to holding only the tools used in writing and speaking on the phone. His eyes were kind, his smile genuine. When Alice or Margaret spoke, the husband would quietly listen, his face showing interest and encouragement of the words being spoken. At their family's dinner table in Bosnia, it had been much the same, Amir's father sharing stories of his day, encouraging the others to do the same by showing his interest in what they had to say.

Amir could see that Alice's husband felt awkward not knowing how to communicate with someone who could neither hear nor speak. Amir smiled back at him in an effort to make the man feel more at ease, but, embarrassed at his own awkwardness, the boy's lips rose in a small upward arc before quickly falling back to their usual place of rest.

For Alice and Paul, the sharing of the dinner table with the young boy struck a deep chord. They had always wanted to start a family but had decided to wait until their careers had become established. Then time, the master magician, performed its ultimate disappearing act: the days vanishing into memory in the blink of an eye, turning present into past as though with the wave of an illusionist's wand, leaving them, nearly a decade later, to wonder where all the years had gone.

The following morning, after saying good-bye to Alice and Paul, Margaret and Amir drove home. As they traveled, Margaret glanced every so often to her right to look at Amir. She was struck by how little she really knew of the boy. Yet part of her wondered whether a more detailed knowledge of his life would provide her any deeper understanding of his being than that which she had already come to find in his silence. There he was, sitting beside her in his small boy's body, his chestnut-colored hair flowing around sea-green eyes that, to those who didn't know him, seemed as mute as his tongue and belied the reclusive intelligence that hid beneath.

How odd, she marveled, that when you first meet someone who draws your interest, there seems a whole universe to explore. Then, after a time, you think you know them: the way they walk, their facial expressions, their gestures, the sound of their voice, the way they laugh, the way they act . . . all become known, and as familiar to you as your own daily routine. But whatever happened to that great, horizon-like expanse of their being that you had seen there within them in the beginning? Did it shrink into something smaller? Or did it disappear? Into what, then? Was the once-vast landscape of their being but an illusion? Or did the illusion come later, when you thought you knew all there was to know about them?

That night when he lay in bed, Amir was unable to find shelter in sleep. Removing the bedding from atop him, Amir rose, dressed, and went downstairs, where he sat by a window in the library and looked out into the dark. He could feel a shift within himself. It manifested almost as a physical sensation, but he unconsciously knew it came from a deeper place. The profundity of it frightened him. After a time, he stood to get his coat and then quietly exited the warmth of the house. There was no moon that night, and the sky was blanketed in clouds. Amir walked into the fields, his feet making their way more by touch than by guide of his eyes. Alone, standing in the middle of the clearing, he felt enveloped by a pervasive sense of loneliness as deep as the black of the night itself. A voice within him called out in need of companionship and, heeding its force, he decided to journey through the forest toward the village center.

In the moonless night everything was colored in such deep obscurity that Amir had to find his way through the woods by means of his feet searching out the hollow of the path he walked upon. His eyes sought out breaks in the leafless branches of the tree cover above him, which signaled that he was safely on the trail. It would be easy to take a misstep or two and quickly become lost in the amorphous skeletal woods of early winter. His steps relaxed when he saw the lights of houses blinking between the trees separating him and the small neighborhood that lay across the forest from his house.

Stepping out from the woods onto a roadway, Amir cautiously traversed the quiet street, like one of the nocturnal animals who lived among the people like invisible inhabitants of a hidden, subterranean land. It was cold outside and the wind was picking up. Amir could feel it bite against his skin, slip in under his clothing, and enter into his body to rob it of its heat. The chill of the breeze moved through his hair and entered his ears, his body's discomfort strangely soothing, distracting his thought from a deeper pain that lay within him.

Amir walked along the street with quiet steps, careful not to disturb the slumber of the darkened homes, their silhouettes barely visible. The serene order of the pitch-black night calmed him, offering an alternate dreamworld to replace the oppressive images that sometimes visited him in sleep. Weeks might pass before such dreams would interrupt his slumber, waking his body with a start, his mind agitated by fleeting images of disturbing scenes, wisps of frightening memory.

Drawn to a massive sugar maple whose denuded limbs reached out into the blackness like arms raised in prayer, the young orphan came to rest. Lowering his body to the ground, Amir leaned his back into the tree, a nook in its massive trunk cradling him against the cold night breeze. Pulling his knees to his chest, he wrapped his arms around his legs and pulled them close, his eyes staring out into the monochrome world of the moonless night. His breathing soon fell into a meditative rhythm. Amir felt each breath of frigid air as it entered his nose, gently traveling from there to lungs and then back again, released to that from which it came. A deep peace settled over him, the perfect black of the night spreading outward toward the heavens, a harmony of being, a kindred emptiness to give meaning to those lost and damaged emotions inside of him that had no name, no destination, nor even path upon which to walk.

The next morning Amir overslept, not rising until mid-morning. Unsure whether or not to wake him, Margaret decided to let him rest according to his own biological clock. Unaware of the visions whose unannounced visits disturbed his sleep, his foster mother was nevertheless fully cognizant of the erratic nature of his sleep patterns and suspected that it was a symptom of some level of emotional disturbance.

Finding herself unable to speak with Amir about his inner feelings to the depth of detail she wanted, the retired psychology professor sought new paths of communication with her foster son.

Later that day, while working with Amir on his homework, an idea came to Margaret. An account of Amir's time at the UN refugee camp had been in her foster son's case file, and it had mentioned the name Josif. Margaret wondered whether the name might be a thread to Amir's past, a thin strand that could lead to the place of the boy's silent refuge.

Sitting alongside Amir in the library, Margaret signed to her foster son that they should take a short break. They had been working on his English reading lesson for nearly an hour. After a quick snack in the kitchen, they returned to the library, but the idea that had come into her mind earlier returned, and she decided to follow its lead instead of continuing with the lesson.

An old book of names rested on a shelf of her library, purchased years ago when Margaret had been pregnant with Alice. Rising from the table where she and Amir had been working, Margaret walked over to the wall of books where the old, clothbound volume rested and brought it back with her, placing it down in front of Amir. Opening it, she began with her own name, Margaret. Origin, Persian; meaning, child of light. Origin, Greek; meaning, pearl. Margaret pointed to her name written on the page and then to herself. She followed by taking a pad of paper and a pen, writing her name down in large letters, then repeated the action of directing her index finger from the word to herself. With the back of her hand facing her chest, she lowered her thumb in perpendicular angle to her extended index finger and rotated it outward in her foster son's direction. "Your turn," she signed.

Meeting his foster mother's eyes, Amir slowly took the pen in hand and wrote his name.

"Good," Margaret signed with a smile, turning the pages of the book backward until she came to her daughter's name, the faded yellow highlight that marked its choice from decades past still noticeable.

"Yes, I know her name," Amir nodded signing his understanding, though perplexed at the exercise's purpose.

Leafing forward through the book, Margaret next stopped at the page that held the name Joseph. Listed beneath it were its non-English equivalents. She pointed to one of its alternates, Josif, and waited for some sign of acknowledgement from her foster son. Amir saw there were many names written on the page. The woman pointed to one that had already caught his eye, one that his mind had immediately pretended it had not seen. But still, the image of his friend began to take on form in his thought. The picture was dull, the face blurred, and though it had been less than a year since he had last seen him, Amir's memory was unable to call up the older boy's features clearly. Nor in his mind could there be found much detail of their relationship other than small, fleeting impressions passing like the thin tails of high clouds in an otherwise clear, blue sky . . . Josif listening to the radio, arms flailing at invisible drums . . . the two of them riding on the bicycle, the older boy pedaling, Amir on the crossbar as they zigzagged crazily down an empty road. The memories weren't much, but they were all his emotion allowed before constricting into a solid wall. Josif was a dam, and behind him were waters so dark and deep that, if they were to break loose Amir would surely be pulled under and drowned.

Margaret caught the boy's nearly invisible first reaction at the sight of the name Josif. She sensed the burden of its hidden weight. So why try and push the child to a place that she intuited was so painful to bear that he had withdrawn not only from the world, but also from himself? Yet as long as it was locked away inside of him, though the pain might be dulled, she knew it would never go away.

Once more making the sign for "your turn," Margaret indicated that Amir should now write down the names of his family members. When her foster son looked back at her with a blank expression, she took out the Bosnian dictionary she used in his English lessons to translate from the one language to the other. She was unsure how to read the boy's expression. She couldn't tell whether his face—his eyes wide, brows furrowed, his mouth open—spoke confusion or shock. Moving her chair closer, Margaret sat next to Amir and took the paper he had written his name on, spelling out the words for father, mother, and sister in his native language: *otac, mati,* and *sestra.*

Staring at the woman, Amir waited for her to write down the names he had neither spoken nor heard in almost a year. The thought of their sudden appearance on the paper in front of him brought forth both a deep yearning and fear inside of him. His foster mother, though, had released the pen from her hand and looked back at him expectantly.

"Me?" Amir asked, pointing at himself.

"Yes," Margaret answered, with a nod of her head. The boy's eyes looked like they were caught in a trance. Margaret could see that the moment hung on a delicate fulcrum that could as easily tilt to paralysis as it could act as the pivot to the opening of a door. Margaret could write the names out herself, but it was Amir, she understood, who needed to bring them forth, who alone could make their memory real. Taking the pen that lay beside him, Margaret placed it in his hand.

Amir's hand received the writing instrument automatically and, without thought and after a moment's pause, began to move on its own. Amir's hand spelled out the first name, slowly, letter by letter, until all four symbols appeared, the brief imprint of ink creating a picture of immense proportion: "Asaf." "Emina," the hand continued . . . "Minka." The pen fell from Amir's grip. As Amir stared down at the words that his hand had just written, he felt as if he had been plunged into freezing waters. How could those names, once so familiar, so short a time ago, now appear like something from a past life . . . distant and foreign to his eyes? And yet the present, in which he sat staring at the written representation of their beings, felt no closer to him than that which had passed. It too seemed to linger just beyond his reach.

Margaret held herself perfectly still, careful to not interrupt the movement of whatever inward journey the boy might be taking. A tear formed in the corner of Amir's right eye, a solitary droplet edging over the bottom lid, spilling downward, and running along the side of his nose, over the corner of his mouth. Another tear fell, and the boy closed his eyes. His head slowly inclined, lowering itself in Margaret's direction, as though his neck and shoulders were no longer able to support its weight. She received the boy's head upon her shoulder, her silence, both within and without, complete. They stayed like that for some time, the only indication that the child was crying was the tears soaking through her blouse.

Chapter 15

Liberated from the dense walls and structured programs of a school system that hadn't known what to do with him, Amir's studies blossomed in the eclectic curriculum Margaret Morgan designed for his homeschooling. Under the freer, more creative methods provided by his new foster mother, the boy's mind felt released to explore its natural curiosity and thirst for knowledge. Of all his subjects, he enjoyed none more than science. Encouraged by Margaret to create a nature journal, Amir spent long periods of time in the fields and woods, even on the coldest days of winter, sketching the various plants, animals, and birds that drew his interest. Returning home, he and Margaret labeled the drawings with their Bosnian, English, and Latin names, Amir engaging in the exercise with enthusiasm.

On some days, though, Margaret's foster son seemed unable to concentrate on even the simplest of schoolwork. These occasions were often marked by Amir rising from bed late, tired and groggy, his physical reactions throughout the day slow and lethargic. In addition to not being able to focus his attention on his studies, he could be irritable, moody, and unresponsive to his foster mother's efforts to engage his interest.

The boy's behavior, while never crossing the line of disobedience, was trying for Margaret. In some ways, she would have preferred that he act out, manifest whatever he was feeling outside the box of his restraint, the better for both of them to see his emotion and acknowledge its existence. As it was, on these days he was like a heavy stone needing to be moved from place to place by lifting its ponderous weight in the smallest of increments.

At day's end, fatigued by the effort, the retired professor had to remind herself that she had known that the honeymoon was bound to end—that, along with the joy of having the child in her life, there would be difficulties as well. Amir was a child war victim. He had lost his entire family and suffered who-knew-what-else in a conflict whose acts of inhumanity were difficult to believe. This was not a university classroom where she could simply walk in, deliver her wisdom, and then leave.

From her observations, Margaret suspected that there were several issues at play in her foster son's off-days. Amir exhibited some of the classic signs of sleep deprivation, and when she had asked about his sleeping patterns, he acknowledged that he didn't always sleep well. When she tried to find out what it was that kept him from resting well, he answered with vague generalizations.

Her professional experience told her that his sleeping problems almost certainly stemmed from a psychological source rather than a physical one. She asked Amir if he was experiencing bad dreams, and though his response was a shrug of his shoulders and tilting of his head in ambiguous gesture, as though it really wasn't something he was aware of one way or the other, his eyes told Margaret another story, something inside of him speaking in a coded language to her. But when she continued to gently probe, he pulled back. This neither surprised nor frustrated her. Having spent her entire adult life in the study of human psychology, she understood that the mind's complexities were many and varied. The fact that she and the boy had begun to bond made their relationship both easier and more difficult, clearer and more obscure, closer and more distant.

Despite the overall success of Amir's homeschooling, there remained the question of his cultural and social integration into the society he had come to live in. In the weeks since the boy had come to live with her, Margaret and Amir's caseworker had been having ongoing discussions about whether or not to enroll him in the local public school. They had met several times with local school officials and had been reassured by the administration's open and responsive attitude toward the boy's special circumstance. The regional elementary school, located near the larger, neighboring college town, was accustomed to accommodating children of diverse backgrounds. The school had both strong ESL and special needs programs that they felt would serve the deaf-mute boy's needs.

Margaret was torn. She felt a deep contentment in sharing the cloister of the boy's silent world, their kinship growing and their communication clear despite the lack of words within which to frame the meaning of their relationship. A part of her would have been happy to continue in that peaceful, monastic silence. Yet she knew that Amir would be best served by entering the public school. A decision was made that he would begin attending the public school after the winter holidays, when the new semester began.

As the winter solstice grew closer and the days ever shorter, the mornings Amir woke up late seemed to increase. At first, Margaret ascribed his tardy rising to the sunlight's own belated arrival. But even when fully awake he seemed to be agitated and restless.

"You look tired," Margaret signed to Amir as she served him breakfast. "Sleep OK?"

"Yes," Amir replied, his fist bending at the wrist, raising and lowering lethargically in ambivalent reply.

"Really?" Margaret asked.

"Don't know," he signed in more truthful answer.

"We'll talk later. When you wake up."

"OK," Amir assented.

But Margaret's foster son never seemed able to break through the languid, sleepy state he had woken with that morning. He showed little enthusiasm for the lessons Margaret had planned for the day's study. Even the hour period of his nature study, when Amir would normally enthusiastically bundle up and head outdoors with his journal, was met with lackluster response.

"Let's stop," Margaret signed, closing the Bosnian–English dictionary she was using for Amir's language study.

Without signing in response, Amir nodded his agreement.

"You still look tired. Are you?" Margaret's hands signed, speaking her question.

"Yes, a little."

"Bad dreams last night?"

"Maybe," the boy signed, his open palms raising and lowering alternately one to the other.

"You remember them?"

"No," Amir shook his head in reply, bringing his thumb and two forefingers together in sign.

"OK. You rest. I'll make dinner," Margaret signed.

That evening Amir ate a few mouthfuls of his dinner and spent the rest of the night absentmindedly leafing through the pages of an illustrated book. Feeling an unusual and heavy tiredness, he went to bed early. Sometime in the middle of the night Margaret was awakened from her dreams by a loud, continuous stream of sound that, when she was coherent enough to focus, she recognized as a shouting voice. It took her a few seconds more to realize that the sound was coming from Amir's bedroom down the hallway.

Switching on her bedside light, Margaret rushed to the boy's room. Opening his door, she was able to make out the form of his body seized in convulsion, as though a strong current of electricity ran through him, while he shouted hysterically. Moving quickly toward the bed, Margaret turned on the lamp and checked to make sure Amir wasn't biting his tongue or having difficulty breathing.

Making a quick decision, she didn't try to interrupt the seizure, but kept careful watch over him until the episode ended with Amir suddenly sitting upright in the bed, his eyes staring directly through his foster mother, as if they held no recognition of who she was or that she was even there. Strange, unintelligible words flowed out his mouth.

After a few seconds, Margaret took the boy by the shoulders and slowly leaned him backward, toward a prone position, his body rigid and stiff. Still talking, but now in more of a soft mutter than a full voice, Amir's eyes stared toward the ceiling. Margaret stroked his shoulders, calming him, then turned off the lamp and sat beside him in the dark. After a time the young boy's eyes closed and his words ceased. Checking his pulse and waiting until his body relaxed, Margaret finally returned to her room. But there was little sleep for her that night. Her mind, caught in a shock of its own, ran through the startling event, trying to analyze the episode's symptoms in an effort to calm her thoughts. *It was almost certainly a psychogenic, non-epileptic seizure*, the retired psychology professor told herself. *There was no need to worry, no need to take emergency action*, another voice said, trying to reassure her anxious mind. *Maybe I should call Alice. No, it's late. She's asleep. She'll only tell me the things I already know: keep a careful watch; if it happens again, be sure his airway is clear and he isn't biting his tongue.*

But no amount of professional jargon or calming internal dialogue could ease the emotional disturbance that roiled within her or the worry that her foster son might suffer another attack. During the hours of her sleepless night a hundred thoughts passed through her head. Had the boy's hearing returned as well? Had he heard himself speak? Would the shock of the episode so frighten him that his mind would block it from his conscious awareness?

Amir awoke feeling confused by his dreams. He remembered that Margaret had been in them. Rolling over to look at the clock on the nightstand next to his bed, his ears were filled with a strange sensation: a soft, low rustling noise, the sheets shifting as he moved to see the time. It was a sound that would barely register within most people's awareness. For the deaf-mute boy, however, hearing the sheets rustle was an experience of extraordinary proportion.

Had his dreams followed him into waking? Or was he still in them? As he got up from bed, sounds continued to follow him. They pursued him as he walked over to his clothes and put them on, his senses suddenly finding an added dimension as the clothing touched his skin: legs into his pants, shirt slipped on over his head, socks tugged on over his feet, and feet slid into shoes—the sound of their movement confirming the weight and texture of their substance.

He felt frightened walking down the stairs, hearing his shod feet touching the treads. In the kitchen, he poured himself a glass of water and was hypnotized by the gurgle of liquid. Then shockingly, he heard a voice. Turning around, he saw Margaret; she had entered the room behind him and was speaking to him. He saw by the expression on her face that she knew he heard her voice. A panic set upon him. It was only in secondary reaction that his brain recognized that the words she was speaking were foreign and he didn't understand their meaning. Yet somehow, he knew what was being communicated.

"I'm OK," the fingers of Amir's right hand spoke.

"Good," Margaret said, signing at the same time she spoke out loud. "Let's eat breakfast."

From the reaction of his facial expression when she had asked, "How are you?" Margaret judged that Amir had indeed regained his hearing. With confusion and anxiety moving about the boy's face like an errant bird trapped in a house, Margaret was careful to move slowly and keep to the routine she and her foster son followed every day upon waking, all the while trying to keep her own surprise and bewilderment of the previous night's startling event at bay.

Conventional wisdom would have one think that instead of being frightened, the boy should have been exuberant and celebratory. But the retired psychologist understood how his reaction might easily be the opposite. The war had taken everything that anchored the boy's identity in the world: mother, father, sister—all of the love that had cradled him in his formation—community, friends, his understanding of what it was to be human. Now he had lost the last vestige of the only thing left to him from that time: his silence. After breakfast, Margaret phoned her daughter and Dr. Caron, both of them expressing great surprise at the sudden recovery of Amir's speech and hearing and relieved to hear how quickly his condition had stabilized from the seizure. Dr. Caron rearranged his schedule and made an appointment to see Amir the following day.

Sound came pouring into Amir's head like a river threatening to overflow its banks. He felt tired and weak from the convulsion he had suffered only hours before. His mind wandered and time seemed to be passing as if in dream. After breakfast he and Margaret moved into the library to begin his day's schooling. But instead of opening one of the books to begin his classwork, Margaret moved them aside. Their eyes met and she smiled. There was kindness in her face, and she took his hand in hers, holding his gaze for a few seconds before letting go and rising, some internal thought within her finding its decision.

Margaret walked to the shelf where all of Amir's study materials were stored. Next to the Bosnian–English dictionary were several cassette tapes and a small, portable player similar to the one Josif had used to accompany his imaginary drums, at the farm in Bosnia. Margaret looked at her foster son, a quiet question in her eyes. He had no idea what the tapes might hold, but he understood what she was asking. He nodded his head in affirmation, his eyes calm and clear, as if he was ready for whatever might come next.

Margaret inserted the cassette into the player, Amir watching, his mind still unable to comprehend the fact that along with his ability to see the action take place, his ears were also able to substantiate the act as the tape clicked into place. Margaret pressed the play button, the sound of the turning tape soon giving way to the music of the plucked strings of a saz accompanied by a drum and the distant, enigmatic drone of a reed wind instrument, the voice of a male vocalist soon joining in. The unusual harmonies, low drones, and asymmetrical rhythms of the songs, played in minor key, sounded strange and exotic to Margaret's ear. It was a collection of traditional Balkan folk music she had purchased on impulse when she had ordered the Bosnian–English dictionary. Although she couldn't understand the lyrics, she felt the music deep within her body and emotion as the melody traveled from melancholy, to passionate expression, and then back. She saw that the boy was entranced, transported to a place of faraway memory.

Amir could not believe what was happening. When he had awakened to the sounds of the day, in their immense and unceasing onslaught, he had been frightened. He had told himself that it was not real, but a dream that had followed him from sleep into waking. But now he was suddenly carried back to a world he'd thought gone forever.

The Bosnian orphan sat transfixed as the music and language from the land of his birth brought forth memories associated with their sounds: images of mountains and hillsides colored in beautiful greens appeared before his eyes, scenes of villages marked by old stone buildings that felt as ancient as the earth they stood upon, their inhabitants going about a way of life so different from the place across the ocean where he now lived. Then he heard something so familiar coming from the tape that his mouth began to move of its own accord, his ears following the gentle melody of an old children's lullaby he had sung in his village school. Amir's lips and tongue moved in attempt to form words around a strange sensation coming from his throat: the crackling, dissonant chord of a lost, disoriented voice—a sound caught between breath and word, neither one nor the other.

Margaret could see the struggle of emotion on Amir's face—happiness, sadness, hope, and doubt merging in attempt to occupy the same space at the same time. When the song ended, Margaret turned off the machine. Looking at her foster son, Margaret spoke slowly, with great encouragement, the hope in her voice speaking as much to herself as to the boy. "Amir," Margaret said, and then, in sign language requested that he speak it himself.

At first Amir looked at his foster mother as if she were asking an impossibility, but then his voice sought to find itself. A noise began to emerge from his mouth . . . stuttering, misfiring, like an engine not wanting to start, until finally a word came forth. "Amir," he whispered hoarsely. Shocked to hear the sound coming from his own mouth, Amir looked into his foster mother's eyes and continued to speak.

"Sta se dogilo?" he asked. "Ne razumijem."

So accustomed to the flow of their simple communication by the signing of their hands, the language of their bodies, and the gaze of their eyes, it took a second for Margaret to register that Amir was now addressing her by means of verbal communication. It was only in secondary reaction that she registered the fact that he was speaking to her in a foreign language she didn't understand.

"Sta se dogilo? Ne razumijem," he repeated. Seeing the confusion on his foster mother's face, he signed his words, "What has happened? I don't understand."

"I don't either," Margaret said pausing, then repeating it in sign, "I don't either," the smile of joy on her face speaking more than her words or the movement of her hands.

The sudden return of Amir's speech and hearing seemed to herald a new and startlingly different situation in the Bosnian orphan's care. That it had come about so suddenly and unexpectedly had caught everyone involved off guard. When they went to see Dr. Caron the following day, Margaret asked if there might have been some psychological catalyst to the event: the boy having come to live with her, the decision that he should attend public school, or even his first meeting with Dr. Caron.

"The truth is, I don't know," the physician had replied. "I can't completely rule out some kind of psychological reaction as having instigated the seizure. But the cause of the episode is much more likely to be neurological than psychological. The exact nature of the neurological function involved will likely remain a mystery. It's a bit like a spring that's become bound and at some point becomes unstuck, then snaps back into place. In this case we don't know where, or what spring was involved. The good news is that it finally happened. That is fairly consistent with what we know of somatoform syndrome: the debilitated motor functions usually return to normal. You must be very happy."

"I am," Margaret answered.

"The recovery of his speech and hearing is very good news, but there are, of course, I'm sure you realize, other major long-term effects involved. It's not over."

"Yes. Yes, I know," Margaret said, the professional in her acknowledging the reality of all of the work still left to be done in the boy's healing, while the maternal in her felt only happiness at the seemingly miraculous event.

For the first few weeks after the recovery of Amir's ability to hear and speak, Margaret was kept busy in back-and-forth communication with all of the parties responsible for Amir's care. Between speaking with governmental agencies, school officials, and health professionals, she had little time to consider the longer-term symptoms Dr. Caron had cautioned her about. With Amir's first day of school growing close, Margaret was kept busy with the small chores of preparing his transition from the sedate comfort of his homeschooling to the more socially vibrant, though challenging, environment of the public school. There were things to be bought—backpack, notepads, pens and pencils, scissors, a calculator, and school clothes.

In the short time remaining before he would begin school, Margaret switched the focus of Amir's English lessons from reading and signing to the spoken word. It felt strange to both of them that the expression of a newly learned word should now be coming from his mouth and not his hands. Even as he began to develop basic verbal English survival skills, he sometimes still asked a question about something he didn't understand in sign rather than with his voice.

The practical details of preparing for Amir's entry into public school helped to distract Margaret from the anxiousness surrounding the recovery of his speech and hearing. There were, his foster mother knew, few social situations more difficult for a child to navigate than being the new kid in school, walking into a classroom for the first time and seeing all faces turning to stare in your direction.

Amir's first day at school felt excruciatingly long. The boy found himself retreating to an emotional survival technique he knew well: closing in and shutting off. His teachers, accustomed to the migrations of families in and out of the nearby university community, understood the anxiety and nervousness the new boy was experiencing and made efforts to ease his way. His second day at school was less intimidating than the first, and his third less so than the second, until, by the end of the second month, Amir told Margaret that she no longer needed to drive him to school each morning. He could, he said in very broken English, take the bus to school with the other kids.

Chapter 16

Standing in the doorway of her house, Margaret watched the large, yellow bus, the vehicle that would take her foster son on his first solo journey to school, come to a stop at the end of the driveway. Wrapped tightly in a thick cotton shawl, she fought the cold of the winter morning and the anxiety she chided herself for succumbing to, as if she were a young mother sending her first born off to begin his very first day of kindergarten. Sensing her eyes following him, Amir turned and waved, then mounted the metal steps that led him past the bus's yellow folded door, where he disappeared among the silhouettes of small bodies framed within the windows of the vehicle.

Margaret laughed to think that her foster son might be making the adjustment to his new school better than she was. The retired psychologist suffered no illusion concerning the difficulties the boy faced, though—not only in the transition of entering a new school in a new home and country far from the place of his birth, but also the added complexity of moving from a silent, speechless world, to one of hearing and verbal expression. Margaret was pleased that Amir appeared to be making a good start at his new school and seemed excited about the things he was learning, especially in the realm of his English-language skills. He came home from school every day now with a new word, a new sentence, and a new sense of his own power.

As the days and weeks passed, Amir's ability to speak English was slowly but steadily advancing toward elementary proficiency; his ESL instructor said he expected the boy to have basic conversational ability by the end of the school year. The reports coming back from his other teachers were for the most part just as encouraging. Although he was somewhat withdrawn and his social integration with his classmates was slow, his teachers said he appeared to be making efforts on that front and was demonstrating an active interest in his school subjects.

Margaret was pleased with her foster son's progress. She forwarded the teachers' reports to Dr. Caron, who had begun seeing Amir regularly since the return of his hearing and speech faculties. The behavioral pediatrician, while happy to hear about the positive developments, cautioned about reading too much into the school reports.

As winter phased into spring, Margaret's thoughts turned to the outdoors and ideas of how she might engage her foster son in outside activities typical for boys his age. It had been a long time since she had worked at the role of being a mother, and even then, she had never parented a son.

Checking out the various options, she discovered that there were a number of different team sports available for Amir to participate in. Of those, soccer seemed to be the one most likely to interest him. He had, he told her, played the game back in Bosnia. But the sport was just beginning to grow in popularity in the US and there wasn't much opportunity for play outside of the fall season.

Margaret spoke with Amir's counselor at school for advice in ways she might be able to create opportunities for her foster son to expand his socialization outside of school. His counselor suggested that Amir sign up for one of the afterschool programs offered by the school, but Amir was reluctant to do so. Margaret persuaded him to attend an afterschool art class because she knew he liked to draw. But he showed little of the same enthusiasm he displayed when he went off alone into the woods with his nature journal and drawing pencils in search of some new plant or insect species he might sketch in its pages. After only several classes, he said he didn't want to attend the afterschool program anymore. He preferred, he told his foster mother, to be outside after having already spent so much of the day inside.

For Margaret, there were both positive and worrisome elements in her foster son's solo forays into the forest. She found herself vacillating between appreciation of the boy's love of nature and concern about his propensity to turn inward to the point that it sometimes seemed like a withdrawal from the world of humankind. The aspect of Amir's outdoor wanderings that concerned Margaret more than any other was his tendency to extend his explorations into the evening hours.

One chilly spring night, Margaret looked out the window next to the patio, worried that Amir had been outdoors in the cold for over an hour. He had come inside at one point and asked whether he could turn off the lights in the adjacent rooms because, as he explained, they interfered with his view of the stars. Not wanting to disturb him by the sudden appearance of bright light, Margaret opened the door to the outside and called out his name. When no answer came she grew anxious. Fetching her coat, she walked out onto the patio. Her eyes, attempting to adjust to the dark, searched about for the boy. Not seeing him, she hesitantly began to make her way toward the fields. She was about to call out his name again when she saw his form quietly moving toward her. When they were close enough so that her eyes could make out his face, she could see that he looked happy and that there was a small, gentle smile calling out to be shared.

"I didn't see you on the patio. I was worried," Margaret said. "I called for you, but there was no answer."

"I am not hearing. Sorry," Amir answered.

"Why don't you come in now? It's awfully cold. Aren't you freezing?"

"OK. You come, please. Yes?"

"I don't understand," Margaret said, confused.

"I show you a thing. OK?"

"What is it? I hope it's not a bear," his foster mother said half-jokingly.

"No, no worry. Come," Amir answered, his smile broadening as he led his foster mother forward, in the direction from which he had come. He stopped in the center of the field and stood there quietly for some few moments before speaking. "Listen," he gently commanded.

Margaret stood still, attempting to hear what the boy wished her to experience. Yet all she heard was silence floating upon the darkness of the night, everything quiet, the breeze noiseless across the still-leafless, budding branches. Only the slightest whisper of wind made its way through the boughs of the pines and hemlocks, and she had to struggle to hear it.

Occasional, isolated sounds emanated from behind the dark silhouette of the trees bordering the fields, echoing through the night. Amplified by the cold air to bigger proportion, the distant, eerie, singular notes floated like lonely ghosts lost among the trees.

Margaret wondered what it was Amir wanted her to hear, unsure of what it could be until he spoke, and the wonder in his voice brought the realization that she had, in fact, been listening to it the whole of the time.

"Is beautiful. The sound . . . is beautiful. Yes?"

Margaret heard it then. Felt it. What to her had been a void was to him a symphony of hearing. Even in the absence of what seemed any distinct audible impressions, a miracle of subtle sensation enveloped her, an entire world of quiet entering her ears.

The retired academic closed her eyelids and drank in the silence, feeling it return her meditation a hundred times over. When she opened her eyes, she saw the boy looking up at her. He had seen that she understood. And through the darkness his eyes spoke his happiness at having her by his side in sharing those few moments of quiet, immense beauty.

With the school year coming quickly to its end, Amir's foster mother was concerned about how she might occupy her foster son's time during the long summer vacation. She considered a number of events she thought Amir might enjoy, though she herself was less than enthusiastic to take part in them: a hike to the top of Mt. Monadnock; a camping trip to the Green Mountains; or perhaps boating on a lake in Maine or New Hampshire. When she mentioned the possibility of these ideas to him, however, Amir could see the hidden ambivalence behind her enthusiasm and truthfully responded that what he wanted most was just to be able to stay home, to have time to play in the woods and read in the library without schedule or plan.

At first Margaret thought to insist, or at least persist, in the pursuit of some special events for her foster son, but she soon desisted, coming to realize that, given the great upheaval in his life, staying at home was what he really desired and needed. And there was, after all, the vacation at the beach in August.

Every year she rented a house on Cape Cod for a couple of weeks. This year she had rented a house in Truro, one larger than she normally would have rented for just herself. There was Amir now, as well as Alice and Paul, who had arranged their own vacation to coincide with hers. Still, she was worried that not having any continuing educational or social opportunities for the entire summer, Amir might lose precious ground. Despite the dramatic recovery of his speech and hearing, Margaret could see that there still lay an intense knot of repressed emotion deep within him. Her foster son was at times nervous, on edge, and continuing to have periodic difficulty in sleeping. Dr. Caron had advised her that those symptoms, along with others the boy exhibited, were consistent with the post-traumatic stress disorders he had seen in other young war victims. It would, he reminded Margaret, take a long time for her foster son to heal from the kind of intense trauma he had experienced.

Acknowledging her foster son's need to have a summer free of the pressures of forced activities and events, Margaret nevertheless felt he needed some structure and routine in his life. Given the importance of his English-language skills for his continued progress in both school and in developing peer relations, she arranged for Amir to be tutored by an ESL teacher over the summer months. Margaret drove her foster son twice a week to the tutor's home, where she left him for the two-hour, intensive session while she occupied herself with errands.

"How did it go today?" Margaret asked when she had picked Amir up from his class.

"Good," Amir answered.

"I'm glad to hear it," Margaret replied, smiling at the boy's one-word reply. "What did you work on today?"

"Things not now. Like happen before and happen later."

"I see. Past and future tenses. Do you find it difficult or easy?"

"Not so easy."

"Well, that will change soon enough. Is there anything you want to do while we're in town?"

Amir shrugged his reply, his gesture saying he was ambivalent. "Is not important," he added by way of further explanation.

"Are you tired from the class?" Margaret asked.

"A little, yes," he nodded.

"Want ice cream?" Margaret signed, switching gears from the spoken word back to the language of hands and facial expression she and her foster son still used on occasion.

"OK," Amir answered back with his own hands, a smile coming to his face as much for Margaret's signing the question as the idea of enjoying an ice cream on a warm summer's day.

After finding a parking space around the corner from the town's main street, the two walked to the ice cream store, made their selections, and carried their orders outside to eat. They sat on a bench beneath one of the maple trees that lined both sides of the street, providing shade and a pleasant aesthetic for the town's center. With much of the student population having gone home for the summer, everything moved at the pace of a more typical, small New England town, allowing residents like Margaret, living in the outlying villages, to once again reclaim it as their own.

Amir ate his ice cream slowly and without words as he watched the people and traffic move past him. Although he had been living in his new country for a year now, there was still a sense of strangeness to it all. It amazed the boy that the people here could move so quickly, with such single-minded intent. Yet at the same time there seemed to be some invisible, mysterious synchronicity that linked the solitary aspect of their movement, as though all of their trajectories were tied to the rhythm of the same beat.

As her foster son sat watching the world go by, Margaret smiled and fell into her own private ponderings, her mind not focused on the world in general, but rather turned in direction of the boy. How similar in temperament the two of them seemed to be, she thought, and how little they needed the reassurance of words as a sonar to each other's presence; the quiet between them acted not as separation but rather as their connection. She was struck by a sense of how much could be communicated with so little, and how much of what was spoken too often had so little to say.

Margaret wondered what caused the silence in Amir even after he had regained his power of hearing and speech. Was it wholly the effect of the war, or was it something of the boy's nature as well? Then, of course, there was also the cultural element to be considered. He was not a child brought up on computers, televisions, cell phones, trips to the mall, taxied to this soccer match and that martial arts class, addict to activity as much as the coffee drinker to caffeine.

Life for the young in a rural Bosnian village would have been of a different order, much more akin, she imagined, to the world of her own childhood over a half century past than it was that of the modern-day American child.

After finishing their ice creams, Margaret and Amir returned home, each to their own orbit: Margaret to work on an article she had promised to write for a psychology journal, and Amir to the small tasks that were part of the household chores he shared with Margaret. Unable to concentrate, Amir went about his work with less than his usual thoroughness, and after a time of simply going through the motions of it, he wandered off into the field and from there into the woods.

It had now been half a year since his hearing had returned, but the wonder of sound had not left him. He loved the whisper of the wind through the trees, the music of their leaves as they brushed up against one another. Lone, distant noises suddenly echoed through the forest growth, and his attention, if having wandered, would be brought back to the present to scan the foliage for a bird or animal that might be furtively moving about.

He could spend hours in just one spot, unaware of any measurement of time other than the sun's slow passing through the treetops. Sometimes he would lie down to watch the sky past swaying branches, to follow the white tail of a distant jet making its way to . . . where? Or he might rise from his sitting position to climb to the top of a tree to look down, his view like that of the bird gazing down watchfully on all that moved below.

Amir had his favorite trees as another person might have favorite chairs or resting places. Usually these were older, large-limbed hardwoods that stood guard near forest paths or streams where wildlife was more likely to be spotted. But even if no animal or bird passed by, Amir was content to sit and watch, especially so if there was the sound of running water, in whose music he could lose almost all sense of self, as though he had become part of the forest itself.

That night, unable to sleep, Amir returned to the fields behind the house. The periodic nightmares he suffered seemed to have no rhythm, no regularity to their arrival. Most often, they came unannounced, shaking him from his sleep with sharp, stabbing thrusts of terror. At other times, though, such as that evening, they would insinuate their visit upon him just before sleep came . . . the fear of the nightmare's images chasing the boy from his bed out into the night before they even had chance to arrive.

He waited until his foster mother's reading was done, her bedroom light turned off, and then walked quietly downstairs and out into the field in attempt to find solace in the dark of the night, alone in a world quiet with sleep. Once outside, with the fresh air bathing his skin and filling his lungs, a calm came over him, washing away the anxiety of unwanted, fearful images that threatened to assault his mind. Sitting down in the grass, he stared up at the stars, the waves of light radiating from those distant, luminous bodies bringing peace to the whole of his mind and body. His gaze lingered upward for a time and then rested upon the land about him, feeling a sense of kinship in it, until, finally, a deep tiredness crept over him, and he made his way back home. There, he lay in his bed, hoping sleep would bring the same still landscape of the night to his dreams, freeing him of those other visions that caused his body to shake and tremble and left his sheets soaked in sweat.

Chapter 17

Summer drifted toward its end in recurrent days of warm, brilliant sunshine with little humidity, blue sky followed by blue sky, broken only by the occasional passing of sculpted afternoon clouds that brought welcomed moments of respite from the sun's rays. Evenings came with cool air and occasional rains, making for restful sleep and moist, productive soil. August arrived warm and lush, prepared to linger. Margaret and her family spent the last half of the month at their rented beach house in Truro; the time spent together providing her daughter and son-in-law the opportunity to bond with Amir. Paul spent a good portion of every day with the boy, kayaking, swimming, or throwing a ball about— Margaret happy to see a positive male influence in her foster son's life, Amir taking to Alice's husband with surprising ease.

All were sad to leave the vacation home, as much for the familial bond engendered in its tranquil setting as for the respite it had given them from the routine of their schedules at home. Although Margaret could see that the vacation had been successful in its effect upon her young foster son, it was still evident to her that the memory and lingering pain of the traumas he had undergone in Bosnia remained buried deep within him. As well as things had gone since he had come to live with her, she still sensed a profound obstruction in the boy's spirit. His nightmares, while less frequent and less intense, were still occurring. Their slow waning was seen by Margaret as a cause for concern rather than as a positive sign. Something was not being let out, and she was afraid it would become burrowed within him, perhaps so deeply that it might never see the light of day.

Both Margaret and Dr. Caron had, over the course of time, slowly begun to address the death of Amir's family. Though it had been clearly established that he was present when the paramilitary had invaded his family's home, Amir couldn't recount the details. All he remembered, he said, was that there had been shooting, followed by the explosion that had caused his head to feel like the inside of a ringing bell, and after that there was only the memory of silence.

Dr. Caron felt that the child was likely suffering from, among other effects, survivor's guilt syndrome. Amir had, after all, escaped while his family was murdered. The doctor explained to Amir that such feelings of intense, often subconscious, guilt were natural, even when they had no real basis in reality. Dr. Caron and Amir continued to talk about this during a number of their sessions, and circumstances did seem to improve after that: Amir's appetite increased; he seemed on edge less often; the times when he would interact with Margaret with a relaxed, open demeanor came more often; and his sleeping difficulties appeared to somewhat decrease.

Since becoming aware of his sleeping problems, Margaret had begun to cultivate a casual dialogue about them with Amir, especially when he awoke looking tired and drained of energy. She spoke to him in mostly general terms so that he felt comfortable confiding in her about those periods when sleep eluded him because of what they had come to term the "bad dreams."

"You look like you didn't sleep well last night," Margaret remarked to Amir one morning as he entered the kitchen.

"No, I not sleep so well," Amir said, rubbing his eyes as he sat down at the breakfast table.

"Bad dreams last night?"

"Yes, bad dreams," Amir let the words out with a long breath.

"Which one?"

Amir looked up toward Margaret, his eyes tired.

"The breaking-door one."

"Ummm," Margaret murmured, looking pensive. "Was it specific, or just the general feeling of it being broken in?"

"No, I saw the things specific."

Margaret glanced toward Amir and paused. The word "specific" was one they used as a key to signal that they were speaking of the actual event that took the lives of Amir's family. She could see by his facial expression and the language of his body that, though hesitant, he was willing to continue. Margaret gently probed deeper.

"Was it more than just the faces this time?"

"Yes, there was the words too. They was talking, yelling, screaming. I think it is just how it is. Then, you know, loud noises . . . " Amir's voice trailed off, indicating he didn't want to go much further into the description of it.

"No explosion dream?" Margaret asked.

"I don't know. I think it is both dreams."

"Was both dreams," Margaret corrected as if in absentminded consideration.

"Was both dreams," Amir repeated in a distracted voice, his mind, like Margaret's, puzzled by some change in the pattern of his dreams that he couldn't quite make out.

The dream of the door being broken down had always been separate from that of the explosion. They had never come together. The one with the explosion was always more intense and also more obstructed. It never came in any detail, as did the dream-memory of the paramilitary soldiers bursting through the front door of the Beganović home. From the latter dream they had progressed quite far into Amir's memory of the event. He could even recall some of the soldiers' conversations in the house. The rest was a blur.

A few days later Amir had another occurrence of bad dreams. This time he was able to go deeper into the memory than he had ever before. He was even able to recall one or two of the names the soldiers had called each other by. It was a small memory recovery, but in its way was a major breakthrough. As Amir spoke, Margaret could see a tremor in his body that seemed to come from deep within, as though speaking the names unlocked the door to the room where all of his suffering lay stored quiet and still, deathly afraid of making any movement that might betray its presence to his conscious mind. The frequency of the boy's nightmares suddenly began to increase, until for several days they occurred every night without break. Margaret called Dr. Caron to inform him of the episodes and ask if he would see Amir earlier than the next scheduled appointment.

"What happened next?" Dr. Caron asked. The physician's voice was kind, yet its encouragement wasn't so much in the gentleness of its tone as in the strength of its neutrality. Steve Caron had heard stories from the mouths of young war victims that few would be able to listen to, even in brief, secondhand detail, let alone while watching the faces of the children as they recounted them. The last thing such children needed was the incredulous, horrified reaction of an adult unable to believe such things possible.

"The man, the captain they called him, he take out all of the bullets from his gun but one and then he make my mother take his gun."

Amir spoke calmly and without emotion. His eyes looked down and away without meeting those of Dr. Caron, whose gaze passed back and forth between his notebook and the boy's face with no attempt to force visual contact. The dream sequences Amir had described to him carried within them a surprising amount of detail, much more than any of his previous accounts of his family's death. Dr. Caron wondered whether the memories had been accessible to his recall all along, Amir unwilling or unable to speak them. Whatever the case—whether his subconscious had opened through dream or he had reached a point at which his conscious was willing to communicate the secrets his subconscious held tight—the boy's mind had begun playing out the full memory of his family's murder for the first time.

"Why did he give her the gun?" the doctor asked.

"Because they are saying they going to take my sister away and do things with her. And my mother she scream no and start crying, then the captain he said if she don't want them to take Minka away he is going to help her, so he make her take his gun and said OK just shoot Minka and then she don't have to worry about the men taking my sister." Amir paused for a second to take in air, the long run of his sentence and the story it recounted having emptied his lungs.

"And then . . . ?" Dr. Caron prompted.

"She could not do it," Amir continued. "My mother, she could not shoot Minka, and she start crying even more. So the captain and the other men they are laughing like it is the big joke, and he take the gun back. Then he said it would have to be me shooting Minka."

Amir quit speaking then. The behavioral pediatrician was not shocked to hear that the paramilitary commander had given a gun to Amir's mother with which to kill her own child. He had heard sadistic stories like this one before, and yet others still even more horrifying.

Dr. Caron saw the boy looking at him. His eyes seemed to beg the man to finish the story for him. "Take your time, Amir," the physician said in a calm, neutral tone. "Just breathe deep and let your mind relax."

"I can't take the gun," Amir replied in slow, nearly whispered words. "The captain, he laugh at me. Then he say since I not going to take it, he is going to do it for me."

Amir fell silent, as though he'd reached the end of the story. Once more the boy looked to the physician, but the man didn't take up the lead, rather just turned it back to him, saying, "Do what Amir? It's OK, just go ahead with what happened."

"He just lift up his arm then and point the gun at my sister's head," Amir said, his voice beginning to break, tears pouring from above his bottom eyelids, as he kept his gaze fixed on the doctor. "And then he shoot her. In front of everyone. In front of my mother and father. In front of all of us."

Dr. Caron struggled to release the air from his lungs without the sounding of a sigh. He fought to keep his eyes balanced in their gaze, calm and compassionate, walking the tightrope of his duty's call. Amir needed to be able to tell his story. He, Steve Caron, needed to maintain his belief in humanity, not fall victim to the hopelessness he so often had to fight from overtaking his spirit at the stories he'd heard. The boy had paused his story again, and the physician waited for him to continue, not wanting to prompt him, not having the words to help advance him onward. But Amir's mind found its footing and returned to the story it had held at bay for so long a time, his words now coming quicker, with more urgency, like he might be able to rid himself of their memory by purging them in sound.

"When the captain shoot Minka, my father scream and try to go to her. The soldier next to my father try to hit my father with his rifle, but my father, he grab it and then there is a shot," Amir recounted, recalling the moment of the soldier's surprise—the hole that suddenly appeared just above the man's nose, blood and bone chips gushing out from the blast. Halting his words, Amir fought to breathe deeply into lungs that seemed to have shrunk so small no air could enter. After a moment's pause, with the physician's silent nod of encouragement, Amir continued, his mind translating the images playing out in his memory into words, his tone of voice almost neutral as the story of his family's death unfolded from its hidden archive. When he was done, both he and the physician sat for some moments in stillness. Dr. Caron was the first to speak.

"I think it is important that Margaret also hear about what happened, don't you?"

Amir nodded but said nothing.

"Perhaps it would be best if you tell her. Do you think you are up to repeating it?"

"Yes, OK," Amir answered, his words riding on a long exhale of breath.

"Good. I'll call her in, then."

With Margaret seated next to him, Amir fought for breath as he began the attempt to revisit the memory of his family's death a second time. His foster mother waited patiently for him to begin, the boy's eyes jumping back and forth in erratic motion, darting about the room as if he were looking for a place of escape. Margaret held her gaze steady and firm, the muscles of her mouth laying limber and gentle, silently waiting for him to speak. Amir turned to look at her in silent question, his eyes struggling to hold their position.

"It's OK," Margaret answered, calming her foster son by placing a hand on his shoulder. "Take it slowly. Just one sentence at a time."

Breathing in deeply, Amir nodded. The first time he had recounted the story of what had happened that day, it was as if he were describing some program he was watching on the television. That the show had been not fiction but an all-too-real accounting from his own life was just now awakening in his conscious mind. With great difficulty he began to repeat the story. He struggled to call forward the images from which he had brought forth the words he had spoken to Dr. Caron, but they wouldn't come at first, and he had to rely on rote memory, as if he were a student repeating the sentences of some tedious lesson assigned at school. The words of the story came forth in a monotonic cadence, his voice in sleepwalk while his heart palpitated in panic-stricken anxiety, fearful of revealing the one thing he'd held back from telling the doctor, the hidden secret his shame could not speak.

Amir paused, at a loss to find a place in the linear sequence of events that might lead away from the place of shocking admission his heart cried out to speak. His voice quavered and quaked as his mind stumbled over too large an obstacle for his rational thought to maneuver over or around.

"I'm sorry. I'm so sorry," he whispered in hoarse voice, the moment of horrible truth coming forth in images too strong to hold from memory.

Both his foster mother and Dr. Caron stepped in to reassure him. "It's not your fault, Amir," Margaret said and then repeated herself. "Those men did a terrible thing. It's not your fault."

"But you don't understand," Amir cried, tears falling. "You don't understand. It is me! It is me that has done it! I am the one who told it to them. I told them where the gun it was hiding. It was me."

"What gun, Amir?" Dr. Caron asked, confused.

"The one my father tell me to hide. The gun the soldiers they are asking about. The one I bury by the big rock in the field. It is all my fault. I told them where it was. I told the captain where it was. I should never have spoken it. I should never have told them."

Margaret's eyes turned toward Dr. Caron in silent question. He responded with a brief, nearly invisible shake of his head. After about a minute of silence, Amir began to speak again, recounting the immediate aftermath of his sister's death.

"After my father shoot the one guy, he start shooting the gun at all the other guys. The soldiers outside, they hear the noise and they are coming to the house. My father, he is yelling for me and my mother to go to where we keep the wood. There is door there to the outside. My mother, she don't move. My father, he yell, 'Go, go!' But my mother, she just standing there. So my father yells at me to go. 'Amir go. Go!' I do like my father tell me. Then there is a big explosion and my head, it feels like it is broken. Then I remember being outside, and I am climbing a tree. But after that I don't remember nothing until I wake up the next day."

Margaret sat still and unmoving, all of the years of her professional life brought to bear. She watched silently as her foster son filled his lungs with air, as though trying to catch his breath. He seemed to look at her then, but she realized his eyes were merely turned in her direction, his gaze passing through her and beyond, to somewhere only he could see.

Chapter 18

Amir's recounting of his family's death shook Margaret to the core. At first, both she and Dr. Caron had been confused about Amir's guilt-ridden admission. It took several times going over the full story for them to finally understand its relevance to the tragedy. The weight of its burden on the boy's psyche, however, had been clear from the moment he spoke it—the dazed, pained look on his face reflecting an anguish he had borne alone, an anguish that had been eating away at his being.

With Dr. Caron's help, Amir slowly came to understand, at least intellectually, that his shame stemmed from an event he hadn't any control over and whose outcome was unaffected by his telling of the hidden gun's location. The soldiers' actions, Dr. Caron assured Amir, were not influenced in any way by the divulgence of a lone, buried hunting rifle. The search for weapons had been a pretext for what had clearly been their purpose from the beginning. The fate of his cousins, his aunt and uncle, his grandparents, and the rest of the villagers spoke of the soldiers' premeditated intent to "ethnically cleanse" the area.

Coming to terms with the tragedy that had taken his family from him, the physician counseled, would be a long-term process. Its aftermath would manifest in both subtle and more overt ways. The important thing, he advised, was for Amir to learn to recognize the symptoms' arrivals for what they were, not judge himself for their presence or shut them off from mind, as if the past had no link to the present. "Don't be afraid to remember your family," Dr. Caron advised Amir. "Remember how much they loved you, and carry that into the future with you wherever you may go. It will always serve you well."

By the time his second winter in New England arrived in earnest, Margaret and Amir had settled into a pattern of comfort in both their routine and relationship. The bond between them was growing deep and strong. Margaret knew she could not have expected a more profound contentment resulting from her decision to bring the orphaned child into her life. Yet she realized that if she were to make too comfortable a nest that same gratification could turn into an impediment in her foster son's social development.

In addition to continuing her search for extracurricular activities Amir might enjoy, Margaret also made contact with a recently formed association of Bosnians displaced by the war. The group held social gatherings at a site located less than an hour's drive away. Part of her mandate in caring for Amir was that she should do everything possible to maintain a link to his ethnic and religious heritage. And even though Amir was at first reticent to attend and showed feeble interest in participating in the occasional gatherings of the Bosnian community organization, Margaret persisted, and the two of them attended the group's events whenever they could.

Amir's progress in school was steady, if not noteworthy. His teachers reported that they were encouraged by his efforts, especially in his acquisition of English-language skills. He was a quiet student, the kind who didn't sit close to the front of the room unless made to do so, answering the teacher's questions only when called upon, and then in a voice barely audible. But despite his shyness and solitary inclinations, Amir eventually found a place among his classmates. His friendships were slow in starting and moved toward the kinds of children who, like himself, were relegated, or who relegated themselves, to smaller groups outside the circles of the more popular students. He was one of those children who learn to blend into the background, understanding, like the smaller creatures of the forest floor, when and where it was safe for their presence to be made known.

When Amir brought home his first friend from school, Margaret felt as if a milestone had been reached. He had twice been invited over to a classmate's house to work on a special assignment—their science teacher, a great believer in team projects, having grouped the two boys together in what had become a successful pairing. Margaret suggested to Amir, as casually as she could, that perhaps the next time the two worked on the project, he might invite his new friend to their house.

"Yeah, I guess so. I can ask him," Amir responded neutrally, in a way that made Margaret feel he might be too shy to ask.

She was caught unprepared when a few days later Amir arrived home with the classmate in tow. It had been unlike Amir not to have informed her of the pending visit, although she in fact welcomed the spontaneity of it. She understood then that Amir must have taken her suggestion as something more, and she was struck with the realization that he had brought his friend home not for himself, but for her.

Even as his social integration continued to develop, Amir often found reason to be outside, to work at some chore or simply wander about the fields or the woods. It didn't seem to matter if darkness had descended or if a cold winter wind was blowing. At times, Margaret grew worried at how long Amir lingered outside in the cold, often until after sunset. She would call him in, concerned both by the harshness of the elements and her foster son's continuing inclination toward solitary pursuit. When called, Amir would obediently come in without complaint, even if he still felt the need to be out in the night air . . . there would always be later, when his foster mother was asleep. That Amir might go outside after she was deep into dream never occurred to Margaret; that a thirteen-year-old boy would wander about on his own in the late evening hours never entered her thoughts.

Alone in the quiet hours, when evening had firmly settled in and established the parameters of its enigmatic shroud, Amir felt as though he could almost physically step from his body and the confines of his reserve out into the night, and there find something of what he once knew as himself. It was like the sense of liberation an outdoorsman might feel after being made to suffer the bridle of formal dress.

In the light of day, Amir often felt susceptible to an anxiety that seemed to envelop him when he was in the company of others. Though it was a fear of neither constant nor intense proportion, it was all the more powerful for the vague, amorphous sensation of its random arrivals. Sometimes in mid-conversation he would find himself feeling suddenly confused and bewildered, his mind for a moment unsure whether he had ever recovered his power of speech or whether it had been but a dream of some memory from the past. At night on his own, out of doors, walking in the open or hidden within the dark cloak of an evening shadow, he was never visited by those anxieties, nor did he suffer the anticipation of their possible arrival.

On the nights when he felt freest, when his evening walkabouts came less from the urge for escape than they did from that for adventure, Amir was drawn to the village center and its surrounding residential streets. If in those late, sleepy hours of the evening he felt freer to be himself, then the town itself transformed into something of the same. The main road, which in daytime saw a slow but regular flow of traffic, lay still, the whirling of wheels rolling over pavement diminished to occasional or singular occurrence. In the lull of the sleepy quiet, there came to Amir's ears not a void, but rather a sound of its own—one so calm and at peace with itself that, like the black of night, it seemed to disappear into a pause of timelessness . . . a lull providing the human world a blessed respite from itself.

Margaret, like the boy, found solace in places of quiet and simplicity. Yet what was a natural ebbing for someone of her age and place in the life cycle was an altogether different dynamic for a boy such as Amir. Margaret's withdrawal might have been analogous to a recession—the retreat, over time, of a natural feature or its process. For the boy, the same tendency to withdraw had the danger of becoming a regression—a reversal of direction in what should have been a process of growth and understanding in his life's journey.

She would sometimes find herself fretting over Amir's progress, worrying that her attachment to the boy was doing more to impede his development than to help it. She chastised herself when her doubts overcame her common sense, but she still had little control over the small anxieties that set about her like vexing flies. Added to that, Amir had begun to act out in small ways. He was beginning to feel secure enough in their relationship that he could be less than perfect and still feel loved. She watched with a sense of both relief and trepidation as the boy's personality slowly began to emerge, the form of the man he would soon become beginning to show itself. He was cautiously beginning to make his way into the world: staying over at friends' houses and attending school and social events with more frequency. Margaret tried to introduce the idea of an allowance to Amir, but his rural agrarian roots couldn't grasp the concept of being paid to do the shared work of maintaining his own household. He was happy to work. He liked it. Earning his own money would be good, he acknowledged. But he would feel bad getting paid by Margaret to do work he considered his responsibility. So in addition to his chores at home, he began working for a neighbor, mowing the lawn, and then another asked for him to help stack firewood for winter, and soon Amir needed to open a bank account, the small box he kept his earnings in not large enough to hold all of the money he stored inside of it.

Spring and summer seemed to sail by so quickly that year that Margaret barely noticed their passing. The time would have remained remarkable in memory only for the comfort of the weather if not for two announcements, one bringing forth the other. The first of these came from Margaret's daughter, Alice, and her husband, Paul, who, while joining her and Amir on their summer vacation again, broke the news that they were expecting a child.

Profoundly happy at the prospect of finally having a grandchild, Margaret prepared a celebratory dinner. It was when mother and daughter were alone in the kitchen, while Amir and Paul were outside attending the grill, that a casual remark from Alice awoke an awareness within Margaret that would lead to an announcement of her own several weeks later: "Amir certainly seems excited at the prospect of becoming an uncle," Alice had commented.

Her daughter's reference to her foster son as the future "uncle" lingered in Margaret's mind through the rest of the evening and only grew stronger in the succeeding days. The ring of its truth slowly began to reverberate through her. She realized she was going to make a life-changing decision. Not wanting to diminish the excitement of the news of her daughter's pregnancy, Margaret waited until after the vacation ended and they had all returned home before speaking with Amir about her thoughts.

"Amir, do you have a minute? I want to talk to you about something that's been on my mind."

"Yeah, of course."

"It's such a nice day . . . let's sit out on the patio and enjoy this last little bit of summer."

"OK," Amir agreed, his expression showing the curiosity he felt at his foster mother's request.

"I've been wanting to talk to you about something. It's been two years now since you came to live here. It's been a very happy time for me."

Amir returned his foster mother's gaze and smiled, secure in the intimate knowledge of her mind and in the depth of their emotional bond. The confidence had no more than breathed its presence, however, before another emotion intruded upon his thoughts, one not as calm and trusting as the first, but panicked and doubtful, ready to hear the worst. Was she going to say it had all been good, but she had grown weary and could no longer handle the responsibility of raising a child? *This is it*, the frightened voice said. *I knew this time was bound to come.*

"What I wanted to say is that I've come to feel as though you are truly my son."

Amir's eyes held his foster mother's and smiled silently back. "Yeah, I feel like that too," he said in a timid voice.

"How would you feel if we formalized that relationship?" Margaret asked.

"What does this 'formalize' mean? I don't understand."

"It means I would like to adopt you, to legally make you my son. Just like Alice is my daughter."

"Really?"

"Yes, really," Margaret replied, smiling, the two of them embracing.

After their arms had loosened from around each other, Margaret cautioned Amir that the legal proceedings to adopt him would be much more than just a simple formality, but she reassured him that his home and hers would always be one, even as he grew old enough to have his own.

The lawyer she hired had told Margaret that the adoption would be a difficult and protracted process. A specialist in international adoptions, he informed her it would be an expensive, emotionally wrenching ordeal. The Bosnian government allowed foreign adoptions only in exceptional cases. She would, therefore, have to make a petition to the responsible government ministry based on special circumstances and, in addition, conduct an exhaustive search for any of Amir's relatives in Bosnia, even distant ones, who might be willing to take the boy into their home.

"You'll have to be prepared," the lawyer advised, "to keep your fingers crossed and your checkbook open. This process will be neither easy nor inexpensive. We'll have to partner with an attorney in Bosnia to deal with the appropriate governmental agencies there, if, after the chaos of the war, they are even functional enough to be able to process the request."

Putting the warnings of failure from mind, Margaret knew there could be no going back for her now. The questions—What if the adoption petition were denied? What if some distant relative in Bosnia was found and wanted to take Amir in? What if peace in Bosnia was suddenly declared and it was deemed safe enough to repatriate Amir to his homeland?—had to be put from mind.

Nearly a year to the day after she applied to adopt her foster son, Margaret received good news from her lawyer. With the war ended, and the governmental agencies in Bosnia now resuming their duties, her petition had been accepted by the responsible bureaucratic agencies both there and in the US. That it happened at all, given all of the obstacles that stood in the way, was a minor miracle. Had the war not devastated the country and Amir already been living outside of Bosnia, the adoption petition would have been rejected. Even given those circumstances, the lawyer later admitted, he'd had little hope for success. But the Sarajevo attorney he'd worked with had strong connections within the government. That, and the fact that Amir's official file listed him as handicapped—a designation that was one of the few exceptions allowed for foreign adoptions—had made all the difference.

It would take almost another year to finalize the adoption. In the meantime Margaret settled into the role of not only mother, but also grandmother, Alice having given birth to a baby girl, Emily. Not long after the birth of her first child, Alice announced that she was pregnant again. By the time Amir entered his first year of high school, a second daughter, Abigail, had been born. In the course of just a few years, Margaret's life had changed dramatically. There was now the sense that their small family circle might enter a larger arena—one where at future family gatherings, chairs might have to be gathered from other rooms to be squeezed in around the dining room table, where conversation zigzagged between the participants in random flow rather than following the smooth, linear conversations of a smaller, more orderly assemblage.

Margaret's life was full, and she felt a deep contentment even as she began to feel age claim more and more of her physical and emotional stamina. The practical work of motherhood itself was simple enough and weighed little on her. It was the emotional aspect of that relationship where she felt the weight: the unconditional investment of oneself to another . . . the identification and intertwining of one's being with that of a child; the trying and the tedious that came along with the moments of extraordinary reward; the unavoidable assemblage of the good and the bad, the difficult and the joyous that parenthood brought to one's life.

Slowly but surely Amir found his way into the current of normal teenage existence, easing much of the anxiety Margaret had felt as he'd entered his adolescence. His English had progressed to the point of native fluency, without the hint of an accent. His mannerisms, his clothing, and the subjects of his conversation all reflected, if not the mainstream or the cool, a recognizable strain of the society's youth culture. He even joined his high school soccer team, in time earning a starting position on the varsity team. His friendships, if not of large number, grew and broadened to include a small group of classmates of diverse nature and interest. Among them were several girls, though Margaret could detect no kindling of any romantic interest from her son. Even as his social skills developed, Amir remained shy.

In the spring of his junior year in high school, Amir finally found something that really brought forth a passion in him. Alice had given Amir an inexpensive camera for his birthday the year before. Seeing how much he enjoyed taking photos, she had followed up with a video camera on his next birthday. Amir took to the device immediately. He began disappearing for hours at a time into the woods to shoot scenes of wildlife and nature and would then come home and get lost in editing the scenes he shot, making short movies. He joined the video club at his high school and became a constant presence in its editing room. Margaret, who could imagine him making documentaries for PBS or employed in some similar fashion that would combine his love of nature and filming, breathed a sigh of relief at the thought that he had found a place of stability and hope.

Margaret understood that Amir's life would take the course it would, whether that would be filming for PBS or becoming involved in some other profession. What was important was that, after the traumatic experiences of his childhood, the boy she'd come to love as her own should find a measure of peace and fulfillment in his life.

Chapter 19

Margaret dabbed the tears that puddled in tiny pools at the corners of her eyes, as gravity caused them to fall down her cheek, breaking the perfect round of their form. Alice held her handkerchief to her eyes as well, and her husband, Paul, found himself sneaking a cuff against the few tears that managed to escape the cordons of his mental dictate that insisted men shouldn't cry in sentimental display. Amir's two nieces, Emily and Abigail, sat in the grass at the feet of their parents and grandmother, the joy of the crowd gathered at the high school graduation and the beautiful summer day creating a happy backdrop for their play.

As her son stepped onto the dais to receive his diploma, a profound sense of happiness spread outward from Margaret's chest to fill her limbs. Her body felt pulled to the earth while her consciousness seemed to float up in the air above her, looking down upon the crowd.

Margaret's contentment was tinged with a wistful, pensive air. She had experienced so many small, ordinary cycles of life revolve beginning to end that at this stage of her life, her appreciation of the moments marking their completion took on a sense of even greater importance. Looking at her son, she saw the boy he once was now clothed in the body of a young man. He wore his hair shorter now, his face was fuller, and shaving had become almost part of his daily routine. He had gone through several growth spurts during his high school years. He was no longer one of the smaller boys in his class, and now stood at average height. His thinness remained, but was carried with strength, a physique built of sinewy muscles grown from athletics and outdoor work.

Finding glimpses of the past in the present caused Margaret to glance in her daughter's direction. She too had changed. Streaks of gray had begun to appear in her hair. Her body was a bit heavier yet still spoke of an active, healthy lifestyle. Some few, small wrinkles that had begun to form in her early thirties were now more prominent. But there inside her daughter's adult body Margaret could still clearly see her little girl.

Letting her eyes pass briefly down upon her own body, a smile tinged in irony briefly appeared on Margaret's face. She could find no glimpses of the past in reflection on her present physical self, the body that now held her seeming to belong to a totally different person. Directing her eyes back to the stage where her son stood with his classmates, she quickly put the thought out of mind.

"Do you have a grandchild graduating?" a woman standing at her side asked Margaret. They stood looking upon the graduating seniors spread in a semicircle on the stage in front of them. "No," Margaret answered without any falter of voice, "a son. He is in the second row, third in from the left." And later, after the ceremony had ended, when the graduates came to embrace their loved ones, a classmate's mother congratulated Alice on her son's graduation. It was Amir who corrected her, introducing Alice as his sister and saying, "This is my mom" as he wrapped his arm around Margaret's shoulder, his smile broad, clear, and as bright as the summer day.

If her son's graduation from high school brought with it bittersweet feelings of his imminent departure from home, it was mitigated by the fact that he would not be moving far away. When Amir began his college search, his list of choices had been made easy because he had limited them to geographical locations within a close commuting distance of home. Margaret worried that Amir was staying close to home because of her. The idea was of tremendous solace, even though the entirety of her belief structure, which held self-sufficiency of the highest value, was loath to admit it. She didn't want Amir to limit his options because of her, and it was only after repeated assurances by him that staying close to home was what he needed that she could accept the truth of it.

Margaret was not surprised that her son's other major criteria in choosing a school was that it have a good film department. Since having first taken up videography, it seemed to Margaret that not a day had gone by when she hadn't seen Amir either with a camera in hand or sitting in front of an editing machine to work on what he had filmed. There were five colleges within easy driving distance of the Morgan home, two of which had very strong film departments: one was a state university, and the other was a well-respected liberal arts college. Accepted to both schools, Amir chose to attend the alternative-minded liberal arts college over the larger state university for the smaller classes it offered and the greater flexibility in designing his own academic program.

Franklin College was built on the grounds of a former dairy farm and encompassed over six hundred acres of field and woods. The school buildings and dormitories that comprised the nucleus of the college's campus were of modern design but built of brick, giving the college the air of a more traditional school. Sitting on the outskirts of a town that boasted three other schools of higher education, Franklin College provided Amir both the peaceful environment of nature and a social infrastructure that would help stimulate his creative drive in filmmaking. But amidst settling into his dorm, getting to know the campus, and fulfilling required courses, Amir had little opportunity to fully engage his chosen major. It wasn't until the spring semester that he was able to embark upon the shooting of his first assigned project in film studies. The assignment's parameters had been simple. It was to be shot in documentary style, five to ten minutes in length, in either video or film, on a subject of the student's choosing.

A number of budding documentarists among Amir's classmates viewed documentary filmmaking as one of the principal paths they might take in order to ultimately earn a living in their profession. But there was little thought in Amir's mind as to possible futures, images of self that he might wear into adulthood to define his identity. He didn't see filmmaking as a means to an end, a way to support himself when he entered the adult world and had to make a living. Rather, he'd been captivated by the process itself, by the sense that through the medium of film he could reflect his own experience of the world. He wanted to find a way to link things of seemingly distinct relation, to travel to places of disparate sources and find a means of uniting them, the instances of his own life narrowed and isolated into singular scenes, an impossibility from which he might find a way to understand his past.

Amir titled his project *Trees*, and it was not so named as a device, metaphor, or symbol. The title of his film was, for Amir, the only explanation necessary to understand his work. It was a short piece, lasting barely five minutes, and on the surface one that most would consider a mood film of experimental nature.

With the help of a few classmates, Amir hoisted cameras up into trees, tied back branches, and filmed random episodes of action and inaction while precariously balanced on branches overhanging the ground. At first Amir's fellow film students couldn't understand what his documentary was supposed to be about. But Amir's enthusiasm for it quickly won them over despite the opaqueness of its story. Amir the filmmaker was different from Amir the student: while still soft-voiced, he was firm and clear in his considerations, more willing to speak out, to express his ideas. His excitement for being up in the trees, edging out onto branches with his camera on his arm, was contagious. The animation with which he explained the idea that the film could show the viewer a differing perspective from that of a person as being the center of all things awoke his classmates to an awareness of their own anthropocentric views.

"Why does it always have to be about us?" he asked. "Why do we always have to be the center of everything? There is other life out there, isn't there?"

For Laura Schwartz, who taught the course, first-year projects were typically a mixed bag, pretty much what you might expect of young, inexperienced students. Even the surprises weren't really surprises: students who didn't get what a documentary was; those who thought they did and had a better idea; the ones from planet X who shot their pieces from outer space; and finally, those who got so entranced with the process that they lost sight of the specific requirements of the project. Of the latter, there was one piece that the professor could call a surprise. Of all of her students' projects it played in her memory the longest. It was difficult, however, to call it a documentary.

"Amir," Laura began as he sat in front of her in her office, "first I want to say that I truly enjoyed your work. But I also have to say that I really don't see how it fits into the category of documentary."

A moment of silence passed. Laura Schwartz looked at her student, attempting to see beyond the boy's outer persona, while Amir looked blankly back, trying to find his voice.

"Yes, a documentary," he said.

To Laura's ears, Amir's words sounded like neither a statement nor a question, but something in between.

"Um-hum," Laura nodded, "a documentary. The presentation of a given subject in a factual mode. The telling of a story as it happened in as objective a way as possible."

"OK, that is what I did, then," Amir said, the timbre of his voice not sounding convinced.

"And the story you're telling, is about . . . ?"

"Trees."

"Trees? Yes, of course. *Trees,* the title of your work," Laura paused, as if the obvious wasn't so obvious at all. "But there weren't any trees, except in the opening and closing shots. I'm afraid I don't quite get what the story is here."

"It was a documentary of the trees, you see? Not about them. By them. They are telling the story of us, of what they see."

Laura Schwartz laughed. There was something in her student's face, in his eyes, that was clear, honest, and devoid of affectation. She suspected that under the quiet, almost distant demeanor was a hidden passion. She was beginning to like this young man.

"Oh, now I see," the irony in her voice unambiguous. "If this is your idea of a documentary, then I can't wait to see what you'll do when you shoot an experimental piece."

Laura Schwartz paused, for the moment letting go of the question of whether the film was a documentary or not. She had other questions, and after all, even though she meant to keep the pressure on her young student, there was a story in the film.

"Why did you overlap the dialogue with the music the way you did? The voices sound more like the babble of a brook than they do people conversing."

"I don't know. It just seemed right, you know? It's like when you're in the woods walking, listening, sort of just hanging out. You hear sounds. To us they're just these kinds of vague noises that don't really mean anything. We never really think much about what their source might be, that they might be a communication of some kind. You don't think the birds are talking to each other. You just think, oh, that's nice, they're making music. You don't think about the sounds the trees make. That they're alive. That they have something to say. So if trees could hear, and they were like us, then everything we said might just be a noise to them, too. They might not think anything was being communicated. The same way we look out at the world and see ourselves, people, as being the center of everything. Most of the time we're hearing only our own voices and nothing else."

The film professor smiled, not knowing quite yet what to make of her student's response. "I'm curious. What made you come up with this idea in the first place?"

"When I was young, I spent a lot of time out in the woods, just playing and hanging out. Like any kid, you know? I liked to climb trees, and sometimes I'd wonder what it would be like to be one. When you gave us the assignment, this idea just popped up in my head."

Laura Schwartz listened intently, her appreciation of Amir's film growing with her understanding of what lay behind its idea. She couldn't help but wonder, however, about his description of playing in the woods, his portrayal of it as an act of common childhood practice. It seemed to her like an old and quaint tradition, the way her grandfathers might have spent their free time as young boys. She couldn't remember the last time her thirteen-year-old son had gone scampering off into the woods on his own accord, if he ever had. If it wasn't attached to an electrical cord or battery powered, an activity was unlikely to hold her child's interest for more than a few moments.

The professor and student talked for a few minutes more about his project before the subject changed to Amir's goals. Laura Schwartz was surprised to hear he had developed no thoughts as to where a degree in film studies might take him. Even as she mentioned possible futures that could bring him both fulfilling and gainful employment, he showed little reaction. She smiled inwardly, appreciating his innocence and at the same time wondering just how long it might last.

Chapter 20

With his first major project completed, Amir refocused his attention on his other courses, which had languished in favor of the film. It had been easy for him to put them off. They were required courses that for the most part were of little interest to him, and that, given the choice, he would have skipped entirely. The lone exception was a humanities course that fulfilled a general education requirement. The course, an introduction to Islamic studies, was taught by Dr. Zakariyya Ashrawi. Zack, as he preferred to be called, had written several books on the Israeli–Palestinian conflict; he was a leading advocate for Muslim civil rights in the United States and one of the more well-known and politically controversial members of the college faculty.

Although Amir did not feel any sense of lost religious heritage that he was drawn to rediscover, he nevertheless wanted to understand more about his former homeland's majority faith and the politics that played into it. The first few classes of Dr. Ashrawi's course reviewed the basic teachings of Islam, traditional Islamic life, and an introduction to Islamic history. Amir was surprised to find the material awaken a sense of the familiar that was as pleasant as it was strange, a distant sensation of the surreal taking him back to a time of innocence and peace. His parents' religious observance had been confined to the occasional visit to the mosque and the traditional

Islamic rites of passage—birth, death, and marriage—where even the least religious and those of other faiths could be found sharing in the social expression of their rural village community. In his mind's eye arose the picture of his father and mother and his sister sitting, smiling, talking happily among all their friends and relatives, little thought given to the lineage of their name or the branding of their religious belief. How that all could have so suddenly vanished into a miasma of hate and violence was only now beginning to find question in Amir's thoughts.

As Dr. Ashrawi's course focused on the more recent history of the Middle East, the tone of the instructor's voice began to change, moving from that of the professor to that of the politician intent upon instilling his words into the ear of the populace. Dr. Ashrawi, who had gained national notoriety for his support of the Palestinian cause in opposition to what he called "the Israeli Occupation of Palestine," was not shy in making his political beliefs known. When the subject of the class came around to the Israeli–Palestinian conflict, Amir began to grow increasingly uncomfortable, his enjoyment of the class beginning to diminish as Dr. Ashrawi illustrated the plight of the Palestinian people with pictures that included dead children, and others showing Israeli tanks bulldozing houses while their occupants stood helplessly outside, pleading tearfully for the soldiers to stop. Those images drew forth others from Amir's past, ones that he would have permanently deleted from his memory, if only it had been possible.

Yet even as Amir turned his eyes away from those disturbing scenes, a part of him, fueled by a simmering, rising anger, challenged him to not look away. Amir felt confused and conflicted and soon found himself making excuses for not attending class.

After Amir had missed several classes, Dr. Ashrawi sent him a message asking Amir to come to his office to discuss the absences.

"Assalamu alaikum," Dr. Ashrawi smiled in greeting.

The professor watched as Amir momentarily struggled with an answer, finally responding with a simple hello and a slight bow in reflection of his teacher's.

"I've been concerned that you haven't been in class," the professor began. "Is everything OK?"

"Yeah, I just had a couple of scheduling conflicts," Amir answered untruthfully. "But I got the notes from the classes I missed from one of the other students, so I have everything covered."

"Well, good then. I'm glad you're keeping up with it."

Dr. Ashrawi smiled and paused, taking the moment to consider the young man in front of him. He looked younger than a college freshman, but then again, in recent years the first-year students had all begun to look younger to him.

"It would be good if you could make an effort not to miss any more classes. We're going to begin a review of the course syllabus, and that will be important to the final grade. You know, I was thinking that it might be interesting for you to meet some other students who have backgrounds similar to yours. We're holding a small gathering next Thursday evening, a sort of *Da'wah*, for students to get together and enjoy each other's company. If you don't mind, I'll give your name to Kemal Abdu, a former student here and now a graduate student in Boston. He'll be organizing it for us."

The professor had used the religious term of invitation to Islam, *Da'wah*, on purpose. He had spoken it in a neutral tone, one that seemed to imply a more general than specific meaning. He sat quietly waiting for Amir to speak, letting the silence force an answer.

"Um, I'm not sure I can. I'll have to check my schedule."

"Of course. I'll have Kemal contact you and you can let him know. But think about it. It's going to be a lot of fun. You'll get to meet some pretty cool kids. I imagine you haven't had many friends you could talk to about being Muslim?"

"No, not really," Amir answered ambivalently, feeling hesitancy at the implied inclusion to Islam, an identity he found distant and not called to.

Yet when Amir received a call from Kemal Abdu that same evening, he was surprised to hear himself answering the graduate student's invitation in the affirmative, afterward wondering why he had accepted the invitation so readily. The following Thursday, as he walked across campus to the room the *Da'wah* would be held in, he hesitated and almost turned back in the direction he had come from. But he had accepted the invitation and felt as though he had an obligation to attend.

When he arrived at the gathering, he saw that the other invitees were, for the most part, people of Muslim heritage near his age. At the center of the gathering was Dr. Ashrawi, straddled on either side by two other older, professional-looking men. They were surrounded by a small group of students who were chatting with them respectfully.

After nearly an hour of random conversations that felt forced and awkward to him, Amir scanned the room looking for a path to a quiet exit. His eyes gazed past, then returned to, a girl standing among a small group of other female students, their heads completely covered by hijabs. Her long, dark hair flowed out beneath a headscarf that was loosely and almost fashionably tied to her head. The picture caused him to smile. There was no reason for his response, no political or social judgment from him on the one side or the other. He hadn't even realized he was staring until the girl looked up from the conversation and caught sight of his face. She looked back at him, her expression at first one of puzzlement, then quickly replaced by a flash of annoyance, before turning her back to him.

Amir gave a small shrug of his shoulders, not an uncommon gesture in his repertoire of expression. He continued looking in the girl's direction for a few seconds more, until he could see by the stiffness of her back that he wouldn't be gifted a second look. There seemed something familiar about her, and he wondered if he'd seen the girl someplace before. His thoughts returning to his exit, Amir decided the time to leave had come, before Kemal Abdu or one of the other student hosts engaged him in yet more comradely chat that always seemed to turn to enthusiastic conversation about faith. Without saying good-bye to Dr. Ashrawi or Kemal, Amir quietly slipped out of the room and made his way back to the lobby of the Student Union, where he lingered, not yet ready to return to his dorm room.

Feeling hungry, Amir decided to get something to eat. At that hour the main cafeteria was closed, so he headed down one of the corridors branching off the lobby, toward a small café that remained open until midnight and was a hangout for students in the film school. Not seeing any of his friends, he sat down alone at a table after ordering a sandwich and drink. He had just finished his meal when, from the corner of his eye, he caught sight of the girl with the fashionable headscarf he had noticed at the gathering of Muslim students. Her scarf was now pulled down over her shoulders and hung loosely around her neck.

Fate can find its opening in less measure than a heart's beat, and it seemed that for the young man and young woman, whose eyes met once again, it was just that way. Their gazes crossed and would have just as quickly passed, had not in that moment an embarrassed smile erupted from Amir's face. The girl, whose natural response to the stare of a male would normally have been abruptly dismissive, caught the disconcerted look on the boy's face and, despite herself, held back from averting her eyes in automatic rejection. Her body slowed and then was halted by his one, quietly spoken word.

"Hi," Amir said with a nod of his head, a hint of red surfacing on his cheeks.

"Umm, hello," the girl responded.

Pausing, she looked him over, her head nodding while her eyes and mouth contracted in ironic expression, as if playfully gauging whether the boy warranted any further attention.

"So," she continued, her humor probing a little deeper, "Zack and his *mujahideen*, they are not your cup of tea?"

Caught off guard, Amir's head moved backwards, as if trying to gain distance to better see the place where the question had come from. His smile remained, though it now appeared even less sure than before. The surprise of the question had momentarily distracted him from the sound of the girl's voice, which held an accent that had immediately grabbed his attention.

"No," Amir answered, then caught himself. "No, I don't mean no. Sorry. No, I mean they're fine. Why do you say that?"

"Hah, I saw you sneaking away. Maybe you are some kind of spy?"

"No, I'm not," Amir said quickly. "Why do you call them Zack's *mujahideen*?"

"It's a joke. You know? They are sometimes so serious. Anyway, you were looking like you wanted to make invisible of yourself," the girl continued, her face in mock seriousness.

Realizing that she was teasing him, Amir laughed, his smile spreading wider in response to hers. He liked her eyes. They were hazel, of a darker shade than his own. Her hair was long, and even with it partially tied back, he could see that it was lustrous and silky. Her face, the one that had looked so familiar to him, was soft and rounded with delicate features that were easily lost to the gaze of her eyes. Like him, she was of average height, though not as thin. He liked the gentle round of her flesh, the smooth, healthy, pale skin that contained her. As his eyes continued to hold hers, he could feel there was something striking about her. He saw her face suddenly grow wary at his continued gaze, and he reflexively turned away before looking back and speaking.

"You weren't wearing a hijab like the others," Amir said, unable to find a better thought to keep the conversation going. He was sorry he'd said it the instant it left his mouth.

"I don't have to prove my virtue to anyone," she responded quickly with a stern look. "If it suits me, I'll wear one. If not, I won't. I don't need to explain myself."

"I'm sorry, I didn't mean to . . ." Amir stumbled to find the right words.

"It's OK, it doesn't matter," she answered. Seeing his discomfiture, she shrugged and half-smiled.

"Are you going to get something to eat?" Amir asked, by way of timid invitation.

"No, just a tea," she answered, letting the unspoken question hang.

He could see that she was watching him, waiting to see what he would say next. His mind raced to come up with some words that might win the moment, but all he could manage was an embarrassed smile.

"I'm going to buy it," she said, and turned without a further word.

As she ordered the tea, her thoughts turned to him. She was glad he hadn't come up with a line, a witty come-on. Because then she would have gone her way, and she didn't feel like being alone. After she paid for her tea, she walked back in his direction.

"So, a big night out then?" she asked, her smile indicating an opening.

"Yeah, a big night out," Amir laughed in response, relieved to find her standing in front of him once again.

"Shall I sit?" she asked.

"Sorry, yes, please do," Amir responded, quickly standing to pull out a chair for her. There followed a moment's pause while she took her place. Feeling her eyes on him, Amir spoke the first thought that found footing. "Where are you from?" he asked.

"You hear my accent? It is strong, I suppose. Where do you think, then?"

"I'm not sure," Amir answered, though the more he heard her speak, the more the tingling of a certainty rose along the surface of his skin.

"I'm from Bosnia-Herzegovina."

She watched for his reaction, accustomed to Americans fumbling about their memory for either geographic or political frame of reference. But in his eyes there had been instant recognition and then even more. At the sound of her country's name, Amir's head had given a slight backward thrust, almost as if having received a tiny jolt of electricity, before quickly recovering into a slow nod of understanding.

"What's your name?"

"Jadranka. And yours?"

"Amir."

"A fine Muslim name," the girl laughed good-naturedly.

"Jadranka. That's not very Islamic," Amir parried with a gentle grin.

"No. But to be Muslim it is not always necessary to have an Arabic name."

"So you are?"

"No, not really. Only half of me is."

This time it was Amir who sat waiting further explanation, something Jadranka normally would have evaded.

"My father was Croatian. My mother is Muslim. I made the mistake mentioning that one time to Zack. So finally I came to one of their meetings just so he would quit making the invitations, you know? And you?"

"Sort of the same, I guess. I'm adopted. My parents were Muslim. But not practicing, so it was never a big thing in our house."

There was a pause and a shift in feeling, both Jadranka and Amir taking in each other's words, the use of the past tense in mention of her father and his parents not having gone unnoticed. And then something clicked in Jadranka's consciousness. Amir's eyes, his skin coloring, the shape of his face. They were all familiar.

"You are not from here, then?" Jadranka asked.

"No. I am from Bosnia."

At the mention of his former home the boy's facial muscles seemed to lose their strength. The brightness of his expression dulled and an aura of sadness, like gravity, pulled the weight of his flesh downward.

"How long have you been here?"

It was a simple question, though one that for a Bosnian could hold more weight than most people could imagine. The subject of dates, like that of family name, was not simply a matter of small talk. It was a topic that could be of important reference in a society where two young people meeting for the very first time could wonder, with strange incongruity to the attraction that drew them together, what the other person's last name might be and just how close their families' histories might touch. It was something that most people could never understand, never fear the worst from: what your father did to mine, or to my mother or sisters; what your brother did to my brother; or what we shared together that we both wanted to forget.

"A long time now. Almost eight years."

Amir saw Jadranka do the math, quickly calculate the year of his arrival, understanding that he had not, by some stroke of luck, arrived in advance of the war, but almost certainly had come as its result. Their eyes held for a brief moment, talking a language neither could translate, the girl finally breaking the silence.

"You don't have an accent."

"No," Amir smiled. "Not anymore."

She had an impulse then to talk to him in their native tongue. To ask if he still spoke it. But she could feel, in herself as well as in him, that it was time to move the conversation away from Bosnia, even though for most Bosnians meeting for the first time the talk would be inexorably pulled in that direction.

The two chatted for a while about things in general, about school, courses, and majors. She was a year ahead of him. She had been granted a four-year scholarship by a foundation active in the rebuilding of Bosnia. She was majoring in English. After a time, she said she had to go. Amir nodded, rising from his chair as the girl stood, saying to her that it had turned out to be a good night after all. Jadranka smiled in response, then turned and began to walk away.

"Oh, by the way," Amir spoke out, "my last name is Beganović-Morgan. Amir Beganović-Morgan. Just in case . . . I don't know . . . you might want to talk again sometime."

"My name is Pušić," the girl replied. "That would be nice."

Chapter 21

Amir wondered how it was that he had never noticed her before. He now found himself running into Jadranka several times a week, and though their encounters were for the most part brief, he could feel a friendship building between them. With the school year's end quickly closing in, they had the pressures of finals and term papers weighing on their minds. For Amir it was a simple matter of getting, if not honors, at least respectable grades. In Jadranka's case there wasn't that same luxury. As a scholarship recipient Jadranka needed to maintain a high grade-point average or risk losing the financial aid that enabled her study. Yet even if maintaining a high GPA had not required a considerable time commitment on her part, it was clear that Jadranka wasn't in the market for a boyfriend.

The Bosnian girl made her feelings about becoming involved in a relationship apparent both in attitude and in dress. The clothing she wore was simple, and although she wore it with confidence, there was also the sense that she did so with complete disregard for how it might reflect her beauty. Though she sometimes wore bright-colored clothing, it was never of a style that accentuated the form of her body or the look of her face, which, when it came to men, she also clothed in a demeanor that said "no trespassing allowed."

She became annoyed when men ignored the clear signals indicating she didn't want to be bothered by their come-ons, no matter how clever or artfully sincere. On several occasions Amir had seen Jadranka approached by men who soon made quick exit from the stare of her eye or, conversely, stood there feeling totally ignored, uncomfortably shifting their weight from foot to foot in her hard silence until they got the message.

It was easy to understand why men would be attracted to her, even as she draped herself in loose, drab clothing, with her hair tied back, and kept her gaze to herself. She was imbued with a kind of Eastern European exoticism that emanated from her being like perfume floating in the air. It was in the look of her eyes, in the way she talked, in how she held herself, moved her head, and even walked.

There was a sense of a deep, rich femininity about her, while at the same time the tenderness of her youthful appearance carried a certain beauty that was made all the more appealing by the mask of plainness under which she tried to hide it. She wore no makeup, not realizing that doing so only served to underscore the delicate, translucent quality of her skin, the unusual proportion of her eyes, her mouth and nose all set on a face that suggested a sculpture of some ancient mix of cultures. She reminded Amir of home, of girls he'd once known, and when he met with her he felt transported to some other dimension that existed somewhere between a dream state and reality. He felt as though one foot had stepped back through time to stand in the rural Bosnian village of his birth while the other remained anchored in the rational present, the rest of him trying to find bearing in a world in between.

Amir saw Jadranka in front of the library, sitting on the lawn bathing in the warm late-spring sunlight. The rich, varied greens of the grass and trees were still a shock to his senses after so many months of colorless landscape. As he came close, her eyes rose to meet his. While the casual observer would have likely seen nothing more than a neutral look from the girl's expression, Amir saw the careful welcome of her eyes and smiled.

"So, you are celebrating?" Jadranka asked as Amir sat next to her.

"Maybe tonight. I still have one more final this afternoon. I can't believe the year is over already."

"And what about the prize? You aren't going to celebrate that? My American boy wins the big honor and says nothing about this to his friends?"

A large grin spread across Amir's face . . . at Jadranka's mock look of disapproval, at the teasing in her voice when she called him her American boy. He wondered how she'd known. Later he would learn the answer to that question: his picture in the college newspaper, the headline declaring him one of the winners of a faculty film award. He had been very surprised to receive it, though he hadn't thought it a particularly big deal. He was one of four film students to have received the special recognition; his short film *Trees* had been voted the most original student work.

"I thought you were talking about the end of the school year. Anyway, it's not such a big deal. Just a piece of paper to gather dust. The best thing about it is that everyone who gets one of the awards is offered a chance to intern on a real film, so I won't have to mow lawns and paint houses all summer. I'll get to work with one of the professors on an independent film project."

"So, now you will stay here?"

"I'll live at home and commute. My house is only about thirty minutes away from here," Amir answered, then changed the direction of the conversation away from himself. "And you? Will you be able to go home for a visit before you start your summer job?"

"No, I cannot. It is the money, you know," Jadranka indicated, rubbing her thumb back and forth against her fingers.

Amir nodded his head in understanding, the conversation ebbing for a second before Jadranka revived it.

"You are finishing with good grades? How did you do? You were so worried about doing well. . . ."

"Pretty good, actually," Amir sighed happily. "I think I'm going to get the first A of my college career."

"That is your film course?"

"Yeah."

"And what about Zack's class? Have you been the good boy and gone to prayers?"

"No, but I am doing work for some kind of charity that he runs. I'm going to edit a bunch of footage he's giving me to make into a short promotional documentary."

"Ah, so maybe now you get two A's"

"Maybe," Amir smiled, hesitated, and then continued. "When do you go down to the Cape?"

"Sunday," she answered without further detail.

"My family goes down there every summer on vacation," Amir said, attempting a casual tone.

"Yes, you have told me," Jadranka nodded, allowing herself a small smile.

"I could come visit you," he said, more in question than statement.

"You would have to leave the big tip," she answered with a look of mock seriousness.

Amir smiled, unable to hide the relief he felt at the veiled assent. "What's the name of the place where you're working?"

"The Blue Whale Restaurant."

"In Harwich Port, right?"

"Yes, in Harwich Port."

"OK."

"OK," Jadranka concurred, laughing at the sound of nervous resolution, the brave look with which the boy held his timidity at bay.

With his internship scheduled to begin the week after school let out, there was little time for Amir to think about Jadranka. The film was an independent production directed by Harold Irving, the most well-known of the school's film professors, whose myriad credits ran from Hollywood to television to art house film. While Amir's job as personal assistant to the director was, in essence, to serve as the director's errand boy, it allowed him to take a close glimpse at all aspects of a film's production. He felt that he learned more in the six-week internship than he could have in a year's worth of courses. His days began at dawn and continued into the night, running nonstop through the entire length of the shoot. Although he was living at home, Margaret saw little of him beyond an early breakfast and a late dinner.

During the postproduction work, Amir's schedule relaxed considerably. On a number of days he was left with time on his hands and he was reminded, by persistent phone calls, of his promise to help complete a documentary video promoting Dr. Ashrawi's foundation. The professor of Islamic studies had given him a rough outline of what he was looking for, a couple hours' worth of random, previously recorded footage, and little else. When Amir expressed doubts as to his ability to put together a cohesive promotional documentary, Zack, as he insisted that Amir address him, responded by saying he had complete faith in Amir's abilities. After all, he had just won a prestigious award, hadn't he?

Seeking help, Amir asked Harold Irving's guidance on how he might best approach Dr. Ashrawi's video project but was surprised to find the film professor hesitant to offer counsel. As a colleague, the film professor felt the need to be politic in his opinion of the man, letting the ambivalence with which he spoke express his feelings about his fellow faculty member. Dr. Ashrawi had been teaching at the college for ten years. In the beginning he had fit in well; he had seemed to be content to teach his courses, publish the occasional article, and not rock the boat. By the time Harold, a refugee from the southern California rat race, came on board, Zack had become a tenured professor and felt freer to express his opinions in a less than politically correct manner. Harold Irving, whose political leanings were opposite to those of Zack's, felt that his colleague's politics were dangerous.

Without directly addressing his real objections to Zack, Harold advised Amir that trying to put something together from bits and pieces supplied to him by others could never serve a filmmaker well. Amir had to be careful, Harold said, what he put his name to. It could come back to haunt him.

Amir felt confused by Harold Irving's evasive response. He understood, to some extent, that the director was trying to get him to read between the lines . . . that there was something he wasn't saying, something he didn't want to come right out and declare. Amir was aware that Dr. Ashrawi had his detractors. But the professor's foundation served a good cause. It raised money for innocent victims caught in the crossfire between two warring factions. Amir didn't care about the politics, felt no pull to take sides in the debate.

But for Zakariyya Ashrawi it was just the opposite. The politics of the Middle East had become his life. As with Amir, his arrival in the US had come by way of war. He had immigrated to the United States with his parents during the 1948 Palestine War. The family's exodus took them first to Jordan, then to Egypt, and from there to Canada and, finally, the United States. They eventually settled in a small city west of Boston, where his father opened a convenience store, to which he added several others over the years. The small chain of mini-stores provided the family a good enough income to send their children to private colleges, where their parents believed they would have better opportunity to seek the American Dream.

Zack did seek that dream, but the memories of moving from country to country and his father's sad tale of having lost everything, of being forced to leave friends and family far behind, had created a rift in his mind and heart. Zack tried to bridge the gap in college by starting a student organization for support of Palestinian refugees.

He hadn't started it with the idea that it would become an Arab student organization; he had imagined it having a more universal membership united to help impoverished refugees displaced by the wars that had forced them from their homeland.

The young student, though, quickly realized his naïveté when he found that the only other students interested in the cause had Arabic surnames, and some students affiliated with the other side of the Israeli–Palestinian conflict complained that his newly formed student club was really a covert anti-Semitic organization.

Zakariyya Ashrawi's years in academia didn't lead him deeper into the realm of peaceful settlement, but rather, further from it. While he became ever more involved in the plight of the Palestinian refugees who were stuck in limbo—welcome neither in their homeland nor in the countries hosting the barren settlements they had been relegated to live in—he found himself spending less and less time trying to bring conciliation to the conflict's supporters in his adopted country. By the time Amir and Dr. Ashrawi met, the professor of Islamic studies had come to be nationally known, and by some reviled, for his advocacy of Muslim-American civil rights, as well as the role he played as the US representative for several Palestinian political and charitable organizations. It was in pursuit of advocating for one those groups that he had asked his student to put together a short documentary film to help forward its cause.

The video footage Dr. Ashrawi had provided him to help make what his professor had called "a documentary of conscience" included some images difficult for Amir to watch . . . scenes of a displaced populace crammed into shanty homes, of orphaned children, and of dwellings reduced to rubble. For the purposes of Dr. Ashrawi's video, they would serve as emotional triggers to gain viewers' sympathy, but for Amir they were more than secondhand scenes of vicarious horror. As he began editing the video footage, his mind was flooded with another set of parallel images, ones that now felt strangely distant, memories of those terrible days in a place whose name still resonated somewhere deep within his identity. He repeated the word in his mind several times, looking to see what might come from it. *Bosnia. Bosnia.* He was not sure what meaning it still held for him, but he felt that for the first time he might be ready to begin talking about it. The subject had remained largely a place of silent exile within him. He had never spoken of it to anyone other than Margaret and Dr. Caron. And even they could understand only to a certain point—could but offer their compassion and sympathy from the distance of those whose blood and tears had never been spilled by war.

As August and the impending time of his family's vacation loomed near, Amir found his mind distracted from its focus on Dr. Ashrawi's video, images of Jadranka winding their way into his mind at odd and random intervals. He began to redouble his efforts to finish Dr. Ashrawi's documentary, finally completing it the same week he was to leave for the Cape with his mother.

Dr. Ashrawi was delighted with the outcome of Amir's work. There was an emotional pull to the simple and honest documentary that drew the viewer's empathy. It wasn't at all the way Zack had outlined it, and he quickly saw that his own ideas had been clumsy and strident in approach. The film student's scripting of it had been better, much better indeed. As he sat with Amir watching the finished product for the first time, Dr. Ashrawi became emotional, wiping a tear from his eye, praising his student, and giving him a hug and a grateful thank-you. Amir was glad to be done with the project, though he was pleased that his work was well received. But the pride he felt at hearing his professor's accolades was mixed with other emotions stirred at seeing the footage of the suffering people included in the documentary, emotions that were strange and confusing. His feelings seesawed between compassion and anger, and from there to yet other feelings, ones he found difficulty putting name to.

During the several occasions they had met to discuss the video project, Dr. Ashrawi had repeatedly invited Amir to join him at the student mosque for prayer. Amir had declined each time, but after they met to review the finished video and Zack asked him once again, he relented. It was the *Jumu'ah*, the day of communal prayer held every Friday, and Amir agreed to join his professor in performing the *salat*, the ritual of prayer. Sitting among a small congregation of mostly young Muslim students in the room that served as the school's mosque, Amir felt both a distant divide and a common bond with the others attending the service.

As Amir came to the last part of the prayer—first looking over his right shoulder, toward the angel who would be recording one's good deeds and then turning to look over his left, toward the angel recording one's wrongful actions—a memory of him and his father, Asaf, kneeling in that same position flashed through his mind. Together, they had repeated the ending words in unison, *as Salaamu 'alaikum wa rahmatulaah,* peace and blessing of God be upon you. When they had finished, his father had smiled and patted him on the back, his look benign and light. It was one of the handful of times Amir could remember when he and his father had attended a service at their local mosque.

As he spoke those same words now in the student mosque, Amir's eyes opened to see Zack Ashrawi smiling at him, yet at the same time looking at him with intent gaze, the older man's eyes speaking a silent question, one that held the expectation of a certain answer. Amir was confused. Was it a call to the celebration of life, or to a life that enjoined him to praise a passion built of stone, a belief built from dogma, a circle drawn upon the ground marking a boundary separating that which lay within from that which lay without—the good and the bad reduced to the simplest of measures?

Flustered, Amir smiled back at Zack, averting his eyes in evasion of an answer he neither had, nor knew if he cared to pursue. For many, the call of religion offered a palladium of both place and identity where question might find answer and search find quench. The professor's smile offered up what seemed a gentle place of faith, but Amir was uncertain whether it would answer the roil of his unresolved emotions or just add another layer of confusion that would make their buried presence within him all the more occult and repressed.

As they walked from the campus mosque and prepared to part ways, Zack Ashrawi asked Amir whether he might be able to help out on another small project, a few video clips for a website, nothing more. Amir knew that what the professor might see as a simple task was not necessarily so. The short video he had just made had taken many hours of work; so Amir answered evasively, explaining that, given his course load for the coming school year, it was unlikely he would be able to be of much assistance.

But Dr. Ashrawi seemed not to hear the underlying apology in Amir's response and instead began to praise his student's work again, saying he was going to prominently display Amir's name on the credits of the documentary he had made and list him as media director of the professor's foundation. The Islamic studies professor then spoke of the importance of their work to the cause of the Palestinian refugees.

Amir could see it was a clear attempt by his professor to win him over, yet despite the manipulation he still felt guilty for trying to excuse himself from further involvement. The Palestinian refugees were a forgotten people, their plight by common consensus erased from the minds of the Western world in place of what were called larger, more important political issues. Amir, hesitating, said that yes, he might be able to help out in some small way, but wouldn't be able to take a lead role in the project and that, in any case, it wouldn't be right for him to take credit as the foundation's media director.

"Look, don't worry about the title," the professor had said. "It's really nothing. I can list you as media consultant instead. It will look good on your résumé. Believe me, anything you can do to build up your CV will help in the long run."

"No, it's OK," Amir replied with an apologetic smile. "I'm not even sure I'm going to work as a filmmaker after I get out of college. I might end up doing something completely different."

"Then it won't matter one way or the other," Zack insisted. "Better to keep your options open."

After a moment's awkward pause, with no further response coming from his student, the professor asked if Amir had considered signing up for another course in Islamic studies. Zack showed his disappointment when the boy replied he'd be too busy with his major courses to do so. But in truth, the class Amir had taken with Zack Ashrawi had disturbed him. Fearful that what had happened to him in Bosnia would haunt him for the rest of his life, Amir wanted to keep his distance from anything that might remind him of it.

Chapter 22

It wasn't until the car was packed and he and Margaret were on their way that Amir realized how much he had been looking forward to their yearly pilgrimage to the Cape. The long hours and excitement of his film internship had helped keep his mind from wandering to thoughts of vacation and to certain unsettling feelings he struggled to keep from intruding upon his summer's heavy workload.

He had thought of Jadranka often, even though he labeled their relationship, as did she, one of only friendship—his mind relegating the call of stronger emotions to less accessible chambers of his conscious thought. But with his internship over, Zack's project completed, and no other demands on his time or energy other than to enjoy his approaching vacation at the beach, the feelings he had suppressed could no longer be ignored. Images of Jadranka started to appear within his mind in larger format and in more vivid detail. Amir's thoughts grew confused as they were pulled into fragile focus in abrupt, random movement, pushing and pulling against one another like a rowdy crowd in a ragged queue.

They were only friends, one voice said. *He liked her very much*, another spoke. *It was OK*, a third voice opined, in reconciliation of the others: *good friends could like each other a lot; it was only normal.* He would go see Jadranka as soon as he got to the Cape, two of the voices agreed—one anxious to see her, another reasoning that it would prove that they were just friends and there was nothing to hide or react to. But he felt guilty abandoning his mother on their very first day of vacation together. Of course, she wouldn't really mind if he went. Then again, she would be left alone without a car. He should wait until his sister came, when there would be two vehicles, and other people to keep his mother company. He could visit Jadranka on that first night, when Margaret was sleeping. But he didn't even know Jadranka's schedule—how late she worked, or even on which days.

Margaret could see that her son was distracted. They had been coming back to the same house in Truro every summer, and the very first thing Amir always did, after unloading the car, was go sit out on the beach to stare at the ocean and drink in the sound of the waves as they lapped the shore. But this time he made no move to kick off his shoes and walk barefoot upon the sand. Instead, he began unpacking the groceries and putting them in their places upon the shelves. He asked his mother if she wanted him to fix her anything to eat. Was she tired, or did she need a rest?

"No, I'm fine," Margaret smiled. "What's going on? You're acting a little too good to be true. Not that I mind, of course. I enjoy being waited on. But it reminds me of the time in eighth grade when you received a D on your report card and made me tea and cookies before you showed it to me."

His mother's words, or perhaps the tone of her voice, brought about a pause in Amir's restless mind.

"Yeah, sorry," Amir said. "That's the problem with having a psychologist for a mother," he laughed, then told Margaret he'd been thinking about going to see a friend who was working a summer job nearby.

"Why don't you go, then?" she said. "I'll be just fine here on my own. Is this a friend I know?"

"No. I mean, you haven't met her," Amir said, color coming to his cheeks. "She's the girl at my school that I told you about, the one from Bosnia."

"Oh, yes, I remember you mentioning her. Well, go then," his mother said, trying to dampen the expression of her pleasure.

"No, I think I'll wait until tomorrow. There's no rush or anything. I mean, we don't have any set meeting. It's just a casual thing, that's all. Tomorrow will be fine. I don't even have a number for her."

Normally spare in his words, Amir realized his internal dialogue had slipped out into his response and that his mother was smiling. To his relief, she let the subject go, saying that whatever Amir wanted to do was fine with her.

That evening, sitting on the back porch staring out toward the sea, his eyes barely able to make out the whitecaps of the waves, Amir found himself thinking about his life with Margaret. His adoptive mother sat to his side in a cushioned wicker loveseat, a book nested between her hands, reading. The soft, rhythmic rumblings of the water rolling onto the sands filled the air. Closing her book, she looked out from the porch and gave her attention over to the ocean's song. She could read anytime, but the opportunity to luxuriate in the sound of breaking waves came for her only this one time a year. Turning her head in her son's direction, she noticed a kindred look of reverie on his face.

"Deep thoughts?" Margaret asked.

"No, not really," Amir responded, then, after a pause, changed his answer. "Well, sort of."

"Care to share?"

"I don't know. . . . I was thinking about how it feels like we've been coming here for so long. I can hardly remember myself back then. I barely spoke English. It seems like such a different world to me now, but listening to the waves I realize they've been crashing onto the shore here forever. It just seems funny how I could think of myself as having some kind of grasp on time, like I owned it or something, when really it's just the opposite. I mean, when you consider it, it hasn't been that long since that first time here. But to me it seems like forever. It's strange."

Margaret, her eyes rising to look out into the dark, paused for a few seconds before responding, "I feel the way you do, that we've been coming here forever, and at the same moment I feel as though it was only last week that we were here for the very first time. I can recall, like it was just yesterday, the wonder in the eyes of that little boy who saw the ocean for the very first time."

Amir smiled at his mother's words. His mind followed his eyes out to the sea, and his thoughts slowed and rested. After a time, he turned to look back at Margaret. She had gone back to her book, her head bent downward in concentration. Observing her as if from afar, he saw that she had aged. Just as a child steps into adulthood, from the one stage of life to the next, Margaret's body had moved from the early, graceful time of retirement into a frailer, more delicate period of decline.

Margaret, feeling her son's eyes upon her, looked up to see some unspoken question within them. And though she could see it wasn't directly addressed to her, she felt drawn to answer by patting the empty cushion next to where she sat on the wicker settee. Her face spoke her love of the boy. He had once asked, years ago after some small incident, whether she regretted having adopted him. Everyone, she understood, no less a child who'd been through what her adopted son had, needed the occasional reassurance of his or her loved ones. The warmth of her smile repeated the words she'd spoken to him then: that his entry into her life had been a great and wonderful gift that had brought with it a profound sense of fulfillment.

Amir rose from his chair and sat next to Margaret; the two of them listening to the wind and ocean, their eyes looking out into the darkness of night. Neither spoke, but they were linked in that quiet moment by the fate that had brought them together and joined their lives, one to the other, as mother and son. It was a state they often found themselves returning to, a bond they shared—the deaf-mute child was still there, indiscernible in the young man's body that had grown about the boy and now carried him into his adulthood.

The next day Amir excused himself from lunch and drove to Harwich Port to find the restaurant where Jadranka worked. After locating it, he parked his mother's car and waited some fifteen minutes before gathering the courage to enter. He told himself there was no reason he should feel so anxious and was confused as to why he would be overtaken by such emotion. Before stepping from the car he looked into the rearview mirror. His gaze met his eyes' reflection in empty stare, then scanned his face as though in search of something possibly amiss: a blemish, a strand of hair strayed from its proper place, or maybe just as much to see if he was there . . . the physical fact of his body not providing the necessary evidence, his mind feeling lost in foreign emotions speaking an unknown tongue. "Shit," he said, "come on." Running his fingers through his hair, Amir breathed deeply, continuing to talk to himself but now without spoken word. *God, get it together*, a part of him commanded. *She's only a friend, so what's the big deal?* a different voice asked. *Maybe I should come back another time. Jesus, what's the matter with me? Come on . . . straighten out.*

Shaking his head, Amir forced himself to open the car door and step outside. Entering the restaurant, he could feel a dampness grow under his arms and a drop of sweat trickle down the side of his forehead. He was met by a young hostess who asked if he was alone or whether there would be others joining him. The girl had a British accent and smiled at him. His eyes glanced nervously from her to the dining room and then back again. He seemed disoriented, and the hostess asked if he was looking for someone. He answered no, that he was by himself. The young hostess led him to a table set for two and handed him a menu. A few minutes later a waitress came by and filled his glass with water. Jadranka was nowhere to be seen. Amir was crestfallen and now felt much worse than when he had entered. He was filled with a despondency that felt infinitely heavier than the jangling nerves of his anxiety.

The waitress returned with a breadbasket, asking if he was ready to order, while the menu still lay unopened in front of him. She spoke in a heavily accented voice, perhaps Polish, Amir thought. During the summer it seemed that foreign students serving the tourist trade on seasonal work visas far outnumbered their American counterparts.

"I don't know if I'm really hungry," he said hesitating, looking up at the girl who simply shrugged, as if she didn't care one way or the other. "Do you know when Jadranka Pušić works?"

The waitress smiled her first real smile. The look on the boy's face was revealing. She had seen it before. "You must be the boyfriend, then?" she asked.

Amir's heart sank. He had never considered that Jadranka might have met someone during the summer. Seeing the boy's face go blank as if in shock, the waitress laughed.

"No, no. I only ask the question," she said, her smile broadening. "Jadranka, she is working now. In the back patio. Come with me. Perhaps you want to sit at her table, yes?"

He hadn't realized there was an outdoor eating area at the rear of the restaurant. Amir chided himself for having been so nervous as to have overlooked the passageway leading through the main dining hall to a large deck that bordered a saltwater creek behind the building.

"You can sit here," the waitress said, leading him to an empty table. "It is Jadranka's station."

As he took his seat, the girl flashed a playful grin in his direction and headed toward a set of doors that led from the deck to the kitchen. It was then that Amir finally saw Jadranka. She emerged from the swinging doors with a large tray hoisted just above her right shoulder, halting her march forward when the waitress who had seated him came up to her side and whispered something in her ear. Jadranka cast a look in his direction, her face seemingly neutral, only a small nod of her head indicating her recognition of him . . . though he thought he could see the light in her eyes brighten, bringing a nervous smile to his face. He watched her cross the deck to a nearby table, where she emptied her tray of its contents plate by plate, serving a party of four. When she was finished, she placed the tray on a stand and walked over in his direction.

"So, just passing by?" she asked.

"Yeah, just in the neighborhood, so I thought I'd drop by," Amir countered, his smile growing larger and surer.

"Hmmm," Jadranka responded, hands on her hips. She nodded her head as if in consideration, looking Amir over as she did so. Then, finally, she smiled too.

Playing the waitress, Jadranka pulled out a pen and order pad from her apron pocket. "You will be having something, then?" she asked. As she spoke, her head tilted back and slightly to the side, her eyebrows rising with the movement while the corners of her mouth returned to neutral position, her eyes assuming a playful, skeptical air. Amir sat silent for some few seconds without response. It was to him an impossibly beautiful gesture that spoke of some silent mystery lingering just beyond the bounds of his conscious reach. The short, graceful movement of her head had been like the trail of a string turning the corner of his vision, making him wonder where it might lead. It wasn't something he'd seen very often in the look of American girls. It belonged to another place and time, another way of life distant from the land he now called home.

"If you don't know what it is you want, it is a help to open the menu," Jadranka offered.

"Oh, sorry," Amir answered, quickly picking up the menu and fingering it, "but actually, I'm not really hungry."

Jadranka gave a questioning look, furrowing her brows to stare at Amir as a mother might to chide her child for some minor offense. The truth was, he was hungry, but he felt discomfited, his awkward presence surely a nuisance to the girl who stood there in front of him waiting for his words to make some sense. Her skin was soft, beautifully translucent . . . he felt its warmth radiate across the distance from where she stood.

"Um, I guess I'll just have an iced tea. That's all."

It was, Amir knew, a lame response. Later, when Jadranka brought him the drink, he finally was able to speak the reason he'd come. "What time do you get done with work? I thought maybe we could do something."

"The restaurant closes at ten o'clock tonight, but sometimes we aren't finished until eleven. Then we begin again in the morning."

Seeing his shoulders sink, Jadranka added that in the lull between the lunch and early dinner crowds she had a break. If he would like, she offered, they could take a short walk. The sky was clear and the sun strong as they strolled along the boardwalk of a nearby harbor. Amir felt a surge of happiness. Surprised at the strength of the emotion, his mind chose to see it as a force coming from the outside in, telling him his elevated mood was provided by the beautiful, brilliant sunlit day. He was unable or unwilling to understand that it might be its opposite: that his happiness traveled from the inside out and emanated from feelings that would continue to linger within him long after the sun had disappeared below the horizon. Before they went their separate ways, they arranged to see each other on Jadranka's lone day off the following week. She said she would love nothing more than to do the same as all of those whose hungry mouths she spent her days and nights satisfying—to go to the beach, swim in the water, and lie peacefully in the sun.

In the intervening days, Amir's thoughts often returned to Jadranka but were made less anxious by the arrival of his sister, Alice, and her family. Emily, now six years old, and Abigail, five, vied for their teenaged uncle's attention and kept him occupied on the beach and in the house, with near-constant requests for his presence. The two little girls were disappointed, then, when one day, as they prepared to head off to the beach, they saw him packing a picnic lunch and were informed that it wasn't meant for them. Amir was going off to visit a friend.

When he arrived at Jadranka's apartment, she was standing outside waiting, a small canvas bag looped around her arm. They exchanged greetings and the kind of small talk people of casual acquaintance might engage in.

"So, where do you want to go?" Amir asked, once they were seated in the car.

"To the beach, of course," Jadranka answered. "It is what we talked about, no?"

"Yes, but I mean, which beach?" Amir responded, feeling like less than the confident leader.

"You are the driver, so you must choose," Jadranka answered, smiling at the boy's nervous indecision.

"OK, let's go to one of the national park beaches then. I know a good one that's usually not too crowded."

When they arrived at the beach parking lot, Amir opened the trunk of his car and began to fill his arms with the cumbersome beach paraphernalia he had brought for their day on the sand, and Jadranka began to laugh. Under one arm, he tucked a beach umbrella, a blanket, two folding chairs, and towels. His other arm grasped a cooler and a large canvas bag.

"What's so funny?" Amir asked self-consciously.

"We are just like the people who come to my work," Jadranka smiled, taking the cooler from his hand. "You only need the funny hat and the sunburn. But it's good for me. I never get the chance to be the tourist."

It was, from her perspective, a distant view. Her days and nights were spent moving from table to table serving vacationers whose freedom to enjoy the sun and beach she could only envy. On her lone day off she normally slept late, went grocery shopping, ran errands, and attempted to keep up with the housecleaning she and the other young women with whom she shared her rundown quarters had put off.

Walking down the long run of sand, away from where the main concentration of beachgoers lay like a resting colony of seals, they spread their blanket, set the umbrella in the sand, stripped to their bathing suits, and walked out into the waves. Despite all of the careful management of their emotions, the two couldn't help but be aware of the other's body, now released from the veil of clothing. Amir's eyes were drawn to the beauty of Jadranka's barely clothed form—to the graceful length of her body, the curve of her neck flowing down to the bare slope of her back . . . to where the clear skin of her flesh met the cut of her bikini, mounding like the gentle rise of a dune. Catching himself, Amir forced his gaze outward toward the ocean.

When he removed his shirt, Jadranka's eyes took in the tanned, smooth skin of Amir's chest and arms. Lithe and wiry, his body could have been that of a younger boy, yet the way he carried it spoke of someone older.

Though they both felt the draw of physical attraction, they were circumspect in the direction of their attention. They spoke of the beach, the weather, school, and their summer, keeping the conversation to small, simple subjects while another communication, wordless and subconscious, carried on between them. They ate lunch, walked, swam, and even napped for a time before finally picking up their things to leave. Driving her home, Amir felt awkward. He was torn between asking her out to dinner and sensing that it was time to part. He was saved the internal debate when they arrived at Jadranka's apartment and she thanked him for the day at the beach, saying she would invite him in but unfortunately had a dozen chores to complete in her remaining free time.

"What about next week?" Amir asked as Jadranka moved to open the car door.

"I don't know which is my free day yet."

"I can call."

"We don't have a phone in our apartment, and at the restaurant they don't like the calls so much, you know? I can call you. Is that OK?"

Amir nodded and wrote down the phone number of his family's beach house, handing it to Jadranka. As he drove back home, his internal dialogue chattered in distracted thought, worried that Jadranka might not call, that she might forget, that something might come up to cause her to cancel . . . or, even worse, that she would decide she didn't want to bother. He was relieved when, several days later, as he was about to leave for the beach, the phone rang and Emily scampered over to answer it, quickly announcing that it was for Amir and that it was a girl. Afterward, while the grownups were, despite their curiosity, respectful of Amir's privacy, young Emily immediately began to question her Uncle Amir about the caller. Trying to maintain a neutral look in front of all the waiting faces, he said it was a friend from school, hoping to leave it at that.

"The same friend you visited last week? The girl?" Emily, as chief inquisitor, demanded happily, and before giving him a chance to answer her first questions added another. "What's her name?"

Her uncle answered in the affirmative to the first questions and "Jadranka" to the last, staving off any more questions with a laugh and a pleading look to his sister, Alice, to rescue him from his niece's prosecutorial zeal. Later, when Emily and her younger sister were out with their father, Margaret introduced the subject again, already having some knowledge of her son's friendship with the Bosnian girl. During the school year, Amir returned home often to spend time with his mother, and once a month he drove her to Boston for a weekend's visit with Alice and her grandchildren. On several occasions he had briefly mentioned his friendship with Jadranka to her, letting the tone of his voice say more than the few words he typically used when telling her about something of import to his life.

"How is Jadranka faring in her job?" Margaret asked.

"Good," Amir answered simply but without sign of reticence.

"So, tell me about this girl," Alice queried, wrapping an arm around Amir's shoulder and chest.

"Not much to tell," he answered, letting his body rest against his sister's. "She's a friend from school, that's all."

"She's from Bosnia, as I recall," Margaret added for Alice's benefit.

"Well, that's cool," Alice said. "Have you talked with her much about Bosnia?"

"No, not really."

"Hmm, what do you talk about then? Is there reason for me to be jealous?"

"No, never," said Amir, smiling.

"That's what I like to hear," Alice said, as she gave her brother a squeeze and kissed the hair atop his head.

"Why don't you invite her here?" Margaret suggested. "She might enjoy having a home-cooked meal after working in a restaurant all summer."

"OK, I can mention it," Amir answered in a tentative tone.

Chapter 23

When Amir invited her to his family's beach house, Jadranka felt several reactions surface concurrently within her. Her emotion had admitted to nothing more than friendship in her relationship with this young man. In Bosnia, to invite a young woman to meet a young man's family had significant meaning and was something she felt herself immediately pull back from. On the other hand, in her country, hospitality was valued and not to be indifferently brushed aside. It was, however, the look in Amir's eyes that finally brought her to accept the invitation. There had been a sense of prepared rejection about the musculature of his face, as though he felt that even to have asked the question had been an imposition. She could see that he sat waiting for her polite refusal. Jadranka felt trepidation about spending the day among these strangers, sure that they would focus keen eyes upon her. Yet she found herself smiling and saying she would be happy to have lunch with him and his family.

They arrived at the beach house just before noon and found Alice, Paul, Margaret, and the girls all in and around the kitchen in the midst of preparing lunch. When Amir made the introductions, Jadranka was surprised to see him indicate that it was the older of the two women who was his mother. Neither Jadranka nor Amir had spoken much about their families to one another. He had told her only the basics. His birth family had perished in the war. In his adoptive family there was no father, only the mother and one sibling, an older sister. Jadranka had said her father was dead. She'd had two siblings, a sister and a brother. But, like her father, the brother was no longer alive.

As she took Margaret's hand, Jadranka briefly held the woman's eyes before politely shifting her gaze away. Margaret noted that the girl stood erect, with shoulders squared and straight in the direction of the person she spoke to. There was cordiality about her bearing. The girl's body stood relaxed, as though in effort that others might feel so as well, a social grace Margaret guessed to have been a result of her upbringing. Yet there was, she felt, a more complex structure than the face of simple pleasantry might imply. She sensed the presence of undercurrents in Jadranka's body language that, along with a quiet reserve in her eyes, spoke of deeper emotion.

Margaret couldn't help but wonder if there could be, as with Amir, something within Jadranka that had been damaged and disillusioned by the experience of war. More than all the years of her professional life as a highly regarded psychologist, it was her time with Amir that had taught her to recognize the signs. She had learned to hear what her son said by what he didn't say, to see behind the apparent calm of his gaze a wariness that flickered like a nervous twitch.

Jadranka could see that Margaret's eyes had measured her, yet she felt no judgment in it. She noted no informality of body or mind in the woman's greeting, no sense of indolence that Jadranka often encountered when meeting other people. Many new acquaintances seemed to weigh and measure her, then wander away the moment they had probed her for the standard data and appropriately labeled and categorized her, as if they had grasped all there was to be seen of her and now, relieved of their social obligation, could return to the comfort of their own orb.

Jadranka followed as Amir and his mother led her to the back porch that overlooked the ocean. The vista was beautiful. Turning her gaze in Margaret's direction, Jadranka noted the way the mother and son stood next to one another with their bodies leaning ever so slightly in each other's direction, like plant to sun, in quiet, unspoken sharing. She wondered whether Amir's mother would feel possessive of him, see her as the interloper, even though she had no designs on him. If the mother was worried, Jadranka could tell her it was needless. She hadn't the slightest interest in becoming involved with her son—nor with any man, for that matter. She and Amir were friends. That was all.

They ate lunch on the porch, an informal buffet of salads and sandwich makings. It wasn't the typical American mealtime the Bosnian girl had become used to in her two years in the country, but rather, it reminded her of one she might enjoy back home. There was a sense of patience, of easy and casual ritual that had them all seated before any one person made a move toward food. Water was poured, plates were passed and filled, and nothing eaten. Only when everyone's meal sat in front of them did they begin to eat, and then but slowly, allowing the conversation predominance over the food.

For Jadranka, the social intercourse brought with it a sense of the familiar. There had, of course, been a few questions asked about her, but they had been of general nature. Alice made an effort to find subjects to put the girl at ease, and that they, as women, found easy link to. Paul and the two little girls, charmed by their visitor, invited her to their play on the beach in sand and water. Jadranka's day ended with a long, delightful dinner on the same porch where lunch had been served, the Bosnian girl's initial trepidation dissipated in an environment that made her both feel at home and miss her own family terribly.

There was little time left to summer before the two college students were to return for the start of another school year. Jadranka had but a few days of vacation between leaving her job and her first day back at school. At Amir's invitation, she spent those days with his family. By the last day with them, she was surprised to find herself feeling in a strangely vulnerable state.

On the final evening of her visit, she sat outside on the screened-in porch with Amir, looking out at the ocean and thinking about her life. The rest of his family had removed themselves to their bedrooms early, partly because it was near the hour of their retirement, though in greater measure because they sensed the young couple wanted time to themselves. Amir and Jadranka's conversation drifted from talk of their impending return to college to a topic of shared experience neither had yet broached with the other. They sat next to each other on the divan that often served as Amir's sleeping place, their backs resting on the cushions that leaned up against the house.

"You are lucky," Jadranka said, turning to look at Amir. "You have a very nice family."

He returned her smile and met her eyes, responding that yes, he was lucky. After a few seconds of quiet, she asked where his home in Bosnia had been, and he named the village he was from. "So, you were a farm boy, then?" she asked. "Yes," he smiled in reply.

"And your other family, there is nobody left?" Jadranka ventured, her voice going soft.

"I have some distant relatives, but nobody I really know," he answered. "Margaret was able to eventually find them after my adoption, and we exchanged some letters back and forth for awhile. But then, I don't know . . . I guess we all just let it go."

The talk of Bosnia and his family began to open doors to rooms of memory long closed, and suddenly Amir was reminded of a girl he had once known. It seemed a lifetime ago. Her name was Sanela, Sanela Oric. She had been a friend of his sister, Minka, and he'd had a nine-year-old-boy's crush on her. She would have been fourteen at the time, almost a woman to a boy of his age back then. Her nose and mouth had been small and delicate, their beauty understated by the high rise of her cheekbones and the round, dark embers of eyes that seemed to always glow with warmth. If you placed Sanela and Jadranka side by side they could easily be taken for sisters. He didn't know why he hadn't seen the similarities in their faces before. He wondered where Sanela was now . . . if she was anywhere at all.

Amir's smile was sad, yet his eyes did not look downward or away, and the conversation edged carefully forward as he and Jadranka volunteered small pieces of their past, one at a time, checking at every interval to see if they had reached the boundaries of the other's comfort. They understood that their relationship was made complicated by circumstances of a past far beyond their control. Whatever the nature of their personal connection might be, it was weighted by a heavier one that, if not approached carefully, could fall down upon them and crush the fragile link that drew them one to the other.

When their friendship had first begun, when the pull of their mutual attraction had forced them to consider the strength of its gravity, there had been an immediate and unspoken understanding that their relationship would for the time remain platonic, and that events long held private, even from their own view, would remain as such, unless or until they were broached by the one who had lived them. Now, resting on the daybed, looking into each other's eyes, the sound of the ocean in their ears, only a few dulled spots of light shining from the curtained windows above to break the dark of the starry night, the two children of the Bosnian War could feel the tectonic shift of deep, hidden emotion. With great caution, they took a step in the sharing of a past they recounted as much for their own ears to hear as for the other's, braving the subject of the war in hope of some small ebbing of its grasp on the present and its seemingly relentless ownership of the future.

Amir began the story of his family's end, recounting simply and factually the general details of the paramilitary soldiers' attack on his family's home. He then went on to briefly tell the events of his subsequent exile, both the external and the internal—the deaf-mute boy by some miracle finding a home in a universe he'd thought forever destroyed.

After a moment of silence, Jadranka said that she and her sister, brother, and parents had been sent to Omarska. That her father and brother had died there. She looked into Amir's eyes as she spoke the concentration camp's name to see if he understood. It was like saying "Auschwitz," except that few people had ever heard of Omarska and its dark secret of hidden genocide. In the beginning days of the war thousands of civilians had been captured in and around the area of Prijedor in northern Bosnia, many of whom were never seen again. How many of the "disappeared" perished in the camp, which had been set up in an open-pit iron mine that lay outside the town of Omarska, was never clearly ascertained. The camp was shut down six months after its inception, when photos of the camp's prisoners appeared in the international press: emaciated men with shorn heads and with bodies whose bones seemed almost to protrude through their sallow skin, their sunken faces framing hollow eyes that belonged more to the dead than the living.

Jadranka saw the musculature of Amir's face and upper torso grab tight at the mention of Omarska. Margaret, who had read every book there was to read on the Bosnian War, had put the best of them aside in her library . . . for when Amir reached an age and a point in his life at which he might be ready to take in their content. In his last year of high school, when the subject of the Bosnian War came up in the course of his studies, Amir attempted to brave the reading of the books. He had not gotten far into the first one when the name Omarska appeared, followed by stories not to be found in high school history textbooks. The recounting of the horrors that took place there—the serial beatings, tortures, rapes, murders, and the infamous white house where much of the camp's most horrific brutality took place—were too much for the boy to bear, and he had quickly replaced the book back on its shelf, never wanting to touch it again.

When Jadranka had spoken the word "Omarska"—her eyes meeting his as the word sounded from her mouth—Amir felt like a coward. She had looked at him to see if he understood the meaning that the name of the camp held. But there was more to her look than that. She wanted someone to share her terrible secrets with. She wanted him, who could understand, to listen, to help free her from some small piece of the terrible pain that owned her. But his eyes stopped her, invoked their unspoken agreement. Without hesitation she moved on, the grace of her acceptance making him feel all the worse for his inability to confront his fears. With his camera for shield, his quiet demeanor for cloak, and his silence for sanctuary, the little rabbit still hid. Then a voice spoke its angry emotion within Amir's head: *And what good is life, if you live it as a coward every day you wake to the sun?*

The voice within him sought no equitable judgment but only condemnation. No matter what rational reasoning that proved his innocence, he had survived while his family had been murdered. Both Margaret and Dr. Caron had tried to help him understand that feelings of culpability stemming from traumas like the ones he had undergone were common but at the same time irrational. As an eleven-year-old, he could have done nothing to change the outcome of the event. Yet even as Amir heard their words and understood them to be true, a sorrow deep inside of him couldn't let go of the guilt.

During this internalized struggle, his body, pulled by a force of gravity beyond his control, moved into Jadranka's arms, who, equally affected, drew into his. There, lost to her warmth, the ghosts of Amir's past dimmed, paled, and retreated. The gravitational pull exerted itself still further and the two lay down upon the daybed, where, cradled in each other's arms, they fell asleep, the pulsing of their hearts falling into synchronous beat with the rhythmic pounding of the surf, their dreams carrying them gently to a safe haven.

Chapter 24

Beginning his second year of school, Amir felt as though he had stepped into a world of larger dimension. His sense of being had begun to blossom and expand, and hope was no longer an emotion he felt he had to hold at bay for fear that it could be nothing more than a dream. It had actually arrived and brought with it more than just a promise, an expectation of good, and a potential of future. There was Jadranka. There was the finding of his talent as a filmmaker, validated by the honor of an award and an internship. There were all the new friends he had made at school.

Amir saw that hope had, in truth, been there all along. It had been there when he was in the refugee camp, when the UN volunteer had found a way to get him relocated far away from the war zone. It was there when Margaret had become his foster mother and then adopted him and given him back a family to love and be loved by. He thought of how his father, Asaf, would have wanted him to be strong, to be brave and not succumb to the voices that would have him hide from life, fearful and without hope. His mother would have wanted him to love, to have braved his emotions. And Minka was there too, in the form of Alice, who cared for him, took interest and pride in him, her touch on his shoulder full of sisterly love.

But even as the voices of gloom within him were pushed to the periphery of his mind, they had not been banished. Amir no longer saw Dr. Caron, but the physician's experienced counsel had taught him that what he had suffered as a child was not a thing that could be shed as might an illness, from simple medication and rest. The results of the trauma would likely revisit him for years to come, if not for the rest of his life. They would come and go, Dr. Caron had said. It wasn't about defeating them, burying them deep within the past. It was about learning how to cope with them, to become aware of their visitations upon him, to recognize their arrival, and to not confuse them with the present moment in which he was living.

Moderating voices within Amir spoke to him of caution about feelings that had begun to spin bright, idealistic futures of himself in his mind. The voices repeated Margaret's advice about pacing himself through the highs and lows, the varying landscapes that all people face in one form or another. Even the luckiest people on earth have burdens to deal with, she had cautioned. Good fortune itself could even potentially become an obstacle to growth and fulfillment.

Leaving behind the relative security of dorm life for the freedom of off-campus housing, Amir decided to share a rambling, rundown, five-bedroom house with a group of students from his school. As the last one in, his choice of bedroom had come by default, yet that room would have been his first pick. What had for his roommates been the room's major detractions seemed to Amir merely minor inconveniences compared to all of its benefits. True, one had to walk up three flights of stairs to the attic to reach it. And then back down a flight again every time he needed to use the bathroom. And the room had no heat. But if you left the door open, the heat from below would rise. That, and a small space heater, he was advised by the others, would make it bearable in the winter.

When Amir first saw the room he immediately felt at home. It was perched high, and if he looked out through the large, mullioned window at its gable end he was greeted by the great, green crown of an old oak that graced the home's backyard. The space was large and open. The room's side walls reached to nearly shoulder height before intersecting the roof, which was supported by beautiful, old rafters, the resulting cathedral ceiling opening up the entire south-facing gable end for the arched window that flooded the room with light.

Amir proudly showed his new living space to Jadranka on his second day in residence, when he had yet to furnish it with more than a mattress and desk. She laughed in appreciation of his enthusiasm and said the room did indeed have real character, leaving unspoken her thought that he might perhaps be a bit naïve to believe his roommates' assurances that the space could be adequately heated in the dead of winter.

As their feelings toward each other slowly advanced in physical expression, Jadranka had been comforted to see that Amir was content to move at the pace she set. It seemed that, for his own needs, he wanted her to take the lead in its progression . . . even though it was Amir who, after their last night spent together at the beach house, braved the acknowledgement of their now more-than-just-friends relationship by taking her hand when they first met back at school. Jadranka's experience in the war had made her intensely wary of men, sometimes, it seemed, irrationally so. She often found herself shuddering at a male's advance, even a benign and ultimately kind one. After what she had experienced at Omarska, sorting men who had good intentions from those who didn't had become an exercise of complex nature.

If a certain amount of anxiety played within Amir's emotions at what appeared to be the beginning of a first love, it was to an extent mitigated by his immersion into his studies, which now, in his second year, allowed him to concentrate more of his efforts on his chosen major. An idea for a film had been brewing inside of him since early summer, and the environs of the film department—the sight of cameras, editing rooms, and students busy about their work—helped to quickly focus his thoughts on the project whose storyline had already begun to play in his imagination.

The idea for his project had begun as a simple visual image that arose in his mind like a photograph, a still shot of an object that lingered briefly in the camera's eye, unmoving, and in so doing had the possibility of turning it into a symbol that held a deeper meaning. He had first been struck by this possibility of view in a Kurosawa-directed film, *Dersu Uzula*. In a number of its scenes, Amir felt the density of the physical imagery pass from an object into something far more profound than its simple, material form.

The young filmmaker's idea was that he would film a single category of objects—doors. He couldn't see exactly what it was he was after, though he could feel it. As integral as wall or roof to any construction, doors abounded in the human realm. They served to permit or deny access, protect and keep out unwanted intrusions, to invite in those whose company was welcomed. They existed, as well, in nonmaterial form. Their manifestation within the human psyche was as myriad as their physical counterparts. Amir had seen the swinging of invisible doors in the act of opening and closing inside of himself and others untold times, the awareness of their action most often lost to the routine of everyday life.

Jadranka and Amir made time to meet almost daily. Each of their schedules was full; between classes, study, and projects there was only limited time, and some days they met only briefly, to share a meal at the dining hall or study in the library side by side. The only free time to be counted on, that each of them always had at their disposal, were the late hours of the evening, the time of sleep. But neither had yet to approach this possibility, the physical nature of their relationship straining to find its way past barriers of nervous caution.

Given Amir's intense involvement with the production of his new film while he was trying to keep up with the rest of his other course load, Jadranka was surprised when he told her that he had agreed to help his former professor, Dr. Ashrawi, create video clips for an Internet website. Jadranka chided Amir for being such easy prey to Zack's imposition and cautioned him about becoming involved with the man, especially given the events of the recent weeks. The 9/11 attacks were not even a month past, and the country was still reeling from shock.

"There are people who do not like Zack's politics," Jadranka warned. "Now he will become like the bull's-eye. It is not so smart to stand too close to him."

"I'm not planning on it," Amir smiled in response. "I don't think it will be much work. Anyway, the attack on the World Trade Center didn't have anything to do with Zack's politics. It's nothing to do with the Palestinians. They're saying it's a group in Afghanistan called Al-Qaeda."

"Does it matter? You haven't seen this before?" Jadranka asked. The Bosnian girl fought to keep her cynicism at bay, but her life experience didn't make it easy. "There are men who make of things what they want them to be. And there are many whose ears are easy audience for their twisted words. It happened in our country. You think it can't happen in this country as well?"

"I know, but I think it's going the other way here," Amir spoke with a nod of his head, a gesture meant to assure himself as much as Jadranka. "People are stopping to think how such a terrible thing could happen, to ask what could cause such hatred in others that they could do something like this."

Throwing her head back, Jadranka blocked the sarcasm about to escape her mouth, allowing it only the look on her face. She knew something about these things. She had little doubt that the time of American reflection, the talk of trying to find ways toward a more peaceful world, would soon give way to those whose purposes were not served by hope but who saw in vengeance a more useful, pliable tool to help direct the path of their interests. Jadranka found herself momentarily annoyed with Amir.

"Look," Amir continued, filling in the pause, "the videos Zack wants me to make into clips are to gather support for the families in the Palestinian refugee camps. That's not a bad thing. They need help. People have no idea what it's like to live in those places. But don't worry, I'm not going to become one of Zack's *mujahideen*." Amir paused, the look on his face changing from serious to lighthearted. "Although I did go to prayer with him after we talked."

"Are you becoming religious, then? Maybe you will have to stop seeing such a corrupted woman like me?" Jadranka responded, her voice taking on the same tone of banter as his.

"I was going to talk to you about that. You know Muslim women are supposed to be obedient," Amir smiled, reaching out to take Jadranka's hand.

"Hummm, and now I suppose you want me to wear the hijab whenever I go out?"

"No, I was thinking of something more proper. Like a burqa."

"Then maybe that is enough of the going to prayer for you. You'd better be careful or soon you will be running off to the *madrasa* college to become an imam."

"I think you're the one who should be careful. You engage in unholy practices like yoga and meditation. The imams will declare you a blasphemer."

"They are lazy old men who do anything to keep from sharing the housework. You think God, she sits in paradise with nothing better to do than keeping one eye on the clock and the other on us? You are all the same, you men. Christian, Jew, or Muslim, it makes no difference. I can see you are trying to make me mad, and I'll prove to you it doesn't work. But just for trying it, you are going to take me to dinner. So do not even think about working on this movie of yours tonight."

Grinning, Amir agreed to the evening out, happy for the distraction from all of his schoolwork and the terrible and unimaginable events that had so recently caused the deaths of so many innocent people. Seeing the news photos of the World Trade Center in flames, the falling bodies and collapsing buildings, he heard a dark, low hum of despair arise in distant chambers of his mind like a sudden wind singing the portent of a coming storm.

When the shooting of his new film, *Doors*, was finally completed, Amir began the work of cutting and re-splicing the lab print he had made from selected footage. He then used the copy print to work out the editing before making the final version from the original, knowing any mistake made on that precious film would be irreparable and cost him dearly. Amir took the print to a viewing room, placed the reel onto the projector, and watched it as if seeing the film for the first time.

After the six-minute movie had run, Amir sat quietly pondering his work. His initial viewing of the film had left him feeling as one might when looking into a mirror on a good day: surprised and pleased to find an attractive and pleasant face staring back. Happy, he replayed the film several more times. With each succeeding viewing, however, the movie's flaws began to grow increasingly apparent to him. It was the same mirror and the same face that he had stared at minutes before, yet now its reflection brought disappointment—the handsome face had vanished and been replaced by one ordinary at best. Returning to the editing room, Amir reclused himself for the remainder of the day, until his eyes grew too tired to focus and his mind too fatigued to function. Suffering doubts that his short film would ever amount to anything more than a jumble of empty and meaningless scenes of doors doing nothing more than opening and closing in pretentious attempt at artistry, he returned home to the comfort of his attic room.

Jadranka had not seen Amir since the day before, an absence unremarkable within the bounds of an ordinary friendship. But both understood that their relationship had evolved, even though their emotional bond had yet to be matched by an equally intimate physical union, something each nervously anticipated though neither had yet attempted to initiate. But even as Jadranka's mind maintained the rationale of a right moment appearing of its own accord on some future day, there was another part of her demanding that she abandon the illusion of such a prescribed construct.

Debating whether to call Amir or to wait for him to contact her, Jadranka decided she was being ridiculous. As she walked up to his attic room, something inside her knew she had come for a purpose whose premeditation her conscious mind would only later come to acknowledge. She had grown weary of waiting for the right moment. The strength of her need had finally risen to decry her mind's cautions; it was in the arms of a lover that she might find her healing, not in evasion of the terrible memories of a brutal past.

Climbing the stairway to Amir's room, Jadranka heard music. The door to Amir's bedroom stood half open, speaking neither an invitation nor a prohibition. Jadranka paused, a part of her stammering excuses to leave Amir to his work, then questioning why she had come in the first place, when she had so much work of her own. The force of her desire shut off the dialogue of doubt, pushing past both it and the door to enter the room. There she saw Amir lying on his bed, quiet and unmoving, his head faced away from her in direction of the large, arched window that overlooked the backyard. His eyes did not move when she entered, even though the sound of the door swinging open made her arrival obvious. A television sat on top of a tall bureau in front of his bed, its glare calling her attention. Nearby, sitting between the television and the bed, a camera mounted on a tripod stood aimed in his direction. Connected to the television by cable, the camera lens pointed at Amir. Neither program nor movie was playing on the set. Instead, the image of Amir's face looked out from the screen, staring so still and quietly that it appeared more like a single frame frozen in place than it did the live video feed it was.

The sound of someone entering reached Amir in delayed reaction, the trance he had fallen into having lulled his sense of time and place into the realm of daydream. Only after a few seconds had passed did his hand reach out for the remote laying by his side. Amir pressing one of its buttons, the camera lens responded, zooming out and taking in a broader swath of the room to reveal the visitor's face on the television screen. Jadranka appeared there, it seemed to him, like a mirage standing in the doorway. Looking into the television screen, Jadranka saw a soft, gentle smile appear on Amir's face. For a moment both remained still and silent, as if in this way they could be freed of not only time and space, but also of all the complications of self that inhibited the words their hearts would speak.

"You are very weird," Jadranka said, finally breaking the silence, shaking her head.

Amir said nothing, his smile broadening, though whether from self-consciousness or the fatalistic acceptance of her words it was not clear.

"Are you making a movie of yourself now, to become the big star?" she asked with a teasing laugh.

"No, the camera isn't recording," said Amir, smiling. "It's just a live feed. Like looking into a mirror."

"I won't ask why you are doing it, then," Jadranka said with another shake of her head. "What is the music you are playing?" she asked, walking farther into the room to sit by his side and meet his eyes without aid of the television screen.

"Nusrat Fateh ali Kahn," he answered.

"It is very nice."

"Yeah, I like it a lot."

"So how is your movie? Why aren't you working on it?"

"Not good. It sucks. I'm taking a break."

"Yes, maybe a break is good idea," Jadranka smiled, taking his hand in hers.

They looked at each other without speaking for some moments, their eyes meeting like naked bodies, a small blush of red coloring Amir's cheeks. A breath, something between a sigh and laugh, escaped from Jadranka's throat. Her free hand reached up to Amir's forehead and moved his hair backward with a gentle sweep. Bending forward, she kissed the cleared area above his brow. He lay there not moving, his eyelids closing at the touch of her lips, opening afterward to take in the smooth contours of her face as it moved away from his. Jadranka's hand went to his cheek and touched it, pausing, then slipped down to his chest to linger in his body's warmth.

Freeing her other hand from his, she ran her fingers along the short, flat curve of his collarbone. Lifting the hand that rested on his chest, Jadranka began to unbutton Amir's shirt. She pulled the fabric to each side, revealing the slow rise and fall of his ribs in silent, synchronous movement with his breath. Her right hand moved to rest over his heart, the thump, thump of its beat reverberating into her palm, streaming up through her arm until it reached the source of her own pulse. Her eyes, which had been gazing at the unblemished landscape of his chest, looked up to see his face. Amir smiled, then closed and opened his eyes in a long, slow blink.

"You look just as beautiful from the back," he said, the low hum of a soft, warm laugh edging forth from his throat.

Jadranka turned her head around to gaze in the direction of the television and saw Amir smiling at her on the screen.

"You are a strange one, my American boy," Jadranka murmured softly as she turned back to face him.

Amir smiled, showing embarrassment, timidity, mischievousness, even a little pride—but most of all happiness. He liked it when she called him her "American boy." Mostly, she said it in moments of affection, though also at times when she became annoyed with him. The pet name she had given him strangely made him feel more a Bosnian boy than one from his new homeland. He lifted his right hand and brought it to her collarbone, where it fell to rest upon her breast, the warmth of the one melding into the other.

Picking up the remote control that lay next to Amir, Jadranka pushed its power button, shutting down the television, the room dimming along with it, only the light of a single lamp illuminating the space. In the dimmed light, the hands of the clock turned in irrelevant motion as the two lovers removed their clothing and lay down next to one another, their time having finally come.

Later, mingled in body and silence, their eyes opened to one another—to smiles, and then to laughter.

"What just happened?" Jadranka asked, the glow on her face like a setting sun.

"I don't know," Amir answered, trying to look back in on the known world, suffering the same disorientation she did.

And the two laughed again, laughed like water flowing. Amir and Jadranka talked in between contented silences, as the clock still turned with wasted effort for the young lovers operating outside its boundaries. Holding each other, they feel asleep . . . for a moment having returned to the homes they'd lost so long ago and thought never to know again.

Chapter 25

When they met now, there was an embarrassed hesitancy, a vulnerability of emotion that hadn't been there before. Both a new intimacy and an uncertainty had come to their relationship, making it at once easier to be in each other's presence and at the same time more tentative and anxious. Jadranka and Amir navigated the beginnings of their love affair slowly and with caution, neither wanting to press upon the other, nor fear being pressed upon themselves . . . attachment and obligation seesawing back and forth in search of balance, the fulcrum hidden from view.

Jadranka began to spend more and more nights at Amir's. Although she still maintained her room in the apartment she shared with two other girls, by the time winter came she had effectively come to live with Amir in his attic perch. On the coldest nights, even with a space heater blasting and the door swung fully open to gather what heat they could from below, the room felt more like a walk-in refrigerator than a bedroom in a heated home. The two huddled next to each other on the bed, a down quilt pulled on top of them and bunched up around their shoulders, while they attended to their studies. After a time, they would rest and chat or perhaps watch the downward migration of a million small, white flakes fall past the window, silhouetted against the black of night . . . or forget the outside world entirely and burrow underneath the down shield of their quilt to hibernate in the warm afterglow of their lovemaking.

On Sundays, Jadranka often accompanied Amir on visits to his mother's house, which brought forth memories of her own home, making the distance from her loved ones seem less acute. Since she had come to study in America, Jadranka had been able to return to Bosnia only one time to visit her family. Her father and brother having been killed in the war, only her mother and older sister were left. She communicated with them often by phone and email. She missed them dearly, though there continued an underlying tension of her having left to attend college so far from home, something her mother had wished her not to do. Her mother had remarried a widower, a Muslim who had lost his wife during the bombing of Sarajevo, and there, too, had risen another issue—one of faith. Jadranka's father, a lawyer of Croat descent, had never been a believer in either his culture's majority faith or any other. Christian, Muslim, Jew, Hindu, it was all the same to him. Although he felt it understandable that in the face of the unknowable people should gather around religious convention to comfort themselves, he had never been tempted to take that road himself.

After the war, her mother had taken solace in her faith. Jadranka's older sister, too, had found a place of refuge in Islam. Jadranka, however, unlike many young Bosnians of Muslim descent, felt no pull to find an anchor for identity in religion after the trauma of the war—something that previous to the conflict held little sway in their thoughts. Intellectually, Jadranka had always been her father's daughter, and she agreed with him in many matters, including religion. Over time, though, her viewpoint had begun to grow less tolerant than his.

If Jadranka could be accused of cynicism when it came to religion and politics, she felt no shame in it, though often enough that within her that still held hope caused her to feel conflicted and confused. The war had cleft her being, creating a great chasm within her—on the one side, a belief in humankind, a hope that its evolution would eventually move human society beyond the kinds of horrors she experienced as a child; and on the other a bitter, despairing conviction that beneath the surface of its civilized face, humanity was motivated wholly by self-interest and suffered a blood lust unmatched by any other living creature.

For Amir, the Bosnian War had become a distant specter and, if not completely exorcised, felt sufficiently remote that he was able to substantially put it out of mind. Jadranka both envied and resented his sense of detachment from it, seeing it on the one hand as freedom, on the other as fearful denial. Amir had escaped the war in its early stages, but she'd lived through not only the whole of it, but also the reverberations of its aftereffects, which persisted in Bosnia to that very day and were likely to do so for years to come.

The warming air and growing daylight lured Amir and Jadranka, like animals waking from torpid winter sleep, from their lair and signaled the approaching end of another school year. As his second year at college drew to a close, Amir felt his past fall into what most people believed to be its proper place: into that which had been and no longer was. The war in his homeland had given way to an uneasy, unhappy peace, and he had settled into a new life in a new country that offered him the possibility of a promising future. Yet he was to discover that the past is not so easily relegated to the memories that wander through the mind in moments of incidental or sentimental recall. Its touch reaches into the present with quiet, persistent persuasion, and if fate so wills it, travels full circle to become the future.

One warm and sunny Saturday, Amir and Jadranka were invited to a "spring blast" at the house of a casual friend. By the time each had finished their schoolwork the day had gone by. They thought about going to see a movie, but none appeared promising, so they opted to attend the party instead, even though it wasn't the kind of event they were inclined to attend.

The evening event, attended by a diverse group of revelers from a variety of schools, was in full swing by the time Amir and Jadranka arrived. After being greeted by their hosts, the young couple wound their way through crowded rooms looking for Jadranka's roommates, who had also been invited. They found the two girls standing among a small group of mutual friends, the gravitational pull of the familiar quickly absorbing Amir and Jadranka into its field.

The light, jovial conversation within their group was suddenly interrupted by a loud chant that arose from across the room, "U-S-A, U-S-A," followed by a loud cheer and the downing of beers. Smiles drew across the faces of those with whom Jadranka and Amir were standing, some sardonic and others indulgent, as they looked across the room to see Brian Larkin, a classmate, standing among the chanters. With a salute and a nod of his head, Brian sent them a mocking wink while waving for them to come over and join in another toast to the USA. His other hand was firmly wrapped around a plastic cup whose journeys to the keg had not been infrequent that evening.

The conversation within the smaller, quieter group dropped off as they saw Brian making his way in their direction. Brian had passed by to mingle with the group several times before. The more he drank, the more inclined he seemed to try and artfully stir some small polemic—his face carrying a smile held just a notch tauter than a smirk, his eyes flashing a twinkle that said he went about it all tongue in cheek. The last time he'd come round, Brian had brought up the subject of Zack Ashrawi, the professor's name recently having commanded headlines in the local newspaper and well beyond. In an innocent voice, Brian had asked Amir how his former mentor was doing, insinuating a close enough relationship between the two that, given Zack's recent troubles, assumed Amir would have intimate knowledge of the man's emotional state.

A conservative columnist had recently printed videotaped excerpts from some talks that Dr. Ashrawi had given in the mid-1990s, in which he had shouted in Arabic, "Long Live Palestine, Death to Israel!" Ashrawi had damned both the Israeli and the American governments for their roles in the deaths of innocent Palestinians. The newspaper article also quoted unidentified sources within the Federal Bureau of Investigation as saying that Dr. Ashrawi and the charity fund he managed for Palestinian orphans were under investigation for suspected ties to terrorist organizations.

Given the tragedy of 9/11, not even a year past, the article had been quickly picked up by a nationally televised conservative news show. The school had been immediately bombarded with hate mail and phone calls threatening violence. Emails arrived containing computer viruses, and the college experienced a sudden and dramatic drop in alumni giving. A raging controversy erupted within the college community when its board of trustees, reacting to the negative onslaught, voted to suspend Dr. Ashrawi with pay. But the school's legal counsel cautioned the board of trustees that they, in fact, had little grounds for firing the professor. Soon thereafter, Dr. Ashrawi was reinstated, the college saying they could find no immediate evidence of any wrongdoing. The trustees, however, quickly ordered a more thorough and comprehensive investigation into the professor's activities, hoping to buy time and ease the brunt of the controversy. Although he was soon back to teaching, it was clear that Zack's troubles were far from over.

"Hey, people," Brian Larkin called out jovially to his schoolmates. "What's up? I want you to meet my man, Lenny, here," he said, introducing a new acquaintance he had brought over from the group of patriotic chanters.

A round of hellos followed in polite reply. Jadranka greeted the two and then turned to her roommate, Chris, to continue a conversation she'd purposely initiated as a foil when she saw the two begin their approach. Jadranka had little use for Brian's game play, his probing for soft spots with smiling sarcasms and joking digs. She had felt more than a little annoyed when he had come by earlier and started talking about the Zack Ashrawi controversy, addressing Amir as Zack's "protégé." Jadranka had been left not knowing who she was angrier at: Brian for his negative charade or Amir for the passivity with which he let himself be made its target.

"So hey, listen up, everybody," Brian spoke out, commanding everyone's attention. "Let's give a big hand for Lenny here. He's just enlisted to go off and fight in the war."

There was no trace of hidden sarcasm in Brian's voice now, for the moment his game forgotten. Lenny was met by a chorus of good wishes but no emotional chant of their country's initials. There were those among the small group of well-wishers whose politics made them hesitate, but the patriotic fervor rolling across the country with tsunami-like force caused them to hold their doubt to private consideration.

"Cool, yeah, thanks dudes," Lenny mumbled. The soon-to-be soldier's eyes rested high in their sockets, floating on a mixture of sangria, beer, vodka, and whatever other drink had been at hand.

"When do you leave?" someone asked.

"Huh?" Lenny answered, distracted by the slug of beer he was drinking, his alcohol-dulled mind slow to realize the question had been directed to him. The future soldier turned in Jadranka's direction, thinking the words had come from her. She repeated the question the other person had asked, indicating it had been they, not her, who had spoken to him. Lenny seemed not to hear the reference to the original questioner. Instead he looked at Jadranka and said that he would be leaving for basic training as soon as school let out. Jadranka smiled and nodded her head in acknowledgement but added nothing to continue the conversation.

"Hey, how about you? Where do you go to school?"

"Franklin," Jadranka answered.

"So, what's your name anyway?" Lenny asked.

"Jadranka," she replied pleasantly, though with neutral tone, her body clearly speaking its wish to end the encounter and move on.

"Danka," Lenny repeated in error, oblivious of the girl's cues. "Cool name. You got a nice accent. I like it. Where you from?"

Jadranka sighed, pausing, and returned his gaze without response. What to the others appeared simply a drunken nuisance was to her something of altogether much less innocent nature. After Omarska, there wasn't a man she didn't look at and first wonder what he might be capable of. She had experienced firsthand exactly how thin the membrane of civilized decorum could be and, once punctured, how easily it could spew out unimaginable evil and cruelty.

"The Balkans," Brian answered in the absence of any response coming from Jadranka.

"Where?" Lenny asked, his head tilting backward as if to gain a better vantage point from which to view the world's geography.

"You know, Serbia, Kosovo, all that," Brian explained, his mind meandering lazily through its intoxication to come up with an answer.

"Oh, yeah," Lenny said, little interested, his eyes scanning Jadranka's breasts. "That's cool."

Brian giggled, seeing Lenny trying to hit on Jadranka. He didn't register the rising tension within her body and the anger growing in her eyes.

"Bosnia and Herzegovina," Jadranka responded in correction, pointedly looking at Brian.

"Oh, sorry," Brian grinned, the whole thing too funny.

"Yeah, yeah," Lenny mumbled, then added his best imitation of a debonair smile. "So how about you and me go get a refill and you can tell me all about Serbia or whatever?"

Jadranka turned her head away from the boy, not wanting to waste words in response. This was her third year living in the United States, and she was well accustomed to its citizens' ignorance of her country and the war that had torn it apart.

"No, no Lenny, it's not Serbia, it's Bosnia and Haresgonia," Brian said, slurring his words as he addressed his drinking buddy. "That's the place we went in and saved the day. Remember? We saved them first, and then Kosovo later."

"You saved us?" Jadranka asked incredulously, looking toward Amir for support.

"Yeah, USA, babe," Lenny answered with drunken assertion.

A smile drew across Jadranka's mouth, an expression that was in polar contrast to the one in her eyes. Her mind engaged two conversations at once: one was internal and spoken in a silent, angry, bitter voice; the second was external and expressed in a calm, leading, matter-of-fact tone.

"And when was that?" Jadranka asked out loud, holding her smile with quizzical face as if she herself needed clarification of the war's history.

"When the Marines came," Lenny answered, grinning at the quickness of his own wit.

"And what year was that, exactly?" Jadranka queried, no longer bothering to hide the contempt of her anger's voice. The ethnic cleansing of Bosnia had been allowed to continue unabated for two years before any intervention by NATO forces that even then had been token and ineffectual.

"Whatever," Lenny answered, not having missed the angry sarcasm in her voice. "What difference does it make? We came and saved their butts, that's all that counts."

Lenny, in fact, knew little if anything of the actual history of the Bosnian War. The few partial and often-enough distorted facts he'd garnered second- or third-hand from school or the news were lost to a thousand other pieces of unsubstantiated information that made up the bulk of his worldview.

Jadranka nodded her head, holding her voice for fear of screaming her anger. Her breath, tight in her chest, constricted her vocal chords, blocking the sound that might exit her mouth and speak words she herself didn't want to hear. "What difference?" she would have asked if she had let her words out into the open. "I will tell you the difference it made. While the world turned its head those bastards came to our town and beat the little boys to death with their rifle butts because they said they were enemy soldiers."

Those words having been spoken, others would have followed, ones whose volume would have grown louder in anger and pain.

"They raped the girl next door . . . not just one of the men, but all of them," she would have shouted. "After they were done, they tied her to a tank and paraded her around the town square. Then they threw her naked, half-dead body in front of her parents. They loaded the rest of us into buses and took us to their camp, the place where they would murder your father and brother . . . the place where they took your mother and raped her in the room next to you, only a sheet for a door. Where you could hear her crying, pleading as one man after another took her. And then they took your sister, thirteen years old. Do you understand? Thirteen years old! And they raped her. Not just once, but all the men in turn. Can you imagine? Can you imagine your mother having to take the gruel they gave you for food and smear it on your eleven-year-old cunt so that when it dried it looked like an infection? And only that way were you saved from them, because they were afraid of getting a disease. Not even an eleven-year-old was safe from them, you see? From men, from fucking men like you."

While the noise of the party around them continued at high volume, the conversation among the others in their small group seemed to have fallen to a whisper, Jadranka's inner dialogue screaming out from her eyes. The intensity of her gaze had grown, until it felt to Lenny like the girl's eyes might pierce him. He could see their accusation, though he had no understanding of what their charge might be. The soon-to-be soldier felt strangely frightened by her look and suddenly grew angry that he should be made to feel that way.

"Jadranka, I think Katy and I are going to head home now," her roommate Chris said, breaking the short silence that seemed to linger interminably long. "Are you guys coming?"

"I don't know," Jadranka answered, casting an accusatory glance at Amir. His silence had angered her as much as had Brian's and his companion's glib, arrogant ignorance. She heard Brian attempt some witty remark to someone on another topic, like a sleight of hand, a change of subject to make the discomfort of the moment disappear. As the casual conversation around her slowly regenerated, Jadranka's anger at Amir grew. "How can you just stand there and say nothing in the face of such shit?" her eyes accused. "What?" Amir looked back. "What do you want from me?" his eyes asked in reply. But of course he knew.

"OK, let's go," Jadranka said, casting a quick glance toward her roommates before returning her gaze in Amir's direction. She was waiting for him to say something. Anything. It didn't matter, as long as he didn't sit there like a goddamned log.

He understood her look, yet now he was angry too. *What do you want me to tell them?* he asked, without the assistance of his voice. *What do you want me to say to them, Jadranka? To tell these people what happened to us? Because if that is what you want, it will do no good. You can tell it all to them, shock their minds, but nothing will change. Because it is easier to believe in a lie, even a terrible one, than it is to see the truth.*

Jadranka would have none of it. She continued to look at Amir, now only to see if he was coming. He saw that she wanted him to come with her, yet he didn't move. A minute later, by the time his obstinacy had calmed to make room for other thoughts, she was gone.

Yes, he could see in the future soldier's eyes that which Jadranka had seen, observed the trace of a snarl that revealed itself on his face for the briefest moment before it was quickly replaced by a smirk meant to say he couldn't care less . . . that dark secret peering through a tenuous veil of civility.

Chapter 26

There can be moments in life, of seemingly inconsequential instance, that later come to stand in memory as having been the catalyst of extraordinary personal transition. What for Amir had begun as a random event, a party he had no real interest in attending, had led him to just such a moment.

Shortly after Jadranka left the party, Amir slipped out unseen, invisible and silent, with no good-byes, hearty words, jokes, or pleasantries to mark his exit. He walked in the direction of Jadranka's apartment but halted part way there. Stopping at a small park, he entered it to seek solace in the quiet whisperings of his old friends, the trees. He wandered to its deepest part and leaned up against a large, leafing maple. Hidden in the dark recesses of the grounds, he was comforted by the shadows and the low, soft song of a gentle spring breeze. With his mind in turmoil, Amir looked upward through branches pushing out newly sprouted leaves, gaps of the night sky intermingling in the gentle flutter of their dance to reveal the light of distant stars.

What did Jadranka want of him? To remember that which he only wanted to forget? To speak it out loud for all to hear? The world had ignored the genocide that had killed their loved ones when it was in the making, so what good would any words of commiseration do now? Nothing he could say would make a difference. And even if he could find the courage to speak, to let those terrible memories out into the open, there were no ears to listen. And even if there had been ears to hear, there were no hearts to act. People believed in war. And even if they said they didn't, their words in opposition were cautious and whispered.

As Amir's mind spat out its denials, another voice rose up within him, this one not loud and angry, but rather like a quiet breeze, gentle and dispassionate. Yes, it said, there was a story he could tell, one as much for his own ears as for those of others. It was what Jadranka had asked of him. He could tell of a day a child woke up in the warm home of a loving family and that same night fell asleep cradled between the branches of a tree, no longer able to hear or speak. He could tell of finding a mound colored with the lifeless faces of his cousins, the grocer, his schoolteacher—the populace of his universe peering out from their death masks like so many broken, tattered, discarded dolls. He could tell of wandering the woods alone or with others like himself, knowing what it must feel like to be a deer in hunting season. He could talk about his friend Josif, tell how the boy had died in his arms, shot in the back by a sniper's bullet, and how, till this day and for all the days of his life, those dying eyes would never leave him.

There was still more for the telling. Stories, all documented and available from any local library, accounts of acts of inhumanity never spoken of on the nightly news, acts of such depraved physical and psychological tortures they would never be read even if printed, their telling too intense, too graphic for people sitting in the comfort of a safe world to take in. Yet truth is for telling, and without it being spoken the inertia of ignorance remains sitting in its place.

Amir began to cry. "Damn them, damn them all to hell," he sobbed, kicking at the ground with his heel.

Had there been anyone there to hear his curse, someone who might ask to whom it was directed, Amir would have been unable to find a specific answer. It wasn't aimed at those to whom he could not find words to tell his story. It wasn't for the militia who had invaded his family's house, or for the country or religion in whose names they killed. There were a thousand names from a thousand wars, names aplenty to point finger and lay blame—the false face of civilization quick to single out villains. And then there was he, Amir. Wasn't his curse thrown inward as much as it was out into the dark night of humanity? Wasn't he who had seen the face of war and felt its foul breath upon his neck, even guiltier in his silence than those who would excuse its cruelties?

The silent dialogue of his thoughts choking him, Amir, one small, dark shadow among the many in the night woods, slumped to the ground. He was tired of his fears and tired of the harbor of his safety. He was just now coming to learn the price of his place of refuge. He understood Jadranka's anger with him. He realized that from silence must come something, or it remained nothing at all but the absence of sound. Yet he felt as if he were back in the woodbin on the day his family was killed: paralyzed and unable to move, the world taking the minuteness of his being and blowing it like the smallest speck of dust into the wind—the infinitesimal into the invisible.

Rising to his feet, Amir stood and slowly walked from the park in the direction of Jadranka's apartment. When he arrived at her building, he stood outside for some minutes debating whether to leave or to enter and speak with her. His emotions had been scraped raw; obscured feelings cached beneath the surface of his sentiment rose up within him, confusing his thought. He wanted to see her, wanted everything to be the way it had been before the party. But it wasn't.

He turned and walked home, where he lay alone in his bed, the roil of his emotions keeping sleep at bay. As his thoughts turned inward, the play of the evening's events evaporated to leave only himself as the focus of his contemplation. The central question of his meditation wasn't a conundrum of who he might be, but rather whether he, Amir, was anyone at all. Tears began to stream down his cheeks in silent answer. As sleep finally overcame him and despair emptied him of thought, he was struck by an awareness of self that was shocking to him as much for its simplicity as its clarity. Though the brief moment of revelation was soon lost to slumber's advance, it remained illuminated in outline long enough for his conscious mind to understand that his question was not a weight he carried alone, but was, in one form or another, shared by everyone.

The following morning Amir drove to his mother's for his usual Sunday visit, but without Jadranka. Margaret was surprised that her son's girlfriend had not come with him as planned and sensed that something was wrong. When she asked, Amir recounted the event of the night before. Margaret listened intently as Amir spoke of the incident and about what he saw as his weakness in facing the past. He was, he said, ashamed of himself and his frailty of spirit. He spoke in a matter-of-fact tone, with his body held upright, his eyes directly facing his mother.

While Amir spoke, Margaret listened, as intent upon the look on her son's face as on the words he spoke. There was a strange aura about him, a kind of desensitized state emanating from within as he talked. It was as if he were speaking not about himself, nor even about another person, but almost as though he was discussing a literary character in a book.

"Why are you smiling?" Amir asked, seeing a gentle, pensive expression appear on his mother's face.

"Because I think you're finally getting beyond it. Or, perhaps better said, that you have come to finally be able to meet it face on."

"But Mom, I feel terrible."

"Yes, I can see that. But I believe something has changed. There is no longer the sense that your past owns you, that you are captive to it. I can hear in your voice and see in your eyes that you've come to a place of change. A part of you has been trapped for so many years by what happened in the war that it can only see things in terms of what it has always known. It's what many prisoners suffer after their release from prison. The bars that have cut them off from ordinary society for so long have, paradoxically, come to represent a place of security for them. They are afraid to live outside of their enclosure, afraid to leave their prison cell when the time comes for them to be freed."

Amir sat looking off into the distance, as if trying to grasp something beyond his mind's reach. He could feel the touch of truth in his mother's words, but he couldn't find a frame of reference from which to make sense of it. It was as if he had been walking along a road toward a destination whose distance lay so far off that all thought of arrival was lost to the endless journey, one day following the other. Then, suddenly, he arrived and found himself struggling to remember why he had come in the first place.

That night, sitting alone in his room, Amir realized that his path forward had been in front of him now for quite some time. It had not been the lack of knowing that it was there that kept him from it, but rather the fear of engaging it. What he had suffered in Bosnia, he now understood, marked his future just as surely as it had his past.

It was only natural that Amir would think of film as the medium to confront the emotions that had held him captive for so long. He wasn't sure, however, just how he might approach it or even what its expression should be. All he really knew was that, whatever it might be, he wanted it to be true. He had no illusion of finding truth in any objective sense of the word. Rather, what he sought was an internal declaration that was honest, and despite his fears, probing and deep. Though he had little idea of how to proceed, Amir braved forward to step into the past.

Jadranka and Amir had been unable to bear their separation for more than a day. Knowing each other's schedules, they crossed paths at the earliest opportunity, their anger and icy stubbornness disintegrating at first look. Their first reaction was to laugh, and then as they hugged Jadranka started to cry, saying she was sorry and that she didn't know why she'd acted the way she had. Amir, in turn, offered the same. They had survived their first real spat.

Jadranka soon noticed a change in Amir. Though he had not directly spoken of his internal decision, he began to speak freely of his former life in Bosnia without being prompted to do so.

"So you really were the little farmer," Jadranka teased. "And did your father take you hunting and fishing for dinner?"

"Yeah, actually he did," Amir smiled. "Not every night, of course. But it wasn't uncommon. It wasn't always game or fish, though. Sometimes we gathered wild herbs and mushrooms. My mom loved mushrooms. She made soup from them, used them in salads, cooked them with vegetables. She made a great mushroom gravy, too."

"They were a good family, huh?" Jadranka smiled at the look in his eyes, catching a glimpse of the rural Bosnian farm boy he'd once been.

"Yeah, they were good," he acknowledged with a gentle smile.

"And your sister? Tell me about her."

"She was three years older than me. We got along really well. Minka was always watching out for me, taking care of me. She was really beautiful, inside and out. She was like the quintessential Bosnian country girl. You know, really pure?"

"'Quintessential'? Such a big English word. But yes, I know what you mean."

In her turn, Jadranka spoke of her family, her father and her brother who had been killed in the war. Describing her mother and sister, she said she hoped Amir would one day be able to meet them. In fact, she had been planning on returning home for a visit that summer, but money was tight and even with a full scholarship she needed to work for as many weeks as she could during the summer vacation to make ends meet. In any case, it would be her last year at school. She would be returning to Bosnia soon enough, an idea Amir had begun giving thought to as well.

Chapter 27

That summer Amir took a job on the Cape to be with Jadranka. They rented a small, rundown, bare-bones apartment in a ramshackle house that had been cut up to fit as many apartment units as possible. Amir worked on a landscaping crew and Jadranka returned to her waitress job at the Blue Whale. When their work schedules kept them apart, Amir busied himself reading all he could about the Bosnian War. After years of having avoided the subject, he had finally begun trying to understand the conflict that had taken his family from him and left him an orphan. Reading about the recent war in his homeland led him to investigate other armed conflicts, and soon he was researching the numerous wars of the twentieth century that had preceded his own country's fall into chaos. By the time summer vacation ended, he had come up with an idea for a film. On his return to school he had been in the final stages of its outline when Zack Ashrawi once again approached him for help.

It was Amir's first day back in class and with his mind wavering back and forth between the film he wanted to make and the reality of getting back into gear for the new school year, he had been caught by surprise at Zack's approach, to see him going about business as usual. Amir had imagined that, after all of the trouble he'd been in, the professor would keep a low profile.

Yet instead of feeling humiliated by the nationally broadcast attack on his character and the ensuing controversy at the college, circumstances that saw him first suspended from his job, then reinstated, Zack seemed to wear the entire event as a badge of honor. Indeed, he appeared to be basking in the glory of controversy, as though he'd received a prestigious award instead of the steady flow of hate mail that condemned him as a traitor and terrorist. In fact, he delighted in showing the hate mail to whomever might be interested, readily reaching into his valise to pull out letters and emails proffering vitriolic and damnatory communications, especially those that spewed confused and fantastic allegation that had little, if anything, to do with his particular case.

"Look," Zack would say, both delight and incredulity marking his face, "this one thinks Palestinians are an Afghan tribe. And here, read this one. It says I'm an agent for Saddam Hussein, who they call the dictator of Iran. They can't even match the names with the proper country. For these people it is all the same, all one big jumble of hate. It doesn't matter whether you are Somali or Pakistani. Every Muslim is the same in their minds. It just points out how the media and the government have manipulated the populace."

Nor was Zack cowed by the government's investigation of him. He had done nothing illegal nor anything to be ashamed of, he declared. His only desire had been to help relieve the suffering of the Palestinian people. The professor of Islamic studies found a number of supporters eager to condemn the government's action. Zack's advocates, who tended to have their geographic and political facts more or less in proper order, chuckled smartly at the more outrageous errors that Dr. Ashrawi plucked from the piles of hate mail he received. Yet their knowledge went little deeper than that, and they, like their right-leaning counterparts, were happiest simply repeating the snippets and sound bites they gleaned from their favorite news source.

If Amir wasn't on the side of those who condemned Zack Ashrawi, for attitude if not for traitorous act, he also couldn't be said to be counted among the professor's ardent supporters. He agreed to help Zack once again because he felt he could hardly do otherwise. If he was going to express his own experience as a victim of war, how could he in conscience not help others who were at that very moment suffering the same? But the more he worked on editing the video footage Zack had asked him to distill into short digital clips, the quicker he wanted to be done with it. Amir's own project was calling out to him urgently and insistently, its germination within his imagination having unleashed a fierce creative urge.

Amir envisioned his new film as one that would have little dialogue but nonetheless would be complex to script for the very simplicity that he wished to bring to it. In his initial research that summer, Amir had counted just over 150 wars or brutal repressions having occurred worldwide in the twentieth century, causing, by very conservative estimate, the deaths of more than 175 million individuals.

Contrary to common understanding, fewer than a tenth of those who died were actual combatants involved in the conflicts. The greater majority, by far, were victims from civilian populations, killed either by direct cause of warfare or by residual effects of injury or starvation. Statistical data made it clear that for each soldier killed in conflict, at least ten innocent civilians would forfeit their lives. When you considered the great number of combatants who themselves were civilians drafted or forced into the service, the data became even more daunting to contemplate.

As he read the statistics, Amir was struck not only by the shocking numbers but even more so by his own ignorance of them. How could war be understood as one thing and yet be so much another? Even for someone like him, who had experienced it firsthand? A search of his own memory easily corroborated the statistical ratio of civilian-to-combatant death. Amir had previously assumed that all of the civilian deaths he had witnessed had somehow been an anomaly isolated to his particular experience. The assumption that the rest of the war had involved soldiers fighting soldiers sat in his mind like the common wisdom of an old aphorism whose truth everyone took for granted.

The idea that his experience of war hadn't been an isolated exception to the norm but was instead a universal result was shocking to both his heart and his mind. In the movies as well as the media, war was always portrayed as the brave soldier coming up against the evil foe, combatant to combatant—war glamorized through the glorification of the heroic warrior. Yet his own experience had shown him a truth far from the entertainment industry's simplistic treatment so readily accepted by the public. The real experience of war was as complex as any of human interaction, the intensity and range of emotions it drew forth marking for life those who were involved. Valor, fear, love, hate, selflessness, and selfishness, mixing, often overlapping in moments of extreme trauma or days of tedious drudgery, of waiting in trepidation for what might come. Amir knew there was no glamor to any of it. He was not surprised that many of those who fought in wars should allow their service to be represented by politicians and film producers as glorious, even when they understood a far more horrific truth. Traumatized emotionally, if not physically, soldiers were easy prey for warmakers who would hail their valor and then quickly forget them, leaving the veterans to endure their nightmares in solitary obscurity.

Amir began to more fully understand that war meant not only soldiers battling each other but also the targeting of those who wanted no more than to escape it. As the young filmmaker read further into the details of twentieth-century wars, he was shocked to learn that it wasn't always the aggressor who consciously took innocent lives. Often it was also those who claimed the side of right, who decried an enemy that would target civilians or use them as shield, who then found justification for their own policies that permitted the calculated killing of innocent nonparticipants.

Collateral damage, that most shameful and cynical phrase of modern invention, had entered the popular lexicon as a rationalization of what amounted to legalized murder. Solemnly spoken by politicians and generals, the two words would float from their mouths to hang in the air for all the world to hear the sincerity of the speaker's regret, as though the calculated killing of innocent noncombatants was a result of some disastrous act of nature and not a decision of their own choice and responsibility. It was a nightmare catch-22 . . . the barbarity of the evil justifying the dark acts of the "good."

The more he read, the more Amir was drawn into that aspect of human behavior, which he had long sought to void from his conscious mind. Not given to political or social passion, Amir nevertheless forced himself to discuss the results of his research with his friends and classmates. When the subject of civilian deaths came up, he was met with comments of universal compassion. However, when speaking of it as resulting from governmental policy there was, on the whole, a reaction of a different order. Sympathy turned to equivocation. When confronted with US involvement in a broader, cumulative picture of collateral damage, people seemed to quickly scurry to the shelter of generalities, weak justification, or patriotic cliché.

Amir was reminded of a news story from a few years past: A young girl had been found murdered in her Colorado home. Her body had been discovered in the basement, the cause of death determined to be strangulation. Amir remembered being shocked both by it and by the media frenzy that kept it front-page news for months. What he couldn't understand then, and even less now, was how such sympathy and outrage could be generated by that one, tragic murder while the deaths of hundreds of children war victims would, if anything, receive little more than a day's passing coverage compressed into a small paragraph crowded among a dozen other minor stories in the back pages of the newspaper.

While Amir was visiting his mother's rented beach cottage that summer, the conversation one evening turned to a recent news report about a bombing in Afghanistan. American warplanes had been on routine patrol when the celebrants of an Afghan wedding party had the unfortunate bad luck to be shooting off their rifles in a traditional festive display as the squadron flew nearby. The rifle fire posed no threat to the aircraft, but at the pilot's report, the central command, assuming enemy hostility, ordered the squadron to bomb. Nearly everyone, including the bride and groom, had been killed. A celebration that should have culminated in joyous union had ended in tragedy.

Margaret was surprised to see her son step forward to take the lead in the discussion, his strong and animated reaction to the story taking her aback. It was as if a switch had flipped inside of him, his normal quiet demeanor suddenly converted from the personality of the meek to that of the impassioned. Even Jadranka, who had been witness to the gradual transformation Amir's research into armed conflict was bringing about in him, was caught off guard by the heat of his words and the anger in his voice.

"It shouldn't have happened," Alice's husband, Paul, sighed in response to Amir's condemnation of the act. "Sadly, in war these things are sometimes unavoidable."

"Unavoidable?" Amir asked, his anger rising.

"Look, I don't want to justify the loss of innocent life," Paul said, well aware of his young brother-in-law's past. "It is a tragedy. It's just that I think that collateral damage is a part of war and there's no escaping it."

"Exactly," Amir stated, his eyes fixing on Paul's.

"Are you agreeing, then?" Paul responded, looking confused. "I'm not sure I understand what you're saying."

"I'm saying that as long as you see collateral damage as inevitable, then it always will be. Then the justification for its continuation will be built in to its very act, the good guys using the bad guys for excuse and the bad guys using the good, and in the end nobody doing anything about what amounts to legalized murder."

When the conversation changed to other topics, Margaret felt relieved, the intensity of her son's emotions worrying her. At the same time, however, she felt that Amir was doing exactly what he needed to do: become engaged in the world. Was he being naïve, or had she lost hope that things could change in a world that seemed to see only in black and white—the breadth and depth of its color spectrum dulled to "us" and "them"?

Amir spent his first few weeks back at school ensconced in the library doing research, reading histories and personal accounts of various wars, searching the Internet for statistics and stories, and writing them down until all the pages of his notebook were filled and he had to buy another. Compiling the data on his laptop, he shared it with his friends, ostensibly to share the results with those who had expressed interest in his project, though really more to observe their reactions.

To Amir, the statistics and stories he'd gathered were shocking. Somehow, though, those waves of shock hadn't penetrated far beyond the part of his brain that dealt with facts. His mind had seized up when it came to translating those quantifiers into visions of reality. His friends' reactions seemed to parallel his own. Listening to the statistics of death and destruction he shared with them, their responses followed in a kind of automatic expression of revulsion that, for all their declarations, sounded dulled and distant to his ear. It was as if they were a passenger in Amir's car and he pointed out some dead animal lying on the roadway as they drove past, the viewer expressing his or her compassion and then quickly looking away, returning their attention to the road ahead of them before the gory scene had time to embed itself in memory.

It seemed that everyone with whom he shared the results of his research, rather than engaging their imagination in the visualization of what they read, wanted to do just the opposite, to block it out. To keep it in the realm where the mind added, subtracted, divided, and could make rational sense of things. It was an impulse Amir could understand.

What was the point in exploring the terrible violence and cruelty of war if its act was but an inevitable fact of human society? It was, Amir slowly came to believe, the feeling of hopelessness that there ever could be an end to war, or even a diminishing of its acts of inhumanity, that caused the statistics that he had compiled to become no more than a momentary, glancing shock to the mind. For any real change to happen, there needed to be real hope—hope that the universally accepted culture of war could end. Hopelessness could do nothing other than bring with it a self-fulfilling prophecy of war's inevitably along with the barbarity that marked its act.

When he sat down to write the script for his movie, Amir had the sense that it was, in its way, already written. It was his story and the story of everyone like him who ever suffered what he had, and worse. It wasn't about the detail of his particular trauma or the particular war that had inflicted it upon him. There was, he felt, a universal link tying him to the past through time, to the present and future of every human who ever suffered or would suffer barbarous injustice at the hands of others. He would have little trouble showing the brutality of war. The problem for the young filmmaker was how he could do that and at the same time still carry a message of hope to the viewer. Without it, his film could be nothing more than an angry cry in the dark. And both darkness and anger served to the advantage of those whose identity and economic well-being depended upon the excuse and ennoblement of war.

Searching through every film and video war archive he could find, Amir began to amass footage in hope that he might later work it into a cohesive whole. Viewing image after image, he came to the same conclusion he had reached in his earlier research begun in the library: there was no clear, visible pattern to war and atrocity, to the whom, the why, the when, and the where. War was a story of the human species, belonging not to a religion or to the color of a population's skin, an ideology, a governmental structure, or a status of wealth or poverty.

Unable to find a thread with which to continue the writing of his script, Amir went out into the world to begin shooting the film. He began by filming children playing in yards, in the streets, and at schools. He didn't know what he was after, only that he wanted to awaken the eyes of those who might shut them tight or turn away, those who would disappear the victims of war, nullify their existence with words such as "collateral damage," steal their individuality, and transform them into statistics and indifferent generalities.

With his filming complete, Amir entered, as he and his fellow film students had termed it, the "time of the dungeon," where he reclused himself in the editing studios in the basement of the film department in an attempt to create a story from all the bits and pieces he had gathered from film archives and the footage he'd shot. He felt like a sculptor caught in a nightmare . . . dreaming himself enclosed in the very material from which he was meant to make a work of art. Trapped inside, he needed to hack his way out in order to begin his work, but in so doing, he was destroying the very object he meant to create.

Having abandoned all of the structure he had previously developed, Amir—without a real script, outline, or storyboard—found himself swimming against the current. It was, he knew, a place no experienced filmmaker should ever be. Yet he couldn't help himself. He didn't know how to approach this particular film in any other way. He was possessed by it, and not the other way around. Eventually he found himself in a creative situation that felt like a place of shattered pieces without structure or order.

It seemed he'd spent a lifetime in the dungeon and had gotten nowhere. Film trims dangled about him, hanging from the wires that traversed the editing studio like tinsel on a Christmas tree. Amir felt as if his head were about to explode. The mass of short video and film clips he'd collected from war archives hung around his neck like the proverbial albatross. He somehow had to make them fit with the footage he'd shot on his own—but not just fit. He was after something much more.

Amir understood that he had arrived at a very dangerous point. The whole project was a mess, a pile of images making no sense, more worthy of the trash can than to be seen by any eye. The words of one of his professors came to mind in frightening portent of his film's possibility: "Every time you make a cut on film, you're destroying it. You can never put it back whole again. Therefore, you must be discriminating about what it is the story wants and not interfere with it by trying to be clever or interjecting extraneous ideas."

Sitting in the dungeon, Amir looked about him, feeling that he had chopped his film to death. Succumbing to frustration, he ripped a handful of film trims from their pegs and threw them to the floor, kicking and cursing. After his outburst, he slumped down into his chair, dejected. A short time later, he bent over and picked up a single piece of trim from the floor. Looking around the room, he was barely able to manage a small shake of his head toward the contents in his hand. Not knowing what else to do, he held the short length of film up to the light, his eyes staring at the image in one of its frames. The face of a lifeless child looked back at him, holding his eyes, refusing to let him go. A thread of something there drew Amir in. Part vision, part idea, it refused to reveal itself, its invitation to follow demanding the freedom to go where it would. Amir gathered up the discarded pieces of trim laying on the floor and hung them back in place. Picking up pen and paper, he began to write the script and storyboard anew, this time trying to listen and let the story tell itself.

Chapter 28

Among the three members of the independent project review committee, Harold Irving, the film department chair, had unexpectedly been the most critical. The other two professors, while agreeing that it was questionable as to whether the film fit the genre under which the student had been granted the permission to pursue the project, felt that its execution had been of high standard and therefore fully deserving of credit. Professor Irving, however, maintained that Amir had been allowed to substitute an independent project for course work on the basis that his film would reflect the same area of focus as the class he dropped. But it didn't. It diverged sharply from the more conventional, observational documentary style outlined in the course syllabus, into a decidedly poetic and abstract work aimed at a specific point of view.

The other professors had been a little surprised at Harold's orthodoxy of interpretation, but then again, he was always toughest on those he thought to have the most promise. There was no doubt that the student had veered off course, yet the work was powerful and moving. The other review members were somewhat taken aback that they should even consider rejecting the film outright on the basis of its failure to meet the project's core criteria. Harold seemed inexplicably agitated by the work.

There wasn't any question that, given the aftershocks of 9/11, the film could be considered, by some, potentially controversial. What the other members of the review committee weren't aware of, however, was that in addition to expecting more from Amir than he did the average student, Harold had grown troubled by a greater concern than simply that of one of his prize students not following the rules. It had come in the form of a more rigorous, severe authority than even the most obdurate college review committee.

Special Agent Joseph H. Tillman of the United States Federal Bureau of Investigation had paid an unannounced visit to the department chair only days before. Though Harold Irving had not expected the visit, it had not come as a total surprise. Zack Ashrawi's troubles, which for a time had seemed to be settling down, had suddenly reignited a week prior, when the FBI, backed up by state and local police, swooped down on the professor's home and office like a scene out of a cheap Hollywood thriller. Warrant in hand, they hauled off computers, boxes of papers, and records from both his domicile and his college office. Rumors of an imminent indictment spread quickly about the campus.

Harold's first impulse had been to tell Special Agent Tillman that he was too busy to see him and that the agent should call to make an appointment. Afterward, the department chair wished he had, even if it wouldn't have made the least little difference to anyone's reality. But fear, like water, was ever resolute in finding gravity's path, and sensing its current within him, the chairman of the film department, putting on his most professorial demeanor, told the agent he would be happy to talk with him.

"You are aware, aren't you, that your department's facilities have been used by Zakariyya Ashrawi?" Agent Tillman asked, after a brief, perfunctory introduction.

Harold Irving looked at the man without immediately responding. He met eyes that returned his gaze with the blank, unwavering expression of one secure in his identity as a representative of hegemonic power. The department chair, though, would not be intimidated; he would not be put on the defensive. Or so he told himself.

"Yes, I'm aware that Professor Ashrawi has made use of the film department's facilities," Harold responded evenly, "just as have many other professors and students at our school. That's what the facilities are here for."

"And are you also aware that the particular purposes for which Zakariyya Ashrawi has made use of your department's equipment are alleged to be in support of known terrorist organizations?"

If the mask of cold calm could have been removed from Agent Tillman's face, it would have revealed a sardonic smile at the reaction showing itself in the professor's eyes and facial musculature, at his inability to respond other than in shocked silence. Tillman's words, though grammatically constructed as a simple question, carried the tone of an accusation. Of course Harold knew, the agent's expression said. Everyone on campus knew.

"We would like to have one of our agents take a look at your department's computers, any that Professor Ashrawi, or anyone acting on his behalf, might have had access to," the FBI agent added, allowing a small, polite smile. "There could be some retrievable files of interest. Your cooperation would be appreciated."

Agent Tillman could see the department chair considering his response. After a second's pause the agent continued, giving Harold little time to ponder.

"We have a list of names that might be helpful to you in determining which equipment would be pertinent for examination. We would like to look at anything that any of these people might have had access to, even if only occasionally."

The federal law officer then began reading off a short list of Islamic-sounding names, ending with "Amir Beganović-Morgan."

"The computers and equipment he's had access to are of particular interest to us. He's credited as Ashrawi's director of communications on a number of the video clips that Ashrawi disseminated on the Internet in support of terrorist organizations."

Harold was shocked. His first thought was to defend Amir, to tell Tillman how Zack Ashrawi used any number of naïve students for his purpose. But his shock quickly turned to anger. At Ashrawi, then at Amir as well. He had warned the student not to get involved with the man. The department head looked at the federal agent and sighed. He wondered then just how deeply Amir might have been pulled into Zack Ashrawi's dealings.

"I'll have to check with the college president," Harold answered, trying to gain more time in which to think. "I'm sure she'll have to check with the school's legal counsel first."

"By all means, feel free to give her a call. But we've already spoken with her. Actually, this conversation is simply a courtesy call to you as the department head. And frankly, it's of no importance what the university's attorneys might have to say. We have a federal warrant."

Harold Irving's body moved backward in the chair he sat upon, drawing inward on itself as if in attempt to find secure footing. Reading the professor's reaction, the FBI agent's expression held tight, maintaining the same dispassionate demeanor, the hubris of his barely perceptible smile belying his words. Fifteen minutes later, having finished the details of arranging the agency's forensic search of the department's computers, the federal agent thanked Harold Irving and left. The department chair sat alone, silent and confused, trying to come to grips with all that had just passed. What could Amir have been thinking to allow his name to be used on the credits of Ashrawi's propaganda? Harold Irving felt a momentary rise of anger at his student's naïveté. Or stupidity. Or perhaps it was neither of those. A thought ventured in Harold's mind, the seed of doubt sprouting in soil made fertile by the agent's visit. Maybe it hadn't been such an unwitting act on Amir's part. Maybe there was more going on with the boy than was readily apparent—his reticent demeanor a veil to more overt, angry emotion.

For the moment putting his questions aside, Harold Irving pondered how to proceed. The boy couldn't have picked a worse time to make a movie portraying war in less-than-glorious light. Although Amir had declared that his film was in no way anti-American, there would be those who would immediately see it as such. The drums of war were sounding from the nation's capital with such force and persistence that they had drowned out all other voices, hypnotizing almost an entire nation with the inevitability of their message. Anyone not dancing to the beat could only be seen as unpatriotic. Now, after the visit from the FBI, it seemed to the department chair that Amir was almost following Ashrawi's lead and looking for trouble.

It didn't take Harold Irving long to realize that denying Amir credit for his film was not going to remove him from the scrutiny of the federal authorities. Nor would it likely serve as a warning to him to keep a low profile at a time when even those who openly questioned the call for war had lowered their voices to a whisper. The professor decided that, given the circumstances, the best option was to request a number of revisions to the student's work, hoping to at least buy time for things to settle down, for the FBI to finish their investigation and leave the campus. He also suggested to Amir that, because the film would be considered incomplete until the revisions were made, he not enter it in the school's annual film festival. The degree of reaction expressed by his student at that suggestion caught the department chair off guard. After a momentary pause, the professor was met by Amir's intent stare and a forceful "Why?"

Harold had expected Amir's response to be vested in his usual quiet, unassuming manner. He was taken aback by the steely challenge of the boy's eyes and his defiant tone. The professor found himself responding with clichés about professionalism and the importance of completion. Not seeing any softening in his student's demeanor, he mumbled something about the times and questioned whether audiences were ready to watch Amir's film, given the tragedy of 9/11. Harold's words sounded hollow and weak even to his own ears, and he quickly backed off, saying inwardly that there was nothing he could do for Amir if the boy didn't want to listen to the voice of reason.

Putting off the revisions requested by his professor, Amir instead chose to submit his movie to the school's film festival. A few days after he made the entry, rumors that Zack Ashrawi had been indicted and arrested by federal authorities quickly spread across the campus, sending shockwaves through the college community. The news was soon substantiated by local and national headlines reporting that the professor had been charged with raising funds and managing finances, through his foundation, for an international Palestinian terrorist organization that sought to destroy Israel. The college administration was quick to disavow any knowledge of Ashrawi's alleged illegal activity and announced his immediate dismissal.

For several weeks after his arrest, the professor of Islamic studies became the main topic of conversation among faculty and students alike. The plight of Zack Ashrawi, however, soon faded from the news and slipped from the minds of all but his few supporters and those who used the professor's arrest as a call for vigilance against enemies of the United States lurking within its very borders.

Harold Irving was relieved to see the Ashrawi controversy die down and things begin to return to normal. He had heard nothing from the FBI since their techs had gone through the film department's computers. Assuming there would have been some continuing investigations or seizures of equipment had they found anything incriminating or illegal, Harold Irving now found himself breathing easier. His relations with Amir, though, remained strained. The professor had received no communications back from his student in response to the revisions he had requested him to make. In an attempt to regain a footing in their relationship, Harold made a point of attending the first showing of Amir's work at the film festival. He hoped to see that it contained at least a few of the changes he'd asked for, some of which, he told himself, had been justly requested.

The movie's opening scene began with the camera looking out upon a small-town park on a beautiful, sunny day, lingering for a few moments before the lens's eye gently panned across trees and green grass against the backdrop of a brilliant, blue sky. A whispering lyric of wind, backed by a chorus of chirping birds, was slowly drowned out by voices of laughing children, nowhere to be seen. The camera gazed across a grassy field, to a playground of swings, seesaws, jungle gym, and merry-go-round, the young voices still singing out in disembodied, enigmatic voices. Then, all of a sudden, the camera caught its focus, zooming in on a group of children running across a schoolyard. Let loose from the confines of their classrooms, they were seen bursting out into the open, their energy exploding, to frolic with friends or chat away their lunch break on the school's playground. The effect of the scene—the way the camera moved in a leisurely, almost mesmeric, gaze through the joyous pandemonium—lulled the viewer into the comfort of the known and sentimental.

The audience's dream state, however, was interrupted by the appearance of a boy, with dirty face and beaming smile, who came running forward to fill the screen. Laughing and contorting his face into comic expressions, he stuck out his tongue in mischievous challenge to the camera's presence. The audience laughed in unison, the scene tugging joyfully at the viewers' hearts. The previous fall, when he had been filming, Amir had stopped at his former elementary school to shoot some footage, and the spirited ten-year-old had come charging at him like a young puppy ready for play.

After a time, the sound of the playing children slowly faded away, the soundtrack changing back to quiet songs of nature imbued with lonely and distant notes, as though composed in a minor key.

As the music of the earth established itself fully within the viewers' senses and settled them into a peaceful calm, the heartwarming scene of children on the schoolyard began to fade, along with the sounds of their play.

When the children's faces had almost disappeared, their apparitions melded into the background of nature's camouflage, their retreat to invisibility paused and then reversed itself. The diminished silhouettes of the young students' visages now came forward again, growing larger, clearer, and more visible, the audience slowly becoming aware that the faces they now viewed were no longer the same as those they had just previously seen. The children who came into view now displayed no smile or expression of playful exuberance. There were no laughs, no bright-eyed looks emanating from the carefree countenance of youthful play. It could be said that their faces were, in fact, without expression at all.

The audio slowly increased in volume and the whispering of a gentle wind could be heard blowing through grassland and forest. There was a distant sound of rustling leaves upon the trees . . . shifting, touching one against the other, like dervishes moving in sacred, ritual dance. It took several seconds for the viewers to realize that the faces of the children they now saw on the screen were not simply resting in repose, but staring out in unmoving and lifeless mask. Against the backdrop of the soundtrack—the steady, rhythmic hum of nature's impartial, ancient song—the viewers' recognition journeyed from the familiar into the unfamiliar.

A silent, communal shock began to work its way through the audience. The smiles of sentimental delight that had spread across their faces in the movie's opening scene had abruptly vanished. Gone were the images of children playfully frolicking about the schoolyard. In their stead were photos collected from news archives of children war victims from around the globe. Amir had made no easy transition, no smooth slide from one world to the other, from the civil to the barbarous. Because that was how it was: the violence of murder took no consideration of feelings, of proper timing, or gentle shift.

As the viewers' breaths caught deep in their chests, the film shifted once again—this time seamlessly back into scenes of everyday life, of people living in complacent comfort. With the parade of deathly images gone, the camera moved with beguiling ease to gently usher the audience back to a sane, peaceful setting, allowing their minds a moment's respite from the lifeless faces that had passed before their eyes only seconds prior.

With everything returned to peaceful order, the camera's lens traveled back to the elementary school, the hour having changed from recess to day's end. Buses and parents were seen parked outside, waiting for the bell to ring and the school doors to burst open with a flood of children. The camera watched the merging of the parents and children, their arms meeting in warm embrace and their faces smiling in greeting. This time, instead of the faces of the children being replaced by those of young war victims, it was the students' parents, waiting patiently for their offspring to exit the school, who found substitute image on the screen. Their stand-ins were parents from distant lands, all of whom shared a common experience: the very worst any father or mother could ever imagine—the loss of their child. There were no children to be seen in these scenes. The grieving faces of parents alone told the story, without need of small, lifeless bodies by their side to explain the broken hearts standing bare and raw before the audience's eyes.

At this point in his first attempt to make the film, Amir had succumbed to outrage and anger. He had sat in the dungeon of his editing room surrounded by still photos, film, and video footage garnered from war archives of image upon image of unspeakable sadness. Encircled by images of death, Amir began to fall into depression, and the depression, in turn, had become anger. Anger at all those who would use war to advance their own purpose, whether for power, for wealth, or to secure their identity in belonging to a cause or tribe. He had wanted to make a statement by including the faces of warmakers in his film. And it would not just be the Hitlers, the Stalins, the Idi Amins, and the Pol Pots. Those were the easy ones to single out. There were others, too: men whose moral authority was thought to be above question yet whose decisions would ultimately be painted in blood.

By the time of his second attempt at making the film, however, Amir had sufficiently freed himself of his depression and anger to keep those emotions from intruding upon the story. If he were to fall prey to his anger, to his outrage at what had been done to him and his family, then Amir understood he would become trapped in the very thing he sought to end. Hate was a doorless wall. Anger was a windowless room. They were what allowed another's humanity to disappear from view, leaving them as no more than cheap objects to be treated without conscience or care.

Without scenes of generals and politicians to bloat the movie's storyline and distract the viewers from their own relationship with what they saw, the film continued on in quiet statement. A slow drift of lifeless faces floated across the screen, their silence saying what no words could. A child of about ten years looked out to the audience, the question in his unseeing, inanimate eyes at once both too distant to understand and simultaneously immediate and intimately close. It caused a great, painful rift to open in the viewers' minds. The image of the boy was followed by that of an infant, then a boy and a girl lying next to each other, perhaps brother and sister—it was hard to say, for the rubble of the fallen building about them obscured the detail of their features.

Other faces painted in silent death mask, both the young and the old, journeyed across the screen in orderly progression, the audience left with the sense that an endless queue of victims waited patiently for their turn to look out onto the world of the living. As each lifeless face took its turn on the screen the viewers were pulled into sorrowful questions: "Who was this person?" "Who had they been?" and "Why? Why?"

But the viewers were left with no time to ponder as the film moved forward toward its end. The camera returned its eye to the elementary schoolyard, the place from which its tale had begun. On the screen appeared the features of the spirited boy who had greeted the audience at the film's start, the child from the schoolyard who'd come running up to Amir's camera and stuck out his tongue in mischievous delight. The schoolboy's face once again loomed close, his playful eyes and delightful spirit lingering, filling the screen for a long moment before exiting. There was a quality about the child, a look that spoke of happiness, of goodness, and of hope. And it was with this scene that the film ended, and left the viewers to ponder. The boy was everyone's child. He was yours; he was mine; he was from our country and from another across the sea; he was a Christian, a Buddhist, a Jew, a Muslim, or from a family with no religious affiliation whatsoever. He was hope, hope that human society, no matter its differences and divisions, could arrive at a place where it could understand its shared humanity. If society could not overcome those things that put one group at angry odds with another, it could at least choose to not kill and maim because of them—nor be manipulated into violence by those whose consciences were lost to their hunger for power or hate.

The audience sat in stillness as the last image receded from the screen. There was some scattered clapping to be heard, but it was subdued and pensive. With the credits scrolling up the screen, the audience slowly began to walk from the theater, a lone, quiet piano playing in the background: Reinbert de Leeuw's recording of Eric Satie's "Gnossiennes No. 1" . . . the slow movement of the notes journeying in minor key, the melody seeming to float above the music itself, a feeling of an impressionist's painting imbued in its sound . . . the music blurring the edges of the literal and leading the exiting listeners' minds deep into thought.

Chapter 29

Jadranka and Margaret sat by Amir's side at his film's debut showing. The film student noted the arrival of Amir's professor, Harold Irving, who greeted him as he entered the theater. Amir felt two opposing emotions as the lights dimmed and the movie began. He was both fearful that Harold Irving's criticisms of the film would be proven true and proudly confident that his film would be well received and the audience would understand the work's intent.

As the film told its tale, Jadranka's body spoke her emotions' struggle by drifting in close to Amir. On his other side, his mother reached over to take his hand in hers. Margaret, who knew her adopted son's story better than anyone, who had been the first to intuit its hidden trauma, was taken still deeper into remote realms of his being as the film continued. Watching the images of death appear on the screen before her, a small trickle of tears ran down her cheeks for the silent child she had taken into her home and who had become her son. He was finally telling his story. She realized then what she had always really known: that compassion not born of experience, no matter how deep and sincere, can never truly understand the burden it offers to share.

Afterward, the three made a brief appearance at a film festival reception. A number of people congratulated Amir on his movie, saying they had been deeply moved by it. There were others, though, whose congratulations were more muted. A reporter from a nearby city newspaper interrupted a conversation Amir had begun with some friends, asking some pointed questions about the film's intent. Amir begged off, saying the man could phone him the following day—that he couldn't speak with him at the moment. Amir and Jadranka left soon afterward to drive Margaret back home.

Sitting at the kitchen table, they spoke about Amir's movie and then, after a time, moved on to other topics. With both spring and the end of the school year within sight, the conversation turned in the direction of the future.

"Jadranka, I imagine you're beginning to see the light at the end of the tunnel, with the end of school just a few months off," Margaret said. "It must feel like it's been a long road indeed. Are you excited about graduating?"

"Yes and no," Jadranka answered. "It is strange, you know? I feel like I was such the young girl when I first came, and now I feel like I am so old."

"Oh, yes," Margaret smiled. "I know just how you feel."

"Come on, Mom," Amir rejoined. "You're young in spirit."

"Hah," Margaret laughed. "You know you've grown old when people start using that line. 'Young in spirit' definitely implies its opposite in body and mind. Jadranka, what are your plans after graduation? Will you be working at the Cape again this summer?"

"No, I don't think so. It's been so long since I have returned to my home. It is too hard to wait another year. My visa permits me to work for one year after graduation, so my plan is to go home first for a visit and then come back and teach."

"That's wonderful for you to be able to see your family," Margaret said, glancing at Amir and leaving her next question hanging. The last time she had talked with him, her son's summer plans had still been up in the air, awaiting the outcome of Jadranka's decision whether to return home. A job opportunity working in a movie production being shot in Boston had also been put on hold. Just as Margaret was about to ask whether or not he'd decided to take the job, Amir answered the look of her eyes.

"Mom, I'm going to go back with Jadranka," he said.

"I see," Margaret replied, caught off guard, not knowing what else to say.

Her brief acknowledgment, however, belied the state of mind reflected on her face. That her son should one day return to his homeland had always been a given in Margaret's thoughts. In the process of helping to rebuild his shattered life, she had long imagined that his return to Bosnia might symbolically represent the last piece put into place—his return to wholeness and the reconciliation of his lost childhood. It was a journey she had always envisioned as one she and her son would make together.

"We are not going for so long, Margaret," Jadranka added quickly. "Amir will still be able to work on the film in Boston."

"Yeah, I talked with the director a couple of days ago," Amir clarified. "I got the job and I'll be able to get back in time. They don't start shooting until the end of June."

Margaret smiled at the concern of their anxious explanations. It was right that her son make this journey with his lover, she who could share his experience in ways that Margaret could not. Time and fate had worked against her own dream of what would be.

"I think that will be lovely," Margaret said, interrupting the momentary pause, and then, in afterthought, another question came to mind. "There won't be any passport issue because of the INS problem, will there? What did the attorney say?"

Amir had recently received a letter from the federal agency asking questions pertaining to the naturalization process he'd undergone when obtaining his US citizenship. When he had shown it to his mother, she had thought it odd that he should be receiving such a letter. Amir explained that in the aftermath of 9/11, many foreign students at the school, especially those of Muslim heritage, were having their status reviewed by the Immigration and Naturalization Service. "But I don't understand. Why would they include you?" she had asked, adding, "You're not a foreign student. You're an American citizen."

"I know, but almost everyone connected to Zack Ashrawi has come under suspicion and practically all the people at school with a Muslim name have been interviewed by the FBI. The lawyer said it's no problem; he wrote the INS a response to the letter they sent me and said that should be the end of it."

But what had really transpired at the meeting with the immigration attorney had not seen so clear-cut a resolution, nor had Amir been given so simple a reassurance as he now gave to his mother.

Sitting across from the immigration attorney, Amir had silently watched as the man read the letter from the INS that he had received. After looking it over, the attorney opened the file Amir had brought along with the letter. In it were documents pertaining to his relocation to the US, his subsequent adoption, and the naturalization process that had made him a US citizen. The middle-aged lawyer spent a few minutes reviewing the papers in front of him, occasionally interrupting his reading to ask a question of his client.

"Well, obviously, there was no intent to willfully misrepresent your past during your relocation to this country," the attorney stated, after having read the last of the files in front of him. "I don't think we have any real problem there. A simple letter in response, outlining the facts, should take care of it. Let's see . . . how old were you at the time of your entry?"

"Eleven."

"Hmmm, and I see here you were naturalized at seventeen. I can't see any cause to think there was any attempt to illegally procure your citizenship or procure it through concealment of a material fact in your naturalization application, which is what the INS letter is essentially questioning. Actually, I'm mystified why the INS would even bother with this, given all they have to do these days."

"Well," Amir spoke, clearing his throat, "I go to Franklin College. You've heard of Professor Zakariyya Ashrawi, the teacher from there who was arrested?"

At the mention of Ashrawi's name the attorney looked up from the files he'd been scanning. His eyes met his client's as Amir explained that he had been a student of the professor and that he'd helped the now-infamous academic on some video projects for his foundation. Amir paused, waiting for the lawyer to say something. The attorney, who could see there was more, responded by simply saying, "Go on."

Amir nodded and continued. There had also been, he said, an interview with the FBI. The day after Zakariyya Ashrawi's arrest, Amir had been approached by an FBI agent who said he had a few questions concerning Amir's relationship with the professor. Given its timing, the encounter had come as a surprise and left him feeling strangely embarrassed: Amir had just sat down to class when the agent entered the room and, making no effort to hide his identity, requested that Amir come with him.

The agent questioned him for nearly an hour before letting him go, handing him a card with his name on it, and saying he would soon be receiving a letter requesting a second interview at the regional FBI office. Amir then further explained to the lawyer that though the agent had been courteous, his questions had been leading and his demeanor clearly skeptical at the responses Amir had given.

"And did you receive the letter requesting a second interview?" the attorney asked.

"Yes, but I didn't go. An ACLU lawyer on campus came to see some of the other students who received letters from the FBI. I spoke with him, and he said it was a voluntary interview. That I could choose to go or not. So I didn't."

The immigration attorney sighed, and he adjusted his glasses before speaking. "OK, what I need you to do now is start from the very beginning again. This time in detail, from the very first day you met this professor, until the last time you saw him. I want you to remember that I represent you and that anything you say is confidential. It's important that you don't leave anything out. I'd like to read you something first. Normally, I wouldn't bother. But given the times . . . "

The lawyer rose from his seat, walked over to a set of shelves lining one side of his office, and selected a book. Returning, he paged through it and, finding the paragraph he wanted, read it to Amir.

"Do you understand what I just read?" the attorney asked when he had finished.

"Yes, I think so," Amir answered, though his eyes showed less than complete assurance of the legal jargon the attorney had read out loud to him.

"Basically, it's saying that if at anytime before or after your naturalization you were affiliated with any organization or group the government feels is a threat to our country, your citizenship can be stripped, along with all of the rights that go along with it, retroactively to the beginning of your residency here. Now, I didn't read this to frighten you, but rather so you understand the importance of not leaving anything out from what you're about to tell me. So please, go ahead."

With the attorney taking notes, Amir recounted his history with Zack Ashrawi. It took him about thirty minutes to do so, the immigration lawyer interrupting here and there for clarification. When Amir was done, the lawyer sat for several minutes jotting down his thoughts and considering the information he'd just heard.

"From what you told me, I still think we're OK. However, I don't think it is a coincidence that you received the letter from the INS and the FBI is interested in talking to you. We'll write a letter of response to the INS and at the same time set the stage, without specifically addressing it, for any possible future question of your relationship with the professor. Hopefully, this will be the end of it. Within the next month or two the INS will come under the umbrella of a new agency called Homeland Security. That could complicate matters or, just as likely, make the whole situation fade into the woodwork. We'll have to wait and see."

A week later Amir received a copy of the letter his lawyer had sent to the INS and considered himself lucky when weeks passed without further communication from the federal agency. Others at the school had not been so fortunate. A number of Muslim foreign students, most of them having some kind of tie to the indicted professor, had received letters stating their student visas were being revoked and that they would have to leave the country immediately. As time moved on and Zack Ashrawi's arrest faded from the news and people's minds, Amir gratefully let it fade from his as well.

Winter that year seemed to drag on interminably, time moving slowly through a miasma of foul and cold weather. Amir and Jadranka burrowed deep into their schoolwork and each other, not looking any further than the day at hand. One weekend in mid-April, they awoke to the chirping of birds outside their window. Raising the sash to better hear the birds' song of celebration, they were met by the sweet smell of a warm breeze and could feel with confidence that winter had finally ended. Time itself seemed to react to the change of season. The hour hands of the clock, which throughout the winter had traveled at a plodding, sloth-like pace, now seemed to turn with more verve and energy, the tempo of the beat quickening with the temperature's rise and the sun's path tracing higher in the sky.

Jadranka and Amir suddenly found themselves thrust out from winter's den to face a future that just a short time ago had seemed a distant prospect. There was much to do and little time to do it in. Projects needed to be completed, details of Jadranka's post-college employment ironed out, Amir's course selection and independent project for his senior year finalized, and the dates for his summer job set to accommodate his trip to Bosnia with Jadranka.

It wasn't until the week before they were to leave that the reality of his coming journey began to awaken in Amir's consciousness. As each succeeding day passed, he tried to keep thoughts of his homeland at bay—yet its images began to build and rise within his mind, threatening to overrun the path of normal and ordinary order that carried him through the day. There was both fear and excitement in this, and in brief moments of clarity, he could see that those seemingly polar emotions didn't exist as separate entities, each reacting to different cause, but shared the same ground, like lovers walking hand in hand.

The closer it got to the time he would actually begin to pack his bag, the more the idea of his upcoming return to his homeland felt strange and otherworldly. He and Jadranka were to fly into Sarajevo, where they would be met by her mother and sister. After a week with Jadranka's family, the young couple would take a short trip by themselves, traveling to Mostar and then on to the Croatian coast to Makarska. Both were places Amir had never seen before. The irony that he would now visit those cities as a tourist from America made his upcoming journey seem all the more surreal to him.

After their short vacation to Mostar and Makarska, the two young lovers would return to Sarajevo to spend more time with Jadranka's mother. There was, however, yet one other place Amir knew he would have to visit before returning home to the United States—the village where he had been born.

Amir couldn't imagine what it would be like to return to his family's homestead. In his mind not only his family's farmhouse, but the entire village, had been destroyed. Yet he knew this wasn't true. It had been only the Muslim villagers who had been "cleansed" from the town. And though many had been killed, a number had survived, having fled prior to the arrival of the invading soldiers. He had no idea how many would have returned to live there. He had distant relatives with whom he and Margaret had been in contact during the process of his adoption and for a few years thereafter, but in the end their communications had trickled down to nothing. When he and Margaret had last heard from them, they wrote that the village was slowly returning to its former self, its inhabitants coming to live together again in an uneasy peace. There had been some question about the family property and Amir's inheritance of it, papers that needed signing, documents that needed finding. But the house and outbuildings had been burned to the ground. Like many Bosnians who had escaped the genocide, Amir was ambivalent about trying to recover any property rights that carried little in financial value and much in the way of sad memory. He wondered whether there would now be others living on his family's property or whether it sat overgrown and abandoned.

The Saturday before they were to leave, Margaret held a small party to wish the young couple a safe journey and to celebrate Jadranka's graduation. Alice and Paul drove in from Cambridge for the occasion with their children. Margaret had fussed all day Friday, chiding herself for being so nervous about something so simple as a small gathering of friends and family. She was greatly relieved when her son and Jadranka arrived early to help her with the small tasks she declared she could just as easily do on her own while they enjoyed a walk in the woods. Amir had smiled and laughed in wordless dismissal of the self-reliance his mother still felt obligated to tender, like the search of her handbag for the few spare pennies the clerk at the market had no care of receiving. His sister, Alice, always responded to such declarations from her mother with debate, the ensuing dialogue having become almost ritual in the expression of their caring for each other.

Including friends from school, there were over twenty guests in attendance. As the party continued on past sunset into the cloudless late-spring evening, brother and sister conspired to keep their mother occupied in conversation with the guests while seamlessly taking over all the responsibilities of hosting. Glass of wine in hand, Margaret sat chatting outside by the bonfire Amir had started on the patio's open barbeque pit and kept ablaze throughout the evening. At one point during a lull in conversation, Margaret looked out across the group to gaze at her two children. Amir and Jadranka stood next to each other, conversing with Alice and Paul, her two granddaughters dancing between them in play. Seeing them like that, she felt a sudden stab of completeness both wonderful and frightening in the depth of its emotion. On the one hand, there was a sensation of perfect harmony, as if there were nothing lacking in her life. And on the other was the feeling of a thing brought to the end of its use—time having both fulfilled her and made her obsolete.

Turning her gaze upward, Margaret glanced into the night sky, past the flickering of the fire's flames, to see the light of the stars arcing in slow, perfect paths. Her eyes suddenly caught the swift stroke of a burning meteor marking the black night with a thin line of blazing light. The meteor was like a human life, she thought, no more than a tick of the heavens' clock. She flinched at the idea, the image of a trailing flame streaking across her mind like a frightening portent of a thing to come. Was it her end she saw? Shaking her head, she lowered her gaze back to earth and saw her son looking in her direction. For a brief moment she saw the child he'd once been, the young, deaf-mute boy watching her in silence. Yet the once-timid smile had disappeared to be replaced by one that now suffered no fear in declaring its existence. She marveled at how he had grown and matured—how much his presence in her life had meant to her. He would be gone for only a few short weeks, but Margaret felt that his departure marked some greater milestone than even this return to his homeland. There was the sense of a cycle reaching its conclusion, of a door closing. Smiling back at her son, she pushed the feeling to the side. In two days' time he would be gone, and she wanted to take in as much of him now, in the moment, as she could.

Chapter 30

It wasn't until he arrived at the airport, received his boarding pass, and checked his bags that Amir began to feel the full weight of the emotional journey he was about to undertake. As the plane taxied for takeoff, he felt a brief moment of panic that his mind blamed on a fear of flying. Yet it was a phobia he had never suffered. Sitting across the aisle from them was a young boy. An image of himself at that age, alone on a plane on his way to a strange and far-off destination, suddenly arose from its place of memory. His body tensed. He felt a comforting hand reach over and take his, Jadranka's touch calming his anxiety.

Later, as the plane carried him thousands of feet above the ground, Amir felt the tension leave his body, and he began to relax. Looking out from their small bubble of isolation, he stared out at the clouds and the ocean below.

When they reached continental Europe, he felt almost as though he was sitting high up in a tree, gazing down at the forest floor. From his window seat he could see towns and cities, small villages, and empty, desolate places, each with its own story to be told. A thousand tales of happiness, a thousand tales of sorrow. His own was, he knew, just one of many.

He and Jadranka changed planes in Munich and soon found themselves on the approach to Sarajevo, flying in and out of cloud cover that partially obscured the broad swipe of valley cradled by mountains.

"Look," Jadranka pointed out excitedly, "Mount Igman."

She'd spoken in Bosnian, something she'd done more of recently to help Amir prepare for his return, his ability to speak his native language having atrophied in the many years of his absence.

"Yes, I remember its name from school. And the river running through the city is Miljacka, right?" Amir answered in the same language.

"Ah, you were a very good student to remember it," Jadranka teased.

"Not so good really. I'm cheating. I just finished reading about it in the airline magazine," he said. "In the English-language section," he added, smiling.

During the landing Amir stared out the window, wondering silently what it would be like to be home. When they disembarked from the plane he let out a deep breath and took Jadranka's hand as they walked to the terminal. She continued to talk to him in their native language while he replied in English, the task of concentrating on his once-native tongue at the moment too trying for his mind. At Customs and Immigration they got in line together, the airport small and basic, with no separate division for national or foreign travelers. Jadranka passed through immigration first, Amir proceeding to the counter immediately after her.

Though Jadranka and Amir were separated by no great distance, the two young lovers threw glances in each other's direction, smiling and making eye contact as Amir handed over his US passport to be stamped. The immigration officer, though, seemed in no hurry to complete the process, thumbing through all of the document's pages and slowly typing into the antiquated computer in front of him. Jadranka became alarmed when the agent signaled Amir to step aside and wait, to let the next person in line move forward. A minute later a uniformed immigration official arrived, followed by a man dressed in suit and tie. Together they examined Amir's passport, the man dressed in civilian clothes rubbing its pages as one might a paper currency to check the authenticity of its material.

As Jadranka saw the two men begin to lead Amir away, her concern grew. Hurrying in their direction, she addressed Amir, asking him what was going on. Amir answered in English that he wasn't sure. The plainclothes agent spoke up then, saying that there was no need to worry, that they just needed to check Amir's passport. It would likely be only a few minutes' delay, he assured her. But his assurances soon proved false, as Jadranka, after having met up with her mother and sister in the lobby, waited anxiously for Amir to appear.

When the immigration officers had taken him with them and sat him down at a table in the middle of their office, Amir had been told it was to validate the authenticity of his passport. But the nature of the questions pertaining to the document's origins and his acquisition of it quickly took a different direction, the tone of the interrogation changing from cordial to hostile. The issue of the passport possibly being a forged document soon showed itself to have been a pretext: the true reason for Amir's detention was that his name had appeared in the databanks of an international terrorist watch list.

It had happened during the investigation of Zakariyya Ashrawi, subsequent to his arrest, at the time the FBI had interviewed everyone connected to him. The names of all of those linked to what were deemed the professor's activities in support of terrorism were passed along to the CIA's antiterrorism unit. Acting merely on a hunch, the unit's leader decided to put Amir's name on the watch list. Al-Qaeda and other terrorist organizations were using the Internet to disseminate their communications between themselves and the public with ever-increasing frequency. Those communications often included video files. They had to be getting technical help from somewhere, the director reasoned.

The uniformed official who escorted Amir to the immigration office had him sit to the side of his desk and then went about other business. His suited colleague, meanwhile, went into an adjacent room where he picked up a phone and placed a call to the CIA station chief in Sarajevo. He was told the American official was on vacation and was put through to the deputy chief, a junior officer who grew excited at the prospect of finding himself at the center of a possible counterterrorism coup.

"What do you want us to do with him?" the Bosnian asked.

"Just hold him until I get back to you," the American answered.

"How long?" the suited immigration official asked, not anxious to sit around all afternoon waiting for the Americans to decide what they wanted to do.

"I don't know," the deputy chief hedged. "I have to check some things out."

"Look, we can find out where he's staying and you can pick it up from there later."

"No, don't let him go under any circumstances," the American said. "I'm going to arrange for your people to pick him up for us. It won't take long. Just keep asking him questions. You know the drill. I'll get back to you soon."

After he placed the phone back on its cradle, the immigration agent returned to the room where his compatriot held Amir. Before sitting down to join them at the desk, he took off his jacket, loosened his tie, and rolled up his shirtsleeves. It was then that Amir realized something was amiss, that there wasn't going to be any five-minute solution to the question of his passport's authenticity. The suited official began to ask him questions, at first simple ones: How long did he plan to stay in the country? Where was he staying? What were his travel plans inside of Bosnia? After a time, however, the questions changed to ones about his political and religious ties, and what groups and organizations he belonged to . . . the tone of the interrogation going from formal but courteous to brusque and combative.

The questions the man asked were confusing to Amir and he grew frightened by the accusatory tone with which they were being spoken. Amir asked to speak to someone from the US embassy. His questioner just laughed, saying he had already placed the call.

The questioning left off when the agent was called into another room to take a phone call. A half hour later, the plainclothes agent returned and handed Amir his passport along with a release form, telling him that as soon as he signed the paper he was free to leave. Relieved, and anxious to be reunited with Jadranka, Amir quickly signed the document. The agent told him to follow him and after walking through what seemed a maze of corridors they came to a door with a wired window looking to the outside. Amir breathed a final sigh of relief as the agent opened it, stepped aside, and indicated his exit with a sweep of his arm.

Amir had come out onto what seemed to be some sort of cargo-loading area and was confused not to see any sign of a pathway leading to the passenger terminal. It took him a moment to realize that two men, who had been leaning up against a car some twenty yards away, were now walking his way, their eyes fixed directly on him. Both were wearing jeans; one wore a leather jacket over his t-shirt, and the other wore a light zip-up coat over a collared shirt that hung untucked outside of his pants.

"You're to come with us," the one with the leather jacket announced.

"Are you from the embassy?" Amir asked defensively, though he knew by their accent and clothing they weren't American.

The two smiled at him in a way that was ominous and frightening.

"Come on," the man wearing the nylon coat stated curtly, his hand reaching out and taking Amir's arm in a painful grip.

"Wait," Amir said, trying to think of a way to buy time. "My suitcase. I have to get my suitcase."

By that time they had reached the car. Both men ignored the boy's plea to retrieve his luggage, as if they hadn't heard him speak it.

"Get in," the man with the leather jacket said, opening the back door. He forced Amir in while the other man went around to the other side to slide in next to him.

"Who are you?" Amir asked, now seriously frightened. "Are you the police?"

"Keep your mouth closed," the driver growled. "Don't ask questions."

Amir was about to protest, but the face of the man sitting to his side halted his words. There was a look in his eyes that he'd seen before. It made his head feel light, his face and hands begin to sweat, and his stomach go queasy. Amir turned and stared out the window, remaining silent and wondering where they were taking him. He soon saw that they were driving away from the city center and he became both confused and frightened. After about fifteen minutes the car pulled up to a motel that sat on the edge of an industrial area on the outskirts of the city. Any momentary hope that he might have felt by their arrival at a place of lodging rather than a prison or police station was quickly lost to the fact that the place seemed to be almost deserted.

Jadranka had grown frantic. Her attempts to talk with any senior customs officer had been brushed aside by their gatekeepers. Her mother and sister tried to console her and tell her everything would turn out OK. Yet their words were unconvincing and rang hollow. Tired of waiting, Jadranka camped out in front of the Immigration office door and began to accost whoever left with questions about Amir's status. It wasn't long before she was told to go home or she would be arrested for disturbing the peace.

"What?" she had responded incredulously. "You'll what? Arrest me? For what?"

She had spoken loudly in reply to the agent who seemed taken aback by the force of her words. The timbre of her voice was filled with anger and drew the attention of several passersby, who stopped to watch.

"Who do you bastards think you are?" she shouted. "Milošević? Do you think you can do whatever you want without answering to anyone?"

The agent, who wanted to react in anger, held himself in check, not only because people were stopping to see what was going on, but even more because the girl's words struck him like a knife, piercing the membrane of officiousness that clothed his identity.

"Look," he said, "just show a little patience, that is all. I'll ask inside, and I'm sure it will all be resolved in a while."

"No, no more patience," Jadranka continued in yet louder voice. "I've been waiting for almost three hours. Either you have your chief come talk to me now and tell me the reason for holding my friend or I'm going to call the police."

The agent responded by laughing at the idea that she would call the police, but at the same time he sensed a clear danger in it. The crowd of people gathered about now numbered nearly a dozen. A few had asked Jadranka's mother and sister what was going on and, having heard the story, began to talk with others, looking toward the agent with disapproving eyes.

"What seems to be the problem here?" a man dressed in suit and tie asked, stepping out from the office.

Jadranka recognized him as one of the men who had detained Amir at the immigration line.

"Where is my friend? What have you done with him?"

"Why, I don't know where your friend is," the man smiled, displaying an expression of mild confusion. "He was released some time ago. Look, I have the release form he signed before he left. Perhaps you missed him coming out while you were waiting here. He's probably wandering around the terminal right now looking for you."

Jadranka took the paper the man proffered and quickly scanned the signature, recognizing it as Amir's. She didn't trust the man, but there was nothing she could do other than hand back the paper and rush to the arrival gate, hoping to find Amir.

It was early afternoon when Margaret received Jadranka's phone call, the first of what would turn out to be many. His mother had asked that Amir call when he arrived, to let her know his trip had gone well. But it was Jadranka's, not Amir's, voice on the line, and the tone of her greeting immediately boded ill and was quickly confirmed by what Jadranka had called to ask.

"Has Amir called?"

"What?" his mother asked, confused. "No. Why do—?"

"I can't find him," Jadranka interrupted, her voice breaking down. "I don't know where he is. They had him in Immigration, and they said they let him go, and now I can't find him."

"Wait, please," Margaret said, suddenly feeling a chill run up the back of her neck. "Slow down. I don't understand."

Jadranka began to sob. It had been her only hope. . . . Amir, unable to find her, might have called his mother as the most logical link to leave a message through which he and Jadranka could connect. Yes, she was sure he would have called his mother. He wouldn't just be wandering aimlessly about Sarajevo looking for her.

When Margaret had finally gotten all of the details straight, she tried to reassure Jadranka that everything would soon resolve itself, something she herself was not in the least sure of. Her mind had spoken the words in attempt to overcome the numbing sensation that had swept over her. It took her some minutes afterward to gather her thoughts, and even then the only thing she could think to do was to call Alice.

Chapter 31

When Amir protested, saying he wouldn't enter the motel room, they shoved him inside. He yelled that they had no right to hold him and demanded that they bring him to the police station, where he would have access to a lawyer or his embassy. Their answer was a strike to his midsection, doubling him over in pain. Then began the endless hours of interrogations.

Upon returning from vacation, the first order of business for the CIA station chief was getting up to date on the capture of the terrorist suspect. He said little while the deputy chief briefed him on the affair.

"And what have our local friends come up with? Anything of interest?" the chief asked, his tone neutral and noncommittal.

"Yes, here's a copy of a statement the suspect signed implicating himself in a broad range of support of terrorist organizations, including Al-Qaeda. It seems Fellini Junior has been involved in more than just making antiwar movies for college liberals. That's his code name, by the way, Fellini Junior."

"Hmmm," the station chief said, taking the paper handed him by his deputy. "Quite the clever tag. Did you come up with that one yourself?"

"No," the junior officer replied, "someone at headquarters did."

The station chief sat in silence, reading the detainee's statement and looking over the file several more times, until his deputy began to fidget. The "confession" wasn't worth the paper it was written on. It was broad, unspecific, and basically said nothing other than "I'm guilty." The chief had no illusions as to how "their friends" in the Bosnian intelligence agency had obtained it. The older agent sat measuring his response. He already knew, of course, what it would be. But it eased his conscience to feel as though he had considered the alternatives. These days, if you even sneezed to your left, you'd be labeled unpatriotic. He closed the file in front of him, looked at his deputy, nodded his head, and then went on to other business.

Amir had lost track of the days. How many weeks had it been, two, or maybe three? He wasn't sure. He felt so weary, so tired of not being allowed sleep, constantly interrogated with the same questions over and over. "Who is Zakariyya Ashrawi?" the interrogator asked him. The question confused Amir. Why would they ask him that again and again? They already knew the answer. When he told them for the hundredth time that he was a professor at his college, they asked, "How do you know him?" Amir answered, "He was my professor."

"What was his name?"

"I don't understand. You know his name. You just spoke it."

"What did you call him? How did you address him?"

"By his name, of course. Zack."

"Zack? You call him Zack. Then he was a friend of yours?"

"No. . . . Yes, I mean a little. He was friendly with all of his students," Amir responded, feeling confused.

"So Zack is your friend, then?" the interrogator continued. "One does things for their friends, yes? What sort of things did you do for Zack?"

"Nothing, really," Amir answered, his eyes wanting nothing more than to close and be carried off into dream.

"Nothing? You did not help make Internet sites for him?"

"Yes, but . . ."

His interrogator didn't allow Amir the explanation his mind was attempting to summon, but interrupted him by holding up a photograph of a man and asking, "Who is this man?"

"I don't know," Amir said. "He's a friend of Zack's. I can't remember his name. It's Arabic. He was from Lebanon, I think. He came to school to visit Zack."

"But you made an interview of him. And then put it on the Internet. What do you mean, you can't remember? Of course you can remember. Why do you lie to me?"

The questions continued coming in small, random probes; the questions had been designed to disorient and trip Amir up on small, inconsequential errors that the man would then use to punish him. After a time, as the men watching him grew tired and bored with the little substantive information they were able to get out of their prisoner, the pattern of questioning changed. The guards worked in twelve-hour shifts, and at the end of one of them the man who was Amir's chief interrogator took the sheets of paper containing the list of questions supplied by the Americans and threw them in the waste can. "I'm tired," he said. "Now we're going to do it the easy way. Not so easy for you, though. But easier for us."

The questions continued, but instead of being punctuated by endless psychological tricks to disorient and demoralize him, they were marked by physical blows and fear tactics that put Amir constantly on edge, never knowing whether or not the moment might be his last. After a time, not able to obtain the information they had been asked to get from their prisoner, the questions began to come with the answers already supplied. Amir had only to agree.

Just the day before, they had him sign a paper they said was unimportant and that he didn't need to bother reading. Now they wanted him to sign another. In the beginning Amir had refused to sign anything. But he had grown so weary, so tired of not being allowed sleep and being constantly interrogated with the same questions over and over that he told himself it didn't matter. The document they now placed in front of him was titled in bold print "Release Form," but his captors had said nothing about his being freed when they had handed it to him. When he asked, they had laughed and said of course it was so, why else would he be signing it? Taking the pen, he signed the document, knowing that in any case, he had no real choice in the matter. He had grown weary of his captors' lies and had little faith that the paper would bring his freedom. When they prepared to lead him outside the motel room, however, he wasn't able to stifle his hope. He felt emotion well up inside him for the first time since his imprisonment. But as he was about to pass through the threshold to the outside, the men pulled his hands roughly behind him, cuffed them, and then placed a hood over his head.

"What are you doing?" cried Amir. "Please, let me go. Please."

A small delivery van was parked just outside the room, its rear wheels snug to the curb. As soon as Amir's jailors had opened the motel room door, the vehicle's rear doors swung outward, pushed opened from the inside. A man stepped out from the back and stood guard as another joined the two holding Amir, hustling their prisoner quickly from motel room to van. There was no one to witness the act, and even if there had been, the men's movement had been quick and their blindfolded prisoner shielded from sight by the guards' bodies. Amir was being driven back to the place from which his ordeal had started, a fact he didn't realize until he was dragged from the van and could hear the sounds of planes landing and taking off. He began to ask where he was and what was being done to him when he received the first blow. More followed. He heard a man say something about softening up the package, but the rest was lost to his pain and the laughter of men his blindfold prevented him from seeing.

His body wanted to fall to the ground but was unable to because it was being supported on each side by hands that refused to let it collapse. Amir felt yet another set of hands taking hold of the hood that covered his head, and then a sudden rush of light momentarily blinded him. What he saw frightened him yet even more. There were half a dozen men, perhaps more, all dressed in black, their faces covered by military balaclavas of the same color. The specter-like sight terrified him. A pair of scissors appeared in one of the masked men's hands, and he watched in panic as the man approached and began to cut away his clothing.

Standing naked, Amir's body could be seen visibly shaking. Suddenly, everything went black as the sack was once again placed over his head. A voice spoke out to him in English, telling him not to move, and he felt the sharp stabbing pain of a needle pierce his skin. The voice that had spoken to him was, he felt sure, American. Without thought he had cried out to the invisible speaker, imploring him for help. The blow to his kidney caused him to gasp. Everything began to grow confused as the injection took hold. He was grabbed and made to bend over. His legs were spread apart and he felt a searing pain as something was inserted into his rectum. His bowels began to expand as though they were a balloon being filled with air until the point of explosion. Afterward, it felt as if they were placing a diaper on him. None of it made sense. He tried to speak once more but could manage only a mumble and began to lose consciousness.

Amir felt his feet walk up a short set of stairs, as if the legs that guided them were not his own but belonged to someone else. There was a familiar noise. The sound of jet engines and then the feeling of being lifted into the air. It was the last thing he remembered before slipping into unconsciousness.

Days turned into weeks, and the weeks into months of tortuous dimension, though of different order for Amir than for his family and Jadranka. Their suffering lay in the agony of unknowing, while for him it lay in understanding exactly what awaited him from one day to the next. When Margaret had first gotten the news of Amir's detention and subsequent disappearance, at Alice's urging, she had immediately called the State Department, who promised they would look into it.

"Look into it?" Margaret had asked incredulously. "It's not a matter to be *looked into*. My son was detained by Bosnian immigration agents at the Sarajevo airport. And now he's disappeared. This is an urgent matter. Don't tell me you'll look into it. You need to have the ambassador contact the Bosnian government immediately."

"Yes, Mrs. Morgan," the calm voice on the other end of the line replied. "I assure you we'll contact the embassy in Bosnia right away."

Not at all reassured by her conversation with the State Department official, Margaret, along with Alice and Paul, called their congressmen and senators, imploring them for help in finding Amir. They kept up the pressure by calling in for daily reports, though they never received anything but proclamations of sympathy and assurances that the authorities were doing all they could to find Amir.

Jadranka stayed in Bosnia in an attempt to discover anything she could about Amir's disappearance. She worked whatever channel she was able to access, both official and unofficial. In the end it was the public outcry, small though strident, that she'd gathered in her support and, most surprisingly, the help of the police that had brought to light the truth of what had happened. The police investigation confirmed that Amir had been taken into custody by Bosnian intelligence agents immediately after being released by Customs. Jadranka felt some hope then, a thread of something that might be followed to find Amir.

Yet in the end, after dragging their heels for weeks, Bosnian intelligence officials, pressed by public and political pressure, came up with another signed release form, which stated that the subject, after his interrogation, had been freed from custody. The form had been filed away, they said, with a number of other inconsequential interviews that had led nowhere and then been relegated to storage, hence the delay in unearthing it. They believed, a spokesman declared, that Amir had left the country, and though they had no exact knowledge of where he might have gone, they had received intelligence saying he'd joined the jihad against the Americans, either in Iraq or Afghanistan.

Jadranka made plans to return to the United States when it became clear that Amir was no longer in Bosnia and she learned through unofficial channels that the Bosnian intelligence agents had been working on behalf of the Americans all along. She was informed, however, that her visa to the US had been revoked and that she was denied entry back into the country. She was given no further explanation.

When Margaret heard the news that Jadranka would not be allowed to return to the US, she was devastated. In the beginning there had been an initial rush of support, both in the press and from her elected representatives, in her efforts to find her son. Very soon, though, the media articles that had been following the story began printing bits and pieces of the same insinuation and innuendo that Margaret was receiving from the government offices. Lead articles such as "Missing American Student" slowly morphed into back-page paragraphs such as "Bosnian-American Disappears From Homeland," "Anti-War Activist Goes Missing in Homeland," and "Missing Student Tied to Terrorist Professor." There began to be mention of rumors from reliable sources that the missing student might have attempted to join up with jihadists fighting the Americans in Iraq.

Meanwhile, after the US invasion of Iraq, the forces of good, in their stirring and successful victory against the forces of evil, were beginning to show signs of trouble in winning the peace. After having easily conquered Iraq, it was being widely reported that hordes of foreign fighters were flooding into that country to make it the staging ground of the war against the West. The story of Margaret Morgan's missing son had become less than a minor footnote to the larger story, and also one that highlighted the dangers now looming from every direction: Sleeper cells, made up of foreign nationals such as Amir, were reported to be planted about the United States, awaiting the right moment to strike.

Amir's mother began to be overtaken by a hopelessness that seemed to wither her body at the same pace it did her spirit. She had come to feel that there was little, if any, difference between the government party line and that which was being presented to the public by the news media. She was being stonewalled by the one, and her only recourse to discover the truth had been the other.

"Alice, I don't know what to do," Margaret said in one of her daily phone calls to her daughter. "Do you think I should fly to Sarajevo? Maybe he's still there."

Alice could hear the tears in her mother's voice, could feel the heavy sadness of her heart. "No, Mom," she replied, "Jadranka says she's sure he isn't there anymore. She's heard Amir was taken elsewhere."

"Oh, god," Margaret said, her voice colored with despair. "I just can't believe it. I don't know. I just don't know."

Alice's concern for her mother grew as summer and fall passed, bringing in the first snows of winter without any new word of Amir. Her mother had become depressed as the State Department continued to deny any knowledge of Amir's whereabouts. When the Christmas holidays came, Alice and Paul canceled their plans in Cambridge and spent the week with Margaret, hoping they and the girls could help her break through her despondency.

"Mom," Alice said, "I want you to come back to Cambridge with us. I mean it. I won't take no for an answer. Paul's spoken to your neighbors, and they'll look after the house. You can come for the winter. In the spring, if you want, you can return. Living here alone isn't good, Mom. And besides, the girls are really looking forward to having their grandmother coming to live with them."

"Oh, Alice," Margaret sighed. "I don't know. I don't think I could live in the city again. This is my home."

Alice looked at her mother with sympathy. She had grown frail. In the last six months she had seemed to age a decade. The rounding of her shoulders had become pronounced, pulling the whole of her inward, like a building whose main support beam had fallen, caving the structure into its center.

"Mom," Alice said, and then paused. "I know it's been hard."

"Oh, I miss him so much."

"I know, Mom. I know. I do too."

"I remember the first time I ever saw him. There was this little boy looking at me from across the table. There was something so sad in his eyes, yet so beautiful."

"Yes, I know, Mom. But what do you think Amir would want you to do now? You know he'd want you to go to Cambridge. Come back with us. Just for the winter. Hopefully, we'll have some news by spring."

"But what if he calls? What if he's able to get to a phone and there's no one here to answer?"

"Mom, he knows my phone number just as well as yours. He would call me," Alice said, forcing a positive look upon her face. "We will find him and bring him home from wherever he is. We won't give up until we do."

"I don't know. I don't know," Margaret answered, her mind closing down under the weight of her sadness.

Chapter 32

Amir awoke from his drug-induced slumber only to find himself in a place of even greater darkness than the color of his sleep, his half-conscious mind unable to recall that his captors had tied a hood around his head. At first he panicked. He could hear nothing but muffled sounds, and he thought that he was dreaming he was once again deaf. His hands and legs, which tried to move, jerked against the manacles that held them, but before he could register their restraint a sharp blow to his legs stung him, bringing his mind back into focus and reminding him of where he was. Or rather of what had happened to him, because in truth he had no idea where he might be. He lay still then, and there were no more painful reminders not to struggle against his bonds. After a short time he could feel the airplane begin to descend and his ears pop under the headphones that covered them and had been placed over his hood.

As the plane touched down, his mind struggled to find some solid footing upon which to stand, while another part of him simply wished for the plane to accelerate, to take off into the sky and resume his journey into oblivion for as long as it might take the nightmare to find its end. He was extraordinarily confused—a state of mind purposefully and skillfully contrived by his captors to rob him of any sense of self or safety. When the plane came to a halt, Amir felt his body being pulled upward. As he attempted to stand, a second pair of hands joined in to help raise him, roughly grabbing his right shoulder and yanking it painfully back at the same time it lifted him.

Amir had no idea where he was. Logic, what little of it was functioning in his mind, told him that he must have been taken back to the United States. He thought he could hear the muffled sound of people speaking in English, and after all, where else would they be transferring him? He felt himself being passed to other sets of hands, and it was no longer the English language being spoken but another he couldn't recognize. The men who had taken hold of him dragged him from the plane, then lifted and threw him onto the floor of a covered truck bed.

The vehicle traveled along a rough road, Amir's body jolting up and down as he made his way toward an unknown destination. Amir's senses could register cool air, dust, and the clang of metal on metal. When he was taken from the truck and his blindfold finally removed, he found himself in a cold, dirty room, barely large enough for him to lie down in. He had been led along a dark passageway and then down a set of stairs, so he guessed that he was below ground level. With one glance at his surroundings, any small, remaining hope that he was back in the United States quickly dissipated. Before his captors closed the door to his cell, he could see several other metal-clad doors across the narrow corridor.

There was no light in his room, and when his door slammed shut, he was left in darkness. Feeling about with his hands, he found nothing in the room but a thin blanket and a plastic bucket to be used as his toilet. He could tell by the blanket's smell and feel that the cloth was filthy, but he was nevertheless thankful for it. In his mind's calculation he thought that it must still be summer, but the room felt cold and damp. He shivered and sought a corner to cradle into, huddling within the foul, threadbare blanket that was his only warmth.

During the long hours of his journey, Amir had done nothing but sleep, yet now he sought sleep's solace once again. His back pressed against the cold, hard surface of the concrete wall, Amir leaned his head back to rest between his shoulders. It was then that he heard the whisperings of other prisoners. Before he could make out the words of the hushed utterings, however, they were drowned out with loud, strange, and discordant music that did not cease for hours, making it impossible not only to hear the other prisoners' whisperings but to retreat into dreams as well.

When the barrage of sound finally ended, he took his hands from his ears and could feel his body release the tension that had seized it, the silence freeing his muscles to relax back into their normal state.

Amir's reprieve was short-lived. The door to his cell was thrown open, and he was blinded by a bright light shining in from the passageway. Two men entered the room and took hold of his manacled hands, raising his arms painfully above his head and shackling them to the ceiling. Both of the guards drew knives, and Amir's heart froze as they moved toward him. In seconds he was stripped of the coveralls he'd been transported in, to hang naked, his feet barely able to touch the ground.

A third man then entered the room. He was different from the other two, who were dressed informally and seemed to have taken pleasure in their work. The gray-haired man stood silently staring at him while the two younger men laughed and exchanged comments in a language Amir thought he recognized as Arabic. The older man's skin was ruddy and of olive complexion, the look on his face all the more hardened for the detached gaze of his eyes. When he spoke, he addressed Amir in a precise and clear, though accented, English.

"Speak only when I tell you to," he commanded coldly and without emotion. "You are in a place that doesn't exist. There is no law here. Nobody knows where you are or even that you are being held." Pausing, the man looked into Amir's eyes to give his words weight and see his prisoner's reaction. Satisfied by the fear he saw clearly written on the boy's face, he continued, "You can make this easy or difficult. It is of your own choosing. It matters neither way to me. If you die, we will bury you in the ground, and no one will ever know. Do you understand?"

Amir nodded as though in a trance. He wanted to ask if his mother knew he was being held. Of all that he'd suffered in his captivity, that was what had caused him the most anxiety.

"Now tell me about the people you worked for," his interrogator commanded. "Start from the beginning. And I warn you, do not leave anything out."

Amir caught his breath, and despite the cold he began to sweat. With his unclothed body chained to the ceiling, a guard at each side, he'd never felt more vulnerable. The gray-haired man began with the same questions that had been put to him in the motel room but then switched to questions of more technical nature: questions about making videos and placing them on the Internet. Amir was relieved to be able to speak of something about which he knew, and he eagerly answered.

"So you are an expert about these things then, are you?" the gray-haired man asked, as if impressed.

"No," Amir answered weakly, swallowing his breath. "I mean, I know the basics, but I'm not really an expert."

Smiling, his interrogator moved behind Amir so that his prisoner could not see him. He asked Amir about Zakariyya Ashrawi, about whether he had taught his professor the technical media skills to pass on to terrorist groups or whether Amir himself had passed them on directly to Ashrawi's operatives. When Amir answered truthfully that he had done neither, the gray-haired man nodded to one of the guards, who took a short length of electric cable from his belt and struck Amir several times behind his knees and on his buttocks.

The questioning seemed to go on endlessly. After a time, Amir felt the places where he'd been hit go from a white, searing pain to a dull throb, and the tears and saliva that had flowed down his face dried, leaving a thin crust from their trail. This interrogator had not been so easily pleased as the previous ones, who were happy to accept the simple parroting of the prompts they had provided. This man wanted specific information and names that Amir had no way of giving. The man eventually announced he was leaving to go eat, an act he knew the prisoner himself had little opportunity to partake in. As the gray-haired man left, he nodded to the two men standing beside Amir and said something to them in their native language. Turning back to Amir, he spoke in a voice that didn't hide its irony, telling him not to worry, that he would return soon to see him again.

Months after having first arrived, Amir was led out of the prison, hooded, shackled, and once more readied for transport. Loaded into the back of a truck, he rode for nearly an hour along a bumpy, dusty road with his feet and hands chained to the bed of the vehicle. As uncomfortable as the ride might have been, he nevertheless drank in the trip's impressions like a parched traveler coming upon a stream. Even the air, choked with grit and exhaust, felt to him like a refreshing breeze after endless days of the stale, dank atmosphere of his subterranean cell. The sounds of life, distant and nearly drowned out by the truck's engine and spinning wheels, were to him like the warbling of a songbird announcing a long winter's end.

When the truck stopped, Amir's chains were released and he was pulled from the truck, his hood removed, and his clothing cut off with scissors and razors by the guards who had accompanied him from the prison. It was daytime, and though he stood in an empty airplane hanger and was shielded from the sun's glare, the light from the open entrance was enough to blind his eyes. It had been months since he'd last seen the light of day. His eyes squinted as he took in the scene.

A group of hooded men stood to the side, chatting among themselves. Nearby, talking with another man dressed in civilian clothes, was his interrogator of the past few months, the one he'd come to know as "the gray-haired man." Neither of the men appeared happy in their conversation, his interrogator lifting his hands in what seemed a dismissive gesture of both the prisoner and the person with whom he was speaking. The other man was clearly a westerner, dressed very much in American style. His demeanor and the way he held himself seemed to confirm this. Amir felt a surge of hope, despite himself.

"Disappointing, very disappointing," the American said as he took the file from the gray-haired man who held it out to him. "It's basically nothing more than a rehash of what we already had."

"I told you, my friend, you could come and ask the questions yourself anytime you wanted if you thought you could do the job better," the gray-haired man responded.

The American replied silently with a sardonic look. The operative words were "plausible deniability"; his foreign colleague knew that as well as he did. If the American official didn't actually see what went on in the prison, then he was free to believe the promise that everything had been handled according to international standards. After all, nothing in the conventions prohibited a wink, a nod, and a turn of the head in the other direction.

"Anyway, you have him now," the gray-haired man said in conclusion. "You can see for yourself. There is no more juice to be squeezed from this lemon. It is dry. Worth nothing, I'm afraid."

The American agent sighed and shook his head. Just another day at the office, his look spoke. He turned to one of the men standing ready and signaled him toward the prisoner. Two of the hooded men walked over to Amir and escorted him onto the plane.

Although he had known better than to allow himself the illusion of hope, Amir hadn't been able to keep its presence from arising and taking hold of his thoughts. Despite the intensity of his experience, he was still a novice at the game, the learning curve of a prisoner not so simple as most might think.

On his newest journey, Amir succumbed to hope's emotion not once, but twice. Its first arising had been dashed by the time he arrived at his new destination: a place of dark, dank passageways and crumbling walls, a gloomy, third-world prison that would have served a filmmaker as a perfect setting of despair. He had not been transferred back home to the United States. When he saw American soldiers, though, hope sprang up within him like a dog greeting its master's return. Amir had no more power to stop his involuntary reaction than the animal had to curb the spontaneous wagging of its tail.

The second collapse came not by the visual but by the purely physical, when Amir attempted a sputtering greeting, to speak his relief and implore his countrymen's help. In response, the soldier nearest him stepped forward and swung his open palm across Amir's cheek, the stinging slap striking away Amir's words just as emphatically as it did the look of hope written on his face. Tears began streaking down Amir's cheeks, and after recovering from the shock of the blow, he cried out that he was an American, the physical pain nothing compared to his emotion's despair. A second soldier responded by grabbing Amir's shirt and then repeatedly slamming him into the wall. Spitting in Amir's face, he shouted at him that they knew all about him, knew that he was a traitor to the country that had taken him in, saved and sheltered him, and that he, Amir, had responded to their compassion with treason.

"So don't fucking tell me you're an American," the soldier yelled, slamming Amir's head against the concrete one more time for emphasis. "You ain't one of us, motherfucker."

After a time, the bleeding from his face and head congealed and dried, the surrounding hair matting into a hardened clump. Amir's new cell was bigger than the previous one, though not by much. The air was as damp and cold, and his body shivered. His thoughts were confused and disoriented, and it took him a few seconds to realize that, wherever he was, it was in a colder climate.

The memory of sunlight lay like the thread of a dream, the touch of a loving hand, a sensation of beauty too painful to recall. Those images belonged to a world that was no longer his to enjoy. Like Alice in Wonderland, he'd somehow fallen into a hole leading to a hidden realm, though not a surreal journey upon a brightly colored path, but a place of terror along a dark road of despair. He wasn't shocked at the netherworld's existence, only that he had fallen into it for a second time in his life. It was, he knew, a place much closer to the surface of things than most would care to believe.

The emotional dejection Amir felt at the hands of the soldiers was far more painful to him than his physical suffering. He hadn't cried out that he was an American in attempt to proclaim his innocence. In fact, he was no longer sure that he was completely free of guilt.

Had he crossed over the line somewhere along the way, heedless or indifferent to its existence? He had felt driven to help those who suffered as he had, yet he knew that, as with the soldiers that hit him, there had been anger within him as well. The other prisoners in his previous place of incarceration often whispered their wrath against the Americans, swearing to revenge themselves against their tormentors, in order to bolster their spirits and persevere, but Amir found himself unable to summon those emotions. Something within him understood that the marriage of anger and vengeance could beget only more hate and suffering.

There were those among the prisoners who sought no other way of life but that. These men were misanthropes at heart—tyrannous, nihilistic people who could speak only of death and violence and sought to herd the other prisoners' thoughts into places of dark and oppressive beliefs. A number of his fellow prisoners, however, if they were enemies of the United States, were ones of more benign nature who had never taken up arms against the invading forces. Since their imprisonment, however, many of them had become radicalized and were now more inclined to follow in a violent path.

The prisoner held in the cell next to his had owned a small electronics business in Kabul. He called himself Abdul Raouf, and he had lived in London for a number of years prior to returning to his homeland. He had been secretly turned over to NATO forces by a former business associate, who claimed Abdul had supplied the Taliban with communication devices. He and the associate had been in a longstanding dispute over a debt. "Of course I gave the Taliban what they wanted," Abdul had whispered during a lull in the guards' watch. "If I hadn't, they would have killed me and taken what they wanted anyway."

Though Amir had once hoped of eventually escaping his ordeal, he no longer had any illusions that his keepers might come to understand he wasn't their enemy. And even if one of his captors sensed the truth, they could do little or nothing to help. They were as much subject to the force that dictated his captivity as he was. The faces of his current guards blurred into those of the men who long ago had burst into his home and descended upon his family in Bosnia. There had been no sign of any pity, no less compassion, in the eyes of the men who had set upon him and his mother, father, and sister. The psychosis that had ignited their blood lust, that dismissed the individuality of their victims, had at the same time consumed their own individuality along with it. Any conscience they might have had to question their acts was lost to the greater cause. There was no "I" in the affliction of any harm done to "her" or "him," but rather it was the "us" doing unto "them." Self was abdicated to the mind of a communal consciousness, one that made no fine distinctions of identity outside the circle it drew around itself. It was a line meant to enclose those within its bounds, close off those on the outside, and redefine the laws of civilization accordingly.

Some of the jailors were better than others. Some participated in his suffering only when they were called upon to do so. Others, though, clearly engaged in it for their own pleasure and amusement. If the conditions of war changed certain people's natural moral inclinations, such that they would act in ways they ordinarily might find abhorrent, there were others who found their way to war because, within its rules, they could find safe haven for their natural predilections without fear of law or punishment. It was a realm where sociopath and good citizen could mix in common purpose.

Amir sometimes wished he could find it in himself to rail at the injustice of his imprisonment, if not externally, then at least internally. It wasn't, however, the futility of it that kept him from trying. Rather, he had been overtaken by an overwhelming sense of sadness, one whose source he was unable to place solely on the fact of his imprisonment and separation from Jadranka and his family. Over the months of being locked in small, dank spaces, shut off from the world of people and light, he had come to understand that the greatest challenge facing him wasn't enduring the physical and psychological abuse his captors inflicted upon him. The abuse was by no means easy to handle, but after a time the purposefully erratic nature of its delivery, designed to disorient him, became a kind of norm. The physical pain took on characteristics of chronic suffering brought on by a disease, such as an arthritic person learning to live with joint pain or a cancer patient coping with the ordeal of chemotherapy treatments.

No, what most challenged Amir was the sense of hopelessness that lived within him, that had entered him like a virulent infection on that last day of his life with his birth family in Bosnia. His imprisonment made an easy pathway for hopelessness to reenter into the seat of his emotions, its false view of life painting a bleak and futile future, a malarial swamp of negativity and poisonous hate. It was not the way his father and mother would have wanted him to live. Asaf would have wished more strength from him than to succumb to the hopelessness that fed evil's purpose. Nor would Jadranka find pride in his giving up, in allowing his silence to once again become nothing more than a rabbit's hole from which to hide from the world. Margaret, who had taken him in, who loved him as her own, deserved more from him than that.

Amir forced himself to think of these things every time hopelessness arose and tried to take over his being, leaving him awash in sadness and despair. When he felt he could bear no more, he thought of the people who loved him, those whose hope for him would be life, not death of either body or spirit. With their image in mind, he would struggle back, force the despair from his heart and mind. He would survive. He would somehow overcome his ordeal and return to those he loved. In the dark, solitary confinement of his cell, when despondency came inching forward into his thoughts, he made movies in his mind, shooting scenes of his loved ones, brief remembrances of home, of school, of going out to get an ice cream, of walking in the woods, of looking into the sky to the bright hope of a sunny day or to the mystery of a starry night. He scripted easy, sweet dialogues, linking the scenes into a documentary of normalcy, a life he might someday live again. The fantasies helped him get through the days—or perhaps they were the nights, he had no way of knowing which—as they blended one into the other in slow, torturous progression.

Chapter 33

If Amir had been disheartened by the animosity of the greeting shown him by his new keepers, he expected that at least the physical tortures he'd undergone at the previous prison would abate in this new one under direct American control. In this, he was only partially correct. There was, it was true, an abeyance of the more overt physical treatments. Yet he found that the psychological and emotional tortures practiced were in many ways more difficult to handle than the physical abuse his previous jailors had inflicted upon his body.

Amir had no reason not to believe the new guards' taunts that they could do to him what they wanted to because he was no longer an American, in fact, never had been. His citizenship, they had told him, was stripped back to the moment it had been awarded, nullifying any claim he'd ever had to its protection. They laughed when he cringed in terror at the snarling dogs let within inches of his naked body, and though they never struck him with closed fists, open-handed slaps seemed to be within the guidelines of their rules.

The interrogations began two days after his arrival. That they were having another go at him surprised Amir. He had already been conquered, had signed whatever paper they'd put in front of him, had told them whatever they wanted to hear. It should have been apparent that he hadn't anything of use for them. Amir couldn't understand why they would go on asking questions he couldn't answer, continue to fracture him into ever-smaller slivers of self in search of what clearly wasn't there.

His new interrogators asked the same questions as had all the others. Amir explained to them that he wasn't in fact a computer expert on Internet technologies, that he was a student filmmaker and hadn't been aware that the groups Zakariyya Ashrawi had been working with had been designated as terrorist organizations. Yes, he had sympathy for the Palestinian people. Yes, he had wanted to do something to help them. No he didn't hate the Israelis, didn't wish to see them harmed or killed.

As in previous interrogations, he started out by telling the truth. When his jailors asked him questions whose answers were not to their liking, they declared that he was lying. But unlike what he'd done in his previous interrogations in the other prisons—waiting until he could tell by the interrogators' accusations what it was they wanted to hear and answering accordingly—Amir began to challenge their assertions. He told them he would no longer sign any papers or acquiesce to their portrayal of him as a willing supporter of terrorist causes, a tech expert who was helping the enemy with their war of propaganda and secret web of communications.

A week after his arrival he once again found himself shackled to the ceiling of a room, his clothing stripped from his body. This time there were no electric probes, no striking of his body with a length of electric cable. Instead his interrogators shouted at him, kept him from sleep, and played music at a volume whose decibels were ear shattering. They doused him with water so that his body began to shiver in the damp cold of the cell.

One of the soldiers questioning him, the one called Berger, finally said that it was late, he was tired and wanted to eat dinner. His partner, Wallace, suggested they let nature do their job for them.

"I don't know," Berger responded. "Let's just go eat and come back. It's late. The temp's dropped."

"What the fuck, man," Wallace replied. "Who gives a shit? He can turn into a freakin' popsicle for I all care. C'mon, don't be a wuss."

"Whatever," Berger said, his tone of voice sounding unconvinced.

The two soldiers released Amir's chains from the ceiling and led him outside into a small, barren courtyard, where they secured his shackles to two iron rings bolted into a wall. Wallace poured one last bucket of water over Amir's head, and the two men left for the mess hall.

The temperature outside hovered just above 45 degrees Fahrenheit, and though the guards who walked the perimeter of the compound were comfortable enough without gloves or heavy winter coat, Amir's naked body began to tremble. To distract himself from his physical discomfort, he forced himself to look up into the evening sky. After a time, he became mesmerized by the stars' glittering light. It had been months since he had been able to gaze into the heavens, and he was amazed by its beauty. Colored by the deepest of blacks, the clear, moonless evening sky reminded him of his childhood home high in the mountains of Bosnia. There, the starlight sparkled through the thin, crisp air unimpeded by illumination of city or town, and he could look upward and feel its touch upon him like the waves of a calm ocean gently lapping at his feet.

Amir's reverie was interrupted by the sudden and uncontrollable shivering of his entire body. He attempted to move in an effort to warm himself, though he was hindered by his chains, which were bound tight to the wall. He tried to hop up and down in place, but his movements were uncoordinated and caused him to pull painfully against his restraints. He felt weak and fatigued. He tried to speak, just to hear himself talk, so that he might gauge whether he was dreaming or awake. Amir heard his words exit his mouth in lazy, slurred monotone, as if spoken in an inebriated babble. His eyes scanned the courtyard with a weak sweep of his head.

The ground in the courtyard was barren, its earth compacted and lifeless. The only thing growing upon it was a scrawny, leafless tree, and even it seemed dead. But as Amir stared at its stunted growth, he began to see it bloom and grow. His body had stopped shivering, and his breathing slowed until it was nearly as still as the air about him. Amir felt his chains give way, as though they had been nothing more than a hologram of their material self and as easily shed as shade by stepping into sunlight. He walked over to the tree and touched its bark—he felt the pulse of its life beating in rhythm to that of his own. He reached up to its lowest branch and effortlessly pulled himself up, as though his body had been freed of its weight and thought alone allowed its movement. He began to climb, and as he moved among its branches the tree grew taller, so that it seemed he might never reach its end. Yet he was glad for the journey and had no wish for it to stop.

After some moments, Amir realized he had reached the tree's highest branches, where it seemed his view was endless. Looking out upon the world, he smiled. Its beauty was stunning. His gaze turned downward to look upon nature's wonders: hills and mountains, streams and rivers, fields and forest floor. His eyes drew closer focus and bore down on the landscape. There was movement in the trees and grass, among the bushes, and in the streams. Deer and squirrels, birds and fish, crickets and bees, ants and insects wandered about. It was endless life. The sound of it all came together in chorus . . . a song that hummed through the air like wind through the trees. The earth teemed with living things, and it was amazing to behold.

He suddenly found himself on the ground again, and the image of a life form suddenly came to his mind, one he realized had been missing from his view from above—that of his own kind. At first there was only the vision of bodies beginning to appear in nebulous form, their faces too indistinct to clearly discern. Then, as though a breeze shifted the air free of a fog, the features of the faceless people began to reveal themselves, causing Amir to smile. In front of him stood his father and mother, Asaf and Emina. Next to them was his sister, Minka. Their eyes were happy and filled with love for him. Coming up behind them was Margaret, and then came Jadranka, who caught his eyes and held them, pouring her love into him with a joyous laugh.

He could see that in the background were yet more eyes looking on. The faces appeared in a patchwork of differing shades of light, some brighter and clearer, others darker and more obscure. Yet the visage of each seemed caught and frozen upon them, as if framed in still photo. He paid little attention to their features but, rather, was drawn to the light that emanated more strongly from the few who, spotted about here and there, helped illuminate the whole.

Amir woke with a start, the vision still lingering in his mind. Lifting his head, he looked around the empty, lifeless courtyard. After a few moments, his gaze lowered and he saw that he was naked. He wondered why he should be without clothing but soon let the question go. He tried to move his arms but found he couldn't; his body was rigid.

Raising his head with difficulty, he looked at the singular, stunted tree clinging to life in the center of the lonely courtyard. Closing his eyes, Amir wished only to sleep, to dream of his family and leave that place of sorrow. He saw Margaret's face. It was filled with love yet lined with worry. Had he disappointed her? He was so sorry to have caused her anxiety and pain. Asaf appeared in his vision and looked at him silently. His father's eyes told him to be strong. Amir heard his father's message as if it had been spoken out loud. One part of him struggled to persevere, but another wanted nothing more than to let sleep carry him away. A noise that sounded like the flutter of wings interrupted his father's exhortation. It started out like a distant and soft vibration but soon grew in volume and intensity: at first like the wings of a bird hovering by his ear . . . and then like a moth trapped within the recess of his inner ear, beating wildly to free itself from the walls of its prison. The sound turned to a drone before changing to a distant hum of consonance, as though emanating from a chant or prayer. His father's face began to fade from view, and Amir's eyes were drawn inward to a blank screen. There was now only a mist of gray light, the sound drawing him deep into a darkness where he found a silence of extraordinary proportion. And in that precarious moment, when the final sleep called out to him to venture forth into it, the surge of a force, primordial and grown from love, from hope, from all the good he had found in life, awakened in his chest. And his heart, which had slowed, reinvigorated, expanding and contracting in urgent, determined movement, pumping and pushing his blood along the pathways of life.

The chains that held him to the wall fell from his wrists. Amir fought the return of the hallucinations, knowing he wouldn't have the strength to come back from them again. As hands took hold of him, took control of his body, he was confused. It took some seconds for him to realize that his body being freed from its restraints wasn't an illusion this time but was an act taking place in real time. Along with the hands taking his body, there were also voices, people speaking words, people who existed not as figments of his imagination, but were real, corporeal, and present.

"Jesus. Fuck," Berger muttered, bending down to take a pulse after having released the detainee from his shackles and lain him on the ground.

"Is he alive?" Wallace asked.

"I don't know," Berger replied, shaking his head. "I don't have a pulse. Call a medic. Tell them it's an emergency, get 'em here quick. I'll get a blanket. Shit . . ."

Berger was wrapping a blanket around the detainee when the medic arrived from the compound's sick bay. PFC Scooter Landon bent down over Amir, searching for a pulse. "What's the deal here?" he asked, although, taking in the shackles lying next to the naked detainee, he had a good idea of the reason for which he'd been called.

"Fucked up," Wallace shrugged. "Left him out a little too long."

Scooter Landon raised his eyes from the prone patient to the two soldiers. His look was hard as he met Wallace's eyes. The medic held Wallace's gaze and then looked to Berger, not even a single blink of his eyelids, as they spoke an accusation stronger than any word could muster. Berger felt queasy. Wallace covered his guilt with a macho uncaring, which a second later turned to anger—a fuck-you, who-gives-a-shit, silent retort.

"Go get a stretcher," Scooter said pointedly in Wallace's direction. The medic had found a weak pulse, but he wasn't hopeful.

Later, when Berger went to the sick bay to check on the detainee, Scooter Landon told him the kid had come as close to death as you could get and still come back whole. Berger took the news with an appearance of more self-possession than he really felt. Wallace had been worried that the event would be reported. Everyone knew, though, there wouldn't be any serious repercussions even if the incident were written up—even if, in the worst case, the detainee didn't pull through. Still, it would be a pain: a likely transfer to another base, a negative on the record that might slow down a future promotion. But this wasn't what had bothered Berger and had caused him to check on the detainee. It wasn't even Scooter Landon's look at seeing what he and Wallace had done to their prisoner. The medic's gaze had been but a mirror, one Berger had already been looking into of late.

The reproof he'd seen in Landon's eyes had meant something. It had focused the self-questioning Berger had been experiencing these last few weeks leading up to the end of his tour and his return home. There wasn't anyone he held in more esteem than Landon. The young medic had proved his mettle on the battlefield more than once. He had run through enemy rifle fire and mortars, taken a piece of shrapnel in his back, and saved two men who'd been caught in a crossfire. He had refused to be evacuated until the engagement was over. Scooter was a southern boy who took his religion seriously. As far as he was concerned, the golden rule applied to everyone, not just the chosen few.

It was just this that had been eating away at Berger lately. "Do unto others as you would have them do unto you" had turned into something altogether different. "Do unto others before they have a chance to do unto you" had become the twisted maxim Berger now lived by. Who had he become? He'd nearly killed the kid, not for any purpose, not for intel that would make a difference, but simply because he didn't care anymore. His view of humanity had been altered. The people he'd been willing to risk his life for, had flown halfway around the world to liberate, he now saw as insects, as lice-ridden, feral dogs, as well put out of their misery as left alive—a discretionary toss-up.

He had enlisted to make a difference, to stop the killing, not to become one of the killers. Yes, there had been some pride in it, some ego, something to show off to the world. He would be a warrior, a patriot. But he hadn't signed on to this war just to become like one of the bad guys. Would this war even make a difference? Would they rid the world of these terrorists, or would the terrorists just return, like cockroaches in the night, after the allied forces pulled out? Would it be like Vietnam, where fifty thousand lives and a few decades later the US was trading with the very enemy they'd said would deliver all of Asia into Communist ruin?

When Amir had been released from the sick bay and returned to his cell, there'd been nothing said about his nearly having died. The guards had given him an extra blanket—that was all. But Amir didn't need anyone to tell him how close he'd been to death. He'd felt his near passage into oblivion, the journey into the void.

Since the event in the courtyard, there hadn't been any more interrogations. The guards came by to check on him and to deliver meals, but nothing more. There had been no apologies, nothing said. The guards didn't talk to him. In a bizarre way, Amir felt himself missing their verbal abuse during the interrogations. It had at least been some form of human contact. The two soldiers who had left him out in the cold rotated in and out with the other guards in shifts that could be four hours or fourteen . . . he had no way of knowing. Time as he'd once known it, measured and ordered in a linear sequence, had disappeared.

Berger was on his very last shift before beginning his journey home, his tour completed. He was returning to Boston. Amir heard the other guards talking with him in the passageway, congratulating him, joking, giving the departing soldier a comradely hard time about leaving them behind. Amir listened intently, as one might listen to a compelling story on a radio show, the opportunity to hear another human voice a rare occurrence for the prisoners held in isolation.

Amir could hear cell doors opening and closing. After some minutes, the hinges of his own door sounded their awakening, and he saw Berger looking in. Amir was in the corner, his head looking out from the blankets that covered him, the cold from the hypothermia feeling as though it still lingered within, there to stay. Normally, the door would have closed soon after it opened, the guard having seen that things were in order, the detainee not having hung himself with his blanket or with torn strips of clothing, his food eaten, no hunger strike requiring intervention. But Berger paused, and in the moment's lull Amir could see that another door had opened, this one not of physical manifestation. Why Berger lingered, Amir had no idea, but in the measure of those few seconds, the time it took to inhale a single breath, Amir found himself speaking. The words came from his mouth as if of their own accord, without thought to the punishments that would likely follow.

"You're going to Boston," Amir said.

Berger's face blinked a brief surprise and then went hard. The music had been turned off; the slip of the guards' conversation had been overheard by the detainee. Amir could see the response in Berger's eyes, its message intense and angry. A physical blow, confiscation of his blankets, a reactivation of the interrogations— any or all of those things were the likely result if a prisoner dared so personal a remark to one of the guards.

"My sister lives in Cambridge," Amir continued. "Her name is Alice Morgan. She's a doctor." Amir went silent then, but he didn't cower.

The soldier's lips parted, as though he might spit out something in derision. His shoulders shifted as if turning back in the direction from which he had come. But his body held in silent deliberation a moment longer. He detected no plea in his prisoner's words. Neither was there challenge, falsehood, or attempt to play on his sympathy or guilt. The kid had dealt the only thing left him: his dignity. Berger knew the young detainee had been "disappeared" and that no one knew where he was or what had really happened to him. Berger knew that Amir had been removed from life as if he were dead, to live in a limbo of justice, a purgatory of righteous vengeance—his family left to wonder whether he was alive or his bones lay scattered and sun-bleached on desert sands or buried in some hidden, godforsaken hole.

Berger observed the detainee without prejudice, a calm finding him between the push and pull of opposing forces within. He'd been staring into the mirror too much lately. It wasn't good. It wasn't what soldiers were meant to do. In his own reflection, he could see others. He could see the boy huddled in the corner of the cell. He could see his own eyes looking back from the kid's face.

"No promises," Berger said.

"No promises," Amir acknowledged, his eyes holding the moment.

Berger nodded once, turned, and pulled the door closed behind him, the clang of metal echoing in the room. For Amir its sound was not one of finality, but rather one of hope, its reverberation a prayer for the future, for all of those who believed that, one day, humanity would fulfill the promise of its great privilege.

A Conversation with
Robert Madrygin, author of
THE SOLACE OF TREES

Due to your father's military career, you traveled throughout your childhood, living both in the United States and abroad. Much of your adulthood has been spent internationally as well. What did this experience bring to you in writing of a child fleeing war?

One of the things you learn early on as a kid moving from home to home and culture to culture is that there is an underlying commonality between all people that gives lie to stereotypes of race and culture. A child is still a child, whether from the US or from Bosnia. This is the simplest, clearest example of our shared humanity. Horrific acts visited upon people in far-off lands are, in truth, not such distant happenings at all. The physical world itself hasn't shrunk, it is the same size it has always been, but the boundaries between the societies and cultures that mark our human presence on the planet have diminished in an extraordinary way. In this sense, the book isn't just about a child from a foreign land, but it is the story of a boy who could as well be living next door. This is, in fact, a scenario that occurs in the story when the main character, Amir, is relocated to the US and in effect becomes the boy next door.

Was your interest in writing *The Solace of Trees* sparked in part by the modern-day humanitarian refugee crisis in Syria? Do you find parallels between Amir's story and those of Syrian child refugees?

The parallels between Syria and Bosnia are painful. Firstly, because of the suffering experienced by the people themselves. Secondly, because the world's lack of response has been essentially the same in both cases. I began writing *The Solace of Trees* before the Syrian War began. But this story is the story of the Syrian conflict, and will be that of other armed conflicts to come, as long as we fail to confront the causes that bring them about. There are today over 65 million people worldwide displaced by conflict or persecution, a level higher than even in the aftermath of World War II. There isn't a wall big enough that you can build that will keep this growing global crisis from landing on our doorstep in one form or another. In the not-so-distant future, these refugees will begin being joined by those forced from their homes by climate change, making the toll of human suffering even greater. It is in our self-interest to address these issues in an immediate and meaningful way.

In *The Solace of Trees*, there are some truly chilling episodes describing war atrocities committed against civilians. How did you become familiar with this subject area and, as a result, passionate about exposing it to a fiction-reading audience?

My research focused on first-hand accounts and documented proceedings from the war crimes trials held after the Bosnian War. The shock I felt at the instances of the inhumanity that research revealed quickly turned to anger and initially caused me to include a litany of atrocities in the book's early draft. But the acts were just so horrific that I ended up editing most of them out. I was concerned they would overwhelm the reader, preventing concentration on the story and the underlying themes the book seeks to address. The recounting of the events I did include is not meant to shock but to build the foundation of the story and give the reader a true picture of the brutality that occurs when the targeting of civilian populations becomes a strategy of war.

What gave you the encouragement to push on and tell this story, rather than become discouraged by the knowledge that such horrific acts occurred in recent history and continue to this day?

It is very easy to feel overwhelmed by a world that no longer fits our image of what we feel it should be. We tend to judge the present based upon nostalgia for a past we've elevated to a place of more idyllic time and become discouraged by the weight of the problems that face us in the here and now—issues that have grown to take on a global, universal character no longer controllable within the environment of our immediate, contained place of habitation. Against such odds you feel as though there is little you can do about anything, so the tendency is to do nothing at all. And that's when we all lose. As individuals we can't do much to affect a war in progress, but we can act on smaller things that are more easily achievable for us, giving what we can in the way of financial, political, and moral support. Cumulatively that can add up to a lot. The more people who speak out against the targeting of civilian populations, the more those voices can become a deterrent to its use as a strategy of war in future conflicts.

Post-traumatic stress disorder (PTSD) plays a key role in the life of the protagonist, Amir, and also more generally in the novel. How did you become familiar with this psychological phenomenon, especially with respect to PTSD in child refugees?

The literature on child refugees suffering from PTSD is just beginning to develop in terms of historical data. For the purposes of the book, I relied on what I could find of literature published by mental health professionals who worked with child victims of war from Bosnia as well as that written about child survivors of the genocides that occurred in Cambodia and Rwanda. The effects upon these children can be severe, with lifelong repercussions. Unfortunately, too many child victims of war suffering from PTSD receive little if any treatment. Their journey into adulthood becomes hindered by chronic symptoms that never allow them to fully integrate into society. The cost of war, then, continues long after the signing of any peace treaty that might end the conflict that brought about their suffering.

Although Amir is from a secular Muslim family, his experience is different from that of many Muslim Americans. How does Amir's experience compare with that of Muslim Americans today?

One of the mandates for unaccompanied child refugees coming to the States is that, whenever possible, they be placed with people of their own cultural and religious background.

In Amir's case, his physical and emotional impairments took precedence over that directive, and it was determined that an individual care placement with someone experienced in dealing with his particular disabilities was the highest priority. His American foster mother did, however, make efforts to get Amir to take part in a Bosnian-American organization, and they did attend some of its events. But he wasn't ready to further explore his heritage at that point. Immigrant children often feel torn between the culture they've been settled in and that of their birth country. I found this to be true in my own case, growing up outside of the US in a foreign culture. My children experienced similar struggles of identity when we moved overseas during their early childhood.

There is a tendency in our country to view Muslims as a kind of monolithic culture, all sharing the same values, lifestyle, and beliefs. The truth of the matter, however, is there is as much diversity among people of Muslim heritage as there is among Christians or individuals of any other religious or cultural identity.

Is there a connection between Amir's PTSD and his eventual passion for filmmaking?

Yes, that's definitely the case. Filmmaking is a way for Amir to see the world both more intimately and at the same time from a safe distance. Child victims of war have experienced an aspect of humanity, or rather, inhumanity, that the rest of us can choose to consider or not as our comfort with reading or hearing about it allows. For a child who has gone through what Amir has, this is not the case. What he has lived through is always there with him. *It* visits him and not the other way around. Filmmaking gives him the opportunity to reverse that dynamic.

As far as his foster placement and eventual adoption are concerned, Amir seems to have been quite fortunate. Is this out of the ordinary? Do child refugees, especially ones with disabilities or mental health issues, often get such acceptance into foster, medical, and therapeutic care in the United States?

The great majority of foster parents are caring, giving people. They come from all social and economic backgrounds. Amir was fortunate in both being placed with a foster parent who could help augment the limited budget designated for helping child refugees, and being sponsored, in the first place, by a religious charitable organization whose efforts over the years have brought thousands of children to the US and placed them in good homes.

Sadly, there are many more child refugees than there are programs and visas available for them to be relocated to the US or other countries of safe haven. For those suffering from disabilities or mental health issues, it is even more difficult to find placements. If Amir's situation were to have occurred in the present day, it would be highly unlikely he would have a chance to find refuge in the United States. The opportunities for child refugees to be relocated outside of the war zones that have created them are, if anything, shrinking, not increasing.

Forests, and especially trees, play a key role in Amir's life. Do you have a special relationship with nature that may have influenced this?

Like most people, I find great comfort in nature. As a child who moved as often as I did—it was something on the order of thirteen or fourteen times—nature was always a sustaining force for me, a relationship I didn't need to worry about having to leave behind when we transitioned to a new home. It's easy to forget that we are part of nature and not separate from it. Our anthropocentrism is such that we forget that nature is not dependent on us, but, rather, it is we who are dependent upon it for our survival. Nature can remind us of the relativity of our true place in the universe, through either stunning beauty or terrifying force. There is no ambiguity in nature.

The novel is in third person throughout, but there are subtle shifts of perspective. Toward the very end, the language shifts to reflect more the perspective of Amir's captor than that of Amir. This leads to a chilling but profound ending. What is your motivation regarding the transitions in perspective in the novel? Why not tell Amir's story from solely his point of view?

The Solace of Trees is about war as experienced by civilian populations who want nothing more than to escape it. Our understanding of armed conflict, for the most part, comes to us filtered through the lens of political and military perspectives. That is the most common point of view we take in when we watch the nightly news, read the paper, or go to the movies. Even when there is coverage of civilian populations caught up in war, it comes to us distilled through those perspectives. It seems distant to us, beyond our control, and makes us feel as though there is nothing we can really do about the sad happenings we glimpse from afar.

The Solace of Trees is written from the opposite view, one that comes from the innards of war's workings. The shifts of perspective that occur in the book are meant to juxtapose the emotional and mental processes of those on the outside looking in with those who are directly caught up in war's brutal act. They link the two seemingly disparate worlds in an attempt to reveal that they are, in truth, one and the same—our place of comfort and safety not absolving us of responsibility for the suffering of those who live in misery and terror. With the world growing ever smaller, the evasion of that responsibility ultimately ends up shifting the problem onto the shoulders of our children and grandchildren. They will be the ones who pay the price of our complacency.

ALSO FROM NEW EUROPE BOOKS

Ballpoint: A Tale of Genius and Grit, Perilous Times, and the Invention that Changed the Way We Write. 978-0-9825781-1-7

Eastern Europe! Everything You Need to Know About the History (and More) of a Region that Shaped Our World and Still Does. 978-0-9850623-2-3

The Devil Is a Black Dog: Stories from the Middle East and Beyond. 978-0-9900043-2-5

The Essential Guide to Being Hungarian: 50 Facts & Facets of Nationhood. 978-0-9825781-0-0

The Essential Guide to Being Polish: 50 Facts & Facets of Nationhood. 978-0-9850623-0-9

Illegal Liaisons. 978-0-9850623-6-1

Keeping Bedlam at Bay in the Prague Café. 978-0-9825781-8-6

Once Upon a Yugoslavia. 978-0-9000043-4-9

Petra K and the Blackhearts. 978-0-9850623-8-5

The Wild Cats of Piran. 978-0-9900043-0-1

The Upright Heart. 978-0-9900043-8-7

Voyage to Kazohinia. 978-0-9825781-2-4

New Europe Books

Williamstown, Massachusetts

Find our titles wherever books are sold,
or visit www.NewEuropeBooks.com for order information.

ABOUT THE AUTHOR

Robert Madrygin spent his early years in postwar Japan, where his father, a US military lawyer, had been appointed defense counsel for Japanese POWs. He attended a local school and learned to speak Japanese. His father's career then brought him back to the US to live on both coasts, and subsequently to Morocco, Franco-ruled Spain, and Paris. The adjustment in cultural shifts and moving from home to home were made all the more difficult due to the illness his mother suffered throughout her life, causing long periods of hospitalization and necessitating that he be placed in a succession of temporary homes during his early childhood. While Madrygin was in his teens, his father suffered a series of massive debilitating strokes and his mother died. On his own at a young age, he continued a life of travel. He worked in Spain as a laborer, in Italy as a deckhand on a ship, and in Alaska on a railroad and as a crew member on a fishing boat. Madrygin first started writing in his early twenties but put it aside when he met his future wife, married, and started a family. During this period Madrygin, his wife, and three children lived in the US, Ecuador, and Spain and traveled widely. It wasn't until years later, while living in Spain, with his children now grown, that the call to writing returned, and Madrygin, informed by a lifetime of experience, took up where he had left off decades earlier. He and his wife live currently in Vermont.